Rescue Child

by

Ann Rawson

For Jacqueline

Thank you so much for all your help & support,

Ann xxx

First edition published 2023 by Ann Rawson

Copyright © Ann Rawson 2023

The right of Ann Rawson to be identified as the author of this work has been asserted by her in accordance with the Copyright, Designs and Patents Act 1988.

Rescue Child is a work of fiction. Any resemblance to actual persons, living or dead, or actual events is purely coincidental. Occasional well-known names and places may be used in a fictitious context.

All rights reserved. No part of this publication may be reproduced, stored in a retrieval system in any form, or transmitted in any form, or by any means, electronic, mechanical, photocopying, recording or otherwise, without permission in writing from the publisher.

Cover art © Tone Hitchcock 2023

*In memory of Paul David Walsh
the very best of friends,
missed more every single day.*

Prologue

I committed the perfect murder. So perfect that the police can't find the evidence to charge me. After that, planning the kidnapping of a child should be easy, surely?

It's a pity, then, that I'm innocent. I didn't kill him. I'm not a murderer. I mean look at me, a middle-class professional woman of a certain age. I'm not the killing type.

All my life I've been a good person. I've barely transgressed against social convention, let alone overridden the highest moral and legal obligations.

Okay, I once ate a piece of shop-bought Swiss Roll with my fingers instead of a fork. My boyfriend's mother was outraged. It didn't help that I laughed when she attempted an etiquette lesson.

I always, always wanted children, you see. For months I cried, in secret, every time my period arrived.

When I forced Matt to face the truth, that it was never going to happen naturally, I endured all the misery of three cycles of IVF. He begged me to consider another way – surrogacy or adoption. I didn't want that, and he was disappointed in me.

'I thought you'd try anything,' he said.

This could be my one chance to become a mother.

Look, I tried the police first. It's not my fault they refused to act. As my Aunt Martha used to say, *If you want something done right, you'd best do it yourself.*

The boy deserves a good home, and I can provide one.

It's not so much a kidnapping as a rescue.

Chapter One

Seven weeks earlier

It wasn't the best time, and it certainly wasn't the best place, to have an existential crisis. I was standing outside Wimbledon Police Station, delaying the moment when I'd have to go in and sign bail.

My Fitbit buzzed on my wrist. It was time. I forced myself up the steps and into reception, where I waited patiently for my turn at the front desk, all the time psyching myself up to tell a deliberate lie to a policeman. It wasn't a serious lie, just the smallest white lie.

It was only when I reached the front of the queue, I realised the desk sergeant was new to me. I relaxed. This man didn't know me. He wouldn't realise I was acting weirdly.

'No Sergeant Evans today?' I asked.

'He's on leave.'

He didn't even look up at me. Rude.

'And you are?'

I blushed, embarrassed. I'm not the *Don't you know who I am?* sort of person, but my face has been on the front page of so many newspapers, and anyway, surely he had a list?

'Jen Blake,' I said. 'Here to sign bail.'

He looked at me at last - curious, no doubt. I would never get used to being an object of fascination.

'Any changes to report?'

'No. Nothing at all,' I said, sounding much too definite. I signed, and said, 'I guess I'll see you next week then?'

He looked at me, steadily. 'Sergeant Evans should be back,' he said. 'But don't rush off. DI Carstairs wants to see you.'

'Oh, okay,' I said. 'Anything to get this mess cleared up more quickly.'

Did I sound too bright and breezy? Surely there was no normal way to behave in this kind of situation. There was the paranoia again. I should slap myself on the wrist.

I expected to wait in reception, but the desk sergeant suggested I might as well get comfortable in the interview room. I raised a sceptical eyebrow at that word comfortable and refused the offered coffee. I'd been conned that way before.

The room was dismal and felt as if it had absorbed the misery of countless unhappy occupants before me. I shivered. It wasn't like me to be so imaginative. How Matt would have mocked me.

Carstairs, though... The man gave me the collywobbles. I already knew he didn't like me. How else could he be so sure I'd killed Matt? It annoyed him intensely that he hadn't been able to find enough evidence to persuade the CPS there was a case to answer, but he was determined to keep looking.

I checked the time on my phone, and as I put it down, there was the unwelcome ping of a text. I knew I should wait and read it later, but when had I ever been sensible?

It was another of *those* texts. Of course. My stalker – whose texts were equal parts mystifying and chilling – had yet again picked the perfect moment to unsettle me.

I had other anonymous correspondents. Ever since it became public knowledge that I was on bail and suspected of murdering my husband, I'd attracted more than my share of nutters. Closing down my social media accounts had helped, but there were a stubborn few with a phone number or an email address who wouldn't let me be. I knew I should block and ignore, but I've always felt knowledge is the key to staying safe.

Taking a long time today. Maybe you're being charged at last. Everyone knows you killed him, even if the police don't.

I deleted the text and put the phone down, my hands shaking. This was escalation. Was I being followed too?

I was already on edge, waiting to find out what Carstairs had in store for me. The extra worry about being followed was just too much. It confirmed I'd made the right decision, though. I would have to be very careful the next day.

I went out to the desk sergeant and asked how much longer I'd have to wait. 'Perhaps it might be best to arrange a specific time with my solicitor,' I added.

'I'm sure he won't be long, Ms Blake,' the sergeant said.

'Could you check, please?' For once, there was an edge to my voice. I was rattled and showing it.

A couple of minutes later, DI Ian Carstairs and DC Suzie Kent joined me in the interview room. Carstairs was tall and slim, with a pale, thin-faced expression of superiority which irritated me. For some reason he reminded me of a vicar – and given my experience with religious men, that did not endear him to me. DC Suzie Kent was the more human of the two, though even she didn't much like me.

I knew it was their job to doubt me and make judgements, but I didn't have to enjoy it.

Carstairs started flicking though a manila folder, looking intent. DC Kent refused to smile, or even make eye contact.

This pair were the officers who'd turned up on my doorstep, that morning, nearly two months earlier, to tell me Matt was dead.

I'd known straight away they'd judged my behaviour unacceptable. I'd been furious rather than distressed. I'd told them the truth – Matt had betrayed me terribly, I'd argued with him, and I'd thrown him out of our home. Permanently.

They'd asked if I wanted someone with me, but I refused. I preferred to be alone. Another black mark. When they asked what they could do for me, I'd only made one request – that they should inform my mother-in-law that Matt was dead. That made me a cold-hearted bitch, I suppose.

It had seemed kinder, given that after my row with Matt, I'd phoned and left a blistering message on her voice mail. She'd colluded with Matt, keeping his secrets from me.

I gathered later, from something Carstairs said, she'd saved the message and played it to them. She'd obviously relished the opportunity to show them how angry I'd been - perhaps angry enough to kill.

'Are you with us, Ms Blake?' Carstairs' sharp voice cut into my reverie.

'Oh, sorry. Was I keeping you waiting?' I asked, sweetly.

After fussing about tea and coffee, which I again refused, DI Carstairs got down to business.

'Some more information has come to light. It concerns the conflict between you and your husband and may speak to motive.'

Surely, they already had motive. What they didn't have was evidence.

'Do I need to have my solicitor present?'

'It's your decision, of course, but that would end up taking more of the day.'

'You could have let me contact her earlier,' I pointed out. 'If you would give me some privacy, I will see if she's available.'

I picked my phone up, waiting until the door closed behind them.

After a productive chat with Chioma, I went to the door. They'd long gone, of course. I imagined them, chatting away in the canteen about how much more of my time they could waste.

I gathered my things together, and returned to the desk, waiting impatiently until the desk sergeant was available.

'Have they finished with you?' he asked.

'They haven't.' I said. 'I've finished with them. My solicitor advised me to say it is time to put up or shut up. If there's still not enough evidence to charge me, then they can arrange a suitable time for an interview in the next few days. And given that this police station appears to be leaky, as some of the stories in the press could only have originated here, Ms Igwe will strongly suggest the interview takes place at her office.'

He looked flustered. I guessed he didn't want to be the one to tell Carstairs that his strategy had failed.

'You can't just leave,' he said.

'My solicitor tells me I can,' I responded. 'I'm not refusing to co-operate. I'm merely objecting to being hijacked when all of this could have been arranged in advance. But I'll give you five minutes to get Carstairs down here so I can tell him myself.'

I sat in the waiting area, but a minute later, the sergeant called me back to the desk.

DI Carstairs says you can go,' he said. 'He'll arrange a more suitable time with your solicitor.'

I smiled.

I can play status games too. I don't like doing it, but I am not a doormat, nor am I defenceless. I swore, once I'd left home, I would never start a fight, but I would never run away from one either. I've not always managed to keep that promise to myself, especially where Matt was concerned, but I have generally made the effort.

I was lucky to have Chioma on my side. It seemed like I'd known her forever. She was on the same corridor as me in our University Hall of Residence. I'd met her weeks before I met Matt. She had a generous spirit, and not once had she made me feel small, in all the time I'd known her.

She'd never liked Matt, and when I married him, our friendship had suffered, reduced to Christmas and birthday cards and a few rare social occasions.

It was a credit to her that she'd been there when I needed her, without a second's hesitation. When I told her about Amy Thompson, and how Matt had described her as a younger, prettier version of me, she'd told me I'd always deserved better, with no hint of *I told you so* in her voice.

We had a running joke that Carstairs was more than a little intimidated by her. As I'd pointed out, I was too, back when I was eighteen.

'You can be quite scary,' I said. 'You're beautiful and brilliant – and on top of that, you have that cut-glass voice which you wield with icy precision.'

She laughed and said, 'Mouse, you were afraid of everyone.'

It was true. Although no one but Chioma calls me Mouse now.

'I'm on your side.' she said. 'Not just because you're paying, although that helps.'

'I'm not afraid of Carstairs, with you in my corner.'

I was whistling in the dark - I was terrified of Carstairs. Every time I encountered him, I was whisked back to that first visit, when I'd asked him to tell me how Matt had died.

'His body was found under the cliffs near your holiday cottage,' he'd said. 'An early morning runner called it in. Matt had been lying there overnight. There was no hope, I'm afraid.'

'Did he fall?' I asked. 'He was always so careless on those cliffs. He would clown around by the warning signs marking the cliff edge.'

'We don't know how it happened yet, Ms Blake. We have a full forensics team down there now, checking the scene. There'll be a post-mortem. We are currently treating your husband's death as unexplained. It's our job to find the explanation.'

In my mind's eye, I saw him lying there, his body broken by the impact. Like a doll or a puppet, limbs splayed in impossible positions, and his head haloed in a puddle of dark blood. It was a vision I could not shake off, and every time it was accompanied by a rush of feelings that threatened to overpower me. The humiliation of betrayal, overlaid with fear and rage, and most of all, grief for all I had lost, and for the future Matt had lost too.

Carstairs thought I was holding back. That's why he thought I'd murdered Matt. He had no idea how much I was holding back, or why.

Chapter Two

I pulled up outside my temporary home, with an overwhelming sense of relief. It was a very ordinary Victorian end-of-terrace – Matt would have hated it – but it was a new adventure. And for the first time in forever, it was all about me, and what I wanted.

I'd set out early, in the dark, to avoid whoever had followed me to Wimbledon Police Station the previous day. I'd taken the scenic route as if I was just having a day out. I'd dawdled on Brighton seafront and eaten breakfast in a small, side street café before making my way to the landlord's office to collect the keys.

It was probably for the best I'd lied to the desk sergeant – that I hadn't said I was moving house. Very few people knew I was moving, and I planned to keep it that way.

I'd been shocked the previous week to be informed my police bail had been extended for another three months. I had every intention of continuing to sign in every week. I would always be available by phone, email and through my solicitor. It wasn't like I was planning to skip bail or anything – I just needed a place where I felt safe.

The house was separated from a convent school by a high wall. The external rendering needed a fresh coat of white paint, and it looked like the windows hadn't been cleaned in years. It reminded me a bit of my Aunt Martha's house – maybe that was the attraction. But it was spacious and comfortable on the inside, and it was mine, all mine. Mine and the landlord's, at any rate.

I dragged my two enormous canvas suitcases out of the car boot and up the steps to my front door. I tried every key on the ring that the landlord had handed over Then I started again, and finally managed to unlock the damn door.

Leaving the suitcases in the long, long hallway, I went back to the car for the carrier bag of goodies I'd picked up at the service station.

Milk, tea and coffee, a box of cookies, a couple of luxury ready meals, prepared salad and vegetables, and a sandwich.

I'd almost dumped the full basket and run away when I saw the shelf full of newspapers - with my photo on front page after front page. *'Is this woman the Black Widow of Wimbledon?'* screamed the headlines. Again.

The first time that had happened was just after the news broke that I'd been arrested for Matt's murder. I'd had a full toddler-style meltdown in the middle of Waitrose.

The day had started badly, with Henry Thompson knocking on my door, pestering me again. I'd seen him and sunk to the floor, leaning against the wall under the windows so he wouldn't see I was there when inevitably, he peered in. He wanted to talk to me about Amy, thinking we had some kind of bond as we'd both been betrayed by our spouses. He seemed to think it was my job to take care of his feelings, and I was so done with that.

The moment he'd driven off I'd escaped to the shops and anonymity. Or so I'd thought.

I'd been spotted by some nosy woman who actually grabbed her phone and started snapping me as I browsed the cereal aisle. She even snapped pictures of my trolley, piled high with cheese, crackers and bottles of wine.

I gawped at her, which likely didn't improve the pictures. I imagined her sharing them on Twitter and Facebook, with barely repressed glee; how she'd spotted the local Black Widow buying cheese, of all things. How dare she buy cheese, when her husband is dead, and we all know she killed him?

In a fury, I'd grabbed the woman's phone, thrown it on the floor and stamped on it until the screen shattered. Then I opened my purse and grabbed a handful of bank notes and dropped them on top of the broken phone.

Of course, that made me look worse. It looked like I thought I could buy my way out of trouble. The woman was bleating about calling the police – as if I hadn't had enough of them already, the way they'd ushered me out of the front door of the police station the day before, straight into the sights of the press photographers.

'Perhaps you would like to borrow my phone?' I'd asked, and then threw more of my money on the floor and the woman crumpled, and sat down in the middle of the shop, acting as if she was the victim.

I suppose she was. I lost my temper. I was ashamed of myself, later.

She wasn't too proud to gather up all the cash, though.

At least I wasn't short of money. I deeply resented all the stories which suggested I was well off because of Matt, as if I wasn't the co-founder of NRS Tech, as if it wasn't built on my technical ability. It was my company every bit as much as his.

'Buy yourself a new phone,' I said, 'and try to respect people's privacy in future.'

Then I turned and fled, leaving my trolley full of groceries blocking the cereal aisle, with half a dozen onlookers recording the whole embarrassing scene on *their* phones.

All my childhood, I'd been a complete pushover, never standing up for myself, pretending to be invisible. When I left home, when I married Matt, when we became successful beyond our dreams, I'd thought all that was behind me. Being a murder suspect, being arrested, being watched and gossiped about sent me back to some dark times in my life. I'd started to creep around, Mouse-like again, hoping to escape notice.

Until I snapped and over-reacted to some pathetic woman taking a photo.

That day, after losing my shit spectacularly and virally, and arriving home with bits of broken phone still stuck in the soles of my shoes, I made an appointment with my hairdresser.

'Even your own mother wouldn't recognise you,' Marco said, as I gave in after years of resistance and let him loose with scissors and colour.

I didn't mention that it was nearly twenty years since my own mother had seen me.

So that was why I'd been terrified of being recognised at the service station. I needn't have worried though. Yesterday's news. Maybe the new hair colour made a difference, or perhaps it was just that I was not in Wimbledon.

I overcame my panicked reaction to being plastered all over the front pages again, filled my wire basket with goodies and paid for my shopping. It felt like a positive sign for the future –as if things were almost back to normal.

In my new kitchen, I unloaded the ready meals and snacks on to the work surface. It wasn't a patch on my old one, but serviceable. I started putting everything away, planning what I'd keep where. The fridge-freezer was small, but adequate.

The house still had that empty house feeling, but the central heating was on. It was far too warm, in July, and I wondered if there might be a problem with damp the landlord was covering up. I like fresh air anyway, so I turned the thermostat right down and opened a few windows.

Maybe this could be the new start I so desperately needed. It might be like being on holiday – living on the edge of Brighton, a stone's throw from the sea.

I put the kettle on, settling at the scrubbed pine kitchen table with a cuppa to phone my best friend, as promised.

'Hi Lainey,' I said, over the racket of barking dogs in the background. 'It's me. I hear the bakery-bark chorus is in fine voice.'

'We have a beautiful litter of pups in,' Lainey said. 'Just your kind – black and tan with the most enormous paws. It's time, you know. You could even have a couple now, without Matt to object.'

'Not yet, I can't. There's too much to do.'

'You know you want to, Jen. I could reserve them for you.'

'Elaine Margaret Westwood,' I said, sternly. 'No.'

'Uh oh, my full given name. I am in trouble. Are you settled in yet?'

'There's not a lot to do,' I said. 'The office removal people will be bringing my stuff tomorrow and setting up in the middle bedroom. Then I'll have no excuse not to get to work.'

'You're going to do it then? Did you talk to your solicitor?'

'It's a stark choice. Keep my shares, and stay on in the company I co-founded, with no say over anything. Or sell up and have a chance to start over and do anything I want. I'll have to stay on for a year anyway, for handover. What joy – I get to train my replacement.'

'No one could replace you,' Lainey said, loyal as ever.

'Thanks,' I said. 'Still, it's good to provide some continuity. It wouldn't be fair on the workforce to just quit – after all, they had less choice than me in any of it.'

'Makes sense, I guess. Have you met any of the neighbours yet?'

'I've only been here an hour, Lainey!'

'Promise me you'll make some friends. Don't push everyone away.'

'It's only temporary. No more than six months.'

'It won't hurt you to take a risk then?'

'No, mum,' I said, shaking my head, exasperated.

'Cheek! You're older than me.'

'But less maternal.' I was aiming for light but even I could hear my voice cracking.

'Aww, Jen. That's not true.' She paused, struggling to find words. 'Seriously, these pups are gorgeous.'

'Maybe. Once I know how it's going.'

The racket of barking dogs resumed, ranging from the squeakiest to the gruffest.

'Sounds like we have visitors,' Lainey said. 'Talk soon?'

'Of course,' I said.

I felt deflated though. On my own again.

It seemed like Lainey, and Chioma were all I had left. When I married Matt, I'd let my guard down. I'd forgotten the hard-earned lesson of my childhood – that I had to be able to rely on myself because I could rely on no one else. I'd let people in, and then I'd been betrayed. Not just by Matt – as much as that had broken my heart, it had been the first of many dominoes to tumble over. Everyone looked at me differently. Even people I'd thought were friends had fallen away, presuming there was no smoke without fire.

I finished my tea, then made my way upstairs to the main bedroom at the front of the house, carrying a pack of wipes. I stood by the window, looking out across the main road. It was a clear bright day. If I stood on my tiptoes, I could just see a sliver of sea.

Moving quickly, I cleaned down the storage units – drawers and wardrobe, put my clothes away on automatic pilot, and lifted the empty cases on to the top of the wardrobe.

There was a new mattress on the bed, as requested. I went down to the car, collected the huge bag with sheets, pillows and the duvet, dragging it up to the bedroom. I tipped everything out and made the bed comfortable.

I almost climbed straight in to hide under the covers, but I couldn't do that forever, so instead I carried on with everything that needed doing.

The house felt oddly unreal, as did my lost life. Everything about my years with Matt had clearly always been fantasy, but I had believed in it until the last. Fool that I was. At least here, I was no longer under constant observation from the neighbours, the journalists, and the police.

As I was unpacking toiletries into the bathroom cabinet, the doorbell rang. Startled, I dropped my shampoo and conditioner, the bottles clattering on the tiles. At least they didn't break. It was an old childhood pattern; unexpected noise always made me jump almost out of my skin.

Matt used to find it funny. He wasn't a cruel man, usually, just insensitive.

I rushed downstairs and peered out of the peephole. Seeing a woman, middle aged, safe, proffering a cake tin, I opened the door.

'Hello,' I said, warily.

'Hi there. I'm Sarah, from next door but one. I guess you're the new tenant. I've brought brownies.'

'Jennifer,' I said, reluctantly stepping to one side and inviting Sarah in. 'Come through, and I'll put the kettle on.'

I had promised Lainey, after all.

'Brilliant,' said Sarah, looking around, openly curious. 'The previous lot refused my cake, and certainly never offered me tea.'

We sat together at the kitchen table, the tin of brownies open, sipping hot tea.

'My wife, Erin, she's a workaholic. She's never home. I can't complain though. She always says I knew what she was like when I married her.'

She waited for me to react, as if it was a 'Welcome to Brighton' test.

I had a mouthful of brownie, so I nodded.

'Are you married?'

'No, it's just me.'

'Oh, that's a shame. I was hoping for a family this time. Maybe with kids the right age to play with my daughter.'

Sarah was one of those people who never stopped talking, I was quickly realising. At least that made it easy.

Sarah grabbed her phone and showed me a stream of photos. 'Izzy,' she said proudly. 'I always wanted to be a mum. Second go at IVF.'

She was an over-sharer. I didn't want to know all the details, although I knew in theory it worked well for so many people. Just not me.

I took the phone she pushed towards me. A small blonde girl with the cheekiest of grins, clearly enjoying posing for the photos. I felt a sharp pang of envy, and quickly clamped down on it.

'She's lovely,' I said.

'Oh,' said Sarah 'She may look like butter wouldn't melt, but she can be a right little madam.'

I helped myself to another brownie. 'These are so good,' I changed the subject. 'I'm no baker, but these are delicious. Thank you for bringing them.'

'I can always teach you. They're easy,' Sarah volunteered.

I cursed Lainey under my breath. This was entirely her fault. Without that promise, I would never have invited Sarah in.

'How kind,' I said. 'Only I ought to finish sorting out the bedroom.'

'You've not brought much stuff with you?' Sarah was nosy.

'Ah. It's mostly in storage, for now,' I said. At least everything personal was – the rest was still in the old house, waiting for tenants.

'There's a van coming tomorrow with all my office equipment and some other essentials,' I added.

I explained to Sarah I was a software developer and talked and talked about it while watching her eyes glaze over. It was a form of punishment– even if she hadn't realised how close to the bone she'd been.

'You'll be working from home?' Sarah asked.

'Oh yes. I have a contract for a year, maybe two. I'll have to go into the office occasionally, but that's all. What do you do?'

'Full-time mum,' Sarah said. 'In the summer we sometimes board language students, too. Izzy enjoys the company.'

It was Sarah, really, who was lonely I guessed. I would have to be careful.

'Thanks again,' I said, standing up. 'I know it's boring, but I do need to settle in.'

'Okay,' Sarah said, putting the lid on the Tupperware box of brownies. 'I'll leave you to it and see you soon.'

'Not if I see you first,' I thought, not altogether serious. There was no harm in her. And Lainey was right – I shouldn't be such a loner. I risked crawling back into the fragile shell that had barely protected teenage me, student me. The girl I was before Matt.

Still, I released a huge sigh of relief as I shut the door. It was good to be on my own in my new home, after all. Solitude and loneliness are not the same. So I keep telling myself, as if I know the difference.

I heated up a ready meal for one and didn't even bother with vegetables. The house was deathly quiet, only interrupted by the ping of the microwave. I hadn't brought the telly, or any music player – all that would be arriving the following day. I hadn't realised I'd be freaked out by the silence.

At least I had the Kindle, so I could read. I locked up and took hot chocolate and the last of the brownies up to bed with me.

I couldn't read. My feelings still hadn't caught up with everything that had happened in the last few weeks. Losing my last chance at IVF, my last chance at having my own child. The terrible row with Matt immediately after that last appointment at the clinic, when they confirmed what I already knew – my too-brief pregnancy was over. That was when he told me all about Amy. The humiliation of it all. That I'd not known about his arrangement with his girlfriend. I hadn't known he'd sold his shares in the company. Amy had known, of course. And his mother, his co-conspirator. It was just me, outside in the dark.

One of the last things he said to me was that my 'goody two shoes act' as he called it, had made it easier for him to sell the business from under me.

'It's not just that you never expect anyone else to take advantage,' he said. 'I mean, that helped a lot. Most of all, everything was so clean and above board, with the accounts kept up to date, all the taxes paid precisely on time. That's why we sailed through the due diligence. All thanks to you.'

If I had been going to snap and kill him, that could easily have been the moment.

I'd gone over and over it in my mind over the past weeks, trying to understand why he did it all behind my back. It wasn't necessary, after all. He and his mother had the majority shareholding between them. They didn't need my agreement. All I could come up with was the way he preferred to avoid confrontation. Or maybe Matt had thought spilling it all at once would be like lancing a boil – that it would let out the poison and our relationship would heal more quickly. He'd really been shocked when I told him his actions were unforgivable, and I'd thrown him out. He had really expected me to come round, to accept every insult to my self-respect.

I'd only told Carstairs the abridged version of the row – I didn't see why he needed to know just how humiliating it had all been. Even so, it was enough to make me a suspect in

Matt's murder. When the forensics team had decided that was what it was, I was already at the top of the list.

Ruminating wasn't doing me any good, I knew, but I couldn't stop the memories whirling.

I'd thought Matt's funeral might help. Closure. What a stupid word.

I'd been determined it should be a dignified affair. I'd even allowed Eve to arrange it all her way, rather than fight. Instead of seeing it as generosity, she had decided it was an admission that I didn't care.

If only that were true.

Outside the church, everyone milling around, I'd discovered that Amy – noticeably pregnant – had left her husband, Henry, and moved in with my mother-in-law. It was hard, seeing Eve so solicitous of her.

Henry had been the one to tell me Matt was having an affair. I hadn't wanted to believe him. Now he was at the funeral, and I was worried he would make a scene. I saw him hovering at the edge of the crowd. He approached Amy, but she turned her back on him. I glared at him, and for once, he had the sense to keep his distance.

Like Henry, I knew what it was to be betrayed. I'd hardly had time to mourn the loss of my marriage when Matt died. My whole life destroyed. In the house we shared I guess I'd been more easily able to pretend he was still there, out of sight. Away on business. Working late.

God, I was such an idiot. Alone in my new home, my new bed, I cried for him for the first time.

How stupid was I, after all Matt had done?

I still loved him.

Chapter Three

I woke looking forward to the day ahead for the first time in ages. Crying myself to sleep seemed to have done some good. Even the phone call from the office removals people saying they would be a couple of hours late didn't dent my enthusiasm.

After a quick breakfast I decided it was time I talked to my new boss.

How I resented him. I hadn't had a boss since I was fresh from university, when we were working in so-called proper jobs as we set up NRS Tech on a shoestring.

Matt did this to me. He knew how much it would hurt. No wonder he kept his plans to himself. And yet, he never once considered I might murder him.

Maybe we never really know each other, however close we think we are. I certainly hadn't known Matt as well as I'd thought.

Of course, my dark, defensive sense of humour explains why Carstairs is so sure I killed him. It didn't help that my personal name for the girlfriend, *that bitch Amy*, slipped out once or twice.

Anyway, enough of the past.

I phoned my new boss, Chris Bailey.

I'd met him for the first time at Matt's funeral. He was American. Tall, dark, smart – every bit the tech company CEO. Yet he'd also seemed kind and thoughtful, which didn't always combine with that role, in my experience. He'd broached the subject of work with me then, apologising for doing it at the funeral. 'I didn't want you to worry about how quickly we'd expect you at work. Please take all the time you need.'

We'd agreed most of my duties could be done remotely. My job would consist of mentoring my replacement, Stefan

Florescu, who I had yet to meet. I promised I would make the effort to go into the office a couple of times a month if necessary – but admitted I was hoping it wouldn't be necessary.

It would be hardly any more difficult now I'd moved, although it might have been polite to talk to Chris about it first.

I'd taken him at his word that there was no pressure, but I ought to be making an effort. I phoned Chris's secretary, asking if she could arrange a time for me to speak to him. I hid my disappointment when she said he had a slot available shortly, and he would call me back. With any luck it would be in the middle of the office installation, so I'd have an excuse not to talk for long.

Of course, he called ten minutes later, while I was eating hot, buttered toast, and brewing coffee.

'Morning, Chris,' I said. 'I wanted to catch up with you. I've made a few changes, and though it shouldn't impact on work at all, I wanted to let you know.'

'Okay,' he said. I thought he sounded cautious, as if he'd been expecting trouble.

'As you probably realise, it's been very difficult for me with the constant harassment from the press. I've temporarily moved into rented accommodation.'

'Ah,' he said. 'Are you still alright for starting work again next week?'

'Oh yes. My new office is being set up later today. I'll still be able to make it into the Wimbledon office when necessary, as we discussed.'

'Shall I update your contact details?'

'Mobile phone and email remain the same. If you need to contact me by post for signatures or anything, there's always my solicitor.'

'If you give me your current address, I can assure you it will remain confidential.'

I gave him my address, hiding my reluctance. I didn't want to appear difficult, or as if I didn't trust him. Perhaps I should have been tougher.

There was another hour to kill before my office gear arrived, so I washed up my breakfast things and went to look at the two spare bedrooms again.

The larger one, at the back, had a great view – over a row of bushes and trees towards the park. On the other hand, it was directly overlooked by the neighbour's corresponding bedroom.

A man appeared at the window opposite – ageing, balding, black-rimmed specs. He gave a little wave – friendly, so I waved back. I didn't want to be observed while I was working, so I checked out the middle bedroom.

It was much smaller, but a perfect size for a home office. It wasn't overlooked – though the view of the convent school's high wall wasn't so appealing. There were enough power sockets, at least. The built-in wardrobe was floor to ceiling shelves rather than hanging space and could easily store office supplies.

The wallpaper though. Clearly this had been a child's bedroom. Dinosaurs everywhere.

I held back tears. I would have loved to create a bedroom like this for my own child.

Could I bear to use it as it was, or would I need to redecorate? Something to think about later.

The doorbell rang and I went down to let the office removals team in.

We all went upstairs to discuss the options. We quickly agreed how they would set everything up in the smaller bedroom.

I showed them where I wanted the TV and stereo in the living room, as well as extra connectivity for the laptop, then left them to the tedious job of fetching and carrying and installing.

They asked if I wanted an extra powerline adapter in the kitchen. 'These old houses, it's often for the best,' the youngest guy said. I agreed to have them everywhere, it would be annoying to have to restrict laptop use to one or two rooms.

When they were done, I had coffee ready and biscuits piled on a plate on the kitchen table.

I was impressed they never once strayed into the personal, or wondered why I'd moved so down market, but then, I had selected the company because of their promise of confidentiality and had made it plain how important it was. Maybe they were fooled by my new hair and had no idea who I was, or that I'd been in the news so often lately.

After they devoured all the biscuits, they asked me to check where they'd put everything, in case anything needed moving.

We all trooped back up to the middle bedroom again.

'Thanks for all your hard work. It looks like a real office now.'

'Except for the dinosaurs,' one of them quipped.

'There are always dinosaurs in offices,' I said, deadpan.

I asked if they had time to unpack the archive boxes into the filing cabinet and line up my box files on the cupboard shelves. All the business paperwork was there, including, ironically, the changes to the Memorandum of Association, which had allowed Matt and Eve to sell their shares without my knowledge. Originally the shares could only be sold with a majority vote – and as we owned fifty percent each that meant we both had to agree. A couple of years in, Eve had stepped in to rescue us when we had cashflow problems. She'd invested her savings, and we'd each transferred five percent of our shares to her. The risk had completely passed me by. I wondered now, if taking away my rights had always been the plan.

I sat at my desk, enjoying the new space, and tried to force myself to stop brooding that the men carried on their work. I was relieved to see my computer was up and running and the internet speed was impressive. I'd been a bit worried.

They were surprisingly tidy and cleaned up every bit of mess, even closing all the doors. I gave them a generous tip, then waved them off, pleased to be alone in my home again.

I put some music on, and lay on the sofa stretched out, listening to Nina Simone.

When I woke up, I was feeling a little stiff, and relieved I still had a ready meal in the fridge. I had planned to go and explore the local shops in the afternoon There was still time, but I didn't feel like it.

After I put the fish pie in the oven, I switched the hall light on and went upstairs to check my emails.

I stopped at the top of the stairs, shocked.

It was the first time I'd seen the door closed. It simply hadn't occurred to me to look. Why would it?

There was a key in the lock. On the outside. And there were heavy duty bolts at the top and bottom of the door. Again, on the outside. I was shaking.

Someone had been locked in the room. I could feel it, an intense pain. And the dinosaur wallpaper made it all so much worse. A young child had been locked in that room. I opened the door and put a heavy box of books against it, jamming it open, so I couldn't see the locks, the heavy bolts.

I took a deep breath, reasoning with myself. Sarah didn't think they had a child. They might not have redecorated – it could be as simple as that. Maybe they kept valuables in the room. That could explain the lock and key, at least.

Feelings were not always a good guide to reality. I was so off kilter because of everything else in my life. I really should not let myself obsess on this. I could so easily be wrong.

I am a rational person. I'm a systems thinker, a mathematician. One plus one makes two. Was I somehow making three? I told myself I was. I must be.

Still, I couldn't stop shaking.

Chapter Four

I woke with a start, from a dream where I'd been hiding from people peering in through the window. It was so vivid, it took minutes for me to remember that I was in a different house now, and that none of my stalkers knew where I was.

For the most part, I spent the weekend relaxing. The only disturbance was whenever I passed the middle bedroom door, which triggered my childhood fears of being locked in. I couldn't help but worry if the child was currently locked in another bedroom, another house.

Monday morning arrived and it should have been my first proper day at work, but as I needed to sort the office out, I decided I deserved another day off.

I phoned the Office Moves people and asked if they could send their team to rearrange everything.

'Was the work not done to your satisfaction, ma'am,' the sweet young woman on customer services asked.

'Oh, it's not that,' I said. 'Far from it. I discovered I'd chosen the wrong room. The view is too distracting, and I will be much better off working in the larger room, I think.'

The same team were available for the following day. I promised to measure up the window and email the details, so they could supply and install privacy blinds too.

I checked my emails and there was nothing pressing.

The moment I settled in my living room, feet up with book in hand and a coffee by my side, my phone beeped.

A text.

Angrier than ever.

'*I don't know where you are, you fat cow. But I will find you.*'

Charming.

A text was as nothing, though. With only general threats, it was easy to brush off, and the admission that they didn't know where I was gave me a real buzz of satisfaction. It felt like a win.

I phoned Chioma and she'd had no contact from the police arranging the promised interview. I allowed myself to hope it had merely been a power play, and it would all blow over. Maybe they'd started looking for the person who had actually killed Matt.

After a very leisurely breakfast, I wandered out on foot to explore the local shops. If Sarah was going to pop round again, I was certainly going to need more biscuits – but it also seemed like a good idea to buy some real food, including fruit and vegetables.

I walked up past the school and through the park until I reached the old High Street, which still housed a row of shops. If I'd walked in the other direction, I could have found everything I needed at the giant Sainsbury's – but I wanted to dawdle and check out the butcher, baker and candlestick maker.

There was a small hardware shop. Not the kind selling blinds, but all sorts of oddments from drain cleaner to plastic buckets and spades – for the pebbled beach, no less. I was pleased with my haul – veggies from the greengrocer; cheese, sausages and lamb chops from the butcher; and a selection of pastries and a fragrant spelt sourdough from the bakery.

I was ready to amble back home when I noticed the most gorgeous wolfhound tied up to the railing outside the small co-op. He was huge, and keen for attention from passers-by, straining at his leash, hoping for some fuss. I could see he was wearing a smart leather collar, but he was tied up not by a leash, as I'd assumed, but by a long piece of fraying rope passed through the collar.

He noticed me paying attention, pulled harder on the rope, and broke it. Delighted to be free, he romped playfully out into the road, running in circles.

Still a puppy – but oh, such a big puppy.

There was a car bearing down on him, far too fast for a residential area, and showing no signs of slowing down. I dropped my bag and ran out into the road. I heard the brakes screech and sensed the car swerving away, as I talked quietly to the still over-excited pup.

'Wolfie, Wolfie,' I said, and he looked at me, decided I looked like fun, and bounded towards me. He slowed just in time and stopped inches away from me, tail wagging, waiting for the fuss which was his by right.

I tried to calm him as I grabbed him by the collar.

The car stopped and the driver got out, actually screaming at me and the dog.

'You dozy cow, can't you keep your dog under control?'

I was so astonished I didn't say anything. That prompted even more abuse.

'Stupid bitch. Someone could have been killed.'

He was a big bloke, all blue-inked tattoos and big bushy beard. He towered over me, still shouting, and I flinched and stepped back. 'How dare you?' he carried on. 'Acting as if I am a danger, when the real danger is from you and your dog.'

Quietly I spoke, still stroking Wolfie and trying to keep him calm.

'He's not my dog.'

He stopped yelling for long enough for me to add. 'He was tied to the railing with this rope, see?'

He sneered at me, but he knew he was in the wrong.

'I saved you AND the dog, right? You were driving too fast. That's why you had to brake, and swerve.'

He got back in the car, slammed the door and drove off. Still too fast.

Just as well I wasn't expecting an apology.

I dragged Wolfie on to the pavement and sat down by my bags. I pulled him down close to me, so I could fuss him some more. One-handed, I managed to fix the rope back through his collar. More securely, I hoped. A couple of women who'd been watching commented on how angry the driver had been, and how sensible I was. Much they knew! No one seemed to know who owned the dog. A kind woman asked in all the shops – so it looked like he was coming home with me, as a detour on the way to the nearest vet.

He rolled over so I could tickle his tummy, and I took the chance to check again that the rope was safely attached. I noticed him sniffing around my shopping. I guessed he was after my lamb chops, but I intercepted him. I opened the bag with the cheese, broke off a corner and shared it with him. He drooled all over me.

I pulled myself off the floor, smiling a goodbye to the little crowd of onlookers.

He walked home with me willingly enough. Someone had tried to teach him to walk to heel.

I took him into the house, and then googled to find the nearest veterinary surgery. He immediately jumped on to the sofa and settled down, making himself at home.

Sighing at the muddy footprints on the white sofa, I grabbed the laptop and took it into the kitchen sure he would follow me, and he did. I let him into the back garden, where he ran round and round with his tongue hanging out, apparently in dog heaven. I filled a casserole dish with cold water and put it down for him, then quickly worked out there was a vet less than ten minutes drive away along the coast road.

I phoned, explained the situation and they agreed to give him a good look over, including scanning to find out if he was chipped and registered. They could fit him in that afternoon.

We had a couple of hours to kill, and I had nothing better to do, so I cut a couple of chunky slices from the block of cheese and chopped it into little cubes. I wanted to see how easy it would be to persuade him to sit and lie down.

He was far too excited. He would, just about, sit on command for a few seconds before leaping to grab a cheese cube out of my hand.

The first time, anyway.

After half an hour it appeared he was perfectly capable and knew what to do – he simply didn't want to do it.

Absolute consistency was key with this exuberant temperament. Absolute inconsistency was clearly what he'd experienced.

I gave up and let him play.

He'd be going home soon, anyway, once the vet had identified where home was.

It was lucky I still had the dog guard fitted in the back of the car, otherwise I'd have had yards of dog crawling all over the car as I drove down to the main road. He settled in the back quite happily, though with an occasional bark to remind me of his existence.

The vet was a lovely Polish woman, Natasha, who Wolfie immediately adored. She gave him a thorough once over and tried to refuse to charge when I said he was a stray.

When she checked the collar, she found a note attached to the inside.

'Nero grew into too much dog for us to handle. Please find him a good home.'

Me and Natasha shrugged in unison.

Unsurprisingly there was no chip. I decided I'd take him to Lainey's rescue. I could trust her to find the best home for him.

I picked out a lead, a couple of bowls, a grooming kit, a knotted rope toy plus a puzzle chewy toy, and bought him a small sack of food recommended by the vet.

'Are you thinking of keeping him?' she asked.

'I'm so tempted,' I said. 'But I have way too much on my plate at the moment. My best friend works at a dog rescue. I'll take him over there tomorrow, and I know she'll make sure he's rehomed properly.'

Natasha laughed, pointedly looking at my big bag full of dog stuff.

'You are seriously tempted though, I can tell. Enjoy your evening.'

I collected fish and chips on the way home – the lamb chops could wait until tomorrow.

After I'd eaten and fed Wolf Dog – I refused to call him Nero – I phoned Lainey to tell her I'd be in tomorrow and why.

'Bring him here and I can keep him at home with me overnight,' she offered.

'It's okay, I can manage one night,' I said.

'Can you?' she asked and started laughing a little bit too much.

As I spent the evening playing tug with the overgrown pup, I could hear her laughter still echoing in my head.

It was lovely having Wolfie for company. Simply not being alone. Sitting quietly brushing his coat as he gazed up at me grinning was so relaxing – almost meditative. Until I found a matted bit of coat and tugged, and he very gently used his teeth to let me know I'd hurt him.

I was sorely tempted to keep him, but really, I knew it was impossible. If I ended up in jail, he'd need a new home, so why put it off? Lainey could be trusted with him.

Chapter Five

In all the dog-related excitement, I'd totally forgotten about the office setup people. I had to phone Lainey to say I'd be late and predictably, she started laughing again.

I didn't appreciate being the source of quite so much amusement.

When the doorbell rang, I shut Wolfie in the kitchen. There was an occasional muffled woofing noise, but he soon settled.

It wasn't my day: the office removal guys laughed at me too.

'We weren't expecting to see you again so soon,' the youngest guy said, with a cheeky grin.

'Are you sure now,' their boss said, 'before we start moving everything?'

I took it in good part though, as there was no malice in them at all – just friendly joshing.

I couldn't help remembering how hard this kind of thing always was with Matt. When we were young, I used to think it was admirable – a determination to be taken seriously. Looking back, he always had this need to be the man. To be right. He could never relax and joke with people.

He was like that at work too, often telling me off for fraternising with the staff, warning me they wouldn't respect me because I acted too much like one of them.

It felt like a major insight when I realised he was the one who was insecure, not me.

Perhaps that was part of what went wrong between us.

Of course, it had turned out he saw me as one of them too, just staff, given that he'd sold our company, with no consultation.

They'd brought three different sets of blinds for me to choose from, and I chose the plainest.

I couldn't explain why I'd changed my mind about the room, beyond the distracting view. I didn't want to make too much of the fears sparked by those external locks. I didn't want to say anything out loud, in case that made it true. I joked about not wanting to be in an office with the dinosaurs, and said it didn't feel quite right, and I'd decided I'd prefer to have more space.

They were only mildly curious, until I made it awkward by spending too much time explaining.

Once the blinds were installed, they started moving the computer equipment and the desks, and my wonderfully comfortable office chair.

I went down to make coffee. Of course, Wolfie escaped and ran straight upstairs.

There was a lot of laughter, but I didn't hear anything fall so I carried on making the coffee, I set out a tray with a plate of biscuits and carried it upstairs.

'The biscuits are for you,' I said. 'Wolfie can't have chocolate, it's bad for him.'

They didn't object.

The whole story of how I'd acquired the dog had to be told, and they too thought I was mad to have him rehomed.

'He's such a lovely dog,' the youngest guy said. 'So friendly. Won't you miss him?'

I didn't say that the longer he spent with me, the worse it would be in the long term, if I had to give him up. If I ended up in prison after all.

Even when the office was moved, and I waved the guys off for what would be the last time. I still had work to do.

I had a quick sandwich lunch then took a huge doggy chew out of my stash for Wolfie, settling him in the corner of my new office, while I booted up my desktop computer.

My phone pinged. I recognised the number and knew the text would be upsetting.

We're both on the same side in this. Why can't you see that?

I took a screenshot, hands shaking. I created a new folder on my computer, typing HARASSMENT in the Rename Folder box. No more deleting them – in case I needed to hand them over to the police at some point.

What did it mean? Could it be Amy? Implying I'd pushed Matt so far, he'd jumped off the cliff?

When Carstairs talked to me about how he'd died, my instinctive reaction had been to deny that Matt could ever have been suicidal. The email he'd left half-finished on his laptop, apologising to me, had made me waver, though. I'd never known Matt so apologetic, so maybe he was more unhappy than I realised. He'd been drinking, of course. Quite a lot, according to the postmortem. Even so, I could believe in an accident more easily than suicide.

I moved on to the build-up of several days' emails.

Most were spam, and worse than spam, as it was junk I'd signed up for. I should unsubscribe to them all, only it was too much trouble.

None of the work emails were personal, merely the usual office mass mailing, telling me lots of stuff I didn't want to know.

I steeled myself to the task and emailed them all again.

Hi folks,

My new office was completed this morning.

Thought I'd let you know I'm really pleased to be back and am looking forward to working with those of you I already know, and to getting to know the rest of you.

Best,

Jen

I paused, crossing my fingers, as I pressed send.

Next, I took the chance to call my solicitor. Chioma answered the phone herself, and before I had time to ask, she volunteered the answer. 'No, Carstairs and his team haven't called to arrange an interview. It doesn't look at all like it was so urgent, does it? Pure intimidation tactics.'

'He wanted me to agree to talk without you being there,' I said. 'That's a bit worrying.'

'I'll ring him up and put a rocket under him,' Chioma said. 'It does look more like a fishing expedition, right now. Are you available tomorrow, if I can arrange it?'

'Yes, of course,' I said. 'I'd like to get it over with.'

'And don't fret,' Chioma said. 'We know the accusations are vexatious. They have nothing more than circumstantial evidence.'

I knew she was right, although I had a suspicion what it might be about. It wouldn't look good for me, certainly, if I'd guessed correctly.

She agreed to call me back later, whether she'd arranged the interview or not.

I checked my email, compulsively.

There were no replies to my broadcast email, which meant everyone – even the folk who knew me, perhaps especially them, was pussyfooting around.

I was contemplating emptying the cupboards in the dinosaur room when I was saved by the doorbell.

I ran downstairs, Wolfie almost tripping me up, he kept so close. I closed the inner door with him firmly inside, picked up a couple of envelopes from the floor, before opening the front door.

It was Sarah. I was going to have to stop this.

Wolfie barked, and she cowered.

There was temptation again - so many good reasons to keep the great lummox of a dog.

'Give me a minute,' I said. 'I'll shut him in the back garden.'

I rushed out the back, dropping the post on the kitchen table, leaving Sarah trapped in the entrance hall.

Wolfie chased around the garden expecting me to play with him. He wouldn't be happy at being shut outside.

I called Sarah through to the kitchen and she interrogated me about Wolfie as I made tea and put biscuits on a plate. She sounded awfully relieved when I told her I was taking him to the dog rescue.

Wolfie was leaning against the back door, howling mournfully.

'Should we let him in?' Sarah sounded a bit worried.

'Not if you don't want mud and fur all over your white jeans,' I said, laughing as she shuddered.

I picked up the post, addressed to a Verity and Paul Gray.

'I guess these were the previous tenants,' I said to Sarah. 'Are you sure they didn't have any children?'

'Certain,' she said. 'Why do you ask?'

'The middle bedroom looked quite freshly decorated for a child,' I said. 'All dinosaur wallpaper. Were they here long?'

'Just over a year,' she said. 'Maybe they never got around to decorating. They were very standoffish, kept themselves to themselves.'

I laughed. 'That's what people always say when they find out the neighbours were secretly serial killers.'

Sarah shuddered again. 'Someone walked over my grave.'

I had to bite the bullet. I knew she'd take it badly, but I couldn't have her calling round every other day.

'My office is all set up now,' I said. 'And I've talked to my boss. I'm starting work soon so I'm afraid we can't go on with afternoon tea every other day.'

She stood up to leave, in a huff.

'Don't take it badly,' I said. 'It was so good and neighbourly of you to welcome me. But you wouldn't be visiting in work time if I were in an office, would you?'

She hesitated.

'Stay a bit longer,' I said. 'I've got to take Wolfie to the rescue in a bit and I'm not starting office hours quite yet.'

I poured her another cup of tea, as she sat down again.

Then my phone rang. It was Chioma.

'I've got to take this,' I said. 'I'll be back in a minute or two.'

I wandered into the living room for privacy, letting Chioma talk. She'd arranged the interview for eleven the following morning in her office. So that was sorted.

As I got back to the kitchen Sarah was finishing up her tea.

'I'll leave you in peace then,' she said.

As I followed her to the door, I said 'We'll do this again soon, okay?' like the people-pleasing Jenny of old.

I tidied up in the kitchen, stuffed a lump of cheese into Wolfie's rubber puzzle toy, and persuaded him into the boot of the car.

It was good to see Lainey again – it seemed like ages though it had only been a few days.

'You've brought him?' was the first thing she said. 'I was sure you were going to keep him.'

'I left him in the car,' I said, 'in case you weren't around. Let's go meet him then.'

'Oh, he's gorgeous,' she said, as he leapt out of the car. She sat on the floor with him right there, tickling under his chin and then scratching his tummy when he rolled over.

'You can't give him up,' she said.

'I don't want to. But I must. Apart from anything else he deserves better than me. I'm so distracted at the moment, and anyway, who'll look after him if I go to prison?'

She scoffed. 'No one could seriously believe you murdered, Matt, Jen. It will all get sorted, I'm sure.'

'I have a meeting with my solicitor and the police tomorrow,' I admitted. 'Apparently some new evidence has turned up.'

I stayed to have coffee with her while Wolfie bounced around the tiny office, somehow not swiping anything off desk, leaflet displays or bookshelves with his tail.

He stayed quite happily with Lainey as I left, tail still wagging.

'Do your best for him,' I said, as I turned the ignition.

'You know I will.'

It was so quiet in the car, and then in the house that evening. I was already regretting leaving Wolfie behind.

I settled down to watch a thriller on Netflix, only it wasn't very thrilling.

Then I had an idea. I did a reverse image search on a photo of the house, tagged Brighton.

And there it was.

A photo of a couple and a boy standing on the doorstep. They all looked uncomfortable – the boy like he might burst into tears at any moment, the woman turning away, with her hand in front of her face, the man scowling directly into the camera. The date the photo was posted made it likely these were the previous tenants – I counted back on my fingers.

There was a child, after all.

I saved the photo on to tablet and phone, and I printed it out, poring over it to see what I could work out.

I clicked again on the image and discovered it was on a home-schooling forum.

A man, with a cartoon avatar, Tintin, was demanding the photograph be removed. It was in a thread posted months ago and no one answered, and clearly no one had removed it.

These were people who did not want to be found.

I took a chance and emailed the forum admin, explaining I was looking for these people as I'd moved into their old home and I had post for them. It was worth a try.

I searched online for anyone else using Tintin as a handle or profile picture. It was hopeless. He had chosen well – there were hundreds of them.

I pondered developing a tool to sort through them all using the AI capacity of my software. Then I remembered it wasn't my software and imagined what Chris Bailey would have to say about me using his software to stalk people.

At least I knew what they looked like now. And Sarah thought they were still living locally. I'd keep an eye open, if only I knew where they were likely to show up.

Obsessive maybe. But I was so worried about the child.

Chapter Six

The meeting with the police and Chioma wasn't scheduled until eleven, and as it was Wednesday it had been agreed I could skip the morning bail sign in. I planned to enjoy a lie in. That was the theory. In practice I couldn't relax. I was up and tidying my office before breakfast.

Then I pottered in the kitchen, searing chicken and sautéing onions before putting them in the slow cooker with curry spices and a tin of tomatoes so I wouldn't have to cook when I got back. Once that was all set, I unpacked the last half dozen boxes of books, roughly sorting them on to the shelves.

At last, the place was beginning to look a bit more like home, even if it was temporary.

I sat at my kitchen table with a coffee. I looked at the post which had come for the previous tenants.

Paul and Verity Gray.

The people who had, presumably, installed locks and bolts on the outside of the door to the dinosaur bedroom.

I went upstairs, to look at it again. I still couldn't quite believe how chilling it appeared. I couldn't bear to see it closed, so I propped it open again.

I went back to the kitchen and called the landlord.

'Do you have a forwarding address for the previous tenants?' I asked.

He laughed. 'Chance would be a fine thing.'

A little gentle curiosity elicited the fact they'd done a midnight flit, owing two months' rent, even taking into account leaving him with the damage deposit.

'You could try the post office,' he suggested.

I rang the local post office and explained, and they said no redirection had been set up, so there was nothing they could do. I should put the letters in a post-box with *Not known at this address* scrawled on the envelopes.

I googled the names again, as if wanting would make results show up. There was nothing on Google Images, nothing on Twitter or Facebook or Insta. It was as if they didn't exist. I was being stupid and obsessive, but I couldn't stop thinking about those locks.

The letter looked personal and had no return address, so there didn't seem to be much point. Even though I was curious, it felt wrong, opening their post, so I left it at the end of the kitchen counter and tried to ignore it.

Somehow the early morning had disappeared so I grabbed a slice of toast and a drink, refilled my water bottle, and psyched myself up for an encounter with DI Carstairs. At least this time I knew I'd have Chioma by my side.

I was there with time to spare. It was good to relax with a coffee with Chioma in her office, as we waited for the police.

I'd been worrying about how the police would cope without recording the interview.

'We have all the gear here – useful for our own records and we also use it in training sessions, so we can see how we're likely to come across in court.'

'Do you have an outtakes reel?' I asked.

'Oh yes,' she said. 'It's the highlight of the Christmas party.'

I wasn't sure if she was joking.

It wasn't long before DI Carstairs and his meek female shadow arrived. Carstairs made a fuss about having to print off his files, especially. As if I'd not seen him wielding his manila folders in the police interview room, like a weapon.

Once they were settled, the interview began in the usual way, with the caution.

'I'm sure you must know what this is about,' Carstairs said.

'Well, I presume you've still not found the evidence needed to clear me of murder,' I said. 'And that's astonishing. Someone must have seen Matt. It's not as if he was that fond of his own company.'

Carstairs sighed.

'You told us,' he said, 'you had no motive to kill your husband. Your share of the proceeds from selling NRS Tech was more than enough to keep you for the rest of your life. You weren't greedy and didn't begrudge him his share, to do with whatever he pleased.'

'Still true,' I said.

'Your mother-in-law told us you'd only recently found out about Matt's girlfriend. That she was pregnant and you would do anything to stop her getting her share.'

'I told you then, I knew he had a girlfriend. He told me she was pregnant. I saw her for the first time at his funeral. With my mother-in-law. You were there. You must have seen how shocked I was.'

'Shocked and angry,' Carstairs said.

'Angry that my mother-in-law had taken her in. Not angry enough to go back in time and kill him.'

'You ought to be taking this seriously.'

'I am,' I said. 'But it doesn't seem to me that you are. You've decided I'm guilty, based entirely on my mother-in-law's view. You don't seem to be looking at anyone else for this.'

Chioma shook her head at me. I wasn't supposed to be aggressive – I was supposed to be reasonable.

'Look,' I said, trying to control my tone, 'I was angry. I'd been lied to about so many things. I told you that I'd thrown Matt out after he told me all this stuff. I was devastated by his betrayal. But I didn't kill him.'

He opened the manila folder and took out a sheet of paper. He pushed it across the desk so Chioma and I could read it.

I recognised it, of course.

'Your point is?'

'You forged this document,' Carstairs said. 'And one of the first things you did after the death of your husband was take it down to the IVF clinic.'

I was angry now.

'After his death?' I said. 'Are you sure? You told me he was found on Tuesday morning. He signed this on the Saturday and I took it to the IVF clinic on Monday morning. The first chance I had. Those embryos, belonging to Matt and me – they were my last chance to have my own baby. Obviously I took it to the clinic – I didn't want them destroyed.'

'You gave the letter to the Clinic Manager and asked for the embryos to be preserved?'

'I did.'

I knew now what had happened. She hadn't liked me, and like so many women, she had been charmed by Matt.

'The Clinic Manager asked you to wait, and talk to your counsellor, correct?'

'She did.'

'And the counsellor said after your last visit, and the failed implantation, Matt had called in with a letter requesting the embryos should be destroyed.'

'She did. She showed me his letter, and the forms he had signed on the Friday. While I was waiting in the car, he went back in – to get his coat, he said. Then she showed me the records of the destruction of the embryos.'

'You were very angry, right?'

'Yes, I was angry! I had gone all the way down to the cottage to persuade him to sign this!' I picked it up.

'I knew he was leaving me, but we'd been together a long time. I thought he might relent if I asked. And he did, he signed. He didn't tell me he'd already asked the clinic to destroy them. Maybe he'd forgotten. Or he was just taking the easy route putting off the inevitable confrontation. He was, after all, a coward.'

Carstairs twisted the knife.

'He signed, knowing full well the embryos had been destroyed. You expect me to believe that?'

'I've said it before. Matt didn't like emotional scenes. That's why he dumped everything on me at once.'

'This is a forgery, isn't it? Carstairs said. 'He refused to sign and so you killed him. Then you forged his signature.'

'Is that what the counsellor told you? Clueless.'

Carstairs looked at me, and I could see he was disturbed his new evidence hadn't bothered me.

'Do you think this is enough to charge me with murder?' I asked.

Carstairs said, 'It shows motive. And it is certainly strongly indicative of fraud.'

'Charge me with fraud then and have done with it. Believe me, I can prove you wrong. This is ridiculous.'

I was angry, and mostly because I knew there were unshed tears building up. Chioma could see that too, I think.

She intervened.

'My client does have a point, Detective Inspector. It's all very circumstantial, and I don't think you have enough evidence for a fraud charge, let alone murder. All you have is a theory, and a story. And it's clear there are alternative stories available.'

Carstairs spoke. 'In my view, Ms Blake has serious questions to answer.'

Chioma, at her most regal. 'I think this interview is over for now, unless you have anything else?'

Carstairs was silent.

'In that case, wait a moment and I'll give you a copy of the DVD. I'm sure when you look at this more carefully, you will see no evidence of deception from my client.'

She pushed the IVF letter back towards him. 'You can keep the copy,' he said.

'I already have one,' I pointed out.

When the police had gone, Chioma said, 'Well, I wasn't expecting that.'

'Me neither,' I said. 'I'd wondered about suing the clinic for destroying the embryos so quickly. But what was the point? They were gone.'

Now the tears flowed.

'I'm so sorry,' she said. 'I didn't know about the IVF.'

'We didn't tell anyone, apart from his mother. Matt didn't want anyone to know. We had three failed cycles.'

'Then he got his girlfriend pregnant. I can see why the police think it's motive,'

I laughed through my tears.

'Maybe. But I wasn't surprised when he signed. He was selfish and arrogant and all but I went down there knowing he would agree. It was leverage, to make me more cooperative. He always liked to have leverage.'

'Only he'd already asked for them to be destroyed,' Chioma said, gently.

'He maybe hadn't expected them to be destroyed so quickly. And he certainly wasn't expecting to be murdered.'

I was making excuses for him again. My tears flowed. I had been right to worry that once I started, I might not stop. I was shocked he had, in the end, cared so little for me.

Chioma continued. 'What Carstairs said, about it not looking anything like his signature?'

'Oh that means nothing. I saw him sign, remember! But his signature was a running joke. It rarely looked the same way twice.'

'Have you got any evidence? It would be useful.'

'There must be loads. Company documents, bank authorisations. I'll get on to various people and get them to send you copies, shall I?'

I felt better now there was something practical I could do.

'Is there anything else?' she asked me.

I didn't want to lie to her, so I didn't answer.

'I do wish they'd look for the real killer,' I said. 'It wasn't me, but it must have been someone.'

Chapter Seven

I'd not reached the kitchen, let alone put the kettle on, when there was a hammering on the front door.

Without thinking, I opened the door and was confronted by a man I didn't recognise. I took a step back, worried for a moment he might be a journalist, or someone looking for me on Amy's behalf. I hadn't read her last email, but I assumed it was as unhinged as the rest of my collection.

'Oh,' he said. 'I'm sorry for disturbing you. I'm looking for Paul and Verity Gray who used to live here.'

I laughed, wryly. 'Good luck with that. I've been trying to find out where to forward their post in case it's important. The landlord has no idea, nor the post office, nor the only neighbour I've met.'

He pulled out a photo ID, showing his details from work. Nick Kennedy. He was tall, blue eyed, and a bit lanky and awkward, and he resembled the photo ID. He was some kind of therapist, it seemed. He didn't appear to recognise me, at least. He looked trustworthy, and of course I was driven by an obsession with the Grays, so I asked him in.

He followed me to the kitchen. As I went to fill the kettle, I noticed the back door was wide open.

'Oh shit,' I said. 'That door certainly wasn't open when I went out. Someone broke in. They could still be here.'

I was furious, frightened, shaking. Was there no escape?

He went over to the door, curious. 'The lock's definitely been forced. Better call the police, I reckon.'

'It's probably nothing,' I said, downplaying even though he'd seen my first reaction. I didn't want to be forced to call the police. 'I'm being stalked by my husband's girlfriend. It's likely her.'

'Stop,' he said, laying a hand on my arm. 'There may be someone in here still. A drunk, a junkie. Who knows?'

I resisted for a minute longer but then realised the truth of it and made the call.

'Someone will be round soon,' I said.

I waited and he waited with me. Neither of us was comfortable.

'There's no noise,' I said. 'I can't wait forever for the police. I'm going to check if there's anything missing.'

There was nothing out of place in the living room. Nick followed me, and we looked round upstairs – bathroom, front bedroom, back bedroom, the middle room – the door still propped open.

'I can't see anything,' Nick said. 'Not that I know what to look for.'

'Me neither. I feel silly now, for calling the police,' I said.

At that moment there was another banging on the door. I jumped out of my skin, almost, and even Nick was startled.

'The police' we both said, at the same time.

I ran down the stairs and let the police in. Detective Constable Dave Elliott, solid and reliable, with tidy grey hair, introduced himself, showing his warrant card. A young woman in uniform was with him, a PC Lucy Shelton.

I explained Nick to them, saying I'd just met him, and they looked at me as if I was mad.

Then I showed them the back door and where the lock had been forced and said that as far as I could tell, nothing had been taken.

'Looks like you interrupted them,' DC Dave Elliott said, 'Perhaps Mr Kennedy here scared them off.'

'I think they must have been gone before I came in, before Nick arrived,' I said.

The police wandered around the house and the garden, checking for access. They gave me a card with instructions to contact them if I had any more trouble, and a case number for the insurance.

When the police had gone, I called the emergency locksmith and then at last I made coffee for Nick, and we sat down at the kitchen table.

'So how did you know the previous tenants?' I asked, genuinely curious.

Nick explained it was awkward as he was bound by confidentiality, but in the circumstances... He was a therapist and had been advising the family, particularly concerning their young son, and was worried when they disappeared.

'Maybe I crossed the line with them,' he said. 'I was so worried about their son, Alex. I suggested a play date with my son Rory, who is autistic.'

Alex. That was the name of the child I was so worried about. He seemed more real, more substantial, now he had a name.

'I'd advised them Alex needed more social interaction. Maybe they didn't like my advice, but I wasn't pushing. I tried to call but the mobile was dead. It's been a few weeks now, and so that's why I turned up on your doorstep.'

We had a long and strange conversation in which we both avoided answering each other's questions but gently probed for more information. It was like a very slow, formal dance of some kind.

I showed him the pile of letters I'd collected for the Grays and told him again, that I'd talked to the landlord and the post office.

Nick let slip that the Grays found him through a referral on a chat forum of some kind, a parenting forum. They were looking for help with a difficult child who they thought might be autistic and one of the families he had helped recommended him.

Nick seemed genuinely to care, and this made me more and more anxious for the child.

I wondered about showing him the bolts and locks on the outside of the middle bedroom door, but decided against it. For now.

He finished his coffee as the locksmith arrived. Clearly he'd been holding on until he could safely leave me, and he gave me a business card, then took it back, and scribbled his personal mobile number on the back.

Nick suggested I could check up on him with his professional association, if I was at all worried. I promised I'd let him know if I found anything out about the Grays.

I didn't think it would come to anything.

Now I had a more solid theory about why they might be locking the kid up. And I was sure the kid existed.

He was a real boy, called Alex, who loved dinosaurs, and was prone to meltdowns.

I had to find him somehow, and make sure he was alright.

Chapter Eight

It was difficult getting back to work after all the distractions, not least because I didn't really want to. I gave myself a stern talking to, pointing out that the year would drag painfully if I didn't find a way to enjoy it. And that, in spite of everything, I really was very fortunate.

I made coffee and toast to take up to my office, in a slightly more optimistic frame of mind. Looking for the signed documents for Chioma and Carstairs could wait until later.

I checked texts and emails first. I had to keep an eye out for interesting new items for my collection. There was nothing from the mysterious anonymous person who'd been threatening to hunt me down. Also, nothing from the estate agent who was supposed to be letting my house, either. I decided a nudge by email would do, until I had the time and energy to care. They were supposed to be holding an open house at the weekend and they hadn't even let me know how many people they were expecting to show up.

There was an email from *that bitch* Amy though. On reflection, I didn't think she was the person sending the texts. The use of language was different, and she was less threatening in tone. Obviously, that was because she wanted something from me. The something being money. Was she clever enough for a two-pronged attack? I didn't think so. Maybe that was just me being cruel.

Matthew would not have wanted me left high and dry, carrying his child. You know that. There are laws about this. I have a solicitor and I will be challenging the will. My son, Matthew's son, will be provided for as he intended. He told you all about me. I know he did. You will pay. Now, or later.

A boy. Matt would have been so thrilled. God, how it hurt, that I would never have his child. Our daughter, or our son – those last two embryos that had been destroyed.

I shouldn't have replied, but I was too angry for self-control.

Why am I supposed to believe this child is Matt's? He had plenty of time to change his will over the past few months. He spent enough time with lawyers, selling the company. That shows where his priorities lay, I suppose. Maybe he didn't care as much about you both as you think? Or maybe he didn't believe the child was his? Why do you think we were having IVF treatment? He didn't have good swimmers, you know.

I looked at the message and considered softening it – as I usually would – at least deleting the stupid lie about Matt's sperm. I pressed send with a tight smile.

I was so very fed up with being nice to everyone. Being the grown up.

Then I forwarded all Amy's emails to Chioma. I begged her to take over dealing with the whole mess, or at least to hand it over to the most junior person in her office. I added that we needed to prepare to make a reasonable offer. In spite of everything, Amy was in the right. Matt wouldn't have wanted his child to go without.

It was ten o clock before I actually started work.

In my work email folder, I had a message from Stefan Florescu, inviting me to phone in advance of starting work proper, so we could set up secure remote access to the system.

It sounded like a good plan – and I intended to offer to make a short trip into the office to meet properly soon.

I messaged him on WhatsApp and he sent me all the information I'd need to set up my login and remote connection, and promised he'd join me on a video call and help me work through it.

I made another coffee and was back at my desk before he was ready to start.

I managed to log in using my new remote ID – apparently my old one 'bossywoman' was no longer deemed appropriate. Probably they'd set up a new one to make sure I didn't still get my previous levels of access. Luckily Stefan was there to hold my hand through the rest of it.

The video chat was awkward at first, but we soon settled into it. Stefan was something of a looker, I decided. All dark curls and intense eyes. All that was soon forgotten as we started talking tech. It was easy to see he really knew his stuff, so I relaxed. I hadn't realised until that moment how stressed I had been. His CV undersold him, by a long way.

After an intense two-hour session – too long without pause, I thought – I was all set up.

We agreed to take a comfort break, then had a long video chat about how we'd approach working together.

Stefan was brilliant, and while I'd been unavailable, he'd made a great start on understanding how the software was put together. He'd assembled a team which incorporated a couple of new technical members of staff and was beginning to consider future developments.

I introduced a couple of ideas from before the takeover that were very early stage and not documented anywhere, while we chatted away happily making plans. I started to get quite excited for the first time in years.

Then Stefan mentioned having to present the various project ideas to the board and I was deflated. I covered it up well enough – he probably wouldn't connect the dots and realise it had all been my decision in the past.

We arranged a time for the first proper work session for the following week.

And I sat at my desk and wept.

Matt had done this to me. He had taken away my last chance to have my own child, and he had taken away my influence in my own company. Without a second thought he had irrevocably altered my life.

For the first time I wondered why I hadn't been angry enough to kill him.

After gathering my emotions into a tight ball and pushing them aside, I phoned our business and personal bank managers – I still thought of them as ours – and asked if it was possible to see copies of the various mandates Matt had signed. They were a bit hesitant until I said it was for legal purposes and they could email them to my solicitor and to DI Carstairs.

'I'm not defrauding anyone,' I said, from my high horse. How long have I been one of your customers?'

Focus on the practical, I told myself. I emptied out the bottom drawer of the filing cabinet and rifled through the documents. I soon found half a dozen with varying examples of Matt's signature. I scanned and emailed copies to Chioma.

There was also a sealed manila envelope. I had no idea what it might be – this drawer was full of papers I'd lifted wholesale from Matt's desk. Unlike me, he was addicted to decluttering – not quite Marie Kondo addicted, but close. Either it was important, or in some way it sparked joy.

I opened it and pulled out a document. It wasn't anything that I didn't know – Matt had told me, after all. It's why I threw him out. Seeing it spelled out in black and white was painful. The whole, stupid, immoral, illegal plan.

Ironically it had the best comparative signature for my document, but it was the one document I couldn't bear for anyone else to see.

I put it back in the envelope, then put the envelope back at the bottom of the filing cabinet drawer.

I missed Wolfie. I needed cake. A little exercise wouldn't hurt either.

I walked to the local bakery and bought a couple of cream eclairs and jam doughnuts.

Sarah was still out in her garden when I got back. I waved the white card cake box under her nose and asked if she would like to join me.

'I thought it was a workday,' she said.

'Don't take the huff,' I said. 'And it's because it's been the most god awful work day that I need good company.'

She was easily persuaded, which boded well. So long as she didn't interpret it as open house.

She left her gardening stuff on my front step and washed up at the kitchen sink as I put the kettle on and put plates with the box of cakes on the table.

I closed my eyes as I had my first bite of chocolate éclair.

'Looks like you needed that,' Sarah said. 'Anything you want to talk about?'

I thought about being on police bail, having been accused of forgery and fraud, and of the loss of my company. It was hopeless – impossible to explain to someone I didn't know, and didn't even know if I wanted to know.

'The usual nonsense,' I said. 'Getting used to working with new people. It's always difficult.'

'The wolf's gone, I see.'

'I was tempted to keep him, but I can't justify it. I'd rather be properly settled first.'

I told her about my idea of setting up my own dog rescue, at some point in the future.

'Wow, that sounds like an interesting ambition. I thought from what you'd said you were totally into computers.'

'Oh, don't get me wrong. I love working in tech. But life is for living and I want to do something else now. Something with a bit more heart.'

'And more bite!' she said.

The letter for Paul and Verity Gray was still on the table. 'I've been trying to find out where they've gone,' I said. 'They didn't leave a forwarding address with the landlord, or the post office. I guess they could be anywhere now. I don't like to throw it away, in case it's important.'

'If they had anything important due, surely they'd have arranged for forwarding? But they are still in the area. I saw him at the Karma Cafe, the other day.'

'Oh, where's that?' I asked, trying to appear just a normal level of curious.

'It's on a side street, up in Portslade Old Village. They do the best vegan food. Ages ago, he told me it was their favourite sandwich place. Mind, last time I saw him, he blanked me when I said hello. But it was him. Just rude.'

Most people look away when there's something uncomfortable going on. They don't see abuse, because they are deliberately, wilfully blind. They leave it for someone else to deal with. And sometimes that means no one does. The Bystander Effect, it's called. When I was a child, I swore I would not be one of those people who stood by.

This was the first opportunity I'd had to keep the most important promise I'd ever made to myself.

After a long chat I waved Sarah off at the front door, and then locked the whole world out. I was home alone, and it was oh so quiet.

I was already regretting taking Wolfie to Lainey.

Chapter Nine

Working with Stefan in the mornings provided something of a structure for my days, though it all felt oddly empty. I was relieved when he said we didn't have to work together so closely. I think I managed to hide it, but I guess he knew. Techies will be techies and many of us are loners.

We came to an easy agreement that a couple of online sessions a week would be enough to keep us on track. I promised to write up some documentation, including producing a report on the system upgrades we'd discussed, which earned me some brownie points. We also had a discussion about which might be most appealing to our clients.

I arranged an onsite visit to the office for the following Monday – just a short one, to give me the chance to meet everyone. Stefan volunteered to organise, which was generous of him.

When we logged out of the NRS Tech network, I checked my email. There was nothing.

There was, however, another text for my "harassment" folder.

You'll never be safe again, you stupid cow!

This one had a certain flair with language and an addiction to the exclamation mark. And it was brief. There was also video attachment.

Foolishly, I watched it.

It was low-resolution and it took me a minute to work out what I was seeing. Someone in my house, face disguised with a scarf, pawing over everything. Rummaging through my knicker drawer in the bedroom. Scanning the contents of the bathroom cabinet. Running gloved fingers along the windowsill in the dinosaur bedroom. In my office – looking in files, and even attempting – and failing – to log on to my computer.

At the end, as this vile person was videoing the contents of my fridge, I heard the sound of the front door opening and slamming shut, followed soon after by a knocking on the door and my voice saying hello to Nick.

I'd only missed whoever it was by a couple of minutes.

If Nick hadn't arrived so soon after I did, maybe it would have been much worse.

I was shaking, now. Really scared. I'd been ignoring it, but I couldn't anymore.

I phoned Chioma first and told her what had happened. She agreed that I needed to report it - this was way beyond a few texts and emails, sounding positively dangerous.

'I don't think it's all the same person, though,' I said.

'It's the police's job to investigate, not yours.'

'You know I ought to have informed Carstairs I was moving,' I said.

'I'll deal with it, should it become necessary,' Chioma said. 'You told me, and you're always available. And the leaks were coming from somewhere. It was perfectly reasonable to take a safety-first approach.'

'I'm not sure Carstairs will see it that way.'

'Meanwhile, you get in touch with the local police who visited yesterday and make sure the house is secure.'

I found DC Elliott's card, but even though I knew I should call him, I couldn't make myself do it. This was not what I had in mind when I moved here to make a fresh start.

I heard the click of the letterbox and the post fell on the mat in the hall, startling me. It was funny how perfectly ordinary sounds seemed to be louder and more intrusive – all my nerves were on edge.

It was mostly junk mail, but there was another letter for the Grays, and this one looked official.

I took it into the kitchen, made a coffee, and sat staring at the letter.

I knew I shouldn't, but I steamed it open and read it through.

Twice.

Dear Mr and Mrs Gray

Further to our letter of 15th May I am writing to remind you, as we were made aware you have a child of school age who is not registered at a school, that we served notice on you under section 437 (1) of the Education Act 1996, informing you that you had fifteen days to demonstrate you are providing Alex Gray with an education which meets the required standards.
As you have failed to comply with our request, we will be applying for a School Attendance order and Alex will be legally required to attend a local school of our choice.

Brighton Department of Education.

I looked at the dates and counted back.

This was why they moved. To escape being inspected by the Department of Education

I knew I was right. Alex, the poor child, was in some kind of danger.

They were locking him up, and they were home schooling. They wanted to avoid even the most basic inspection. When Nick said he thought the boy was isolated, he was right,

This was all so familiar to me. I felt sick, thinking how the child was being deprived of a normal life. I'd been one of the lucky ones. I was already in school when my mother married Richard, and it would have been too blatant to remove me – though he had wanted to. Other kids who attended the chapel didn't even have the luxury of daily escape into a more ordinary world.

I searched online again. I could find nothing referring to them by name. Not a single mention. I had perhaps been a bit too trusting with Nick. Maybe he had something to do with the break in? I couldn't quite believe it, though. Whoever had broken in had wanted me to be scared. Nick might have been lying, but I was pretty sure it was because he wanted something. And he had stayed with me until the locksmith came, out of what had felt like genuine concern.

I absolutely refused to distrust everyone. I'd been there before and nothing good ever came from it.

Most of all, I was so worried about the child. Alex. Locked in his room. Not even going to school. It sounded as if he was almost a prisoner.

Chapter Ten

I wondered how the open house viewing had gone, and if the letting agent had any prospective tenants lined up. I was about to ring to find out, when I had a slightly hysterical phone call from Lainey.

'Have you seen The Mail,' she said, almost gibbering.

'No. Why would I want to?'

My heart was already sinking though. I was imagining another story about the Black Widow of Wimbledon, leaked by Carstairs' team. A fishing expedition. Now with added details about my skill at forgery and my hormonal state, thus showing I'd been driven to murder not – as previously assumed – by greed – but instead by some form of hysteria brought on by my wandering, barren womb.

'I'm not going out to buy The Mail,' I said.

'Look online then,' Lainey pleaded.

There it was. A huge picture spread with photos of the house, and all the details of how it was available to rent.

'Oh, for heaven's sake. I am paying the letting agent more because they promised to protect my privacy. I will have their guts for garters.'

Lainey said, 'I was worried they might try to track you down at your new home, given it says you've moved out.'

I didn't tell Lainey my new home had already been desecrated. I decided to set aside my fears that the police might see the article – I would cross that bridge when I came to it.

'Maybe I will go home for the day and make sure they know I'm there. I will say I was out for the open house. Make them look stupid.'

I could easily fit it in around my visit to the office, but I was seething with resentment at the waste of my time.

'More importantly, how's Wolfie?' I asked. 'Has anyone shown an interest yet?'

'He's a delightful boy,' Lainey said. 'Missing you though.'

'Ha, so long as he's fed, he won't care. Anyway, I bet you're giving him loads of fuss.'

'I am. He's a big dog though, won't be easy to find the right home for him. I wish you'd reconsider.'

'I might pop in later,' I said. 'As I'll be in the area.'

Not that I was having second thoughts about Wolfie.

Also, I wouldn't be phoning the letting agents. It would be far more effective to give them a bollocking in person.

On my way I called in at the pet superstore to buy a new rope toy for Wolfie. Completely ridiculous, but still.

In front of me in the queue I saw a young boy having a meltdown, and his parents struggling. I was watching them a bit too closely and the dad saw me and gave me the evil eye.

'Oh, I'm sorry. I was miles away. Can I help?'

I distracted the boy by talking about my dog. I showed him a photo of Wolfie on my phone, and then the toys I was buying as we all slowly progressed in the queue for the till.

Looking at the boy's parents I could see how different they were from Alex's family. Not at all likely to lock the boy in his room. They had a child who was having difficulties, yes, but they were working hard to help him get used to being out and about.

A brief flash of memory, and I was back in the dark cupboard, back in my childhood. I could hear the voice of the pastor, my stepfather Richard, talking about what it was like living outside the light of the Lord, to be cast eternally into the outer darkness. How I had screamed, terrified he would never let me out.

Suddenly I was back in the bright lights of the store and it was my turn to step to the front of the queue and pay. I apologised for my ditziness.

Awkwardness over, the boy's parents waved to me happily enough, but it was a warning. I needed to be more situationally aware, and less obsessed.

I decided to check the Karma Café, the vegan place Sarah had mentioned. It was a bit out of my way, but only a small detour from the main road out of town. It was set back from the road, so I didn't see it at first, but I quickly found a parking space, which was lucky.

I went in and bought a coffee and a sandwich to take away.

It was surprisingly roomy inside. Looking around there were a few people working at laptops, so they'd provide me with cover if I decided to start keeping a regular look out for the Grays.

I spent some time reading the crammed noticeboard. I smiled, as it was all very Brighton: yoga and T'ai Chi classes; courses of all kinds, from self-care to promises of spiritual discovery; various groups of Green and other political progressives, including one for home schooling parents – intended to create opportunities to socialise their children without exposing them to dangerous influences. If only I had a child... Perhaps I could borrow Sarah's daughter?

Well, that was probably a step too far.

A young waitress spoke to me, asking if I was interested in any of the groups.

'I thought I might try T'ai Chi,' I said. 'I loved it, but lapsed a long time ago.'

'Andrea's a brilliant teacher,' she said. 'You should sign up.'

'I'm new to the area,' I said. 'So pleased to have found you all here.'

I put my drink and sandwich down on the side table, and took some photos of the noticeboard, making it look like I was considering the classes and groups. Really, I was collecting leads, I thought. Perhaps one of these threads, if I tugged, might lead me to the Grays.

Of course, I didn't see either Gray – I knew that was a long shot.

Just as well, actually, as I was booked up for the day.

I drove back to my old house – how quickly I had stopped thinking of it as home.

I let myself in then wandered all around, making sure to spend time at the windows. I wanted to be seen. It was odd how quickly I'd lost any emotional connection to the place.

I'd put a big hat on to hide my new hair colour. My neighbours were likely to assume that was the disguise, and the thought amused me.

As I locked up, I noticed my neighbour had suddenly decided to wash his car. I leaned on the fence and chatted to him about the weather, and how the coming rain would ruin the polish on the Merc. He was lost for words. He couldn't even find a hello.

The letting agents were next.

When I walked in, the usually busy, chatter-filled office fell completely silent.

'I guess you know why I'm here, then,' I said. 'Not one of you had the courage to call me and tell me what happened?'

After I'd extracted an apology and negotiated a much-reduced fee, given their failure to protect my privacy, I left them to it.

Bumping into one of the younger agents, outside on a cigarette break, I asked him if he fancied earning a little bonus. When I told him what I wanted, he happily took my money to leak to the Mail I'd blown up at them for failing to stick to the privacy clause, and to accidentally let them know I was still living there.

I was early for my appointment with Stefan at the office, but only by about half an hour. It felt a bit weird, anyway. It was still hard for me to imagine the company without Matt. I sat in my car for a few minutes, holding back tears.

I was pleased to see the NRS Tech sign was still there – I had wondered if they would change the company name, but it looked as if that would stay.

I was noticed, so I had to go in before people started talking and making up stories. Even if they were true stories about how upset I was.

Kerry was on reception and instead of signing me in she ran round the desk squealing and hugged me.

'We've missed you so much,' she said. I was sure not everyone had. Maybe some of them even suspected I'd murdered Matt. He wasn't an easy boss, and a few of them had probably fantasised about killing him themselves.

She sat me down and brought me coffee, telling me Stefan was running around but would be out soon.

To my astonishment, Chris Bailey appeared as if by magic, all smiles.

'So pleased to see you again,' he said. 'Welcome home.'

Expecting a business-like handshake, I was surprised by another hug. This never used to be a huggy office, I thought. What has happened here? Invasion of the Body Snatchers?

I was overwhelmed with sadness again, that I couldn't share that thought with Matt, and that I'd never see his terrible Donald Sutherland impression again.

'I'd normally be offering to show you around, but it seems a bit unnecessary in the circumstances,' he said.

I managed a laugh. 'It feels odd to be back. So much has changed, but I very much appreciate the warm welcome.'

'And here's Stefan, looking for us,' Chris said.

I happily shook Stefan's hand, saying how good it was to meet him properly, and how much I was enjoying working with him. He was even more charming and attractive in person, but also just as self-effacing.

I added I was impressed with how quickly he had a handle on the innards of the software.

Chris praised him too. 'Stefan is our technical genius,' he said. 'Which is necessary, given that he will be your replacement.'

Stefan said, 'Come through and meet the rest of the team,' shepherding me into the large meeting room, which was full of people I knew, as well as people who were new to me.

On the meeting-room table there was heaps of food – properly good food too, not just sandwiches – and bottles of actual champagne.

Chris gave a short speech welcoming me back to work and then everyone pounced on the food and drink. I soon met all the new people, realising there was no hope I'd remember all of their names. It was bittersweet to talk to the rest, the familiar faces, knowing they'd be thinking about Matt and maybe wondering, *Could she really have killed him?*

It was like a leaving party, without even getting to leave.

After my scheduled hour and a half, I decided it was probably okay to escape. Chris and Stefan saw me off the premises, and I waved goodbye as I drove off.

I found a safe place to park and sat in my car and wept again for all I'd lost. It helped that they were lovely – of course it did – but still, my grief was real.

And of course, my phone pinged. I couldn't even be left in peace with my sense of loss.

I only wanted to talk to you. There was no need to run away.

For a moment I was confused, and thought it was someone at the party I'd just skipped out on. Then I realised. It was just more of the same.

I ran away so all you ghouls would leave me alone, I thought. I didn't answer. I knew it would make things worse if I did.

I needed solace, so I drove over to the dog rescue. Lainey would make time for me, and being with the dogs would be extra comfort.

Of course, she fetched Wolfie to join us, so I sat on the floor with him, giving him his new rope toy.

'That dog has too many toys already,' Lainey said. She was going to say more, but I glared her into silence, and told her all about the office party.

She sympathised with my mixed feelings, but even though she didn't say a word on the topic of me adopting the dog, I knew it was on her mind.

Wolfie gave a single desolate woof and a lazy tail wag as I left, breaking my heart.

I couldn't though.

I didn't have time for a big lummox of a dog who needed lots of basic training and socialisation. I kept telling myself that on the drive home.

Home, to Brighton. Whatever else, I'd been right to move.

Chapter Eleven

The next day, after dashing to Wimbledon to sign in for bail, on my return I took my laptop to the Karma Café to begin work on my report for Stefan.

I was greeted by the young waitress, who said it was good to see me again so soon.

As I was nibbling on a rather solid flapjack, and typing my draft report, I was interrupted by the sound of my mobile ringtone. The one which alerted me to a call from Matt.

It had to be Amy. She had his phone, like she had everything else he'd taken to the cottage. I hadn't objected. At that point I hadn't cared. It was beginning to seem like an oversight.

My heart beating fast, I answered.

I nodded to the waitress, mouthed I'd be back, and left my laptop on the table with my cake and coffee as I went outside to take the call.

I paced up and down the pavement as I talked.

'Did it occur to you that it was an unpleasant thing to do, to phone me on my dead husband's mobile,' I said, after I caught my breath.

She'd been ranting for five minutes by then, but even when I tried to rewind in my mind, I couldn't remember anything she'd said.

'I heard from your solicitor,' Amy said, not answering my question.

'Please deal with her, not with me,' I said. 'I have no interest in speaking with you.'

'I want this sorted out,' Amy said, as if she hadn't heard a word I said. 'Matt would not have wanted me to be struggling like this.'

'This is harassment.' I was loud, and angry. 'I am grieving the loss of my husband, and you are hounding me. It's not my fault Matt didn't provide for you. Look. I didn't know about you. You knew everything. One of us is at fault here, and it isn't me.'

That wasn't quite true of course. It was my story, though, and I was sticking to it.

'Of course you knew,' Amy said. 'Matt promised me he'd told you. He was in love with me.'

I laughed. 'Love? Do you think he knew what love was?'

'He was leaving you for me. You begged him for a last chance with IVF He only gave you that chance out of pity. It's not my fault that I'm pregnant and you're not.'

Amy burst into noisy tears – she wasn't the type to cry quietly. In a snotty, muffled voice she said. 'I know what you know. And I know what you did. Bear that in mind.'

For a few moments, I couldn't speak for the pain. I was winded, as if gut punched.

'He lied to me, over and over,' I said. 'He was already lying to you. Consider yourself lucky he didn't live long enough to betray you, as he betrayed me. Talk to my solicitor.'

I felt a slight, momentary satisfaction as I hung up on her. That bitch.

As I turned to go back into the cafe, I saw him, coming out, carrying a cake box.

Paul Gray. I was sure of it.

I stood watching him walk up the road, at a brisk pace. I wanted to follow him, but I couldn't leave my laptop.

They were living in walking distance though, surely? Of course, it was impossible to know how far he'd walk for his favourite cake.

I went back to the report, but I couldn't settle. He wasn't going to come back to the cafe today though, so I paid my bill, packed up my laptop and went home.

Wandering around the house, a new wave of grief for Matt washed over me. Angry as I was, that was not going to go away.

I couldn't stop fretting about the break in, and wondering if Amy was behind it. Briefly I considered phoning DC Elliott, but I still couldn't make myself. I'd had more than enough of dealing with the police.

An email pinged, from the web forum person. A long rant about stalking and privacy and how I needed to learn to leave people alone.

We are a community, he said, *and we look after our own.* I messaged back and said he had me confused with someone else, and I didn't need an address for them – but if he could pass their post on, I'd be glad enough to be rid of it.

It was so over the top, I wondered what was wrong with him, but I guessed it didn't really matter. I didn't need him anymore. Karma Cafe was my way forward.

I admitted to myself I was already half-planning taking some kind of direct action. I wasn't hanging around the café every day just so I could find the Grays and give them their post. I wanted to know where they lived now, so I could check it out for myself. I needed to know the boy was safe.

Then I'd be able to relax, let go of this compulsion, and get on with my life.

Chapter Twelve

I had a very troubled night. It wasn't surprising, really. I was suspected of murder. I still missed Matt; the bastard. I was worried about the child. I was stressed out of my mind, knowing both my homes now felt unsafe.

How much darker could my life get?

That was not a challenge to the universe. If only I were superstitious, I could touch wood.

Perhaps I should have called the police, as Chioma had advised. Instead, I drove over to visit Lainey.

As soon as she saw my face, she started laughing. She went to collect Wolfie, who rather too enthusiastically jumped up and put his paws on my shoulders. That would be one of the first things to train him out of – endearing though I found it.

'Shall I start on the paperwork?' she asked, as soon as she was able to pause for breath.

'Yes, please,' I said.

'Technically, I should do a home visit since you're living in a different place now. But if you fill in your official address, there'll be no need and you can take him today.'

I signed the form and paid up, including a generous donation.

'I knew you wouldn't be able to resist him for long,' she said. She rummaged on the shelves behind her desk and found a bag, which she passed to me. It contained all the doggy stuff I'd bought for him.

'I shouldn't,' I said. 'All my reasons were valid. But there are good reasons to give in too. I need the company, and if he's not exactly guard dog material, my stalker won't know that.'

'I've done some work on training him,' Lainey said. 'He needs a lot more work on the lead – and off lead. But he's better at sit, down, and stay than I expected.'

'Everyone needs a hobby, as Aunt Martha used to say, and it looks like Wolfie will be mine for the next while.'

Lainey hugged me.

'I think you're doing the right thing,' she said. 'It's beyond time you took on a new dog.'

'He'll be good for me, I'm sure.'

I took Wolfie home. I let him bound into the house in front of me, but very quickly followed and checked all the ground floor doors and windows. No one had broken in when I was out, anyway.

It was probably too late to catch Paul Gray at the cafe, if he had a regular time. But it would be useful to get Wolfie used to being left on his own. I made sure there were no tempting food items lying around for him to steal. Then I stuffed some peanut butter into the rubber puzzle toy and left him, without any fuss, playing on the kitchen floor.

An hour would be enough to see how he coped. I put the radio on quietly to keep him company.

I parked near the café, in what was becoming my usual spot.

I decided against cake – there's a limit to how much 'healthy' cake any one person could excuse, and I had passed it. Fortunately their coffee was very good. I briefly imagined the horror of being limited to herbal teas and was thankful they were not quite that puritan in their approach. I'd left the laptop at home and taken a book so I sat at a window table, reading.

I'd only been there for twenty minutes when Gray arrived and bought sandwiches. He had a long conversation with the waitress talking about clean eating, organic food and the dangers of pesticides.

I gathered my stuff together, waved goodbye, went to put my book in the car, and waited to see where Gray went.

He was on foot again, so I took a chance on following him. He started walking towards the path on to the South Downs Way, so I could pretend I was exploring local walks. And of course, he wasn't expecting to be followed, so I didn't need advanced surveillance techniques.

I'd watched too much television drama.

He went into a house only five minutes up the road. I was startled it was so close – I had to walk past, then look back, pretending I was out of breath, taking the chance to enjoy the view down to the sea.

I needed to see more. Perhaps I could explore behind the house? I counted doors carefully then walked up a narrow lane between the rows of houses. A twitten, as they're called in Sussex.

At the back, I could see the whole street had long gardens, backing on to the Downs.

There was a path edging the field – the kind of place where people walk their dogs. I would be able to bring Wolfie, assuming he'd behave well enough for me on the lead.

It occurred to me that not only would Wolfie make a good alibi, he would also be a good way to make friends with a young boy for long enough to find out if he was okay. Maybe. Although I remembered the time when I was very far from okay and telling everyone who asked that I was fine.

I walked back down the road, past the cafe and to my car. My phone rang. It was one of the numbers that had been sending unpleasant texts. I listened but whoever it was didn't say anything and eventually the phone clicked off.

Next time I went spying, I would have to remember to turn my phone off. I didn't want to draw attention to myself.

When I let myself in, I was prepared to see the house in chaos, with a mad, dog dashing around, wild with anxiety.

What I found was a huge wolf dog sleeping on the sofa, legs everywhere, and with a slight peanut butter moustache.

Chapter Thirteen

In theory, the next day I was scheduled to work with Stefan. That was all derailed from the start.

Wolfie insisted on being in the office with me. I'd shut him out but the occasional mournful howl was a distraction. I gave in and opened the door. He bounded in so I introduced him to Stefan, telling the whole story of how I'd found him. Once he was in the office, he was happy enough to settle on the floor, making no more fuss than the occasional grumble or snore.

Until the doorbell rang.

I ran downstairs, and it was DC Dave Elliott – on his own this time.

'Where's your PC?' I asked. 'Lucy something, wasn't it?'

'Shelton,' he said. 'I don't need a chaperone, do I?'

'I'm theoretically in a business meeting. If you could just give me a moment, I'll go and ask to postpone.'

Who on earth had called him? I'd told Chioma I would, but I'd lost interest. Perhaps she had realised how likely that was?

I apologised to Stefan, and explained about the break-in. Given that everyone at work knew about me being on police bail, I felt as I was making an excuse to cover some greater sin on my part, and I imagined he was worrying about what would happen to his job if I ended up in prison. It's so easy for me to catastrophise on no evidence.

I knew I was innocent, and I knew I had a great legal team. Everything was going to be fine. Not that I didn't sometimes lie awake at night, worrying, especially as I knew DI Carstairs had convinced himself of my guilt.

When I went back downstairs, having reassured Stefan as best I could, DC Elliott was talking to Wolfie.

'Not much of a guard dog,' he said. 'He's far too much of a softy.'

'He's mostly for company,' I said. 'Although if anyone were to upset my dog, they'd have me to answer to.'

He approved the new lock arrangements and the camera I'd had installed at the back of the house.

'So why are you here?' I asked, gracelessly.

'To follow up on your break in,' he said.

'You gave me a card to call you if I needed to,' I pointed out. 'It didn't look as if automatic follow up was on the agenda.'

He looked at bit shifty, and I thought for a moment he might be one of those policemen who ends up in the news for sexually harassing lone women who need protection. He made me feel uncomfortable in some way I couldn't quite define.

'I was worried,' he said. 'Especially because of the coincidence about that chap turning up at the same time. What was his name?'

'Oh,' I said. 'I don't think it was anything to do with him.' I conveniently forgot Nick had given me a card.

'May I?' Elliott asked, gesturing at a chair at the kitchen table.

'Of course,' I said. 'I'll put the kettle on, shall I?'

He was charm itself, DC Dave Elliott. Especially when compared with Carstairs. I assumed he was working on the theory he would catch more flies with honey, so I was on my guard.

Once the drinks were made I reached for my phone and showed him the video.

He was gratifyingly shocked.

'That is deeply unpleasant,' he said. 'Not kids – this is someone who is deliberately trying to frighten you. You should have called me.'

He was so genuinely sympathetic I told him about the harassment I'd been getting – the texts and the folders of emails I'd saved.

He asked me to send them to him and promised he'd see if their digital harassment team could investigate. He also asked if I had any idea who might be behind it all.

At that point, I had to tell him more, or suddenly decide against letting him see the emails and texts.

I told him an abridged version, including the death of my husband, being accused of his murder and put on police bail. I even told him about Amy – but pointed out she had been quite open in her demands and I thought this must be someone else. Perhaps more than one person. 'Maybe it's general nastiness,' I said. 'It all started after the arrest, and the pieces in the news which had hinted I'd killed Matt for the money.'

'I'd check out that therapist guy too, if I were you,' he said. 'Sometimes people like to see up close the distress they cause...'

That did worry me a bit, but I shrugged it off.

DC Elliott was surprisingly fair. He thanked me for coming clean and trusting him. He made me feel he cared, even saying, 'Please call me Dave.'

'Is there anything else?' he asked. 'I can see there's something on your mind.'

I decided, on impulse. Not like me, but what did I have to lose?

'I have been worrying,' I said. 'Come upstairs and I'll show you.'

He led the way, and I stopped him by the middle bedroom door.

'Look,' I said, showing him the lock and the bolts. Then the dinosaur wallpaper.

'What are you saying?' he asked.

'This is a child's bedroom, look at the way it's decorated. These locks are on the outside. I'm worried a child has been locked in here, and maybe is still being locked in somewhere now.'

'The previous tenants,' he said. 'Did they have children?'

'Sarah, from next door but one, she says not. But that's even more worrying.'

I took him back downstairs.

'There was post for them,' I said. 'The Grays. I asked the landlord and the post office, but there was no forwarding address.'

'I don't think that's a police matter.'

'I opened one of the letters,' I said. 'It was from the education department, about a home-schooling inspection. They have a son, called Alex.'

'That, you shouldn't have told me,' he said. 'You know it's illegal, to open other people's post.'

'I'm worried,' I said. 'I would like someone to check up on Alex for me. To see if he's safe.'

'Without knowing where they are...'

'I know where they moved to.' I said. 'I saw him, at the local cafe, and I followed him. I can tell you where they're living.'

Genial Dave disappeared then, and he flipped into rage. I'd seen that pattern before.

'You confessed to tampering with the mail and to stalking,' he said. 'I should arrest you. Or tell, what did you call him? DI Carstairs? He'd think all his Christmases had come at once.'

I looked down, hiding my fear.

'I'm worried for you, Jen,' he said. 'If I can call you Jen?' He switched back so abruptly, I wondered if I'd imagined it.

I nodded.

'You've been through such a lot, and I'm worried you're losing it. None of this sounds anything like the sort of thing you've done in the past.'

I couldn't tell if he was joking. It wasn't very funny.

I remembered how Richard used to claim I was possessed by demons. Perhaps I was. Demons he had raised in me.

I tried to explain.

'You'll have seen some terrible things in your job, the kinds of things people can do to each other,' I said. 'I have too. I can't simply walk away from this. Please, if you could check up on the child?'

'If I do, will you promise me you will let this nonsense go?'

'Yes,' I said. 'Of course. All I need is to know he's safe.'

'I can see you're a good person, Jen. I can see you care about all the right things. I will try, okay? As long as it means you let it go.'

'I will,' I said.

'Promise me?' he asked.

Maybe I'd landed lucky at last – I'd found a good policeman.

I still didn't send him the emails and texts though. I couldn't. Not even when he sent me a gentle reminder by email.

Hello, Ms Blake,

Please do get in touch and let me have those emails and texts. No one should put up with harassment. Let us deal with it, please,

Dave

Chapter Fourteen

DC Dave came back on Monday, as promised.

I took him through to the kitchen, where I was working on the big table, with my laptop, so I could keep an eye on Wolfie who was out in the garden.

He was in stern mode, and refused my offer of a hot drink.

'I went to the address you gave me, and the residents confirmed they used to live in this house,' he told me.

'Paul and Verity Gray?' I asked.

'How do you know their names?' he demanded, sounding quite cross.

'Their post,' I said, handing the letters over. 'Should I pop up there and deliver them now I know?'

He snatched the letters from me, almost. 'Best not,' he said. 'You have crossed the line here and if you're not careful, you'll find yourself being arrested for stalking on top of everything else. Think about how you feel, about these texts and emails you've been bombarded with.'

'I didn't mean any harm. I was worried. That's all.'

'You can relax now,' he said. 'They are perfectly nice people. Even though they had a right to be angry, they were very cooperative and understanding. They totally get that people should care about child safety. The boy was with them and was fine. Very well behaved.'

'And the locks on the door?' I couldn't help myself, even though I could see it was annoying him. I should have simply accepted his word, I supposed.

'I did ask,' he said. 'His mum explained. Alex is autistic and sometimes has meltdowns when he's overwhelmed. It's a sensory thing. The best thing to do is to lock him in a safe place, where he can't fight and can't hurt himself. They have a baby monitor set up so they can always see him, and he's never left alone in the house. And now he's getting therapy, so they're hoping to find a better way forward.'

Dave suggested we go upstairs to check, and he quickly found and pointed out the space where the baby monitor had been fitted.

It all seemed so reasonable and yet I was still uneasy. If Alex was prone to meltdowns, how come he was so quiet and well behaved with a stranger in the house?

I said it all still sounded a bit worrying and wondered if they had enough support.

DC Elliott blew his top.

'I listened to you, and I made a fool of myself. They could report me, if they were that way inclined, for acting on malicious gossip instead of going through the normal channels and passing the information to social services.'

'I'm sorry,' I said, feeling guilty he'd risked trouble on my behalf.

'It was my decision,' he said, calmer now. 'With everything you've been going through, I thought you needed the reassurance. There is nothing wrong in that family. You're acting out of care, but you're projecting your own distress – and it's not good enough. You've already crossed the line – opening their mail, tracking down where they live, watching them. It's borderline illegal. Hell, it's not even borderline.'

I was wobbling now, on the verge of tears. Dave was right, wasn't he? It sounded so much worse than I had realised when it was spelled out like that.

'Promise me that's it,' he said. 'If you won't promise, I will have to take you to the police station and charge you.'

'What with?'

I mustered a tiny amount of defiance.

'Tampering with the Queen's mail. Harassment. Stalking. Wasting police time.'

Wolfie howled and went to lie in the corner with his back to us. He didn't like emotionally charged situations.

'You're scaring my dog,' I said.

'You're scaring me,' he said, quieter now. 'Promise, please.'

I promised.

My phone pinged. Another damn text.

I tried to phone you, but I couldn't speak. I want to talk. Talk to me. Please.

'Is that another of those texts,' Dave asked. 'You forgot to send me the rest of it. Do it now, before you forget.'

He stood over me as I logged in to my laptop. I opened the email folder named Harassment and typed his email address, to forward them.

'And the texts?' he asked.

'I took screenshots,' I said. 'They're all in there too.'

'Good,' he said. 'Though I might need your phone at some point. It's likely a stern warning is all that's needed here, so I'll pass it straight to the digital harassment team.'

'Ok,' I said, knowing full well I had no intention of parting with my phone.

'If Amy gets in touch again, or you get any more threatening texts, please do call me. You should take this further.'

I was suitably grateful. It might work, I suppose. Or at least slow down the constant flood.

DC Elliott left, more cheerful now. Seemingly we were on good terms again. I was used to that – being on good terms so long as I did as I was told. I still resented it, even if there was some sense in it.

I'd always thought I might have to move again. So that was another possibility to ponder. But first, I had more to do.

Chapter Fifteen

I needed to see the child, and maybe talk to him. That was all.

I called Wolfie.

'Walkies!'

It was beginning to get dark, but not too dark for a walk and a nose-around.

He sat, letting me attach his new lead to his collar. He was patient and well behaved because he could smell the bag of cheese cubes in my pocket.

We were soon walking up and down the street outside the Grays' home. I held Wolfie's lead tightly, but he didn't pull.

A car pulled up right outside their house, and the Grays got out. I recognised him, with his lanky hair and pale face from the cafe, but I'd only seen her in one, out-of-focus photograph. She still had long, straight hair, but what had been blonde was now brunette.

My hair colour had changed just before I moved, so I guessed I had to allow it.

Alex wasn't in the car with them. Had they left him? On his own? I was raging.

I allowed Wolfie to sniff at a lamp post as I watched them unpacking their car. They carried piles of empty boxes, folded flat, which they heaped on the doorstep.

Shit.

They were moving house. Again. Probably because of me, and DC Elliott's visit.

I walked down the street, Wolfie walking perfectly to heel, just to prove he could. I slipped my hand in my pocket for a cheese cube. I could hardly stand there pretending to walk the dog as cover for my surveillance without actually walking him. How ridiculous I sounded, even in my own head. Surveillance, for fuck's sake.

Unfortunately, that meant I missed them taking the boxes inside.

I turned around in time to see them coming out of the house, locking up, and driving off. They'd left the kid locked up in the house on his own. Again.

I speeded up, Wolfie trotting beside me as we dashed up the twitten and turned back on ourselves, into the narrow path dividing the houses from the Downs.

Wolfie was my cover story. It's no way to treat a new rescue, I know, but I gave him another cube of cheese, then pushed him over the wall at the back of their house. Thankfully he didn't need much encouraging. He was so tall he could almost step over it.

He barked enthusiastically, and the back of the house next door lit up before I had time to clamber up after him.

I held my breath and stayed very still.

"Is there a dog in our garden?"

"Nah. Up on the Downs, probably."

They shut the door and the light in their kitchen went off and I breathed again.

I followed Wolfie, my partner in crime, my alibi, over the wall. He rushed at me tail wagging furiously. I fussed him, tickled behind his ears, fed him more cheese, then we bounded up to the back door together.

I tried the back door. It was locked shut. Somehow I was going to have to break in. which was not in my skillset.

Unless.

I ran my hand along the wooden ledge above the door and found a splinter. No spare key. Perhaps the Grays were ultra careful. There was always the doormat, or under the plant pot.

When I wobbled the big terracotta pot planted with a fading bay tree, I saw a glint of metal. There it was.

It was filthy and had obviously been there for an age – much longer than the Grays. It was stiff and creaky in the lock but with a bit of wiggling it worked.

I opened the back door, then put the key in my pocket. Perhaps they'd believe they'd just left it unlocked.

As we went into the house, I softly called out. 'Wolfie, Wolfie.'

I turned on the light in the hall, and called out, louder, 'Have you seen my dog? He got off the lead and jumped into your garden. The back door was wide open, so...'

There was no answer. I looked into the living room. Packing was in progress, full boxes, half-full boxes, and empty boxes taking up most of the floor space.

I climbed up the narrow staircase, Wolfie close by my side.

There was only one door locked upstairs, and the key was in the lock, on the outside.

I unlocked the door and opened it. The light was on. A child in dinosaur pyjamas was sitting on the bed. He looked terrified.

I sat in the doorway and made myself look small, and persuaded Wolfie to lie down.

'Do you like dogs?" I asked. "He's a bit scared of people, is Wolfie, but he's very gentle. Do you want to give him a treat? He loves cheese.'

I helped myself to a piece of cheese, threw the small bag with Wolfie's cheese to the kid, and he picked it up.

I showed him how to offer cheese to the dog, putting my little cube on my open palm.

The boy smiled and followed my example. He held his hand out.

Wolfie swiped the cheese off the kid's hand with his giant tongue. The kid ate some of the cheese himself and then gave more to the dog.

Wolfie licked the boy's face.

"He likes you," I said.

The boy wiped his hand across his face.

'My name is Jen,' I said, very quietly, not looking at him. 'You're Alex, I think.'

He nods, hesitant, but interested.

'I'm friends with Rory's dad. You know Rory?'

He looked less frightened, now, and was fussing Wolfie.

'I've not met Rory,' I said. 'But his dad seems nice.'

'Yes,' the boy said. There was no real feeling there and I wondered how much he understood what I was saying.

He wasn't scared any more, though.

'I'm Jen,' I said again. 'I wanted to know if you're okay.'

The front door opened and I realised I must leave. They were back home.

'I have to go. But I'll come back. I promise. Very soon.'

I quietly locked him in again, although it was so painful to do it, and I stood at the top of the stairs in the dark, listening, holding tightly on to Wolfie's leash.

I could smell Indian food. They'd been out for takeaway. They wouldn't be bringing any up for the child – he had a plate of sandwiches and carrot sticks, and a bottle of water on his bedside table.

Damn, I thought. They would be going to the kitchen to eat. I couldn't just sneak out the back.

I stood very still and listened. Cutlery clattered on to the table, following by the crackling of paper bags and I could see in my mind's eye the foil trays being uncovered. The curry smelled good.

Praying Wolfie would stay quiet, I slowly and carefully walked down the stairs hoping to avoid any creaking steps.

There was one extra loud one and I paused but thank God they were still clattering dishes, and sharing out the food.

Once we were off the last step, I almost ran down the hall and opened the front door.

A moment's inspiration and I turned around and slipped back into the house. There were two bunches of keys hanging from a hook by the door. I carefully lifted one set, pulled the door shut behind me, and quickly followed Wolfie down the steps and then the road, and back home via the Indian takeaway. The smell had been irresistible.

I had a key to the back door and the front now. Belt and braces.

Chapter Sixteen

I barely slept.

I lay in bed, tossing and turning, unable to get comfortable. In theory Wolfie was supposed to be sleeping on the floor. In practice he'd crept up on to the bed next to me and was snoring in my ear.

But that wasn't what kept me awake.

I couldn't stop thinking about what I'd done. I'd broken into someone's house, sneaked upstairs and talked to their child.

All the different things that could have gone wrong!

If they'd come back earlier, while I was in the hall. The idea they would have believed I'd been looking for my lost dog, after DC Elliott's visit, was ludicrous.

What had I been thinking?

Or they could have come straight upstairs and checked on Alex when they brought back their takeaway.

They could even have seen me on the baby monitor.

Never mind what DC Elliott would have had to say, DI Carstairs would have had a field day. There's a theory that people who break the law in small ways, are more likely to break it in big ways. I'm not sure anything I'd been accused of doing counted as small, and as for what I have done, well. I'm clearly on a new path as a career criminal.

I was up early, drinking coffee, preparing to go over to Wimbledon to sign in for police bail.

Sergeant Evans was back on the desk. He was brisk, and there was no time for talking, and even better, there was no request for me to stay.

I thought about asking how much longer the investigation was going to take, but realised it was more sensible to leave all that to Chioma.

'See you in a week,' I said. He smiled and nodded.

I'd left Wolfie roaming the house. When I returned, I found him fast asleep on the sofa, with his head dangling off the side. It seemed to be one of his favourite positions.

Sleeping was his superpower. Which was lucky, really. I've had insecurely attached dogs and they could be such hard work.

I left him where he was, heading up to my office to work. It was one of the days where I was scheduled to work with Stefan – but a short day as I'd had a late start, and Stefan was leaving early for a dentist appointment.

My mind wandered all day, fretting about Alex.

What if he'd said something to his parents?

'Mum, there was a strange lady and a big dog in the house last night.'

Perhaps DC *Call Me Dave* Elliott was right, I thought. I'd gone off the rails, driven mad by grief and trauma. He'd visited the family unofficially, to reassure me, and he said everything was fine. As an experienced policeman he would have some idea of what to look out for. But I had my own experience, too. And my instincts were on fire.

I couldn't ignore it. That would make me complicit, like all those who've turned away in the past.

I put Wolfie in the boot of the car. I parked where the road petered out into a dirt track up to the farm, branching off towards the South Downs Way. It was only a couple of minutes' walk down to the Grays's house.

Worried sick they might have already moved, I peered through the window. They were in the living room, him and her, surrounded by boxes waiting to be packed. The boy was probably still in his room.

Wolfie pulled me further down the road, where a woman with a beagle was walking towards us.

The dogs went mad for each other – sniffing bottoms and circling, tangling up their leads.

'I saw you here the other day,' the woman said.

'We're new to the area,' I replied, gabbling. 'I'm still exploring, looking for good places for walking the dog.'

I'd said way too much. Nerves.

Luckily, she was a talker. She started listing the best places to walk, including the parks where the dogs could run free, and threw in a lecture on the rules of the beach for good measure.

The Grays emerged from their house, slamming the front door behind them. They walked off down the road without a care in the world. And without their child.

Beagle Lady had said something and was waiting for an answer. I tried a mental rewind, but I hadn't been listening.

'Sorry. Miles away.'

'It's raining,' she said.

It was. Just a drop or two at first, but then it began in earnest. The weather gods were on my side. Or against me. One or the other.

'Must go. We'll get soaked.'

I smiled in sheer relief. 'I'll see you this way again. Or maybe in the park.'

I watched until she disappeared in the distance, then quickly raced up the twitten again, with Wolfie loping alongside me.

It was already muddy. I would have to risk the front door. Thank goodness I'd lifted their spare set of keys.

There was no one on the street, so I decided to risk it. I fumbled a bit with the lock, but the door opened and Wolfie and I were safely inside.

I ran straight upstairs and unlocked the child's door.

'Hi Alex,' I said. 'Remember me? Jenny.'

He looked up from where he was sitting on the floor with his toy cars and smiled.

'You're real,' he said.

Wolfie licked him again and he laughed.

There wasn't much time. I was terrified the Grays were going to come back. This is madness, I thought.

'How old are you?' I asked, as if it made any difference.

'I'm eight.'

'Eight is much too old to be locked in your room,' I said. 'Do you like being locked in?'

'No,' he said.

'Do they lock you in a lot?'

'Sometimes. When I'm naughty or a nuisance. I get in the way.'

I felt my anger rising.

'You know the policeman who came the other day?' I asked. 'I sent him because I was worried.'

'They said he had come to take me away. To lock me in a cell. With no toys or anything.'

'That's not true,' I said, as calmly as I could. I didn't want him to think I was angry with him.

'They do tell lies,' he said.

'If you come with us, I promise I won't lock you up.'

He looked at me. I wanted to rush him, but it had to be his decision.

'Do you want to come with us?'

'Promise?' he asked.

'I do.'

He petted Wolfie and stood up. Of course, if you're going to kidnap a child, the best way must be to take a dog with you. I wondered how long I'd been unconsciously planning this. Maybe since I decided to adopt the dog.

'Let's be quick, before your mum and dad get back. Pick up anything you want to bring.'

He picked up a tattered old stuffed panda.

'Nothing else? I asked.

He shook his head.

He followed me and Wolfie downstairs. I was conscious of keeping his choices open, so I asked again if he was sure.

'There's still time to change your mind,'

He looked down and said nothing. But he followed me, holding on to Wolfie.

No matter how wet and muddy, we had to leave via the back door. The front was too risky, now I had the child with me.

We went down the garden path and this time I was able to unlock the gate.

It was pouring with rain still and we squelched up the muddy path behind the houses, round the side of the last house, and there was the car, waiting for us.

I hustled Wolfie into his cage in the boot, and strapped Alex in the back seat, careful to show him how to undo the seat belt. I was worried about him feeling trapped. 'You can have the window open if you like.'

I drove him home, all the time thinking and worrying.

It shouldn't have been so easy. Didn't that prove there was something badly wrong? And all he wanted to bring with him was a threadbare, one-eared panda.

Chapter Seventeen

I parked in front of the house. I hadn't thought this through properly, as I'd still been pretending to myself I was only checking on Alex. I hadn't packed any of my stuff, I had nothing ready for him, and – I finally saw the expression on his face as he sat stubbornly in the car – I hadn't thought about how he would feel about going back into another house where he'd been locked in his room.

I jumped out of the car, then crouched next to the open car door.

'It would help a lot if you could come in and look after Wolfie while I get a few things packed.'

I grabbed Wolfie's leash and he jumped out of the boot of the car, and pulled me toward Alex.

Wolfie worked like a charm, and me, boy and dog were up the steps and in the house in no time.

I asked if he was hungry. He said he'd eaten, but I got some cheese and some fruit juice out of the fridge and sat him at the table.

I cut up a few pieces of cheese and said he could feed them to Wolfie – but no more.

'We don't want him getting sick in the car,' I said.

Alex looked solemn, promising not to give him too much.

'You can have some fruit as well,' I said, pushing the fruit bowl towards him.

I didn't want to leave boy and dog alone, so after Alex had fed him some cheese, I shooed Wolfie out into the back garden and closed the door on him, trusting that Alex would stay put until I returned.

I rushed upstairs. I grabbed my washbag and toiletries, and packed my laptop in its bag and then collected a few days' worth of clothes, sweeping them into one of my big suitcases.

I could see from the hall that Alex was happily eating a banana. In the background there was an occasional mournful howl from Wolfie.

'Just packing the car,' I called.

I ran down the steps, cramming the suitcase on to the back seat, leaving plenty of room for the boy.

Back in the house I looked at Alex.

What on earth was I going to do with him? I should have taken five minutes at least to grab a change of clothes and shoes. He was so muddy.

I could at least try to clean the worst of it off – but the rest would have to wait for tomorrow.

I found a washing up sponge to wipe the mud off his legs. I cleaned up his shoes too, so they didn't look too bad.

Picking up a bag, I suggested Alex put some fruit in to eat on the journey, while I filled another bag with Wolfie's toys, his food bowls and a big water bottle.

It felt sad, to see how much Wolfie had, and how little Alex had. I vowed I would fix that as soon as possible.

Right now, we needed to get away. The Grays were probably back home, wondering where Alex was. If they'd even gone upstairs to check on him.

I quickly emptied the perishables from the fridge into a bin bag and took them outside to the dustbin. With Wolfie following me, I dragged it out into the lane at the back in the hopes that the bin men would forgive me for not taking it out to the main road.

Back inside, with Alex and Wolfie watching me, I locked the back door.

Then I thought again.

I turned off my security camera, grabbed a screwdriver from the kitchen drawer, unlocked the door and went back outside. There was no one around, so I scratched hard at the new lock and the newly painted woodwork.

Now it looked as if someone had tried to break in again.

Systems thinking skills – good in tech, but useful for a life of crime too.

Alex was watching me, with interest.

'Let's go get in the car,' I said. 'Wolfie first!'

I locked up, picked up the bags, but couldn't manage the laptop bag as well. I left it on the top step, planning to go back for it.

I ran down the steps, bundled the dog into the boot, dumping the bag with Wolfie's bits and pieces in the footwell.

When I looked round, Alex had managed to carry the laptop bag down for me. I thanked him. He was a good kid.

I strapped him into the back seat again, and stood by the car, thinking. Was there anything I'd forgotten?

Sarah was approaching from down the street, with her daughter Izzy.

Just what I needed. I was getting more and more worried about the Grays catching up with us.

I could imagine the scene in the street with accusations and screaming and then me getting arrested for kidnapping.

Carstairs would love that. And imagine the field day the press would have.

She managed to block me at the bottom of the steps.

'Sorry, Sarah, a bit of a rush.'

She wasn't having any.

'Who's the boy?'

Sarah was nothing if not direct.

'Alex. He's my nephew.'

I opened the car door, planning to get right in and drive away, only Sarah popped her head in the door, and said hello to Alex. He looked down, staying quiet.

'You've only been here a couple of weeks,' she said, turning to me. 'A bit soon for a holiday.'

She'd clocked the case and the bags.

'Just a short trip,' I said. 'Family emergency.'

I could see Sarah won't be satisfied with less so I came up with a complete story, off the cuff.

'My sister is in hospital,' I said. 'I'm taking my nephew to stay with his grandparents.'

'Pity,' Sarah said. 'It would have been great for Izzy to have someone to play with.'

Izzy was standing with her arms folded, looking exactly like her mum.

'He's a baby,' she said, under her breath.

Three years is forever at that age.

Sarah's interrogation wasn't over. 'Where do your parents live? Are you making a break of it?'

'His father's parents. Ours are both gone,' I said. I was on pins, worrying about the Grays showing up, but I was getting the hang of lying. 'I have friends nearby, so I might stay a few days. We can have a bit of a holiday, right, kiddo?" I said to Alex.

He didn't say anything.

'He's very quiet.' Sarah said.

'He's worried about his mum. And he's worn out, poor lamb. We'd best be off.'

As I got into the car, I called out, 'I'll send you a postcard from Cornwall.'

As I drove off, I explained to Alex.

'It's not a good idea to tell lies. But sometimes it's necessary.'

As we drove past the turnoff up to the Grays' house in the old village, I noticed two people running down the hill. It was them. I was sure it was them.

DC Elliott's visit had tipped them off about me, and they knew where I lived because they used to live there.

We'd cut it a bit fine.

I didn't ask if Alex had seen them.

Chapter Eighteen

It was eight o clock, and I had to find somewhere for us to stay. I didn't know where I was going – or indeed, how I'd found myself where I was.

How easily I'd kidnapped a child.

I'd had fantasies about it, when I feared I would never have a child of my own. Wandering around the shops, I would see parents screaming at their children, sometimes even hitting them in public, and I would wonder at how unfair life was. They had children and didn't appreciate how lucky they were.

Maybe that was where this had started – the thought that some people didn't deserve their own children.

Then Amy, pregnant with Matt's child and living with my mother-in-law. Eve had known me for fifteen years, yet assumed I was capable of murder. A double whammy.

Did Amy deserve her luck? I knew way more than she realised I did. I knew she didn't deserve it.

All the same, it wasn't wishful thinking that led to me finding the locks and bolts on the outside of that middle bedroom door. I had evidence to suggest they had moved house rather than have their home schooling assessed. And after DC Elliott's visit, they were packing up to move suddenly, once again.

There was something they were hiding.

The boy had come with me so easily too. I was genuinely worried for him.

It wasn't well thought out and planned. On impulse I'd told Sarah we were going to Cornwall. I thought it best we went in that direction, at least for long enough to lay a false trail.

If anyone showed up on my doorstep – Amy, my stalker, the police – Sarah would be sure to send them to Cornwall, so we couldn't actually go there.

I suppose I'd always known there was only one place I could go.

I'd promised to stay in touch with DC Elliott about the nasty texts and emails. In just a week I was supposed to turn up in Wimbledon to sign on police bail. All these thoughts running on tracks in my mind, round and around.

Sufficient unto the day is the evil thereof.

What a time for one of Pastor Richard's constant biblical quotations to float to the top of my mental whirlpool.

Alex was asleep in the back seat and Wolfie was snoring too. I kept driving west. I needed to buy some basic supplies, and maybe find a Travelodge or Premier Inn. Somewhere impersonal, where we could settle for the night. If we were noticed – so much the better, at least for now.

I stopped for petrol off a roundabout on the double carriageway and noticed a service station and a Travelodge well back from the main road. The place was tucked out of the way.

I woke Alex so we could go shopping. I managed to pick up toothpaste and toothbrush, and a superman tee shirt which drowned him, but he liked it. I suggested he choose a comic to read and instead he asked for a colouring book, so I bought some crayons too.

Then I bought us both fried chicken and chips to eat straight away, plus drinks and sandwiches for breakfast.

'Mum doesn't let me have chips,' Alex said, cramming them into his mouth as if I might change my mind. 'It's dirty food.'

'I don't think we should eat like this all the time,' I said. 'But once in a blue moon it's fine to have a treat.'

'That's what my nan used to say,' Alex said. 'Mum didn't like Nana Lilian. I'm not allowed to see her anymore.'

I was longing to ask much more but didn't want to make him feel interrogated, as if he'd been naughty. I made my mind up there and then I would always allow him to lead in conversation. I wouldn't force anything, but I would always be ready to listen.

He finished his chicken before I did mine. He sighed, contentedly.

'My body isn't a temple anymore.'

It was no big surprise they were big on food purity, his family, given that they bought so much takeaway from the vegan cafe.

I booked us into a ground floor room with twin beds and was delighted to find out that for a small charge plus a cleaning deposit we could have Wolfie in our room.

I let Alex pick a bed. Without hesitating, he chose the one by the window.

We each sat on our beds with Wolfie lying down between us, which was useful as we were both oddly uncomfortable with looking at each other.

I didn't want to make him nervous. I was terrified. What did I think I was doing?

Not having any clothes or anything for Alex was upsetting. I made a mental note to prepare better next time I kidnapped someone and just about managed to stop myself from laughing like a maniac.

I found a spare flannel for him and took the label off the superman tee shirt.

'Time to get ready for bed,' I said.

'Where's Panda?' he asked. 'I always take Panda to bed.'

'Oh shit.'

I said that out loud and he stared at me, aghast. So much for me being a good person to be in charge of a child.

'We must have left him behind,' I said. 'I'm so sorry. I didn't think. Where did you last have him?'

'In the kitchen,' he said, in a very small voice. 'Can we go back and get him?'

'I'm really sorry,' I said. 'I don't think we can.'

For the first time he looked like he might burst into tears.

'Perhaps we can imagine he's on his own adventure,' I said. 'While we are on ours? We will be able to collect him soon, I'm sure. And you can tell him all about our adventure, and perhaps he will tell us about his.'

He looked at me with disdain, like a child who is fed up with having to pretend to believe in Father Christmas.

'You still have to get ready for bed though,' I said. 'But perhaps we could take Wolfie out first.'

Once we were back, I gave him the clean tee shirt, the toothbrush and toothpaste, and flannel, suggesting he have a quick wash.

I hoped an eight-year-old would be capable of all that without supervision. I wasn't ready for this at all.

'It's like camping,' I said. I had no idea where that came from. When had I ever been camping?

He went into the bathroom. There was a bit of splashing but it wasn't long before he came out, in the superman top.

'I'll just go and have a wash,' I said. 'I don't know about you but I am worn out. If we have an early night, we can make an early start tomorrow.'

When I got back Alex was in bed, eyes too tightly shut for him to be asleep.

Too late, I realised I shouldn't have left them alone together, again. Wolfie seemed like a softy and Alex was quiet and well behaved, but a strange dog is always a risk. And Wolfie was a stranger to both of us, still. I would have to be more careful in future.

I locked the door – I thought it was okay with both of us on the inside – and climbed into my bed. Of course, I lay there, eyes wide open and unable to sleep. My mind went round and round.

All along I'd known I would go home, eventually. Well, to the house I lived in as a teenager, anyway. When Aunt Martha had died three years ago, I discovered she'd left the cottage to me. It was reasonably secluded in a small village north of Manchester, and no one knew about it, so it should give me some breathing space before anyone tracked us down.

I knew it would be upsetting to go back. I'd always sworn I wouldn't, and then Aunt Martha died, and it became harder. I should have gone back earlier for her sake, while she was alive. Going back now seemed like a betrayal.

She'd have rescued Alex. Just as she'd rescued me. She was that kind of woman.

I turned on my phone, scrolling the news sites, looking for anything about a kid reported missing from Brighton.

There was nothing.

I tried various Brighton news pages and Facebook groups. Sussex Police on Twitter. Still nothing.

All I could think was the police might be keeping the information back, because they knew who I was and were out looking for me.

That made sense. I remembered a spy novel I'd been reading about going dark. With clumsy fingers, I fumbled the back of my phone and removed the sim card, putting it in my wallet. That wouldn't help if they were looking for the car. I'd have to do something about that too.

I must have fallen asleep somehow, but I woke up early and Alex was sitting on the edge of his bed, watching me very closely, Wolfie lying next to him, curled up around him and still snoring.

I felt a bit spooked and for a moment wondered exactly why they had kept Alex locked up.

If it had been a horror film, I might be about to find out.

He'd been very co-operative so far. Weirdly well-behaved, if anything.

I decided he was probably scared. How bad must it have been for him to simply agree to leave with some mad woman who broke into his home and unlocked his bedroom door?

Thinking back, with my rescue dogs I'd always had some idea of their background, and why they'd been rehomed. An assessment from the rescue centre of their temperament and any issues they had.

Ben, the last one, was a rough collie who had been too much for his family. They'd let their kids get rowdy with him and play too roughly – and alternated that with locking him in the garage on his own all day.

He'd been terrified of his own shadow – but I'd expected it and knew how to handle it. I'd let him be and always waited for him to approach me, and eventually he had relaxed.

Probably it was the same with kids.

Probably.

Anyway, there I was with two unknown quantities, and by the looks of it they'd bonded with each other. Hopefully they weren't planning to gang up on me.

'You hungry, kiddo?' I asked.

He nodded.

I got the sandwiches and juice out and we breakfasted. I was ravenous. While he was still nibbling round the outside of his sandwich, I slipped the SIM back into my phone and checked all the news sites again. There were still no reports of a missing child.

I was beginning to fret. What if they were out looking for me already? I made a decision.

Before we checked out though, I thought I'd best try to chat to Alex.

'Have you ever lived with a dog?' I asked him.

'No,' he said. 'Mum doesn't agree with keeping pets. Dad used to have dogs though.'

'Wolfie is a gentle dog,' I said, 'And he clearly likes you. I saw he was cuddled up to you this morning.'

Alex smiled. 'He's very snuggly.'

'You're a sensible boy, I can tell,' I said. 'Just remember that dogs are not exactly like people. We have to be gentle with them, and very careful not to frighten them with sudden movements and loud noises.'

Alex said, 'I'll try to remember.'

He reached out and petted Wolfie on the head very gently, and the dog licked his face. This was either going to be very easy, or very difficult. I hoped they weren't going to gang up on me.

We checked out, and I drove to Southampton airport. I hired a car on the company charge card, and transferred everything but the dog, and parked the hire car in short term parking.

Then I parked my old car in long term parking as if we were off on holiday for two weeks, instead of on the run for as long as possible. Maybe forever.

Alex didn't ask any questions except for the moment he was worried I'd forgotten the dog.

'No, I would never forget about Wolfie. Or you!' I said. I guessed he was worried about being abandoned.

I dismantled the dog guard, praying it would fit in the hire car, then transferred dog and guard, thankful it was a cool day.

'Now how about we go shopping?'

First stop, I bought myself a burner phone – all that time watching thrillers and reading spy fiction had not been wasted. I paid for it on the company charge card so I couldn't so easily be traced that way.

I didn't expect an eight-year-old boy to enjoy clothes shopping. I helped him pick out underwear and PJs, and then we started on jeans and tee shirts and hoodies. I thought three changes of clothes would do for now. I asked him what his favourite colours were. He didn't have a preference, but I noticed he picked out bright tee shirts –

oranges and yellows. I saw a red hoodie and took it off the rack, and turned round to show him, but he was gone.

My heart started beating very fast and I panicked. Where was he? Surely they hadn't been able to follow us?

My panic caught the attention of a store detective.

'What's the matter, madam?' he asked.

'My nephew,' I said. 'He was here a minute ago and I can't see him anywhere. He's eight, this tall' – I gestured with my hands. 'Blond, blue eyed.'

'Have you got a photo on your phone, ma'am? I could circulate it round the store and the shopping centre. We find it helps.'

I floundered. 'Well, no. I haven't.' I started to make excuses. 'It's a new phone, and I've not seen him for a while and he hates...'

He looked at me, and I could see his brain was ticking over. Was I reporting an imaginary kid had been lost? I felt so guilty, I was sure he could sense that.

'I'm sorry,' I said. 'I am panicking. My sister is in hospital and now I've lost her child, who I am supposed to be looking after.'

I really was on the verge of tears.

'We can use the sound system, ask him to come back to the fountain. Don't worry, it will be fine. What's his name.'

'Alex,' I said.

As I spoke his name, a small hand tentatively touched my arm. I turned, and there he was.

Without thinking, I hugged him. 'There you are. I thought I'd lost you!'

He wriggled away from me, uncomfortable with the contact.

The store detective seemed a bit concerned, still. 'All's well that ends well,' he said. Then he turned to Alex, and asked, 'Is everything okay, Alex?'

He nodded, too quiet.

'Sorry,' I said to the detective. 'He's autistic, gets very shy. That's why I was so worried.'

'Do you like this red hoodie?' I said to Alex. 'Do you want to try it on?'

It looked good on him.

'Come on then, we'd best pay for this lot. Maybe you can wear that now, if you like?'

Alex was keen.

I asked if the store detective could point me to the nearest place to pay and he escorted us there, carrying an armful of the clothes we'd picked out.

He stood watching as everything was rung up. I dithered – what card should I use? I decided on my personal debit card, just in case. Given that we'd drawn so much attention to ourselves. Once Alex's face was on the front pages and TV news, this store detective would be on to it, I knew. How very stupid I'd been.

Once I'd finished paying and everything was bagged up, barring Alex's new red hoodie, I thanked the store detective, and we left the shop and walked back to the car. I checked occasionally and, thankfully, we were not being followed.

He'd really paid a lot of personal attention to us, that store detective. Maybe he recognised me from the news. Maybe he just had a sixth sense there was something wrong. But I was uneasy.

The back seat of the car was piled high with bags. Wolfie raised his head and woofed.

Most of the morning was gone and I was exhausted. I wanted to trek onwards and lay a false trail to Cornwall. After finding a park to walk Wolfie, who needed to stretch his legs after spending ages curled up asleep in the back of the car, we clambered back in there and I drove west.

I wasn't the only one who was tired. That dog could sleep for England, and the boy followed his lead. I opened the window so the cool breeze would keep me awake.

I kept to the coast road until we reached Exeter. I'd been tempted by Lyme Regis, but decided that me, the boy and the dog would be too noticeable in a smaller place.

I found another Travelodge and we all settled down and had a nap, we were so tired. I woke up and found Wolfie snuggled up to Alex again.

Kidnapping was hungry work, so I suggested we go out for fish and chips. Alex was a bit picky about the food and refused, saying he'd rather have a sandwich. But he couldn't resist picking at mine and discovered he loved it – apart from the mushy peas.

He ate more than half my meal and then apologised.

I laughed at him, very gently.

'Not to worry,' I said. 'We'll buy some sandwiches and share them with Wolfie later. How does that sound?'

We walked past Boots, and I had a thought, so turned back.

I kept a very close eye on Alex in the shop. I sort of wished it was acceptable to have those toddler reins, but for eight-year-olds.

At the display of home hair dyes I asked, 'Would you like to try a different hair colour?'

He pulled a face.

'It would wash out,' I said. 'But for now, it might be a part of the adventure. In case they're looking for us.'

He looked at all the different colours on offer and picked out a medium brown that would work nicely.

I bought him some fancy sunglasses too, to cover his blue eyes, but didn't fuss when he wouldn't wear them.

We ambled back to our room, and for a moment he put his hand in mine, and then jumped as if shocked, pulling away. I carefully didn't look at him, as if he was a skittish kitten, but I was smiling inside.

He was a likable kid, picky eating apart. That seemed imposed – it was all about rules and so on – not innate. He wasn't afraid of me, and he'd been very quiet and co-operative. Quiet to the point where it was a bit worrying. It must have been so bad if this weirdness I was inflicting on him was an improvement.

And he wasn't stupid. I could see intelligence in his eyes and his behaviour. He was always watchful, working things out. He didn't ask questions – as if he preferred to make his own observations. A little scientist, I thought. Or an anthropologist – observing human behaviour in all its forms and quietly fitting in.

It reminded me a little of living with my stepfather, the good pastor. Then I was walking on eggshells in case I triggered one of his frequent rages; but now I was worried that I might add to Alex's trauma, whatever it was.

I remembered when I was a teenager, I'd played one of my records – rescued from the chapel jumble sale – on the stereo in the living room. He'd been enraged.

'The devil is in that music.' And he had taken it and scratched both sides, making sure it was unplayable ever again.

I didn't know what was in Alex's past. Perhaps he had cause to fear rage too.

He could certainly be said to be behaving too well, for an eight-year-old. Perhaps he was very used to having to control himself – if the adults in his life were on a hair trigger and he was so compliant. Trying to please could be a necessary survival skill.

Not, I thought, that I wanted him to be naughty and demanding, or to have tantrums and meltdowns. There'd be enough time for that later, when I got him home.

Home.

Like it had ever been home. Once I escaped to Uni, I was determined to make my own home. And here I was, having to do it all over again.

We were almost back at the room when I spotted a supermarket. I suggested to Alex we go and buy snacks. I made a detour first to collect binbags, protective gloves and cheap towels. Then we filled a basket with sandwiches, and I got him to choose his favourite biscuits. He picked out some salads and fruits too, and we chose juice. I added milk, and some treats and doggy kibble for Wolfie.

Back at the Travelodge we dumped the bags and put Wolfie on the lead.

He was boisterous, having spent too much time asleep. Eventually, with some well-judged bribery, he calmed down. At least he was staying close to the treats he knew I had in my pocket. When I stopped and he sat automatically, I rewarded him with a chew.

Back in the room, I let Alex watch TV.

I took my phone into the bathroom to avoid the noise, and fortunately there was a strong signal.

First I checked to see if Alex had been reported missing yet. All it needed was photos of him plastered all over the news and I just knew that store detective would be on to the police straight away. He'd had a very good look at me, and at my debit card too, I thought.

I called Stefan and talked to him – said there was a family emergency and I was taking off for a week. I told him I'd found my credit card was refused because there'd been some mix up at the bank over my change of address, so I'd used the company charge card.

He said I didn't need to tell him, but I was happier with him knowing. 'It will all be automatically paid off from my bank account,' I added.

I also called my landlord and explained I was away for a few weeks on business. I reassured him – I knew his previous tenants had done a midnight flit. I transferred three months rent right away.

I was using my old sim card so it would be established if anyone looked for me that I was on my way to Cornwall, as I'd said to Sarah. I suddenly realised for all my thoughts about buying myself a burner phone, I had no idea how I was going to manage this in practice. I hadn't got time to watch The Wire again, and anyway, it was probably all different in America.

Finally I emailed DC Elliott. I explained I'd moved out of the house – that I'd been getting more texts and phone calls and someone had tried to break in again.

I thought it was a good cover story, assuming the Grays would have told him about Alex's disappearance. I would easily be at the top of any list of suspects if he did know. In the email I suggested I'd be back in a week or two, but I simply needed a break from being on red alert all the time. I was exhausted from all the stress – which was true enough.

Then I joined Alex, and we watched kids' TV together, eating sandwiches and salad and fruit, washed down with milk. I could have murdered a glass or two of wine, or even some fizzy pop. I was probably eating more healthily than I had in months because of the kid.

Chapter Nineteen

I was totally absorbed in the TV news when I noticed Alex had half lain down on his bed and fallen asleep, with Wolfie next to him.

I was so keyed up I'd forgotten how very young he was - he should have been tucked up in bed earlier. He needed his sleep. Given how tired I was, how much worse must he have been feeling?

'Come on sleepyhead,' I said. 'Time to put you to bed. Do you think you can manage a proper bath, without falling asleep?'

He looked unhappy.

'I think you're old enough to bathe on your own, if I run the water for you,' I said.

He smiled, so I asked him to choose which of his new PJs he wanted to wear. He went for the dinosaurs, so I piled them on the heated towel rail and ran a couple of inches of water in the bath, worried about his safety.

'I'll leave the door ajar,' I said. 'Call me if you need me.'

'Ajar?' he asked, warily.

'Just a little bit open,' I said. 'You can be private, but I can hear if you call me, if you need help.'

He disappeared into the bathroom, and I was relieved to see he carefully left the door a little bit open. I'd been wondering what to do if he'd pulled it shut.

I sat on the bed with the TV on, sound turned right down, listening.

It was a few minutes before I heard some reassuring splashing sounds. Then a loud woof as Wolfie joined him in the bath.

I started to laugh, helplessly. I couldn't go in there and do anything – I had to give the kid his privacy.

I could see I'd be paying a hefty amount on top of the bill to cover the extra cleaning.

A few minutes later the door opened wide, and a still slightly damp Alex appeared with new PJs plastered to his body. Wolfie followed, soaked to the skin, shaking water everywhere.

I quickly grabbed a big towel and dried the dog off, laughing all the time. Wolfie barked. The person in the next room knocked on the wall.

Fortunately, it was warm enough that I wasn't too worried about Alex catching cold, but after drying off the bathroom I sent him back in there with my towel and the other new pair of pyjamas to change into.

I wondered if I should read some parenting books and if there were any that helped say foster or adoptive parents cope with a ready-made eight-year-old. Perhaps there were. I'd have to look.

I was pretty sure it wouldn't hurt to talk to him gently about getting properly washed and dried. But not today. We were both exhausted. Wolfie, however, was wide awake.

I tucked Alex into bed and then went into the bathroom to have a wash and get ready for bed myself.

His clothes were all in a puddle of water on the floor, so I hung them, and the damp pyjamas, on the heated towel rail. I cleaned up as well as I could after boy and dog, still laughing.

In the middle of the night, I was woken by the sound of screaming – and more hammering on the wall. Wolfie was pacing round the room, looking nervous, and emitting occasional high-pitched whines.

I got up and sat on the side of Alex's bed. I touched him gently on the shoulder and he woke up and stared at me, uncomprehending, unable to move.

'It's a nightmare,' I said. 'You're safe now. I promise you're safe. Me and Wolfie are here. We'll look after you.'

He gradually relaxed and became less rigid.

'Do you want to talk about it?' I asked. 'Sometimes it makes everything seem better, to say it out loud.'

He turned away.

It was too soon. Of course, it was. I should have known better. I would let him be and not pester him with questions until he felt safe. Just as if he were a rescue dog.

I carried on talking to him quietly. I held back from offering a hug, although I longed to comfort him. I told him I'd sit up until he went back to sleep.

I shifted into the armchair and carried on talking quietly while his breathing signalled he was still hyped up, still wide awake.

I talked about how I used to have nightmares back when I was his age, and sometimes I still had them. But they didn't scare me anymore, and I didn't have them very often.

I rambled on about how it's possible to consciously intervene in your own dreams, and how you can learn to recognise you're dreaming and take charge of what happens. You can decide whether to confront the scary things, to fight and win, or run or even fly away.

He soon fell asleep. I couldn't help but remember Matt who used to say I could bore anyone to sleep when I started on my hobby horses and that he should rent me out as a cure for insomnia.

I still missed him. He wasn't always cold and distant – we had once shared a lot of laughter. And I couldn't help wondering what he would have made of this adventure.

Alex and Wolfie were now curled up asleep, but of course I was wide awake.

What did I think I was doing? Stealing a child. Taking him back to my home, where all my own nightmares had started.

A psychotherapist would have a field day.

Was DC Elliott right? Had I been driven mad with grief, by new trauma heaped on top of old?

He seemed to think the Grays were lovely people. Then again, my stepfather was an admired and respected pillar of the community.

I snorted. Who could I trust, if not myself?

My phone pinged. I panicked at first – which one was it?

Of course it was my old phone, but I'd left both of them turned on. How stupid was that?

I checked the text.

Why did you tell me? I know I started it, but you must have known how I'd feel.

I took a screenshot and uploaded it to my collection, then put both phones on to charge. It would be like me to have two phones and for them both to run out of juice.

I tried to work out what to do with both phones. I knew I was probably overcomplicating things in my panic. I had to keep switching my old phone off, I thought. Maybe it would be okay to check it, perhaps in the middle of the night. I set up my email on the new phone – that was more generally useful. As far as I knew, no one would know which phone my emails came from.

Some techie I was.

I knew nothing about how to use tech as an actual criminal. Maybe there are classes I could have taken, or more likely, these are skills you pick up on the job.

I set up Facebook and Twitter so I could check out reports of missing children. I scrolled my way through all the local groups and checked news sites. I googled for missing children.

There was nothing. Still not a word to say Alex was missing.

Surely by this stage it should be all over the media? What the fuck was going on? Why wasn't anyone looking for him?

Chapter Twenty

We were all up early. Before breakfast we took Wolfie out for a walk in the nearest park, and Alex cleaned up after him without being asked.

Back in the room, I checked our stash, giving Alex a choice of smoothie. As we were drinking. I checked out the instructions on the hair dye.

I'd forgotten – how stupid was I? – about the allergy test. I didn't even want to risk doing the test – after all, I had no idea if Alex had any sensitivities. So it would be at least a couple of days before I could dye his hair.

I hadn't wanted to show up in my old home-town with this gorgeous blond and blue eyed kid who would be instantly recognisable once his photos showed up in newspapers and on TV.

I'd have to buy him a baseball cap or two on the journey.

For a moment, I panicked.

Wouldn't people think he should be in school? What could I say if anyone asked?

On my phone, I quickly googled and discovered we were only a couple of days off the summer break, so I'd have weeks to work out a proper solution.

I suddenly realised I hadn't given anyone my new phone number, and there were some people I wanted to keep in touch with.

On the new phone I called everyone on my good list, telling them I was getting nuisance calls and giving my new number, and asked them to please remember not to give my new phone number to anyone.

Stefan agreed and asked when I'd be available to work again. I told him it wouldn't be long – the family emergency would soon be under control, and I'd let him know. I asked if there was anything he was having trouble with and he said it was fine.

I let Chioma know too. She was more trouble.

'Jen,' she said. 'You have to sign in at Wimbledon police station in five days. They could jail you over this, you know?'

I laughed, hysterically. I had totally forgotten for the first time in weeks that I was a murder suspect. I didn't tell her it was very minor considering what I'd actually done, but she wasn't stupid.

'What are you up to now?' she asked.

I asked her to smooth things over if she thought it was possible, but said it was probably best if she didn't say I'd been in touch.

'What have you done?' she yelled.

'Client confidentiality,' I said.

'That's not what it means. Keeping secrets from your own lawyer.'

I hung up while she was still squealing.

Lainey was a lot easier, especially as I distracted her by saying how lovely Wolfie was, and how well behaved. Unlike his owner.

I didn't phone DC Elliott.

I thought I might keep in touch occasionally by email, in case he let some useful information slip, but was hyper-aware I might let something slip too.

After all that, I had Alex help me pack everything in the car, including Wolfie. It was strange having the hire car, but at least we had a bit more space for everything.

'We've got a long drive today,' I said. 'We'll make a start and get some breakfast in an hour or so, yes?'

He dropped off back to sleep in the back seat, so I assumed he wasn't hungry.

I woke him up when I'd parked on the outside edge of the carpark at the motorway services.

We wandered around looking at the various food choices. I suggested a big breakfast with egg and bacon, but he wasn't interested.

'Choose anything you want,' I said.

He picked a giant chocolate cookie and I picked out a cream cheese bagel for me. We could have something else later, at the next services a few miles further north.

I had a coffee while Alex had a glass of milk and we sat at a little table watching all the people go by as we ate our breakfast.

'We're going north,' I told him. 'It's quite a long drive, but I want us to get there today so it's going to be a bit boring. If you want to buy a comic or something to entertain you on the journey, you can.'

He shook his head. 'I wish I had Panda,' he said.

'I'm so sorry we forgot him, but we can't go back,' I said. 'I already explained. I know it's not the same but we can take a look at what they have in the shop over there.'

He stood up, half his cookie still on the plate.

'After breakfast!' I said.

He took another bite, obediently.

'We're going to stay in the house where I grew up,' I said. 'When I was young.'

'When you were the same age as me?' he asked.

'I was a bit older,' I said. 'But not much.'

Well, it wasn't much to me though he would have thought it was a lot.

This was a more difficult conversation than I expected.

'It's a stone cottage,' I said. 'On its own, nearly, at the top of a steep hill.'

'Are your mummy and daddy still there?'

'No,' I said. 'I'm quite old, you know. I lived with my Auntie. My mum's sister. She died a few years ago,'

For the first time he volunteers some information.

'I don't know about my daddy,' he said.

I didn't know what to say. It was only two days.

'He was alright on Friday night, when I...collected...you,' I said, stumbling over my word choices.

He looked at me, as if I was disappointing him.

I was too scared to say anything, at first. Then I realised.

'Is Paul your stepfather? Are you worried about your real daddy?'

He looked away, and didn't say anything.

I decided not to push it. He would talk when he was ready and at least for now we had time.

'Look,' I said. 'If you've changed your mind, I can take you back home. Is it what you want?'

'Home,' he said. 'I don't know how to get there. I would have tried before, if I knew.'

'I can find my way to the house you were living in?'

'No,' he said. 'I don't want to go back there. I want to go back to my dad's house.'

'Do you know where that is?'

'London. Somewhere godless, that's what Mum says.'

He was so upset it seemed more sensible to leave it, while we were in the middle of a busy service station.

'We'll work it out,' I said. 'Let's pretend we're on holiday for now. If you're sure you don't want to go back?'

I was starting to think it must be some kind of custody thing. Maybe his mum was awarded custody but he'd rather live with his dad. Perhaps they locked him up because he'd been running away?

But maybe there was a good reason his mum got custody. Sometimes it's the way it is. Sometimes, in a nasty divorce, people lie.

What a mess I'd walked into. Now it was my mess to sort out, somehow.

I took him to the loo. He was happy go into the ladies with me. I didn't want to leave him anywhere public on his own, just yet, any more than I would leave Wolfie.

While I was waiting for him, I checked my phone again. There was still total silence on the news and the Brighton pages about a missing child.

It was beginning to weird me out.

At the shop I encouraged him to pick out a soft toy to stand in for Panda. He chose a sheep, and I laughed. 'You'll see lots of real ones where we're going.'

I picked out a baseball cap, pulling it onto his head so it covered up his blond hair.

I also added some basic groceries. We weren't going to want to go shopping when we got there. So tinned soup, bread and cheese, plus a bottle of blackcurrant squash.

We gave Wolfie some food and water by the car, then walked him around on the grassy bits of the service station, before carrying on with the next leg of the journey.

We were stopping at alternate service stations so that boy or dog could use the facilities and we could all stretch our legs. It made the journey take a lot longer, but maybe that was a good thing.

I hadn't checked for missed calls on my old phone, but it would have to wait until the middle of the night. I wished I knew if anyone was trying to contact me.

God, I was so hopeless under pressure. All I'd achieved by having a backup phone was that I was missing people getting in touch with me who I wanted to hear from, and now I was worried about getting harassing texts and calls on two phones.

At least I had email access though. Thank goodness for Google's memory – that was easily installed.

There was just one email from my stalker.

You're not answering your phone and the voicemail is turned off. Don't think you can escape me that easily, you cow. Here I am haunting your inbox again.

Who on earth is this blond kid you told your dozy, nosy neighbour was your nephew? I know you don't have a nephew.

You moved out in time, though, I'll give you that. I didn't think you'd have moved on yet. I thought you'd feel safe a bit longer. It's not as if I've been pulling the stops out. I'll find you, even if I have to trek all the way to Cornwall.

Aha, I thought. Perhaps this is Amy.

It didn't really make sense though, as she'd taken my advice and found a solicitor.

I was about to forward the email to DC Elliott, then I realised it would tell him nearly everything I didn't want him to know. Instead, I emailed to let him know I was still being pestered.

I didn't add anything else, but I thought keeping him informed made me look more innocent, somehow. Or deceitful. One or the other.

'Just one last big push up the motorway,' I said to Alex, 'then we'll go to collect the keys to the cottage.'

He was still unnaturally quiet and well behaved, I thought. I don't know much about autism, but it seemed to me this behaviour didn't make sense of their story. Meltdowns? This boy was altogether too good.

If meltdowns were something to do with sensory overwhelm, a long journey with someone he didn't know would surely be difficult? How could a kid with problems cope so well through all this. It didn't make any sense that his parents had to lock him up. Maybe not all autistic kids react the same. Perhaps some go quiet. Alex was certainly quiet, to the point of invisible at times. But why would anyone lock a kid up for being quiet?

It was all a bit confusing.

At some point, I thought, it might be worth consulting Nick. He had personal experience, after all, as well as being a therapist. Maybe it would give me away though. He'd been keen to find Alex, so he might have discovered the boy had gone missing. And as a therapist, he had a duty of care – and he was bound to interpret that as needing to get the police involved.

Why wasn't a missing boy, just eight years old, all over the news by now? I didn't understand it.

Although I'd been dreading going back home, there was something comforting in watching the landscape change. I loved the South Downs, walking distance from the Brighton house, but the soft green rolling chalk hills seemed tame compared with the Pennines and the moors.

I wasn't expecting the rush of happiness I felt seeing the darker greens of the grass and foliage and realising that some part of my heart still found itself at home in the North West. Of course, the local countryside had been my escape – I'd spent many happy times out on my own with a library book, a sandwich, and a soft drink. I had actually missed being here – I still felt connected to it as my home. My place.

Alex was still asleep when we reached my home-town, so I left him in the car sleeping while I went into the solicitors' who had dealt with Martha's will.

'I'm here to collect the keys to the Blake property' I said. 'I'm Jenny Blake.'

The receptionist looked at me astonished and said, 'You look nothing like Jenny.'

I recognised her though. She was one of my school friends. If they counted as friends when they had mostly been bullies.

'Yasmin Nawaz,' I said. 'Well, I remember you.'

I took my passport out of my bag.

'Here's my ID,' I said, 'OK, my hair's shorter, and a different colour, but I'm still recognisably me.'

Flustered, Yasmin said 'Oh, I'm sorry, Jenny. I didn't recognise you. Your mum's been in few times, to ask if you'd decided what to do about your aunt's house.

Oh, so she is alive then, I thought. I knew, of course. There had been plenty of letters I'd binned unread.

'And what did you say?'

'Oh, nothing, of course.' Yasmin backtracked. 'Our client's business is their own affair.'

I looked at her, steadily, and waited.

'I'll see if Mr Havilland is available.'

Within minutes I was in his office, coffee and biscuits brought in, which I ignored.

'Sorry,' I said. 'I'm very tired. I'll like to get to the house and get some rest.'

'If you'd let us know you were coming, we'd have had the house all ready for you,' he fussed.

'It was a sudden impulse.'

'The power's on, and we check the place every week,' he said, 'And we do have a cleaning service do a regular deep clean, so it will be liveable, if not homely and welcoming.'

'It never was homely and welcoming.'

He looked at me askance.

'It will be fine. I can soon sort the place out. I'll be staying for some weeks while I sort out all Martha's stuff and decide what to do with the house.'

He sniffed. 'We were expecting you to deal with this three years ago.'

'I was busy.'

He handed the keys over and I rushed back to the car where Alex was still sleeping. I realised I was going to have to come up with some convincing story. And soon.

I drove up to the house, slowly, reluctantly. I had to force myself to get out of the car. It felt so strange to be back.

I woke Alex up, shaking him gently.

'We're here?' he asked, rubbing his eyes, looking at the forbidding stone cottage. 'Is this your home.'

'Our home,' I corrected him. 'At least for a few days, maybe weeks.'

That made it feel better.

Once inside, I turned on all the lights. It looked more welcoming that it had in the unflattering light of dusk.

Alex's eyes were wide open, now, interested in everything. I grabbed Wolfie from the car, and he and Alex set off exploring the house while I brought the bags and the shopping in.

In the kitchen, it all came back to me. The heating first – luckily, it was a knack I'd not lost, and I heard it start to grumble and bang as the pipes warmed up.

I found a new sponge in the drawer by the sink to wipe the surfaces over. I was astonished to discover Martha had caved to the demands of the modern age and had installed a microwave.

That made it easier. I started fixing some food – heating up a big tin of tomato soup, while toasting a couple of cheese sandwiches.

I called Alex. I could hear his footsteps on the wooden stairs before he appeared at the kitchen door with Wolfie ahead of him.

The dog begged for a bite of cheese sandwich.

'You can have yours after we've eaten,' I said. Then I persuaded Alex to wash his hands and we sat at the table to eat.

Later, I checked my emails and there was a reply from DC Elliott. He was quite brusque demanding to know where I was. He hoped I'd found somewhere safe to stay. He apologised for not realising I was right to be paranoid – he'd been to the house and there was evidence of an attempt to break in. He'd been prowling round the back, then. He hadn't taken my word for it.

He didn't say anything about the kid. Surely he would know if Alex was reported missing? After I'd sent him round to the house, and he'd taken their side, wouldn't he be the first person they'd turn to when the kid went missing? Surely he'd ask me about it?

Unless he was hoping to lull me into a false sense of security and track me down.

Maybe they all thought the kid had run away?

But then, they'd go to the papers for help in finding a runaway, right?

None of it made the slightest bit of sense.

Chapter Twenty One

The bedrooms were uninviting with a musty smell. The whole of the cottage needed airing.

I rummaged in in the airing cupboard looking for blankets but they weren't there. Eventually I found them, vacuum packed, in the built in storage in the spare bedroom. When I opened the first one, it smelled fresh, so that was a good start.

I carried a couple downstairs chivvied by boy and dog.

In the living room, the two big sofas were covered in dust sheets. Taking them off without thinking meant that all the dust they'd kept off the sofas hovered in the air for a while. All three of us had sneezing fits.

'I think we'll settle down here for the night, then work out what we're going to do with the house tomorrow. After we've taken the hire car back.'

I smiled when Alex took his stuffed lamb, dubbed Sheep, to bed with him. It wasn't Panda, but it was something.

In the morning, Wolfie was lying next to Alex's sofa and cuddling Sheep with his teeth and soaking him with slobber.

I took Sheep off Wolfie, planning to wash him, but Alex stopped me. 'I gave Sheep to Wolfie,' he said. 'He was lonely when he couldn't fit on the sofa with me.'

We didn't want to snooze again on the sofas, even though we were up unaccountably early. We ate biscuits and drank blackcurrant squash. Wolfie breakfasted on dry kibble, and we gave him fresh water, then we let him out to run loose in the back garden.

The garden looked secure enough, although a determined wolfhound could probably escape if he wanted to. It was the first time Wolfie had run free since the house in Brighton so he was full of energy.

I took a quick inventory of the house. The fridge needed a clean – I added bicarb to my mental list – but other than that it looked like it was working. The cooker was ancient but I was used to it, and it was still going strong.

In the living room, the TV looked reasonably new. To our delight, it worked without any messing about.

I left Alex watching kid's TV while I sat at the kitchen table making a huge list for a supermarket shop – vast quantities of cleaning supplies plus healthy food for me, boy and dog.

Sheets and duvets too, I decided. On impulse I added electric kettle and toaster.

Wolfie had worn himself out, so I decided it was best to leave him at home, shut in the kitchen.

I hated shopping – I decided one of the next things to do would be to see if I could transfer my online shopping account to deliver to my new address. Surely no one would be able to work out where I was that way? Or I could set up a new account and pay via PayPal. That would probably be safer.

Before we went out, I put Alex's baseball cap on his head, pulling it down over his blond hair. He accepted it. In the big supermarket he was still on his best behaviour, doing a great job of collecting what I asked for and adding to the trolley. I didn't let him out of my sight for a moment. Back home we unpacked the shopping on to the kitchen table, deciding where to store it all.

I plugged in the new kettle and toaster. Before long we had hot squash and hot, buttered toast – just a snack to keep us going until we'd returned the car.

Just before we left, I checked the garage, opening the door from the kitchen, while blocking boy and dog. Martha's car was still there, white and polished under its own dust cover. It must have been years since she'd driven it, plus the three years since she died. She'd told me she was keeping it in good condition so if I could drive it if I came to stay. I'd told her I had my own car, but it never sunk in. To her, I was still the impoverished student who had last visited fifteen years earlier, with Matt.

They hadn't liked each other at all. It was something of a pattern with Matt.

Maybe Aunt Martha had been right though. I'd have to get organised with an MOT and transfer my insurance, but her car could save me a lot of trouble, as well as not being easily traceable.

After dismantling the dog guard and leaving it in the hall, I strapped Alex in the back of the hire car and drove the twenty miles to Manchester airport. I returned the car to the franchise, and Alex was astonished. 'I thought we'd have to take it back to the place we got it.'

'Just as well not,' I said. I'm getting bored with all this driving around, aren't you?'

He nodded enthusiastic agreement.

We found a cafe for a late breakfast. I was ravenous and had egg and bacon, but Alex chose toasted cheese sandwiches. The boy did like his cheese.

As we sat in a quiet corner, I talked to him.

'I'm going to have to come up with a story about you,' I say. 'Telling lies is usually a very bad thing, but for now it's necessary. Unless you want me to take you back?'

Ouch. I was worried that sounded like a threat, but it didn't seem to bother him.

I wasn't sure it was the right thing to do, to keep asking, but I thought not giving him any control was the psychological equivalent of keeping him locked up.

'Which do you choose? More adventure or go back to your home.'

'More adventure!' he said.

'Would you like to choose another name? Just for this adventure?'

I thought it might make it easier if he ever was reported missing.

He looked at me, solemnly.

'I never liked Alex.'

'What name would you like?'

'Lucas,' he said, with surprisingly little hesitation.

'You can call me Jen,' I said, realising he hadn't called me anything so far. I hadn't even thought about it.

I felt a bit guilty for drawing him into lying this way, even though he didn't seem to mind.

I paid for our brunch and asked the waitress where a taxi rank could be found.

Chapter Twenty Two

There wasn't too much to do to make the house habitable. It was nothing like as bad as it had seemed, so I decided we'd make a start, and see how it went.

I'd almost forgotten about the hair dye allergy test, but it was a good time to do it. I opened the pack and placed it on the draining board in the kitchen.

Then I realised it was pointless.

Lucas still hadn't been reported missing so no one was looking for him. There were no front-page photos, nothing on the TV news, nothing online. I would make a mess of an amateur dye job. It would look fake and flat and then his roots would soon need sorting.

I realised I had been over-reacting and threw the lot in the bin.

Lucas was watching me, astonished.

'I thought it was a waste of time and effort,' I said. 'We have such a lot to do. I'm going to make a list. Do you want to help?'

First things first. We went round the house opening the windows to get some air in, Wolfie following us everywhere.

Between us we decided to thoroughly clean the bathroom and the kitchen first, then sort out the bedrooms. Mr Havilland was right – the house had been cleaned relatively recently so there wasn't a great deal to do.

I asked Lucas which room he would like. There were three bedrooms on the same floor as the bathroom, plus upstairs there was an attic which was mostly used for storage, but which had natural light, heating and a huge floor space.

I'd have been tempted by the attic if I were Lucas' age, but thought it was probably sensible when he picked the bedroom which had been mine, once upon a time.

That suited me – I would be happy enough in Aunt Martha's room and I had no desire to revive memories of my teenage misery.

The beds were still in good condition, and only needed the dust covers removing before making up with the new bedding.

Otherwise, a quick run round with the vacuum cleaner would do for now.

We made the beds together. I thought for a moment I'd lost Lucas entirely in the duvet cover for my bed as we wrestled with it. Wolfie was busy helping too, until we decided to shut him out until we were done.

It was such a normal sort of experience, and we were so relaxed and laughing so much, it was almost possible to forget what a strange situation this was.

I could almost be his mother, not his kidnapper.

Once my double duvet was done, his was much easier.

We collapsed on the bed afterwards.

I noticed the bookcase, still full of my childhood books – every single one bought for me by Aunt Martha.

There was me fantasizing about us being a proper family and I'd been treating him like a small adult, not giving him time to play or be a child.

Fine damn mother I'd make.

'Do you like reading, Lucas?' I asked.

'Oh yes,' he said. 'I have a lot of books at home. My nan bought me books all the time, and she used to read to me.'

Not his mum, I noticed. I remembered how empty his room was...

'Here,' I said. 'These are all my books from when I was young. If you want, you can find one to read – either here in your room or bring it downstairs.'

He was taking the books off the shelves and looking at them before I'd finished speaking.

'Or you can always watch telly. Only I ought to go and do some work now, okay?'

He picked up Winnie the Pooh and lay on the bed, reading. The moment I opened the door Wolfie ran in to check on us.

Calling Wolfie, I left Lucas in his room, went downstairs and set up the laptop on the kitchen table.

I wasn't convinced using my mobile phone was the best solution for online access, so the first thing I did was google and explore my options.

Would it be sacrilege to have broadband installed in Aunt Martha's house? And how long would it be before they could do it?

Luckily, I was easily sorted out with a mobile router which would arrive the next day and being on top of the hill with a direct line of sight to the nearest mast, reception was likely to be pretty good.

I was only putting off catching up with work. There were very few emails to deal with. Stefan was obviously trying not to bother me too much while I was handling my family emergency.

But of course, there was another email from DC Elliott which made me roll my eyes.

Ms Blake,

To remind you I have seen the attempt to break in at your back door. With any luck your camera will have recorded the perp. It would be great to have access to the property so I can do something about this. In the meantime, I have added your house to the list of properties at risk, so it will be covered on patrol.

Dave

He could spot a property at risk, but not a child. I was no criminal mastermind. I'd disabled the camera and forgotten to turn it on again.

All of this was exhausting. Especially DC Elliott paying so much attention to me. Who knew the police could be so diligent?

Lucas came down to the kitchen, carrying Winnie the Pooh. He put the book on the table, and sat on the floor next to Wolfie, making a fuss of the dog. They were so comfortable together, I was beginning to think I could stop worrying quite so much about keeping an eye on them.

However, it was time to settle Lucas into some kind of routine, so I asked him what his usual bedtime was.

He thought for a moment and said, 'Eight 'o' clock.'

Google suggested that nine might be reasonable, if there was no reason to get up too early.

When I announced my decision, he slipped up and said, 'Mum insists on seven.'

I was so happy to have found him out in some ordinary naughtiness, I couldn't stop grinning.

I said, 'I bet she usually had you getting up early though, and here we're planning to sleep in until at least eight. It's about time in bed, and how much rest you need.'

'What if I wake up early and you're still asleep?'

'Well, then, you can get yourself some juice or milk, cereal if you're hungry, and read quietly or watch TV until I wake up. Probably best not to go outside though, until I've made sure the fence is properly safe. We don't want to lose Wolfie.'

He seemed happy with my answer.

By nine pm his eyes were closing even as he fought to stay awake. I let him go wash and get ready for bed on his own, but said I'd be there to check on him in fifteen minutes.

By the time I went to look he was fast asleep.

I breathed a huge sigh of relief.

I felt safe, at least for now. As far as I knew, no one knew about Aunt Martha's house. And it wouldn't have been easy to trace my movements, once I'd hired a car. I wasn't even expected to sign in for bail yet. I could relax for a while.

I went downstairs determined to enjoy some time on my own, but I was exhausted too, and in bed before ten.

Next morning we went shopping again. This was getting to be ridiculous, but I guess it's one of the problems of inadequately planning a kidnapping. I called a taxi to take us to the big supermarket – thinking it was past time I sorted out Martha's car, if possible.

We wandered around with a trolley, picking out more clothes for Lucas first, then we went to look at the toys. He still had Sheep, although Wolfie seemed to think it was his now. He chose a teddy. I said he shouldn't let Wolfie steal that one too. Mostly what he wanted was art supplies. Sketchpads and crayons, paints and paintbrushes. His mum had thought all that stuff was too messy, he said, prompting me to buy aprons and huge silicone surface protectors for the kitchen table.

Once we got home, he wanted to paint, so I set him up at the kitchen table.

I had to work again. I dealt with emails then I WhatsApped Stefan at the office, to tell him I was still away but would be available for work every morning from the following week.

Lucas was in the next room, at the breakfast table, colouring in, drawing. He spilled some water and cried out, and I helped him clear up.

My phone pinged. I'd forgotten to turn it off. It was Chioma, and I just didn't want to know, so I didn't answer. I decided I'd check and call her back later.

Late afternoon, after the mobile router had been delivered, we took Wolfie out for a walk, checking out the big park. It was in much better shape than I remembered. There were more benches and places to sit, a really impressive children's playground, and saplings had become grown trees.

Afterwards, once Wolfie was tired, though Lucas was still full of energy, I asked Lucas if he wanted to learn to groom the dog. He was enthusiastic, and listened intently as I explained about being careful to watch out for matts on his coat, and not to tug hard. I had some cheese handy, to distract the tired dog in case Lucas was a bit too enthusiastic with the dog rake. I had no need to worry. Lucas was very gentle – much more careful than I was.

Without thinking I rewarded them both with cubes of cheese.

I reflected on the past few days and thought it was odd the way my life had resolved into an adventure with interludes of work and domesticity.

Lucas went to bed, without prompting, exhausted by a full day.

I checked my phone again and realised Chioma had left a voicemail.

'Jen,' she said. 'This is really urgent. I've heard from Carstairs, and he wants to see you as soon as possible. I can't cover for you for much longer. Please call me.'

I just couldn't face it. I would deal with it all the following day. It wasn't as if I could go back, after all.

Instead, I started to set up the mobile router.

It took a bit of working out, especially as I could only google instructions on the phone, but once it was up, I connected my laptop to the Wi-Fi. It worked perfectly.

At last, I could do a proper online search – on the phone it was so easy to miss things.

I thoroughly checked the Facebook local groups again. There was still no reference to a missing child.

I wondered again if it was because someone, DC Elliott for instance, knew I had him. Maybe the Grays and even the police were on my trail already.

The more I thought about it, the more frightening it was that there'd been no mention.

I looked up rental cottages online. We might have to move quickly. This luck couldn't continue, could it? I contemplated paying a deposit just in case, but decided we were safe enough for the time being.

Even contemplating giving Lucas up was painful. I'd had so much loss lately, and I was already attached. From starting out with a determination to do what was best for him, I was now all about what was best for me. I needed to give myself a good talking to.

With that in mind, I looked up autism sites. ADHD, too. I read a bit and couldn't find any real points of similarity. That worried me. Nick had said the parents had a diagnosis, though he'd too had doubts about its accuracy.

I sat staring into space for a while, trying to be objective about what was happening, and what my part in it all might be.

I kept coming back to how easily he had come with me – it must have meant there was something wrong. But I had to admit it meant nothing at all about what should come next. My desire for my own little family – my heart almost burst thinking of me and Lucas and Wolfie as a family – that wasn't justification.

If I cared about the boy, I had to do what was best for him. And my running away with him, not trusting the authorities was only acceptable if I used the time and space I gained to work out exactly what was best. Best for Lucas, not just for me.

I opened a document and started typing.

Thinking on paper – or virtual paper – is always clearer. It was also useful to keep a record for my own sake – so I wouldn't forget things I had already learned, under the influence of my own desire, my own bias.

What did I know?

From observation – the boy had spent far too much time locked alone in his room, at two separate houses.

He was left at home on his own, locked in, solely for the convenience of the Grays.

They had moved house rather than be subjected to an official inspection of their home-schooling setup.

I didn't know how much or what kind of home schooling they did – if any. I knew sometimes it was an ideological thing, to protect children from a politically impure world.

The police, in the form of DC Dave Elliott, thought there was nothing wrong and the Grays were an average, happy family.

Lucas seemed like a bright and observant child. He was perhaps too eager to please.

Apart from weirdness about food – his mother seemed to be very food purity oriented – he was well adjusted, or at least well behaved.

But there were the night terrors.

He missed his Panda, and his Nana.

Lilian who used to give him sweets and other forbidden treats.

He didn't seem to like Paul Gray. At all.

There was still no sign online he'd been reported missing. No newspaper stories local to Brighton. Certainly nothing nationally. I checked again, to be sure.

Nothing.

I wondered...

I searched again for missing child stories. For the first time, I thought of looking for a boy called Lucas, not Alex. I didn't restrict my search to the Brighton area. And I went further back in time.

There was nothing on the first page of Google results, but there was on the second.

Maybe this was why I hadn't looked before. I hadn't wanted to know.

There he was, my Lucas.

A man in Wood Green, London – Simon Ward – had been awarded custody of his son at the culmination of a very nasty divorce and custody hearing in the family court.

Soon afterwards, the child was taken by his mother, who convinced a teacher at the school gates she had his father's permission.

I read the interview with Simon Ward with tears in my eyes. He was afraid they might have gone to Spain, as the new boyfriend used to have a business there.

The names weren't the same. Lucas' mother wasn't called Verity, but Kim. Kim Ward. Her boyfriend was the same man – but his name was Jed Shepherd. It was them – I could recognise them in the photograph.

There was a photograph of Simon with a boy holding a toy panda. It was Lucas's sixth birthday.

It all fitted.

But this was only one side of the story. The courts have been known to make wrong decisions. Lucas' mother – it was understandable she would want custody of her own child.

I needed to know more before I decided what to do.

Or did I need to have more time with Lucas?

I searched for Simon Ward on Facebook. There were a few, so it took a while to narrow it down. Finally I stumbled on one sharing news stories about the missing boy. I bookmarked his page, so I could keep an eye on it. A friend request seemed too intrusive, or at least, too soon. Why would he accept?

After checking his friends who posted regularly on his page, I found a woman who posted a lot publicly about her rescue dog.

I added a friendly comment on her most recent photo of the dog, saying I had taken on a wolfhound, and he was a delight, although a handful. It's easy to make friends with dog people.

On impulse, I picked up my phone and called Nick.

He was reticent at first, then I realised he wouldn't have recognised the phone number.

I explained who I was, and that it was a new number – I'd been sick of nuisance calls. I mentioned Carphone Warehouse and he laughed.

'Sorry to pester you again, it's getting to be a habit. I wondered if you'd managed to track down Verity and Paul Gray.'

'No,' he said. 'The trail ran cold.'

'You said your little boy had played with their child?'

He made an affirmative grunt.

'I should have said before, but I was afraid to seem insane. What bothered me was the locks on the outside of the child's bedroom.'

Nick was shocked.

'Are you sure?'

I couldn't tell him how sure – that the same setup was at their next house.

'It was like Fort Knox,' I said. 'Not just a key, but two large bolts.'

'They seemed fine to me,' he said. 'He was a quiet kid. I can't see why they'd lock him up.'

'OK, I know there's an issue with confidentiality. This is gonna sound bad. Please excuse my ignorance. You said your son is autistic. I've read that autistic kids sometimes, well, they go into meltdown.'

Nick went so quiet, I felt awkward.

'My son, Rory,' he said. 'It's a thing. You don't want to see him on a bad day in a supermarket. Alex, though. They said he'd been diagnosed, but I wasn't convinced. I kept telling them to take him back to the doctor, get him assessed properly. He was super quiet to me. Too quiet, maybe. Shyness, or social withdrawal, can be a sign of autism, sure. Not all autistic kids are the same.'

Then I made a partial confession.

I told him how I'd tracked the family down and even talked to the police. The detective had visited the family and said everything was fine, but I didn't believe it. How DC Elliott had made me promise to let it go – told me he'd have me on charges for stalking and wasting police time.

'But I'm still worried,' I finished. 'I mean, is it possible he was being sedated?'

'Some parents do,' he said. 'I can't say I saw any sign. But it's possible.'

'I know I might be catastrophising,' I said. 'I just can't bear the idea of a child being locked up in his room like that.'

'I understand. Would you take me to where they live?' he asked. 'I could try to talk to them?'

I apologised. 'I'm away for a few weeks. I have to go where the work is. I could give you the address though?'

He wrote it down, and said he'd visit them when he could.

'I'll let you know what I find out,' he promised.

Last thing before bedtime, I went online again, looking for missing child stories.

Still nothing. Didn't they care? Was there something else going on? Was it really because they'd taken him without his father's permission. Perhaps they thought Simon Ward had tracked them down and taken him?

The police should have been after me by now. Asking questions of my work colleagues, my lawyer. DC Elliott knew I was concerned – surely I would be the first person he'd ask. He could email me, after all.

There was nothing.

The silence was unsettling.

Chapter Twenty Three

I tossed and turned yet couldn't find a comfortable position to sleep. I blamed the bed and the bedding. I stripped the sheets and remade it, even though I knew it was all the worry going round and round in my head that wouldn't let me settle.

Eventually I must have fallen asleep. I woke at one point after dreaming about being locked up in the dark and not being able to breathe. Again, I had to straighten the covers out – I'd somehow become all tangled up.

I tried calming breathing exercises – breathing in slowly for a count of four, and then out for a count of six. The next time I awoke I was haunted by images of Matt standing on the top of the cliffs, and me pushing him so hard I almost followed him on to the rocks below.

I knew it didn't happen like that and I certainly hadn't pushed him. But I still felt guilty. Responsible.

Maybe I'd pushed him in less literal ways.

He'd fallen, I thought. Or maybe, he had killed himself. Jumped. He'd always been less careful than me. When we walked along those cliffs together, I'd paid attention to the 'Keep away from the edge' signs, but he was always a daredevil.

Of course, the police thought I'd pushed him. Murder.

My guilt was off the scale and all bound up with my worries about what was happening now. Or was it the other way round? Perhaps all this was a distraction from Matt's death? And from the risk of being arrested, when they caught up with me. Maybe I was on the run to avoid that, not just to keep Lucas safe.

Could I have done anything differently? Maybe I could have behaved better with Matt. With Amy.

How could I find out more about Simon Ward, and Lucas' Nan?

The next time I was woken up it was because Lucas was screaming. Another nightmare.

I knocked on his bedroom door and went in very quietly. I sat on the bed next to him and said, 'It's a dream, Lucas. It will pass. Don't worry.'

Wolfie, who had somehow beaten me into his room, was pacing and whining.

The boy woke, rigid with fear, but slowly, gradually he relaxed.

I said, 'I'll stay here until you go to sleep.'

I moved to the bottom of the bed to give him a bit more space, thinking it might be a good idea to find a small armchair to go in the room.

I must have fallen asleep soon after him.

I woke up half snuggled up to him, and from his breathing Lucas was also waking up. Wolfie was in there too – all three of us on a single bed.

We were kind of embarrassed looking away and pretending it hadn't happened. Except the dog, who slobbered on both of us. But it did seem to me we felt more comfortable with each other, all the same.

Like family.

After breakfast I left Lucas watching kids' TV.

Putting off starting work, I phoned Chioma.

Well, I planned to call her. I was interrupted by another text.

I suppose you think I should face the music. No chance. You are as much to blame as me, if not more.

I tried to put it out of my mind and carried on with my call. Chioma answered the phone and was as cross as I'd ever known her.

'Why didn't you get back to me sooner? I told you it was urgent.'

'I'm sorry,' I said. 'I'm still getting all these texts so I had my phone turned off.'

'Haven't you told the police about them yet, like I told you?'

My voice squeaked a bit. 'Yes, DC Elliott has them. He was going to pass them to the Digital Harms Team.'

'Block the numbers,' she said. 'Easy.'

'I can't,' I said. 'I need to know.'

'More than you need to know what Carstairs wants?' she asked, snippily.

'I know, I know. I just want to escape from it all. I need a break. That's all.'

'Well, you'll have to come back. Carstairs wants to interview you, and it sounds important.'

'What's it about?'

'He's not going to tell me, is he? He wants to interview you. The murder suspect, remember?'

'I can't,' I said. 'I'm sorry, I can't explain why, but I just can't come back at the moment.'

'Where are you?' Chioma asked. 'At the Brighton house? I'll come to you.'

'No,' I said. 'I couldn't stay there. Not after the break in.'

'Where are you?'

'I can't say.'

'How can I be your lawyer if you keep me in the dark?'

That was fair.

'Look,' I said. 'I understand. Perhaps this will help. I should have told you, and Carstairs sooner. I was just afraid because it made me look guilty.'

'Go on,' she said, as I paused.

'I drove down to the cottage on the Monday. I was angry, after the confrontation at the IVF clinic. I wanted to see Matt. I wanted to rage at him. How could he do that to me? But I didn't see him. There was no one in the cottage. His car wasn't there. I waited for half an hour but realised it was all pointless, so I drove home. That's it.'

'You have to talk to Carstairs,' she said.

'And I will, but not yet. Look, if I write it up and email you, could you please submit it as an addition to my statement? Perhaps that will hold him off for a while.'

'It will very likely have the opposite effect. He will want to question you more than ever,' she said. 'But if it's all we have, I'll give it a try.'

'I'm sorry,' I said. 'It's really important or I wouldn't do this to you.'

'You're hurting yourself more than you are me,' she said. 'I'm worried about you, Mouse. What could be more important than being the main suspect in a murder investigation?'

'I'll tell you when I can,' I said. Then I hung up and turned my phone off.

I spent an hour composing the best email I could, together with a weak apology to Carstairs.

Then I finally started work.

I was still on reduced hours, so it wasn't long before I could escape to do something with Lucas and Wolfie.

I missed having a car, so I needed to do something about that.

I checked with Mr Havilland, and discovered they had transferred ownership, so that was one problem solved. Now all I had to sort out was servicing and other admin, like adding it to my insurance.

I called Aunt Martha's garage and explained who I was. The owner remembered me, although I didn't remember him.

'Are you back home for good, Ms Jennifer,' he asked me.

'I haven't decided yet,' I said. 'But do call me Jen.'

'Oh, sorry', he said, 'Only Martha always called you Jennifer. She was so proud of you, you know.'

I couldn't tell from his tone whether he knew I was suspected of murdering my husband. I decided to think the best of him, as I needed the work doing.

He promised to send someone over to collect the car and was very optimistic it wouldn't take much, if anything, to get the car on the road again. 'Your Aunt was meticulous,' he said. 'She never missed a service. She kept that car in the best condition.'

Lucas was still engrossed in watching the telly. I wondered if he'd not been allowed to watch very often. I was probably guilty of being too permissive, but it seemed like an essential rule when you've kidnapped a child – let them do more or less what they want.

I checked the kitchen drawers and sure enough, Aunt Martha's car keys were where she always kept them.

My car keys now, I supposed.

I took my laptop into the living room so I could sit with Lucas while we waited for the mechanic.

My phone pinged and stupidly I checked straight away. Pavlovian.

It was another one of those mad texts. This time there was a series of pings. One text just wasn't enough anymore.

I know you're in Cornwall, stupid cow. Did you think I wouldn't find you?

See, I have your new number. Not as clever as you think you are.

You won't get away with murder. I will see to that.

I was angry now. Instead of ignoring, I replied.

What do you want of me? Is it you who's been making the creepy silent phone calls? Did you break into my house? If you don't stop, I'll be reporting all this to the police.

I went back online, checking Brighton groups and newspapers. I added Sussex Police on Twitter and Facebook to my search.

Still, there was no report of a missing child.

The phone pinged again.

You're on the run. There's a reason you don't want the attention of the police. They have more evidence, don't they?

Murderer.

I switched the phone off. Perhaps they'd get bored if I didn't answer.

There was a knock at the front door, and I picked up the car keys from the coffee table and went outside to see the mechanic in overalls and baseball cap trying the garage door.

'Oh,' I said. 'I hope the key's on here.'

I passed him Martha's key ring.

'If not, I can go through the kitchen and open it from inside.'

It was soon sorted, and to my surprise the car actually started. He drove off, saying they'd be in touch to let me know what the damage was.

At last, we could go out.

Luckily Lucas was bored with watching TV, so was happy to get his shoes on and go for a walk with Wolfie. The dog was happily snoozing on the sofa, but jumped up quickly enough when I jangled his lead.

I wasn't quite ready to let him loose even in the park or on the hills – I needed to be certain he would come when called. One day soon we might do some training in the park, with an extended lead. He would enjoy having more freedom to run.

I picked up the poop bags and stuffed a bag of treats in my pocket. Lucas was already at the door with his shoelaces badly tied. That was something else we were going to need – more shoes, especially if it turned out he liked walking on the moors and down in the valley, by the brook.

Once I'd tied his laces a bit tighter so he wouldn't trip over them, I followed him outside.

'Would you like a walk up the hill to look at the old church, and walk up past the farms to the top of the valley?' I asked. 'Or would you rather walk around the village?'

He picked the village. A bit of a townie, I guessed. We could do the hill and the valley another day.

We walked down to the main road, then along the short parade of shops. They'd all changed, of course, since I was there fifteen years ago.

Lucas wanted some sweets. It was so new for him to want something – and more than that, something his mother would not have approved of – that I gave him some cash and stood waiting outside with Wolfie.

He came out with a bag of jelly babies and gave me the change.

'I'll have to think about pocket money,' I said. 'You shouldn't have to ask every time you want something.'

'I've never had pocket money.'

'It's time we started a new tradition, then.'

I had no idea how much was suitable. I would have to resort to Google again. How did people manage before the internet?

As we turned the corner to go back up the hill, I saw her, in the distance. The same hair – only her helmet of stiff curls was greyer now. Feeling sad, I remembered her hair from the days before Richard – long and loose, naturally straight and so dark brown it was almost black. She had allowed me to brush it – a hundred strokes – every night before I went to bed. Long hair was vanity, though. He'd made her give it up. She still had the same awkward gait, as if she was a stranger in her own body.

I backtracked.

'Tell you what, let's go home the long way round, instead of the way we came. We'll see a bit more of the place, right?'

Lucas looked at me and nodded.

He offered me a jelly baby, which was kind of him.

I gave Wolfie a treat as we started walking quickly along the main road to the next turn off.

We walked up the lane, and again I marvelled that so much had changed. Detached houses had been demolished and replaced by flats. What had been a down-at-heels pub – the sort my stepfather used to rail against from his pulpit – was now a posh looking gastro inn and very middle class.

The whole area seemed much more upmarket than it had been.

I wondered if Pastor Richard's chapel itself still existed. I hoped not. Perhaps we could explore some more another day.

Back home I put the kettle on to make myself a pot of tea. Lucas preferred milk, so I poured him a glass and put out a plate of chocolate biscuits.

Probably too much sugar, along with the jelly babies that had already disappeared.

Half-way through a biscuit, he asked me a question which had me choke and splutter.

'Auntie Jen? Who was that woman who was staring at you?'

I wondered where the Auntie came from. Sure, I'd told everyone he was my nephew, but he'd not called me anything until now, although I'd told him he could call me Jen. I decided I liked it.

I didn't want to talk about her, but I didn't think I should lie to him.

'That woman was my mother.'.

'Oh.'

Before he could ask any more difficult questions, I added, 'We argued a long time ago. Remember I told you I went to live with my Aunt Martha, in this house, when I was sixteen?'

'Oh yes,' he said. 'Have you still not made friends with her?'

'Sometimes,' I said, 'When a person has done something very bad and has hurt you a great deal, it's not easy to forgive and forget.'

'Was she not sorry?'

I laughed, bitterly. 'I don't think she's ever been sorry in her life.'

This was too difficult and emotionally awkward for Lucas. It felt like such dangerous territory, as he was so young, and had his own pain to think about. It was coming out in his nightmares, if nowhere else.

He was going to need some proper help at some point. But not yet.

'Let's turn the TV on,' I said. 'And you can watch while I cook us a proper dinner. With vegetables.'

Later that evening, once he had gone to bed, I sat at the computer again, fretting.

I logged in to Facebook and to my astonishment Simon Ward's friend Rosie with the dogs had sent me a friend request. I accepted immediately – I'd thought I would have to work up to that.

She sent me a message saying she was always happy to meet new dog people, and so I sent her a photo of Wolfie.

I followed a link one of Simon Ward's friends had shared, to a Facebook Page about the missing child.

As I scrolled down, I found a link to the same news story I'd found through Google.

On the comments someone else had posted a link to a YouTube video, below which several people were shouting, all block caps, tagging Simon, while the other Page Admin – the woman with the rescue dog I'd talked to the previous day – suggested they delete.

I was glad it was still there, though. I followed the link and sat watching, then followed all the way down the recommendations rabbit hole.

I didn't watch all the videos, just bookmarked them for later. The first one was horrific enough.

A man was talking, voice over a montage of news clippings and family photos, claiming Simon and his mother Lilian were part of a paedophile ring based in Wood Green. Then there was a brief interview with the Grays. Worst of all, an interview with a policeman in uniform, his face pixellated out and his voice altered, claimed these were credible allegations and suggested senior police and judges were part of the conspiracy too.

I googled again, checked on the school where Lucas was taken from. Their summer fair was next week – a fundraising event to pay for textbooks and art supplies and school trips.

It sounded like a good cause. I made a note of the time and place. It was possible to work a lot out online, but I needed real human contact to be sure.

I was so worried. How could I ever find the Grays again, if it became necessary? What if they'd moved again, with no forwarding address. What if they were in the right?

Maybe I did need to make long term plans. I might not be a great mother, but I was sure I could be a good enough mother. Holding on, for a moment, to a smidgeon of hope.

Chapter Twenty Four

My notes, where I'd tried to make sense of what was going on, only served to prove how confused I was. So far it was comparable to the stage in tidying up, when it gets more muddled. Clarity was a long way away. Were the phone calls and the texts related? And the emails? Surely there weren't that many people obsessed with harassing me.

I knew about Amy. Her emails were signed. She wanted money and was obvious about it. She'd also phoned me using Matt's old phone. I made a note to cancel his account, send a copy of his death certificate and pay the closing bill. If she wanted to carry on phoning me, it could be at her own expense. It seemed very unlikely she could be behind other calls and texts. The language was just too different. What did she have to gain?

Who else could there be? There had been dozens of people who I didn't even know who'd sent vile messages on social media – that was why I'd shut down my Twitter and Instagram accounts, and why my Facebook account was now private. I'd also had a spate of blocking people I didn't know or didn't trust.

Once I'd made it more difficult would any of them have carried on – made such an effort to find my phone number and email? Maybe one or two.

I ought to check if DC Elliott and the Digital Harms Team were making any progress.

Who had my new phone number anyway? Lainey – who knew better than to pass it on to anyone else. Chioma – not a chance in hell could it come from her. I trusted my landlord, and Stefan. I had made them all promise. It could be one of the idiots at the letting agents – except they only had my old number and I'd told them to contact me through my lawyer.

Nick was a possible culprit. I trusted him, but only on instinct. I met him only once, at the moment I was stressed by the break-in. My trust for him was based on the very loose idea we were on the same side – because I intuited an obsession in him that matched my own.

I got his business card out and checked the professional association website where he was registered.

It all seemed legit. He was listed and everything. I tried to phone and email them – but it was all voicemail and out-of-office autoresponders.

The phone rang – it was Chioma. I answered, even as my heart sank. She would no doubt have heard back from Carstairs by now.

'How bad is it?' I said, pre-empting her.

'Oddly, not as bad as I thought,' she said. 'Perhaps Carstairs is holding back and has already ordered a nationwide search for you, but somehow I doubt it.'

'Oh,' I said, more nervous now than I was.

'He said your statement helped to clear up some issues, and the CCTV evidence confirms your story. He also suggested that you might consider sharing any other information you've kept back, just to make his job easier.'

'If only he didn't think his job was to get me convicted of murder.' Back to the dark humour. None of my therapists would have been impressed.

'Have you still got the text with the video of someone rummaging through your house?' Chioma asked.

'I do.'

'Forward it to me, and I'll make sure Carstairs gets a copy of the video. I think it will keep him off your back for a while, and it does provide a good explanation for why you've disappeared.'

'I did get a text a few weeks back, when I was signing in at the police station. I don't remember exactly what it said now, but it made it clear I was being watched.'

'Can you send me that too?'

I scrolled through my texts.

'Sorry,' I said, at last. 'I must have deleted it.'

'Never mind,' Chioma said, obviously not meaning it at all. 'I wish I knew what you were up to.'

'I promise it has nothing at all to do with Matt's murder,' I said.

'Why does that not reassure me at all?' she replied, before rushing off to her next meeting.

I needed to walk off some of the stress and empty my mind of it all, just for an hour or two. I couldn't help worrying though. Carstairs was being too generous. Perhaps even now he was tracking me down and would show up on the doorstep at any moment.

'Do you two want to go to the park?' I call to Lucas and Wolfie.

Wolfie showed up first, tail wagging as if he knew what was on offer. Lucas trailed behind, open book in his hand.

I took the book from him, marked his place with the dust jacket and put it on the table.

'You can carry on reading when we get back,' I said. 'I thought you might like to help me training Wolfie.'

We collected dog treats and more cubed cheese, then we all walked to the park, Wolfie pulling a bit in his excitement.

In the park I did a bit of work with Wolfie, persuading him to walk to heel. Lucas was paying attention, so I decided to let him have a go.

I handed him the lead, all the while teasing Wolfie with a lump of cheese. I didn't want him to take off at speed, dragging Lucas behind him.

It was clear Wolfie wasn't a beginner – he simply had his own ideas about how walks should be conducted. With a handful of treats and some encouraging words, Lucas soon had him walking close.

Unsurprisingly neither dog nor boy was up to concentrating for long. I wouldn't be letting them walk together anywhere but in the park any time soon.

'Right,' I said. 'Let's have a go at some basic commands. Sit, Stand, and Down. I'll go first, then you have a go.'

I cycled through the commands, rewarding the dog when he complied. He was very good at sit and stay, but not so keen on lying down. Even with cheese. I thought he was a bit too excited at being out in the park – and also perhaps a bit lazy. It's harder for a dog to lie down and get up again, than to cycle between sit and stand.

'You have a go, Lucas,' I said. 'Just try Sit and Stand and reward him with a bit of kibble when he gets it right.'

Lucas wasn't quite quick enough to respond to Wolfie's lackadaisical compliance, so the dog was probably rewarded for not obeying commands. I very much got the impression Wolfie knew what was expected. He merely thought it perfectly reasonable to decide for himself whether he wanted to do it or not.

Lucas said a very firm *Sit* and Wolfie sat beautifully for a moment. Just long enough to snatch the cheese. Then he actually lay down and rolled over, grinning and showing his tummy.

'One last try,' I said laughing, 'then we'll walk round the park and stretch our legs a bit longer before we go home.'

I took hold of the lead and explained to Lucas what I was going to do next.

'I'm going to change the order of the commands,' I said. 'Just to make sure he doesn't learn to expect them in a particular sequence. We want him to respond to the words, not the pattern.'

The first few goes, Wolfie was perfection itself – responding to the command, and slobbering up the reward.

But then he got faster and faster and more random.

I started to laugh.

'He's trying to read my mind,' I said. 'He thinks this game is about guessing what I'm going to say next.'

Lucas said, seriously, 'He's watching you for clues.'

'He's a clever dog,' I said. 'Now, let's walk around the park just once more, then go back. I think we've earned tea and cookies.'

'Or milk and cookies,' Lucas said.

As we walked along together, I realised how Lucas was like Wolfie, watching for clues, how to fit in, eager for rewards.

'If Wolfie is bad,' Lucas asked, 'or slow to learn, we won't starve him, will we?'

I shiver, a little.

'Of course not. Training rewards are an extra. Even if he was the naughtiest dog in the whole world – and he isn't – he won't go hungry. He will always get his dinner.'

I saw Lucas relax a little.

I knew he was worried about the dog. But that wasn't all he was worried about. I knew then sometimes they'd let him go hungry as a punishment and I raged inside.

When we got home, I put out milk and cookies for both of us and asked Lucas what he wanted for dinner.

'Takeaway is naughty,' he said. 'It's bad for growing children.'

I'd sworn I wouldn't do any of this yet, but I couldn't not.

'Sometimes we have funny ideas about food,' I say. 'We're all different about it, and it depends on how we're brought up.'

I knew I was on dangerous ground here.

'Food is for fun and enjoyment, too. It wouldn't be good to eat takeaway all the time, but it doesn't hurt once in a while. We've had lots of fruit today, and yoghurt. It's okay to have Chinese if you want to. We can have Chinese from the takeaway tonight, and we'll eat home cooked chicken and veggies tomorrow, okay?'

He nodded.

I laughed at myself. This was the sort of mother I would have been. Long talks, until I bored my children into submission.

We were interrupted by a phone call from the garage. There were a couple of minor repairs needed before it would pass its MOT, and they were waiting for parts, but it would be ready tomorrow if I gave them the go ahead to do the work.

I said yes, of course. It would be great to have a car again.

Lucas had already picked up his book, so I called my car insurance people, asking them to add Aunt Martha's old car to it. It was all reasonably straight forward.

Lucas tucked into the sticky barbecue ribs with stir fry noodles. I'd forgotten how messy it was likely to be and was glad it was finally possible to keep up with our laundry. There were noodles everywhere and of course, our resident living garbage disposal made them all disappear.

'We must put these bones in a bag and out in the dustbin,' I said. 'I know Wolfie would love them, but they could splinter and hurt him badly inside.'

Lucas, barbecue sauce on his nose and chin, helped me sort it all out and we went down to the dustbin together.

On our way back inside, Wolfie was waiting on the kitchen step and with his big tongue, licked Lucas' face clean.

By clean, I mean covered it in dog slobber.

The plates on the kitchen table looked suspiciously 'clean' too.

I found a flannel and encouraged Lucas to wash his face, then dished up a big bowl of fruit salad I'd made while he was reading.

While I was clearing up, without being told Lucas got Wolfie's grooming kit out and sat on the floor brushing his coat. Obviously it was more fun than being persuaded to dry cutlery.

We sat and watched TV until it was Lucas' bedtime. He was very sleepy and went up without any complaints.

I switched through channels and checking online news and still no one was looking for the boy.

My phone rang. It was Nick.

'Hi,' I said, rushing straight to the point. 'How did it go?'

'Hello, Jen,' he said. 'It was weird. I went to that address and they'd moved. I asked the neighbours and they went a couple of days ago. They hadn't lived there long at all. Just two, maybe three months.'

I was more scared now than ever. It was bad enough they weren't looking for Lucas. They'd made it impossible for me to take him back. How would anyone find them now? Did they not want to be found? Was that more important than Lucas?

'It's disturbing,' he said. 'The more I think about it, the worse it seems. Who moves so often, without a reason?'

You don't know the half of it, I thought.

All the news stories I've ever read, of parents with kids who have gone missing – even when it's clear they're probably never coming back – they all stay in their homes, in case.

This felt like the opposite of that. As if they were glad to be rid of him.

That couldn't be true, could it? There must be some other reason.

I couldn't tell Nick though. I wasn't sure if I could trust him. I couldn't admit what I'd done.

'The neighbours have no idea where they've gone,' he said. 'Could you let me know the name of the policeman, the one who went to visit them for you?'

'Of course,' I said. 'You know he won't like it. He was so angry with me.'

I found the business card and gave him DC Elliott's name and phone number.

'I'm not sure what else to do,' Nick said. 'But I'm not happy letting it go.'

'I understand. Let me know if you find anything out.'

I went back on to Facebook and chatted to my new friend Rosie. Simon Ward turned up in the thread, talking about childhood dogs, saying maybe he'd have another dog someday, but it didn't seem like the right time yet.

On impulse, I sent him a friend request. There was no immediate response, so I closed down for the night and went to bed.

Chapter Twenty Five

The following day Martha's car came home. It would always be Martha's car to me.

We did a big shop at the supermarket. After that, we went clothes shopping yet again, and then to the shoe shop. Lucas chose new shoes – a smart pair, some sandals and some trainers. The assistant who fitted them said Lucas was being spoiled, and I laughed. 'Not possible,' I said. 'He's the best kid.'

For the next couple of days, we walked around the village, Lucas wearing his new trainers every day. He wasn't interested in the other pairs at all.

We sometimes went out without Wolfie. I didn't want it to always be about the dog, because good as he was, he needed plenty of attention. Lucas needed attention too.

I had a text from Chioma, confirming that the video had persuaded Carstairs to hold off for a while. She'd failed to get any useful information from him, other than to say he was pursuing new leads.

I hoped those leads didn't involve me but was afraid perhaps they did. I hadn't exactly done anything to convince him I was trustworthy, after all.

Every day I checked online, and nothing changed. There was still no news of a missing child. It was driving me crazy. Crazier, some might say.

Simon Ward had quietly accepted my Facebook friend request, which felt exciting, like I was making progress. There wasn't much on his page which wasn't open to all, though, just some old family photos. I looked back at those early photos of Lucas' childhood, scrolling through backwards, watching him get younger and younger, with tears running quietly down my cheeks.

I liked a couple of recent posts, just to show I was engaged.

I worried a lot about missing signing in for police bail. I had odd fantasies of driving down and doing it – but what was I going to do, take Lucas with me?

There was no one I could ask to babysit, not least because what would happen if they decided to charge me, if they didn't let me leave? I couldn't do that to the boy.

But now I'd been home for a while, it felt like it was time to walk round the lanes, past the old stone chapel building. Time to confront my past, to face my demons.

It was a beautiful walk, past farms and up a steep hill. There was a fork in the path, one track leading to the valley, the other curving round the chapel, then back down towards the village, and home. I thought Lucas might be interested in the tumbledown mill, once powered by a waterwheel, or the scrappy bit of roman road, should we walk that far.

We didn't get that far.

The stone building wasn't a chapel anymore. It was now a potter's workshop. The large shop window likely meant it wasn't so dark inside now.

This seemed to count more as gentrification than the gastro pub. It gave me some satisfaction – Pastor Richard must be spinning in his grave, now his domain had been colonised by the evils of the arts and commerce combined.

Lucas was transfixed.

'Can we go in and watch?' he asked.

I didn't want to. I felt queasy looking at the place and remembering... But I couldn't resist the hungry, excited look on his face.

I recognised the potter. I couldn't remember his name, but he was in my class at school. I think the teacher even made me tutor him in maths one time.

Again, the memories flooded in.

'Maths. It's not even a girl's subject. What is wrong with you, child?'

That was before Pastor Richard decided what was wrong with me was demonic. A demon with a talent for maths. Legion, maybe.

Lucas was looking at the pots displayed on shelves which lined all the walls. I didn't have to even warn him to be careful – he was such a sensible child. Careful. Maybe too careful.

Not that I wanted him to be breaking things. Just as well we'd left Wolfie at home.

I spoke to the potter. Even sitting down at his wheel, he looked tall, and when he looked up, blue eyes peered through dark curls. He had a very serious expression, as if he were considering me. Maybe he was trying to work out where he recognised me from.

'Is it okay if Lucas watches you work for a while?'

'Of course,' the guy said. 'That's what I'm here for.'

I wished I could remember his name.

Lucas watched and the potter talked to him about what he was doing.

'Would you like to have a go? If your mum doesn't mind,'

Lucas smiled at me shyly, not saying anything about me not being his mum. He wanted to try.

I was getting more and more stressed by being in there, but the child didn't ask for much.

'I have a spare smock,' the potter said. 'He won't get messy. Well, not too messy.'

I agreed. Of course.

I wandered along looking at the different pots on display – mostly inexpensive mugs and bowls. Then I saw the array of more complex work, his art, behind glass. Fantastic vases and larger bowls. Beautiful pieces. The kind of thing that would make an heirloom.

How funny that the boy who couldn't do his sums had grown up into a man who could make such art.

All at once, I realised this display used to be the vestry cupboard.

I snatched a quick breath, steadying myself. It was not the time for a panic attack.

There used to be high shelves where the hymn books and bibles were kept. And the lower part was for bags and there was hanging space for coats.

That was where I had been locked, in the dark by Pastor Richard, when I was sixteen.

'I'm going outside for some fresh air,' I managed to say, as I regained the use of my voice, and my feet.

Lucas spoke. 'Are you okay, Auntie Jen?'

I nodded. 'I'm fine,' I said. 'I'll be back in a moment or two. You have fun as long as Sean is willing to put up with you.'

Ha, funny how his name came back to me, inspired by panic.

After a couple of minutes, I went back inside, and this time avoided the back of the shop.

'It's a long time since anyone called me Sean,' the potter said. 'I should have recognised you sooner. Jen Blake, isn't it?'

'Yes,' I said. 'What do they call you now?'

He laughed, embarrassed. 'I thought Joseph sounded more artistic, less like a farmer's son. I began using it at Art College.'

He started helping Lucas to clean up, taking him to the back to wash his hands, taking off the smock, talking all the time.

'If you come back in a few days, you can collect this young man's pot, if it survives the kiln.'

'Oh, that's kind. Thank you, we will be back.'

'I was explaining that sometimes pots break. Mine too. There's an element of chance in it. But this is a fine vase for a first try. The boy has talent.'

Lucas looked thrilled.

We waved our goodbyes, saying we'd be back soon.

Lucas put his hand in mine.

'Aunty Jen,' he said. 'What was wrong in the shop?'

'Oh, nothing much,' I said. 'Just memories.'

'No. You were upset. I could tell.'

I couldn't tell him everything, but I had to tell him something.

'My stepfather was the pastor of the chapel,' I said. 'He insisted I called him Pastor Richard. All the time, even at home.'

'You had a stepfather too?'

'I did. And he didn't much like me.'

Lucas nodded, seriously.

'Anyway, I would rather have spent Sundays playing outside, but instead I had to spend it at chapel. There were lots of boring sermons, and they didn't stop when I got home.'

'My mum's religious,' he said. 'Dad said it was all rubbish, though.'

I realised he meant Simon and I wanted to ask questions, but still felt I shouldn't push.

'She said I was a devil child,' he said.

'Oh Lucas,' I said. 'That's what Pastor Richard said about me. You don't think I'm a devil, do you?'

'No,' he said. 'You're nice.'

I wanted to cry. A nice, mad, kidnapper. That was me. Maybe Pastor Richard was right. He said I always thought I knew more than anyone about what was right and wrong.

'Nobody is a devil,' I said to Lucas firmly. 'No one. And certainly there are no children who are devils.'

I gave him a quick hug, for the first time. He hugged back, but I didn't push it.

It was time to leave this conversation behind. I thought we needed a distraction.

'I'm looking forward to seeing what your pot looks like after it's been fired,' I said. 'But for now, I have an idea.'

For someone who had always hated shopping, I was doing a lot of it. Truth was, I couldn't resist buying things for Lucas.

When we got home, Wolfie was asleep, so we tiptoed back outside, and got in the car.

Google told me the nearest specialist arts and crafts store was in Bolton, so that was where we went.

I let Lucas loose in the aisle devoted to clay. The kind that can be air dried and baked in a conventional oven. He was in heaven.

We picked out lots of different colours, some tools for shaping, some moulds – an Egyptian set with scarabs and little figures and a set for making Roman coins seemed educational, so easily justified. I also picked out a book. There'd be some instructional videos on YouTube, I thought.

When we got home with all our parcels, Wolfie was very pleased to see us. Tail wagging furiously, he jumped up at me, Then he tugged at his lead, which was hanging by the front door.

'Wolfie wants a walk!' Lucas said.

'He always wants a walk,' I pointed out.

'But he showed us. He's a clever dog,' Lucas said.

We all went to the park and enjoyed the rest of the afternoon trying to train the dog to walk to heel.

He was much better at it now. When he wanted to be...

One day soon it might be time to see how he would be if we let him run free.

The devil was playing on my mind, so once Lucas – and Wolfie – were safely asleep in bed, I settled down at the laptop and found the YouTube videos I'd bookmarked.

The first one was a very intense man speaking to camera. He had a slight Northern accent and spoke quite fluently, but there was something a little off. He was more than a bit obsessive.

Truth Is Everything.

That's what his YouTube channel is called. He's covered all the conspiracy classics, from replacement Beatles to the Great Replacement.

He knows all about crisis actors.

On my pinboard in the office, I used to have a quotation from Merlin Mann. "My gut is that most conspiracy theorists have never been project managers."

That was when I was a project manager. Maybe it made me immune.

This mad YouTuber though. His staring eyes. His looks. His affect. He was so intense.

I had to laugh at myself, there. Who was I to criticise anyone for being obsessive?

He told a story of powerful people networking and making connections. He reminded us of our own recent history. Cyril Smith, an MP and member of the Liberal Party, had for years been manipulating the people of Rochdale. He had taken money from a business in asbestos and covered up the damage asbestos was causing to working people. He talked about the horrors of mesothelioma, and how it meant nothing to Smith, compared with the pay off. Then he reminded people Smith was also accused of abusing children, young boys. The police and the Liberal Party elite had known about the abuse and had covered it up. Maybe they weren't looking away. Maybe there was more going on.

Then there was Jimmy Saville. The all-round creepy entertainer, who had abused so many people, for years. A few had spoken up - people like Johnny Rotten and a not-very-well-known comedian. It was widely known he was an abuser, yet he was welcomed into NHS hospitals, given the keys to Broadmoor. He was friends with politicians like Thatcher, and even Prince Charles asked him for advice.

Surely there was enough evidence here to show there was an actual conspiracy – it wasn't paranoia, it was really happening.

He made mention of other rumours about more modern entertainers and more politicians. People in children's homes. Local dignitaries. These monsters were in positions of power and influence everywhere.

Many of them were actual Satanists, he claimed. In the nineties, people had begun to uncover the truth – social workers had taken children into care. It looked like the powers of good were going to prevail. But the system fought back. Judicial reviews were rigged.

Those who had bargained children's innocence in exchange for political power were not going to give it up so easily.

It was still happening, he said, and we had to fight for the sake of all our children.

It was happening right now, in our community here in London. Schoolteachers and headmistresses. Small businesses – the owners of a launderette here, a posh restaurant there.

One woman, he said, had been brave and rescued her son. His father, a key figure in the local network, had won sole custody of the child. It could only have happened because of the top policemen, psychiatrists, social workers and even family court judges were all in on the conspiracy. All part of this evil, power-hungry cult.

He finished with a promise. A call to arms.

'We will be stronger than they are. We will prevail. We have many good people on our side, all over the country, people are fighting back.

We have officials on our side too. Social workers, psychologists, even experienced detectives.

Fight the good fight.'

The keyboard warrior spoiled the impact of his message by highlighting the links to the merch. 'Buy your tee shirts and baseball caps here!'

He also shared a link to a video of one of their own detectives interviewing a six-year-old child.

I caught my breath. It was Lucas.

I couldn't face it yet. It would have to wait for another day.

But I was sure now. This could not be true. Lucas' mother was at best, not well. At worst... she was a monster.

Chapter Twenty Six

After all that I needed a quiet Sunday.

We ate breakfast together, then spent time in the park, playing with the dog. We read, watched TV, and I made a proper roast dinner with Yorkshire puddings and everything. All the kinds of everyday things needed to stay sane and healthy.

Even so, on Monday morning I was not keen to get back to work.

After washing up the breakfast dishes, I set Lucas up with a big silicone mat to keep the table clean. All his new clays and moulds and tools were piled up by the side. I propped up my iPad, with a playlist of videos about how to make things in polymer clay.

'Do not let Wolfie eat the clay,' I said. 'It won't be good for him, and we don't want to have to take him to the vet.'

I also gave him a baking tray, covered in another silicone mat.

'Anything you want to keep and fire in the oven, put it on here, and we'll sort it out when I've finished work. Okay?'

I left him to it, hoping when I was done, I wouldn't find scenes of total devastation.

Lucas seemed happy enough.

I needn't have worried about Wolfie. He followed me into the living room, settling on the sofa next to me as I worked on my laptop.

I missed my office, with its printer and all my files, but it was perfectly possible to do everything necessary with the laptop.

Again, there were no missing child posts on the various local and national news sites. It was compulsive to check, but I was beginning to see it wasn't going to happen. For whatever reason – and I suspected I now knew why – they couldn't or wouldn't turn to the police for help.

Trust me to kidnap a child who had already been kidnapped - although by his own mother.

I settled down to work. It wasn't one of my days working with Stefan, so I kept my own pace, working on the report about possible new functionality for the software upgrade, together with some informed speculation about likely client preferences. I kept an ear open for Lucas.

Once I was finished, I tiptoed to the doorway to see how he was doing. There wasn't much mess, and he was still engrossed, so I turn backed to see Wolfie watching me, debating whether to move or not. When he saw me on my way back, his eyes closed and the snoring soon began again.

Back at my laptop, an email pinged. It was from DC Elliott, and he wasn't happy with me for sending Nick Kennedy his way.

So what if they've moved house? You moved because you claimed all the attention from journalists was a nuisance. A few random phone calls and emails made you uncomfortable.

*Have you no empathy? I am inclined to think it's all projection and **you** are the stalker.*

You agreed to let it go, remember. To stop harassing them. I really don't want to have to take this further.

And I will be checking with the Met to see if you reported for your bail meeting,

I am worried about you, Ms Blake. You continue to cross the line and I think your behaviour is now actively criminal.

Let me have your phone number so we can talk. I need some reassurance from you.

Dave.

I was going to need Nick's help – if I could ever find a way to ask for it.

I went into the kitchen, where Lucas was so excited to show me what he'd made. There were marbled beads with big untidy holes poked in them. Multi-coloured Egyptian scarabs, slightly distorted from being removed from the moulds – enough to fill a Pharoah's tomb. Flowers and leaves, and lots of buttons.

I admired them and helped to wrap the polymer clay up so it would stay fresh for another time, clingfilmed and then placed in ziplocked bags.

Standing on a low stool in front of the sink, Lucas washed all his moulds and tools in soapy water, and then put them to drain on the side, while I read the instructions for baking the clay, and put the oven on.

With oven gloves on, he slid the tray into the oven, and we set the timer for 30 minutes.

After cleaning the table, I made tuna and sweetcorn sandwiches which we ate while waiting for the timer.

I took the tray out of the oven, and I set it on the cooker top so we could wait for it to cool, making Lucas promise not to touch yet.

All the time, I could feel the weight of unshed tears building up.

This quiet domesticity – it was all I ever wanted. If only he were my child. If only it were possible.

He seemed contented enough.

And yet, no matter how I wanted to justify, I knew better than that. Just as I was holding back my tears so as not to upset him, he was bottling up his own wants and needs to hide them from me.

He was so young, and I had all the power. He had already suffered – I knew that from the video. And although I was not so cruel or so insane as to tell him he was possessed by the devil because he wanted his father, I was still at risk of thinking more about myself, than about him.

I needed to understand what had happened to him, and then I had to make sure he got the best of help returning to his family. The right family. And I would learn to be happy about that, because that was best for Lucas.

We spent the afternoon out with Wolfie. I drove us to the far side of the valley. We walked around the reservoir and down a narrow dirt path, then up the steep slope to the Roman road.

'When I was child everyone believed this road was built by the Romans, a long, long time ago. I still call it the Roman road, and I bet lots of other people do too.'

'Who were the Romans?' he asked.

I managed not to add, 'And what have they ever done for us?' There was only so much explaining I could do in any one day.

It looked like I was doing some home schooling after all.

'We'll see if we can find some good books, on our way home,' I said. 'History is fun'

He looked at me and smiled, a very sweet smile.

'I like it when you tell me things I didn't know,' he said.

'Well,' I said, 'this is the interesting thing. People now think perhaps it isn't a Roman road. They think it might have been constructed in the eighteenth century. Which is still a long time ago, but not as long ago as Roman times.'

It was quite steep walking, so I had to stop talking as I was a bit out of breath. Wolfie and Lucas were fine, though they were walking twice as a far as me, the dog running ahead on the extending lead, and then back to collect me. When I got my breath back, I carried on.

No one knows if it's Roman or an eighteenth century turnpike. I want to think it's Roman because it's more romantic, I guess, thinking it's older. And imagining Roman soldiers, maybe from Italy, or from other parts of the Roman Empire, walking across this very hill on this road eighteen hundred years ago.'

Lucas said. 'That's a long time. What's an Empire?'

I laughed. 'We should get those history books and read them together. What do you think?'

He smiled, which I took as acceptance.

'But other people think it was built three hundred years ago, to bring people to work at the water mill in the valley, perhaps.'

Lucas asked, 'Which is true?'

'That's the funny part. We really don't know. There might be ways to find out. If someone found Roman coins here, for instance.'

We'd reached the top of the hill and again, I needed to stop for breath. In my time living down south, I'd obviously gone soft. I knew it was more that I'd been spending too much time at my desk and not enough out walking.

'Look at that view!' I said to him. 'See how far we've come? The car is parked by the reservoir, that way.' I pointed. 'You can see the sun glinting on the water.'

'And back over there, over that hill – that's where our house is.'

He looks hard.

'It's behind the hill, so we can't see it from here. But I'm glad we're not walking back all that way!'

We started the long trek back to the car. It took us nearly an hour and all the way Wolfie was longing to run free. I needed to do the training and make sure he would come back when called.

Back at the car, I got a big bottle of water out and filled up Wolfie's bowl. While he splashed more on the ground than he drank, I grabbed a couple of cans of fizzy pop from the picnic cool box for me and Lucas.

Once we were all refreshed, and splashed with water, I sent Lucas off to throw the empties into the bin and packed up Wolfie and his water bowl into the boot.

We drove home, via the bookshop in town. Together we picked up a kid's book about Roman Britain, and one about dinosaurs.

'Were there dinosaurs when the Romans were here?' Lucas asked.

The shop assistant laughed, and said 'No, of course not, silly.'

I glared at her and said, 'There are no silly questions. What did you know when you were eight?'

She said she was sorry, but only because she could tell she had to. That was good enough though. It was only such a little thing, but I could see Lucas wasn't used to having anyone stand up for him.

On the way back to the car, we passed a vet's. We went in and bought a long training lead for Wolfie.

Back home, we all collapsed on the sofa watching TV. Lucas at one end and me at the other, and the dog stretched out between us.

'I think he should have a sofa of his own,' I said. 'There's not much room for us, when he stretches out, is there?'

Lucas and Wolfie actually dropped off to sleep. I would have too, if it were not for the need to sort out our tea.

I hoped Lucas liked sausages. There were still so many everyday things I didn't know. But they were quick and easy, with jacket potatoes and cabbage and gravy. And if Lucas didn't like them, Wolfie was sure to eat his share.

While we ate at the kitchen table, with Wolfie watching every mouthful disappear, Lucas was still talking about the Roman road.

'So people believe it's Roman but they could be wrong?' he said.

'Oh yes. Or they could be right,' I said.

He ate another bit of sausage, though he scraped the onion gravy off first.

'People can believe things, and they can be wrong?'

'Yes,' I said. 'Anyone can be wrong.'

'I could be wrong too?'

I laughed. 'Sometimes. But what matters is knowing that. And being able to change your mind.'

'What does that mean?'

'Well, if you believed it wasn't a Roman road, and then you found a Roman coin, you would change your mind, yes?'

He nodded.

'It's not always easy though,' I said.

'So when Mummy said I was a devil child,' he said. 'She might be wrong?'

I said. 'She was definitely wrong. There's no such thing as the Devil. No child can have a devil in him.'

He nodded and finished eating.

'Can I give my last sausage to Wolfie?' he asked. 'I'm full.'

'Yes,' I said, but the dog had swallowed it whole before I was able to suggest cutting it into pieces.

I wanted to talk more about this devil thing, but decided we'd had enough intensity for the day.

Pity no one let my serial texter know I was tired and frazzled.

Without you, without your refusal to help me, none of this would have happened.

It was all I could do to keep my promise to myself and not text back. It only encourages them, so the advice goes.

Lucas didn't last past eight o clock and I thought I'd probably have an early night too.

But there were couple of things I wanted to do first.

I logged back into Facebook and took another look on Simon Ward's page. He seemed obsessed with various cults and conspiracies, but in a critical way, which makes sense of his story.

I wonder what makes some people vulnerable to these beliefs.

His wife had accused him of being involved in a satanic cult – a paedophile ring. It sounded mad, but it could actually happen. Not that he was a satanist, but surely there were cases where people pretended, to scare children into silence. Maybe she was genuinely worried for Lucas. People could believe things and be wrong.

That included me too. Maybe I was wrong.

What if she was right?

If I handed Lucas back to the authorities – well, I knew they could get it wrong.

They had with me. They'd even believed Pastor Richard's claim I was angry because I'd stolen jewellery from one of the chapel ladies, so I had made up the story about being locked in the vestry cupboard as revenge for my punishment.

At the same time, not trusting the authorities – well that's always one of the key features of conspiracy theorists, right?

I could keep going round in circles or I could do something to find out.

My head and my heart hurts so much.

I realised I couldn't put it off any longer. I had to watch that YouTube video which featured Lucas.

It was a compilation.

It started with a shaky image, taken on a mobile, perhaps. He, Paul Gray, was talking to Lucas. Quietly at first, then louder.

'Were you afraid of him, your dad?'

Younger Lucas said no, quietly. He must have been maybe six – it's such a big difference to how he was now.

Again, Gray pushed. And Lucas did look a bit scared then.

'Did he make you do bad things?'

Lucas was more confident.

'Yes. Dad was very bad. Mum says.'

Gray – no, Shepherd – looked pleased, but then his face dropped at the 'Mum says' part.

'What did he make you do?'

'Pizza.'

I was shocked. Surely not pizzagate here? That was all American, Trumpian nonsense, wasn't it?

I mean, I knew we had home grown conspiracies. All the way back to watching David Icke on Wogan.

We weren't laughing now.

But no, I could relax. He didn't mean that – he was talking about fast food.

Shepherd pushed more and got nowhere.

Dad was naughty because of the fast food, nothing more. Lucas admitted he was naughty too because he liked it.

Shepherd grimaced and looked at the camera.

'He's too frightened of his dad, of the whole damn lot of them to talk. That's all.'

There was a pause and then a new video started.

A respectable looking older man introduced himself. He was a retired police officer, from the Met. I googled him, and sure enough he was telling the truth. He had even been awarded medals for bravery.

Unlike the mad Truther, this guy was serious, and convincing. Enough to make me doubt myself.

He introduced the next segment of the video, which showed a small room, and a table and chairs.

'What is about to happen here is what we call a disclosure interview. It's difficult with younger children to get them to talk about what has happened to them, so we have some techniques we have developed to overcome the problems. They might be frightened of the people who have harmed them. They might be frightened because those people have told them they too have done wrong and could go to prison.'

The uniformed policeman sat down on one side of the table and Lucas, a very young Lucas, was led to the chair opposite. He was shaking with fear.

The policeman put two anatomically correct dolls on the table. By anatomically correct – well, they had exaggerated features – big boobs and open mouths. Large willies and big vulvas. You'd maybe think they were funny in any other context. Joke gifts perhaps.

Here, they were chilling.

I couldn't even begin to describe what was said and done next. Lucas, trying to look away, and the policeman, well, using the dolls to perform sexual acts in front of him.

And his mother was there, standing in the background, making Lucas stay and watch. His appropriate adult. I felt sick.

At one point the policeman was trying to persuade Lucas to talk about an erect penis. A hard penis. Lucas was confused. He clearly had no idea what the man was talking about.

I couldn't watch anymore, and I stopped the video.

Tears flowing down my cheeks, I thought about what they put that sweet boy through. I was devastated – sad, and angry at the same time.

I reported the video to YouTube, that one and many others like it. They should all be taken down. This was horrible stuff. The number of people who watched them was horrifying.

And yes, I counted myself in that too. I wished I hadn't seen it. I wished I had put my faith in the court judgement.

I was as bad as they were, distrusting authority.

But I realised this was almost enough to help me decide. No matter how respectable the retired detective might appear, this was not right.

One side was posting news stories and rational calls for people to look out for their missing child.

The other wasn't even looking for their missing child. They had created videos showing the child – name and everything - being bullied by a police officer into telling the story they want told. A story that makes no sense, of his father feeding him junk food and forcing him to "do sex" with other children and adults, and making him eat roasted babies, for heaven's sake.

The more the bastards pushed, the more it became clear the poor child didn't even know what "doing sex" was, thank heavens. He thought it was perhaps kissing, and when prompted with the word willies, he looked amazed.

Perhaps I was too quick to say there's no such thing as devils. It was nothing less than torture they put him through.

Piecing the story together, it hadn't worked. The court appointed psychiatrist, the judge, everyone had realised it wasn't true.

Which made them all part of the conspiracy and the paedophile ring, of course.

It was difficult to tell whether these people – the mother and her boyfriend, their supporters, truly believed it all – but it came across that they did.

Maybe it had started off as a way to get custody – to make these wild allegations about her ex. And then it had all escalated, until it involved so many people. Teachers and restaurateurs. Other parents at Lucas' school. Anyone, perhaps, who had looked at her funny.

I guessed too it was exciting. More fun than real life – this big adventure. To see themselves as participating in a mythic battle of good against evil, and not just a nasty custody case.

I knew now what I had to do.

Chapter Twenty Seven

The next day, after a big breakfast of bacon and egg with heaps of toast, we went to the park.

It was time, I said, to teach Wolfie how to come back when called, so we could let him run off the lead when we went for longer walks.

We started with him on the long lead, and with the help of more cubes of cheese and lots of praise persuaded him to lie down and stay while we walked away, leaving the long lead loose on the ground and being very careful not to tug on it.

Lucas, in a rare mischievous mood, tugged on the lead after I said not to, just to see what would happen.

Wolfie, of course, ran straight towards us and almost knocked Lucas over in his excitement.

I laughed and laughed and explained to Lucas that was not sensible.

'Let's give him some freedom and see what happens,' I said. 'Perhaps he's ready.'

I gave Lucas a handful of cheese cubes, and Wolfie, on the long, loose leash.

'Careful now,' I said, 'And see if he will stay close and walk to heel.'

The cheese worked its magic.

'Okay, now let him run free.'

I unclipped the leash from Wolfie's collar.

Immediately Wolfie ran a mad circuit of half the park, delighted with his freedom.

Lucas called him, and Wolfie ran towards him, giving me hope, but then he zoomed past at the last minute.

Lucas panicked. 'What if he doesn't come back?'

'I think he will,' I said. 'And when he does, we must reward him with lots of fuss and treats, not shout at him.'

Wolfie ran past again, tongue lolling out, almost grinning.

'Let's try my favourite trick,' I said.

'Wolfie!' I shout, and when I had his attention, I started running towards him, but made a sharp turn and ran away back towards Lucas.

Wolfie chased me down. I let him catch me, and rolled on the ground, the dog standing over me, triumphant.

I gave him cheese and lots of fuss, all the time laughing so much.

Lucas ran over and gave Wolfie a treat, and then slipped the lead back on while he was distracted.

We did some more practice with stay and come on the long lead, and Wolfie was remarkably obedient.

'We'd best let him run free a bit more,' I said. 'We don't want him to think the lead is a punishment.'

Wolfie ran around the park and when Lucas called him, this time he rushed back for his cheese straight away.

My phone rang, and it was Chioma.

'Practice walking him to heel,' I say to Lucas, and clipped Wolfie's lead on, before handing it over. 'I have to take this call now.'

I sat on one of the benches at the side of the park while Lucas walked the dog up and down.

'Will you be here to sign in for bail this week? It should be tomorrow, you know. Carstairs wants to know.'

'I don't think so,' I said. 'I am working on it, but it's going to take time. Maybe next week?' Under my breath, I added, 'or next month.'

'What the hell are you thinking girl?' Chioma, calm, serene, Chioma, is raising her voice. 'You missed signing in last week. Tell me you're going to come back? Tell me you're not actually on the run.'

'It's a long, long story,' I say.

'Go on,' she said. 'I have time.'

'I can't tell you.'

'I'm your lawyer,' she said. 'Our conversations are covered by lawyer client confidentiality.'

'I haven't actually checked,' I say. 'But I think this might be an exception.'

'Oh.'

There's a long pause while she thinks through the implications. It's not a good thing when Chioma thinks at you – in person or on the phone.

'Carstairs spoke to me again today. He has some questions for you, he says, but they can wait. He just wanted me to say if I thought you would really come back. And to tell you his patience wouldn't last forever.'

'I am working on it,' I said. 'I hope to be back soon to face the music. And thank you, Chioma.'

'I don't know why,' she said. 'But I am trusting you on this. And I told him I trust you. Don't let me down.'

After lunch I got Lucas's clay out, as we sat at the kitchen table.

'These beads and buttons are brilliant. Do you want to try them with a bit of polish,' I said. 'Shall we experiment?'

I'd looked up instructions ahead of time, but I still didn't know what I was doing.

'There are varnishes, like this bottle here – you can paint it on and then leave it to dry. Which might take ages. Or we can just use this sandpaper and polish.'

Lucas wasn't keen on the idea of waiting, but I persuaded him to try with at least one so we could see how it looked.

'This one,' he said, picking the ugliest bead he'd made by rolling together all the left-over bits of coloured clay. It was a horrible mucky brown.

I found a saucer in a cupboard and covered it in clingfilm, and he painted the glaze on the bead, rolling it around. There must be a better way, I thought. It was bound to stick to the clingfilm.

We put it on a high windowsill – glad Wolfie was still snoozing or he would have been bound to investigate.

The rest of the beads and scarabs we polished with medium and then fine sandpaper.

'Auntie Jen,' Lucas asked. 'Have you got any thread?'

'Aunt Martha's sewing basket is bound to be somewhere in the living room. Shall we go and have a look?'

We found it, an ugly basket on legs, by the window.

There were little embroidery scissors with a stork-shaped handle, lots of threads of different kinds, and a needle case. Lucas asked for permission, and I told him to take whatever he wanted into the kitchen.

I sat watching him working it out, a frown on his face. Checking which needles would fit through the holes he'd made in the beads and the scarab, then choosing a black linen thread. I watched him stringing them on, one by one.

He clearly wasn't satisfied with the result, so he took them all off the thread, and then alternated, scarab and bead, with clumsy and uneven knots to hold them in place.

'How did you know to do the knotting?' I was curious.

'There was a video on stringing pearls,' he said.

I laughed. 'You're a natural artist. Which is to be, potter or jeweller?'

He looked at me seriously.

'I want to do everything,' he said.

My kind of boy.

Once he'd tied his last knot, making the string of beads into a necklace, he handed it to me, smiling shyly.

'Try it on, Auntie Jen,' he said. 'It's a present.'

I don't know how I managed not to burst into tears as I started to tidy up after our crafting session.

Later in the evening, after a lazy afternoon of reading and television, Lucas asked what would happen if Wolfie ran away for real.

'He has a microchip,' I said. 'It's a little bit of electronics under the skin on his neck. It was put there by a vet when he was at the rescue centre, and it can be scanned by any vet, anywhere. So if he runs away, we would be able to go and get him back.'

'Oh' said Lucas. 'I didn't know.'

'He might run for home though. This is where he gets fed.'

Lucas asked, 'What about his previous home?'

I realised I was on dangerous ground.

'He might go back there, too. Even though we are so far away.'

'What if a bad person stole him and took him to their home?'

Ouch. That hurt, even though I knew he wasn't talking about me. But I knew I couldn't duck this. He was beginning to trust me.

'Is that what happened to you, Lucas?'

'Yes,' he whispered. 'Why don't they put microchips in kids?'

'If they did,' I said. 'I would scan you and take you home. Even though I love having you here with me.'

'That's because you're not a bad person,' he said.

My heart almost broke. I knew I had to do the right thing by this boy who I already loved more than I'd ever thought possible.

After Lucas's bedtime. I poured myself a rare glass of wine, feeling reasonably sure there weren't going to be any police hammering on the door any time soon. Carstairs wasn't after me – unless he had deliberately misled Chioma – and still no one was officially looking for Lucas.

My phone rang and I was pleased that it was Nick. I'd been dithering about phoning him, and he'd saved me any more agonising.

'Hi Nick,' I said. 'I had an email from DC Elliott. I knew he wouldn't be pleased.'

'I thought you might have heard from him. He was very dismissive, even when I told him I'd originally turned up on your doorstep because I was worried about the child.'

I could tell Nick was miffed. Probably not as used to being brushed off as I was.

'He even implied you had somehow manipulated me into it!'

I could sense his driving anger over the phone. I wasn't looking forward to how angry he might be if I told him what I'd done, and how I'd been deceiving him. But although in one way it would be safer to do it on the phone, I knew it had to be in person.

It was important.

'I pointed out to him they'd been doing the midnight flits long before we started worrying, but did that get through to DC Elliott?'

'It did not,' I said.

He laughed. We had a common enemy, or at least a person we were both frustrated with.

'That reminds me,' I said. 'They moved from my place when they heard from the Education Department. That was what got me worried.'

'Yes?'

'Well, in my experience, home schooling tends to go with a certain set of people, at least some of the time. There are a few who are driven to it unwillingly, because their kids are excluded, or the schools won't deal with bullying, I know. But the others, well.'

'Go on...'

'I've known a few who are religious extremists. In my childhood, for instance – well, my stepfather was the pastor of a small evangelical church. The kind that didn't want their kids exposed to the outside world. The influence of mammon, he used to call it.'

'Ah,' he said. 'I'd like to talk some more to you about that sometime.'

'What?' I thought. 'I don't need therapy!'

'It's also used to hide real abuse too. We read about sad cases in the news and it's part of the pattern too often. I wondered if the religious thing might be a clue. Perhaps they're in a kind of home-schooling network?'

'Good thinking,' he said. 'I have contacts in the Education Department. I'll have a chat and see if they can share any information.'

'DC Elliott will think I'm manipulating you again,' I teased.

'Perhaps we could meet up sometime for a proper talk,' he said,

'I'd like that,' I said, stalling. It was true too. But it was a bit too soon. 'I'm away on business at the moment. But I'll let you know when I'm back.'

Chapter Twenty Eight

Most of a very quiet Wednesday I spent on the laptop.

Lucas was occupied with the dog, chasing and playing fetch around the house and garden. He also did a whole lot of colouring and even finished reading Winnie the Pooh.

In the afternoon, I let him watch TV.

I spent the day researching online. The feeling of needing to find out everything for myself took me right back to my childhood.

My earliest memories were of wanting to be able to read so I could know things. And then when Dad died and Mum married Pastor Richard (I still hear his name capitalised in my mind) so many of the books I wanted to read were not allowed in the house. They were harmful influences, and the fact I was drawn to these forbidden books, this forbidden knowledge, was more evidence I was under demonic influences.

I mean books about maths and history! It wasn't that I was off the rails. Instead I was told to stick to the bible or terrible Christian books.

Weirdly the kind of Christian books I was allowed to read were packed full of sinfulness. Many of them were American and talked about sex in weird baseball metaphors I didn't understand – first base and second base. I probably spent more time thinking about sex in its possible permutations in trying to figure those out than I ever would have otherwise.

My favourite British one was a long confession from a woman who claimed to be the Queen of The Witches, who had attended sabbats skyclad, and enthusiastically participated in orgies and rituals involving the sacrificial deaths of babies and virgins.

The books, second-hand when they were given to me, all fell open on the most salacious parts of the story.

I sometimes wondered if I was the only one who read the handful of pages at the end about making amends and repentance and handing over one's whole life to the Saviour Jesus Christ.

The effect of the books was to make me a devout atheist. It wasn't until much later in life I realised not all Christians were like this and saw for the first time how extreme my childhood had been.

I was very fortunate to have support from teachers at school, who understood – having been lectured by Pastor Richard on the evil of teaching girls maths they would have no use for as wives and mothers – who encouraged and supported me in my studies and my application to University.

I also escaped regularly to the brilliant local library where I could read anything I wanted.

I've often thought how ironic it was that what I had longed for most of all – to be a mother – was what life itself and my treacherous biology had denied me.

Pastor Richard no doubt would have said it was a judgement on me imposed by God in all his wisdom.

I scrolled through Facebook's local news pages. There was still no sign Lucas had been reported missing. I was almost ready to relax vigilance on that front.

Then I went back to his father's page. Simon Ward.

I followed links to news articles and interviews going back to when Lucas was first reported missing.

One of the earliest showed a young Lucas photographed with his nan, and what was a very new looking toy panda.

The photo brought a tear to my eye. I was sure Panda was still in my rented house in Brighton, likely somewhere in the kitchen.

I desperately needed help and Nick was the obvious choice. I couldn't drag Lainey into it and there was no one else. I didn't know much about him though, beyond seeing he was genuinely registered as a therapist. There was just one reference on the website of the Professional Association for Experiential Therapy – nothing else showed up online.

I checked out his qualifications as listed on the Association website. It looked like one of those American diploma mills. The sort of thing that's a scam – where people submit some half-baked thesis and for a hefty fee are awarded a 'professional' qualification.

I began to feel seriously uneasy.

Maybe DC Elliott had been right, and I had trusted Nick too easily.

I changed the search terms, adding in the name of the American diploma mill.

Bingo.

There was a news article, a long investigative piece, about the dangers of therapy with barely trained counsellors.

I start to read, and it all sounded very alarming, especially the ease with which people can acquire these qualifications.

We're all too easily impressed by a stream of letters after someone's name, if printed on good card stock and accompanied with a certain amount of charm.

The article included the example of science writer Ben Goldacre's cat – actually, his deceased cat, who was an accredited nutritional therapist.

Nick was not as honest as he seemed.

I did a Google Image search and there was no Nick Kennedy who looked anything like the man I'd met.

On impulse, I searched for the name of the journalist who wrote the article.

There he was.

Not Nick Kennedy. Nicholas Gamble.

I looked up other articles he'd written.

He'd clearly specialised in writing about health scams – everything from homeopathy to herbal medicine. He'd written about over-the-counter sugar pills from reputable chains of chemists, all the way to clinics charging vulnerable people with intractable health issues thousands of pounds for treatments were neither effective or safe.

More recently though, he'd been writing about the rise of dangerous alt medicine groups online. He'd written about chelation therapy and the 'Miracle Bleach' cures for autism – which are not cures at all, but dangerous nonsense.

He'd also written about a renewal of the old Satanic abuse panic. The article described how people online were obsessing over cases where there was absolutely no evidence of harm, dismissed as rumour and lies by police and social services, yet people were claiming that proved there was a network of paedophiles. How even in England there was a new growth spurt in conspiracy theories – where old fashioned satanic panic and recovered memories stories met a modern English version of the QAnon political conspiracy. Instead of Hilary Clinton's paedophile ring were supposedly meeting in the cellar of a pizzeria, here in England there were members of the Royal family involved, and the tunnels ran underneath Buckingham Palace.

I had one of those aha! moments. He was actually looking for Lucas. That was why he came to my door.

That was almost certainly why the Grays hadn't reported Lucas missing. My earlier intuition was right.

They were so deep in conspiracy thinking they probably thought social services and the local police and media were in on it. Including DC Elliott.

They were running from him as much as, or more than from me.

Perhaps they even thought he had been the one who had kidnapped Lucas. He'd been in their house, after all. He'd have had much easier access than anyone. A child would willingly go with a policeman. Especially one they'd already met.

I knew I could trust Nick now.

And yet.... It was still hard for me to trust my instincts. All the anxiety from childhood had been revived by Matt's betrayal.

Lucas' father was obsessed with these cults because he knew his ex was deeply involved, and she took his son. He knew that was how Lucas had been hidden, in a community which as far as possible, stayed off grid.

I decided I must talk to Nick, and that together we would work out a solution that was easy and safe for Lucas, and him back to his father and his nana as soon as possible. I needed to persuade Nick to come north and visit me.

Chapter Twenty Nine

After breakfast, Lucas, settled with his crayons, watercolours, paintbrushes and mixing palette. There was a glass of water too – and I remembered the mat to protect the table.

He was already making a terrible mess mixing colours by the time I headed for the living room and logged into the laptop to start work.

A couple of times I had to apologise to Stefan and get up and go to help Lucas – mopping up water, rescuing his crayons from Wolfie, and admiring his work.

In problem solving mode, I suggested a game of tug of war in the garden.

'Wear Wolfie out by playing with him for half an hour, then you can get on with your painting undisturbed.'

And I could get on with my meeting...

After we finished the last pass of edits on the proposal for the development project, Stefan heaved a huge sigh, and I laughed.

'Well, that took longer than expected,' he said.

'Like every stage of every project ever,' I answered, grinning.

'Look, don't take this the wrong way,' he said. Of course I steeled myself not to show I was already taking it the wrong way, whatever it was.

'I'm taking my annual leave from tomorrow. And if you want to, you can carry on and work with Alicia. I wondered, as your family emergency isn't over, by the looks of it, if it might be easier if you take yours too?'

'Oh,' I said. 'That's thoughtful. But I took a whole six weeks that weren't expected when Matt died. I can't for shame...'

'Course you can,' Stefan said. 'Look, I've worked with Chris for years and there's no way he would classify that time as holiday. You are still allowed holiday. Either now, or later in the year if you would rather fly off to the Caribbean or whatever.'

If Carstairs returned my passport, I thought.

Lucas and Wolfie appeared at the living room door again, woofing in turn.

'Listen, Auntie Jen, I'm teaching Wolfie to count!'

He was too. One woof from Lucas, followed by one from Wolfie. Then two, and three.

I laughed and so did Stefan, who had heard it all.

'Looks like that might be a good idea,' I said.

'Fill in the form and submit it before five tonight, and I promise I'll sign it off before I go on my hols.'

'Where are you off to?' I asked, belatedly remembering to act like a human.

'Visiting family in Romania. We have baby Elena to introduce to her grandparents.'

'How fabulous,' I said. 'I hope you have a wonderful time.'

As soon as we were logged off the system, I found the holiday form and sent it, as well as ordering a Steiff teddy bear to be couriered to the office before five for Elena.

Another day, another anonymous text.

You are the cause of so much pain. Just because you are barren, a shrivelled-up shell of a woman who can't bear your own children. You've caused so much destruction because of your bitterness, including the death of your husband. It was your neediness that trapped him, your neediness that drove him down the road that led to his death. Your fault, not mine.

Did this writer mean a metaphorical road, or the actual road to the cliff edge?

I couldn't help trying to decipher the meaning in this missive crammed with hatred and blame, even though I knew it was no use. We were all capable of disordered thinking. We all interpreted events to put ourselves in the best light.

I added it to the harassment folder. Maybe one day the Digital Harms Team would find out who was hounding me, and DC Elliott would get back to me.

But for now – well, I didn't want to address it. I had my own reasons for not wanting to talk about Matt's death and whose fault it all was. Maybe I did carry some share of the guilt.

I wasn't a murderer though.

There was a knock on the door.

I answered, holding back excited dog and child.

It was my mother.

O perfect day.

'Can I come in?' she asked. 'I don't want to air our dirty laundry on the street.'

I looked up and down and there was no one in sight. I couldn't bring myself to say anything, but I stood aside, allowing her in, and closing the door behind her.

'Make that stupid dog and child be quiet, will you. I can't hear myself think.'

I was enraged.

'This is our home, and you are here on sufferance,' I said, sounding unbearably pompous even to myself. 'Are you sure you're actually thinking?'

I pointed her towards the living room. 'As you're here, we'd better talk, I suppose.'

I watched as she marched in, ramrod stiff, and perched on the edge of an upright chair.

'Lucas, take Wolfie out and play in the garden, would you?'

Wide-eyed, he nodded and picked up Wolfie's rope toy.

My turn to go on the offensive, I thought, on my way into the living room. I lounged on the sofa, looking up at her.

'Richard must be spinning in his grave, knowing you're here in this house of sin, visiting me.'

'You're still not fit to even speak his name,' she said. 'You know why I'm here. I wrote to you often enough.'

Ah, those letters.

'I binned them, unread,' I said. 'You're going to have to say it now, out loud.'

'This house should be mine. Martha inherited from our parents. She had no right leaving it to you.'

'Have you run that past a lawyer?'

She blushed. Of course she'd tried that first. Anything rather than talk to me.

'It's not as if you need it,' my mother said. 'You're rich enough. Did you murder your husband by the way?'

'Aunt Martha used to say, *You catch more flies with honey than with vinegar.*' She said she learned that from your mother. Another inheritance you missed out on.'

She sat there, stubbornly. Refusing to move. Refusing to give way.

It was all too easy for me to believe in mothers who abuse their children.

'Not once did you stand up for me to Richard. Not even when he locked me in the vestry cupboard. Aren't you even the slightest bit sorry?'

'I'm not,' she said. 'Richard was right about you all along. Here you are, sitting in judgement on me. You were a thief. You were disobedient. You always went your own way. You did whatever you wanted. You knew you were right. And look at you now.'

I shrugged. I knew it was pointless.

'Were you even going to keep my grandchild from me? Is he adopted?'

Now she sounded hurt.

'Leave Lucas alone,' I said. 'He's not yours in any way. If you hurt him, or do him the slightest harm, I swear you will answer to me for it.'

'The new chapel has dry rot in the roof,' she said. 'Without donations, the chapel won't survive.'

I started to laugh. I couldn't help it. She wanted me to fund the chapel, for the congregation who had had attempted to pray my imaginary demon away?

She got up, stiffly. Arthritis, perhaps? I felt a slight pang, as she walked down the hall to the door and let herself out.

Later, Lucas talked to me. 'Was that my gran?'

The poor love. He was confused, I supposed.

'No, darling,' I said. 'Just my mum, being silly.'

'Oh,' he said, looking sad. 'I know. I forgot.'

'Your nan gave you Panda, right? She seems like a nice lady. We'll look for Panda. I can't promise, because Panda is lost, but we will try.'

He sniffed, holding back tears. He was such a brave kid.

'But I do promise we'll find your dad and your nan. Very soon. I have stuff to sort out first, but I promise. I will take you back to them when I can.'

That evening, once Lucas was in bed, I cried. I hadn't realised how through all of this I'd been holding on to a fantasy of family. I'd secretly hoped somehow it would work out that I didn't have to give him up.

I remembered another of the Bible stories from my youth. This time it was one Aunt Martha told me. It was about the judgment of Solomon, in a case where two women claimed the same baby. Solomon declared the baby should be cut in two, and one half given to each woman. One woman said, 'No, give the baby to her. Better that he should live.' And Solomon decided she was the true mother – the woman who wanted the best for the child.

Looking back, I realised Martha too, like me, had wanted children and not been able to have her own. In her case, she had been my true mother, as she allowed me the freedom to be myself and choose my own path in life.

My choice was perhaps harder. I had to find it in me to restore this son of my heart to the family who loved him.

Chapter Thirty

We were both reading at the breakfast table. Lucas had found the Roald Dahl collection on my bookshelves and had started reading Charlie and the Chocolate Factory. I had my laptop open, checking the online news and then my email.

The first one I opened was from Stefan, confirming my holiday time had been booked, and adding a lovely photo of baby Elena chewing the ear of the cuddly lamb I'd chosen for her.

After all my fears of what would happen now the company belonged to someone else, it had so far been a mostly pleasant experience. Perhaps, after all, Matt had been right. And perhaps there was more to live for than work.

The second email also included a photograph of a baby – this one a new-born boy.

Amy had given birth.

Her email seemed gloating and cruel – or perhaps that was only how I was reading it.

Matt's baby came early. The doctors reckon it's all the stress and we all know who is responsible for that.

Isn't it time you paid up what is owed to Matthew's child? Baby boy Jamie Taylor. It's what he would have wanted. And do remember, I know you know.

I was so angry and so hurt – seeing Elena's photo had brought me nothing but joy, but this baby, Matt's – it roused a whole volcano of jealousy in me.

All the same, I thought it was time to start being the grown up. No one ever wants to be, but sometimes we have to behave better than we want to. At least there was some comfort in knowing I'd be able to live with myself.

I phoned Chioma.

'At last,' she said, before I was able to say anything. 'Tell me you're coming back to face the music. I've had Carstairs on at me again this morning.'

'I am working on it, seriously,' I said. 'But this is something else. Amy's had the baby.'

Chioma knew how I was feeling.

'I'm so sorry,' she said. 'I would have held back on my rant if I'd known. I know how distressing it must be.'

'It is,' I said. 'But I've decided now. It's best to get this over so it doesn't have to invade my life any longer. Can we get started on the legalities? Make sure Matt's baby gets his due. In a trust, preferably.'

Chioma said, 'Whoah, slow down. This is a legal process. We do not do these things at breakneck speed.'

'I want it done,' I said.

'And Amy is in a rush too,' she said, 'Pushing your buttons? Hurrying you into a decision?'

'Yes, but I still want it over with.'

'Let's make sure the baby is Matt's first,' Chioma said. 'And work out the details of the trust.'

'Of course, it's Matt's,' I said. 'I followed him. I checked his card statements. He was having an affair with her for months.'

As usual, there were things I didn't talk about. How much money he'd already given her. At a time when he was complaining to me how costly the IVF treatment was – as if we couldn't afford it.

'She also has a husband, right?' Chioma said. 'Trust me, you have to be sure.'

'Fair enough,' I say. 'But I would like to transfer a lump sum, as evidence of good faith. Maybe £100k.'

Chioma sighed. 'That's way too much,' she said. 'It's not your good faith I have any doubts about. Make it £10k and I will arrange it, but there will be a legal disclaimer. This is a gift and has no bearing on your future liabilities to the child, which will only be negotiated after DNA testing has proven Matt's fatherhood.'

'I'd rather be more generous,' I said. 'I know it sounds manipulative, but I don't trust her. Amy is a user. But I can dangle the promise of more in front of her if necessary.'

'Amy is the manipulative bitch, I'd have said. You're just taking defensive action.'

'Is that the legal terminology?' We both laughed.

'I am worried about you,' Chioma said. 'Please take care of yourself.'

After lunch, followed by half an hour playing in the garden with Lucas and Wolfie, I suggested we walk up to the potter's studio to check whether Lucas' vase had survived the kiln.

'Shall we take Wolfie this time,' Lucas asked.

'I don't think that's a good idea. A wolfhound in a potter's studio would cause absolute mayhem.'

'What's mayhem?'

'It's a general word for lots of trouble, but in this case it means lots of broken pottery. Imagine the damage his tail could do!'

'I don't like leaving him behind.'

'He'll not mind,' I said. 'He'll curl up on the sofa and sleep. But we can take him for a run in the park afterwards, if you want?'

Once it was settled, we set off up the hill, round the lane and walked right back into my childhood again.

It didn't feel so bad this time, I realised. Making new memories was a good way of dealing with the trauma.

It was a sunny day and Sean had propped the door open for air.

The studio was empty, though. We went in and hovered, looking at the pots, and then Sean came out of a room at the back carrying a coffee.

'Oh,' he said. 'I thought you'd forgotten all about me.'

I blushed.

'Of course not,' I said. 'I said we'd be back and here we are.'

'Would you like a coffee?' he asked. 'The kettle's boiled.'

I shook my head, but neither of them were paying attention. Lucas had spotted his vase.

'It came out well,' Sean praised him. 'You're a proper little potter. Do you want another go?'

Lucas said yes, of course.

Sean set him up with smock, and clay and slip and suggested he make some coils and stick them together.

As he demonstrated what he meant and Lucas faithfully copied him, Sean smiled up at me.

'Sorry for not checking with you first,' he said. 'But I was busy making sure you'd have to come back again.'

It was a long time since anyone had flirted with me, but I still recognised it. Not that I knew what to do about it, so I pretended it didn't happen.

'He's talented,' Sean said. 'My own two aren't interested at all.'

'Oh, do you have children?' I asked, relieved. I was making too much of it after all.

'Twins. Boys. Both monsters. Benjy and Sammy.'

He grabbed his phone and scrolled through, showing me photos. They were a little older than Lucas, I reckoned. Maybe ten or eleven. I have joint custody,' he said. 'I have them alternate weeks, but Jessica is nearby and we manage it all very well. Better than when we were married.'

Lucas is listening avidly. I wonder what he makes of it. If he wishes his parents were like that.

'Jessica,' I say. 'You were married to Jessica Riley? The sweetest girl in our class?'

'She's still sweet. Just not on me. But we are good friends.' Then more quietly, he added. 'Would you like to come out for a coffee,' he said. 'If you can get a babysitter?'

Lucas was still listening. 'I'm not a baby,' he said, outraged.

'It's not a good time at the moment,' I said. 'There's too much going on. What with work, and sorting out Aunt Martha's house...'

'You don't have to let me down gently, you know,' he said.

'It's not that,' I said. 'Really. I'd love to. I can't explain right now.'

'Little pitchers,' he asked.

'Something of the kind.'

He went to stand outside in the sunshine and gestured for me to follow him.

'Tell me what's wrong,' he said.

'Well, to start with, I'm on bail for murdering my husband.'

'Oh,' he said.' I know about that. I can read you know.'

I blushed.

'Did you do it?' he asked.

'No.'

'I didn't think it likely,' he said. 'Unless you've changed a whole lot.'

'Or got possessed by a demon,' I said.

'Oh God yes, Pastor Richard. You had a rough time, I know. The new guy is supposed to be much better.'

'A low bar.' I said.

We both kept peering back into the workshop. Lucas was totally caught up in coiling clay.

'Can you prove you didn't?'

'They can't prove I did,' I said. 'And I have good lawyers. But the real problem is actually something else, and much worse.'

He laughed, assuming I was joking, until he saw my face.

'I'm sorry I can't tell you,' I said. 'But I promise I will when I can.'

I must have been convincing enough, because he smiled and accepted it.

I followed him back into the workshop.

Lucas had used his coils of clay to create a mad coiled animal of some indeterminate species. He had added eyes, and asked Sean to glaze them so they stood out.

'I want them white, and staring,' he said. 'It's a snake!'

Looking at it I was a little afraid the end result would look rather like the poop emoji and I tried not to laugh.

Sean looked at me grinning and I could see he was thinking the same thing.

I took Lucas' finished vase, carefully wrapped by Sean, and put it in my bag.

'Don't forget to come back for errr, Lucas' spirit animal,' Sean said.

I laughed a bit too much.

'We won't.'.

'Also, in a couple of weeks I'm doing a summer school for local kids, at the community hall. You could sign Lucas up, if you like.'

'Oh, he would love to, wouldn't you Lucas? Only I'm not sure if we'll still be here.'

Sean picked up a leaflet and scribbled on it.

'Let me know. Either way,' he said.

Outside, I looked at it before stuffing it in my bag. It was his phone number. And, thankfully, his surname. Sean Hunter, of course. I blushed, again.

Once home, I gave Lucas his pot and he unwrapped it carefully and placed it in the middle of the dining table.

'It is beautiful,' I said. 'What do you want to do with it?'

'I'd like to give it to Nana Lilian,' he said.

He had remembered her name, I noticed. I was so pleased for him his memories were coming back, or that he was no longer scared of talking about his family.

'That's a good plan. In the meantime, shall we put some flowers in it?'

I added water to the vase and Lucas ran outside and picked some flowers from the overgrown garden.

I looked at the table as we enjoyed our dinner, and it did feel like a home. My heart was full, and also breaking, at the same time.

It was going to be hard to let him go.

Chapter Thirty One

Watching as Lucas dug messily into his cornflakes early on Monday morning, I made a decision.

It was all very well investigating things online, but there was only so much I could judge from newspaper articles, court documents, Facebook pages. Sometimes it mattered to look people in the eye. And I knew it was the week of the summer fair at Lucas' old school.

It was my best chance. I had to create some kind of cover story, and I could hardly take Lucas with me.

I supposed I could learn a thing or two from Nick.

Once we'd cleared up after breakfast and Lucas had chased Wolfie round the garden to tire him out, or vice versa, I suggested we go into town, with a promised bribe of another visit to the big craft store.

'We can top up your clay collection, and buy some more moulds,' I said. 'That would be fun.'

It didn't count as bribing him, as he wouldn't have asked and wouldn't have made a fuss anyway – just cheerfully tagged along with me.

First things first. I went to the local print shop. I should have done this days before, but I hadn't thought it all through – what I would say, what I would do, even if I would go.

I'd googled and discovered they did same-day printing services. If need be, I could go back later in the day to collect, but I was hoping an hour in the craft shop, and maybe lunch in a cafe would be enough elapsed time.

I talked to a salesman who seemed very concerned I didn't want to have their top end design service for my new business cards.

'It makes all the difference, Ms Blake,' he said. 'Prospective clients will take you more seriously.'

'I'm sure you're right, but I don't have time at the moment. I need them today. I'm happy to pay whatever it takes, including for your premium design service, so long as the cards are done by close of business.'

'Our designer is out today,' he said. 'But she will be available tomorrow.'

'Can you do me a short print run?' I asked. 'Simple, clear, heavy card stock. 50 cards.'

He agreed, with a final show of reluctance.

"How long will it take?'

'No more than two hours.'

'Excellent, thank you. I'll be back this afternoon then. I'll pay now.'

I put it on my company credit card again. It was ridiculously expensive, but I didn't quibble.

'What do you want on the cards,' he asked.

He pushed a pad and paper towards me. 'Better if you write it down. That way we won't make any mistakes.'

I wrote:

Jennifer Blake. Freelance Investigative Journalist.

Then I added my phone number – the second phone – and my GMAIL email address.

'Anything on the reverse?'

'No,' I said. 'Plain white card, embossed black text please.'

He started asking me about the typeface and it was all I could do not to scream, *Just pick one. Dammit*

Instead I asked him to show me some examples. I chose the cleanest, simplest, most readable.

At last, we were done.

'I'll be back,' I said, trying not to sound like Arnie. 'Two hours, you said?'

At least Lucas had fun in the craft shop, rummaging around in the treasure, choosing moulds and more colours of clay.

Then we walked past the art section, and I saw him looking at a wooden box filled with watercolour crayons in lots of different colours.

'Oh look,' I said, 'You can use them wet or dry.'

His eyes spoke, but he didn't ask for them.

'Let's buy them,' I said. I asked the assistant for guidance with sketchbooks, and she helped me pile the trolley high with all kinds of things – plain sketchbooks, books which led stage by stage through how to draw castles and dragons and knights and princesses, and packs of blank postcards and greetings cards.

After I paid, we'd only used up an hour of the waiting time. We took the shopping back to the car and put it on the back seat, then went to look for a cafe.

Lucas had toasted cheese and I had bacon and mozzarella panini. He drank orange juice, while I had coffee.

We ate and talked. He was excited about the crayons as much as the clay.

'Lucas,' I said to him in a serious voice, 'I have to go away for the day – not tomorrow, but the day after.'

He didn't say anything. He just looked very worried.

'I promised you once I would never abandon you, and I won't. I'm sorry that you can't come with me, but it's impossible. It's lots of grown-up stuff, that's all, and it would be very boring.'

Lucas spoke. 'I would be very quiet,' he said.

'I know you would. What I thought, if it's alright with you, was I would ask Sean, the potter, if he could look after you for the day. What do you think?'

He looks thoughtful.

'That would be fun.'

'He might not be able to,' I said. 'But if not, I will find someone else, okay?'

He nodded.

'I promise I'll come back, Lucas. And you'll look after Wolfie for me, won't you?'

That seemed to convince him I wasn't abandoning them, and he managed a tentative smile.

After we finished our lunch we walked to the print shop, where the cards were ready and waiting.

'These are exactly what I wanted,' I said. 'Thank you.'

The salesman was still disappointed in me.

Back home, and we unpacked the arts and crafts haul from the car into the living room.

Then we took Wolfie for a walk in the park and detoured past Sean's studio on the way home.

He was packing up for the afternoon.

'I hope you're not here for your pot, young man,' he said to Lucas. 'It's not going into the kiln until it's dried out. It will be another couple of days.'

'I'm sorry, Sean,' I said. 'I'm here to ask you for the most enormous favour. I wouldn't ask if it wasn't really important, but there's no one else.'

'Well that was a long build up without actually telling me what you're asking. Spit it out, woman!'

'I have to go to town Wednesday, and I need someone to look after Lucas. I can't explain what it's all about, but if you could... If not, I will use an emergency babysitting service, but I'd rather leave Lucas with someone he knows.'

Lucas spoke. 'I'm not a baby. You could leave me on my own.'

'No need,' Sean said gently. 'And you're certainly not a baby. Of course, you can spend the day with me. We can spend the morning in the studio, and perhaps the afternoon at your house?'

'I'll find the spare keys,' I said. 'I'm afraid the afternoon will include Wolfie. He will happily sleep all morning, but if he's too much trouble, so long as you feed and water him, you can always turf him out into the garden.'

'Oh, we'll manage somehow, won't we Lucas? How early are you starting out?

'How early are you up?'

'Usually 7 am,' he said.

I looked at him like he was some kind of monster.

'Is that okay?' I asked. 'That early.'

'Of course,' he said. 'I'll make him breakfast.'

I could feel tears starting to well up, 'You're a lifesaver,' I said to him. I gave him a quick hug, with Wolfie pushing in between us.

'See you Wednesday morning, then' I said, as I turned and virtually ran away with boy and dog, before I embarrassed myself more.

Once home I ordered takeaway for tea. Again. I was certainly making up for all those months of clean eating Lucas had endured.

I spent Tuesday preparing lunch for Lucas and Sean and panicking about what I was going to say on Wednesday, should anyone at the school agree to speak to me.

I sorted out my smartest clothes, regretting I hadn't brought anything more business-like with me. Mind, freelance journalists probably dressed less formally. How would I know?

I checked train times, If I set out early, I'd be in London by eleven, which would give me plenty of time. I'd be able to track down a few people and talk to them. If only they'd talk to me.

Chapter Thirty Two

First thing on Wednesday morning, I put Wolfie out in the garden. I then made sure Lucas was dressed, dragged on my brightest red silk jersey tee and my black linen trousers. I made sure to pack my phones, a spare battery pack, notebook and pen – maybe a bit old fashioned – and, of course, the business cards. My only attempt at a disguise.

Wolfie was settled on the sofa when we left. On the way out I picked up the spare house keys for Sean.

The studio door was already open when we arrived. Sean welcomed Lucas and accepted the keys.

'Just a minute, lass' he said, as I was about to dash off.

He came back to the door with a foil parcel.

'Bacon sandwich,' he said. 'I hope you're not a veggie.'

'I'm not,' I said. 'Thank you. Again.'

He and Lucas waved, as I walked back to the house to collect the car.

I put Sean's bacon sandwich on the passenger seat, my handbag in the footwell, and set off for the station. I'd already bought my e-ticket, checking several times it was on my phone. When I arrived at the station early, I found somewhere to sit and devoured my bacon sandwich, enjoying the feeling that I was being looked after. I just had time to buy a takeaway coffee before the train arrived at the platform.

I snoozed for most of the journey, waking with a start as we approached London.

I took a taxi out to the Wood Green primary school Lucas used to attend, Tuning out the driver's chatter, I tried to gather myself together. The entry fee was £5.00 but I was prepared to pay more if I could persuade the headmistress to talk to me for a few minutes.

I wandered fairly aimlessly around, looking at stalls selling second hand school uniforms, home-made cakes of varying quality, and the children's artwork. There was a book stall too so I grabbed a couple of suitable looking paperbacks for Lucas, and then couldn't resist an extra one about dinosaurs. They just about fitted in my shoulder bag, which had been heavy enough to start off with.

Eventually I realised I was going to have to actually talk to someone. I picked an efficient looking woman who appeared to know what she was doing. I had an idea from her ethnic background and her bearing she might be the very person I was looking for.

'I'm looking for the headmistress, Miss Patel, I think?'

'Yes,' she said. 'I am she, as you very likely guessed. What do you want with me?'

I handed over my card. 'Just a few minutes of your time,' I said. 'And in exchange I'll make a sizeable donation to your art club fund.'

'How sizeable?'

'How about a grand?' I asked.

'I can endure ten minutes or so, I suppose,' Miss Patel said, and led me to her office.

It was an old-fashioned school in an old Victorian red brick building. Miss Patel seemed totally out of place. More like an entrepreneur, I thought. Brisk, business-like, efficient. Although I had been an entrepreneur and never looked like one, so maybe that wasn't a thing.

'What do you want to talk about, as if I can't guess.'

'I'm working on a story about cults and conspiracies,' I said. 'And I know this school was unfortunately, through no fault of your own, caught up in one when one of your pupils was snatched from here around two years ago.'

'Another ghoul,' she said. She wasn't happy, and who could blame her?

'Give me ten minutes, and I'll prove that's not it.'

Miss Patel looked at me steadily, and then said, 'Go on.'

I explained I'd been living in Brighton and had a run in with a strange family who were home-schooling their child.

Well, it was a variation on the truth, at least.

'They lived next door but one,' I said. 'I was concerned about the home-schooling because, well, I grew up in a strange family.

'My family attended a fundamentalist chapel, and the pastor was a complete separatist. He didn't think children should be exposed to the outside world. That it would guide them into sin. And he pressed his flock to take their children out of school.

'I was lucky. I had a sympathetic aunt who took me in, so I could continue my schooling.

'But I was concerned because I never saw this child leave the house, and so I reported the family to the education department and suggested an inspection.

'And they did a midnight flit.'

Miss Patel looked more and more worried.

'I discovered they were connected to a sort of cult, through an online parenting group, and a local vegan cafe. Brighton, of course.' I shrugged.

'In the end, I couldn't get any further. No one would talk to me.'

'I wonder why,' Miss Patel said.

'I know you had the same kind of problem here. I need a bit more depth for this story. I think it's important that parents and teachers are forewarned. It's not as bad or extreme here yet,' I said, 'as QAnon and pizzagate are in the States. But it is worrying. I've been talking with a guy who's been working on the story a long time. He was the one who put me on to what happened to Lucas Ward. Nicholas Gamble, he's called. I'm sure he'll vouch for me.'

'I know Nick,' she said. 'He's talked to us all.'

I hoped that was a good thing, and that she wouldn't decide to phone him to check on me.

'From the inside, it's been appalling, and the boy still isn't home. His father and his grandmother – well, they are devastated of course. As are we all.'

She looked me in the eye, challenging.

'Now,' she said. 'Why should I trust you? Can you show me your publications?'

'No,' I said. 'Look, I'm not a journalist. But everything else I've told you is true. I know Nick. I'm trying to help him. The story about my neighbours and their child, it's all true. And I am a respectable person, really, although it's difficult to prove.'

I told her who I was. That I was on bail for murder. And that I hadn't done it.

'Thank you, Ms Blake,' she said. 'I recognised you, and your name. I'm glad you decided to tell me the truth. Now how can I help you?'

I asked her to tell me about the family. Did she ever suspect the mother had gone off the rails?

'Well,' she said. 'She was an aromatherapist. Training to be a homeopath. All nonsense, of course, but not illegal. But she did start to go a bit mad about food stuff. Lucas wasn't coeliac or anything, but all his food had to be gluten free, and 'clean'. He wasn't allowed to eat in the dining room with all the other kids in case of contamination. This was after the divorce, so I asked Lucas' father Simon, and he was in despair. He said sometimes the child came back hungry after spending the weekend with his mother. We knew she was flaky, but...'

'And I know there were these awful accusations against Simon?'

'Simon and countless other people in the community. A restaurateur. A hairdresser. A local magistrate. Other parents. One of my teachers. I could go on. It was all nonsense, I promise you. I am not naive. I know abuse is real. I've had to deal with it throughout my career. Some heart-breaking cases. But these stories were too mad. And Lucas was too happy when he was here, in all truth.'

'You had no worries about Simon.'

'Absolutely none at all. He was not abusive. I would stake my life on it. Is there anything else I can help you with,' she asked.

'Is there anyone who might talk to me. One of the parents, perhaps?'

Mrs Patel thought for a while.

'Yes,' she said. 'Louisa Scott. She's the mother of one of Lucas's best friends. And she used to be very close with Kim, his mother. Louisa was also accused of unspeakable crimes.'

'Could you put me in touch with her? Perhaps she's here, today?'

'She was supposed to be running one of the stalls, but her little one is unwell. She called in. But she might be able to spare you a few minutes.'

'That would be useful.'

'I'll phone her, now,' Miss Patel said.

In minutes I had a meeting set up at her home, only a few minutes' walk from the school.

As I thanked her and turned to go, Miss Patel looked me in the eye.

'There's no chance the child you're talking about could have been Lucas, is there? The family are suffering so much.'

Very firmly I said, 'I'm afraid not, Miss Patel. This child was older, and a girl. But it's a whole community of people, and I do wonder if there may be a connection somewhere, that could help the investigation. I think Nick does too.'

I was pleased I had some confirmation of my sense Lucas should be returned to Simon. I got the impression Miss Patel was a reliable judge of people. Of course, that was because she chose to trust me... A woman who was on the lam, had broken her bail conditions, and not only that had kidnapped a child. Worrying.

It was difficult, this issue of trust. Maybe the sad truth is that none of us can be trusted.

Who was the psychoanalyst who said all that was necessary was a 'good enough mother'? I googled on my phone. DW Winnicott. Mind, that was all I knew him for, but perhaps he was a good enough psychoanalyst.

And maybe, most of the time, most of us are good enough people.

The problem is how we deal with the ones who really aren't.

I checked the address on my phone before I knocked on the door. The woman who opened the door had a crying baby in her arms.

'Are you the journalist Miss Patel phoned about?' she asked.

I said yes, and she showed me through into the kitchen.

Louisa introduced herself and apologised for not shaking hands. 'I'm all sticky with rusk,' she said. She was bubbly and friendly, with her brown hair in a messy bun that perhaps hadn't been intended to be quite that messy.

'Don't worry about Jack here, he will quieten down in a minute or two. He's noisy, but not persistent.'

She put him down in a crib in one corner of the kitchen and after a few more snuffles he fell asleep.

'Coffee?' she asked. I accepted as she apologised for not meeting me in a cafe. 'It's a bit too much at the moment, to impose Jack on the general public. I hope he grows out of it soon. Until then it's instant coffee at home, I'm afraid.'

'Don't apologise,' I said. It's good of you to talk to me. Especially about such an upsetting subject.'

She paused, before carrying on stirring and pouring milk.

'It is upsetting' she said. 'I'm glad Arthur's out with friends today. He misses Lucas very much. They were best friends.'

'Miss Patel said. How well did you know the family?'

'Not terribly well. We sometimes socialised as a big group – all of us with kids in the same year.'

'I gather it all became very nasty when they divorced.'

'Oh yes, I've never seen worse. And it was divisive. There's all this guff about not taking sides, but in this case, it was just awful, impossible not to.'

'Did you think the allegations Kim made against Simon were reasonable?'

Louisa looked down. She didn't want to catch my eye.

'I didn't know. I mean we never do from the outside, do we? Someone may seem perfectly pleasant – but these people are pleasant, aren't they? It's part of the cover story.'

'So you did wonder about him.'

'Yes, but that's natural, right. I wondered about Kim too. We all know sometimes mothers make stuff up in custody cases.'

'Yes,' I said, 'That makes a lot of sense. It really is difficult to know.'

'But then the rumours started, a massive paedophile ring here in Wood Green. And the people she was accusing and the sheer extremism of the ideas - Satanic rites and so on. Well, it was like that moral panic in the eighties and nineties, right? And innocent people were accused.'

Miss Patel had mentioned Louisa had been accused too, but Louisa didn't mention it. I could understand that.

'It seemed mad to you, then?'

'It did. Then the family court awarded Simon custody and explicitly said there was no evidence to support the idea of a conspiracy... well.'

'Did it surprise you when Kim kidnapped the child, took him from school without permission?'

'Not really. I mean, not if she believed it all. A mother would do anything to protect her child.'

'And you didn't have any idea Kim was caught up in all this conspiracy stuff?'

'Not before it all came out.' She laughed. 'Kim was always selling us essential oils. Vitamins. We thought the main danger was to be recruited to an MLM scheme, not a cult.'

I grimaced in sympathy.

'She was always on about vaccination, that kind of thing. She could get very intense about it. I remember seeing her browbeating a young mother about the MMR – actually shouting in her face. We had to stop her; she went much too far. But we all thought it was because she cared too much. Even if it was wrong headed.'

'Poor Simon,' I said. 'To go through all that and have lost his son too. Did many people believe the conspiracy stuff, do you think?'

Louise thought for a moment.

'I think lots of us wondered at first. But by the end, maybe a handful still thought there was something in it. No smoke without fire and all that.'

'Would you be able to give me a name or two? I'd like to talk to people who did believe. I won't say you sent me, I promise.'

Louisa's face closed down. 'I don't think I can, sorry. I am not comfortable with that.'

'I understand,' I said. 'I won't push, but I had to ask.'

She smiled, relieved.

'Thanks for your time, it's been helpful. Could I use the loo before I go? I have a long journey ahead.'

It's a cliche of TV drama investigations, but I did need to go. I was lucky there was no downstairs loo and I while I was upstairs, I could hear Jack's squalling had begun again, and Louise walking up and down trying to soothe him.

I took my chance and had a quick peek in Arthur's bedroom, as the door was open. I didn't expect there would be anything to see, but there was...

By his bed, a framed photo, of Louisa with pushchair and baby, and Kim, Lucas and Arthur, I presumed. In Brighton, by the pier. The baby surely meant it was recent, and anyway I knew Lucas quite well, so I was certain it was taken weeks ago. Not months. Long after he was abducted by his mother. I got my phone out and snapped a photo of the photo.

She talked a good talk, Louisa. But that was all it was. Talk.

She had taken sides, and it wasn't with Simon. That accusation against her – had it been deliberate? A cover story?

I flushed the loo and went downstairs,

'Thanks,' I said, over the noise of Jack crying. 'I do appreciate you talking to me. I'll leave my card here on the table, so if you think of anything else, do let me know.'

'I will,' she said. 'Do you think there's any chance of anyone finding Lucas?'

I could tell now she was worried, as well she might be,

'I don't know,' I said. 'I know Nicholas Gamble has been looking for him for a long time. Did Miss Patel tell you I'm looking for an older child, a girl, who disappeared in the same way?'

'Oh, I didn't realise,' she said. 'I thought you were looking for Lucas.'

Louisa seemed relieved and Jack started wailing even louder, so I decided it was time I made my escape.

'Thanks again,' I said. 'It was good to meet you.'

I didn't know how finding this out would help, but somehow it might come in useful. But I did know now I was on Simon's side. How awful to have the community turn on you, and even after the court has decided in your favour, people still think of you as a monster?

One last thing before I rushed back to the station for my train to Manchester. I wasn't planning to talk to him, but I wanted to get a look at Simon and see how I felt. If I was lucky, he'd be at work – he was surely very unlikely to be at the school fair.

I walked up the road and turned left into the High Street. There it was, the artisan bakery. Simon's Sourdough. He'd shown a lot of courage leaving his name above the shop, I reckoned. But good bread is good bread, and the place was busy.

He was serving customers. I watched him, relaxed and easy, chatting to everyone, but I thought there was a hint of sadness. Of course.

I bought a sourdough loaf and didn't even wince at the price. 'Do I know you?' he asked. Oopsy, maybe he recognised me from the news, or from Facebook. 'No, I'm not a local,' I said smiling. 'This loaf's going back with me to Manchester in an hour. Do you know where I can find a taxi?'

'I'll call one for you,' he offered. And did so immediately on his mobile. 'Hi Tom,' he said, 'A lady in the shop needs to catch the train to Manchester, quick as you can please.'

True to his word, the taxi arrived in less than five minutes. I thanked him and waved goodbye.

On the train, my phone pinged. My new phone.

You're as much to blame for this as Matt. You should have kept him in line.

Yeah. This was from someone who knew how marriage worked. And that confirmed my suspicions.

When I arrived home, Sean, Lucas and Wolfie were all on the sofa, snoring in front of the TV.

I put the kettle on and woke Sean up. He tried, and failed, to get up without disturbing the other two.

Lucas was pleased to see me but happy enough to go off to bed. I let Wolfie out into the garden, and he ran around for a while.

I looked at the kitchen table, astonished.

It was piled high with drawings and clay modelling tools, and there was a tray of baked beads sitting on top of the cooker.

They were beautiful.

'Are those millefiori?' I asked.

'He has got a talent for this,' Sean said. 'and, I am, err, sorry I didn't finish tidying up.'

I laughed at him.

'I'm not complaining,' I said. 'I'm far too grateful for that.'

'Here,' I said. 'I brought you a present from London.'

I gave him the sourdough loaf from Simon's bakery. I had already taken the precaution of putting it in a plain paper sack.

'Thanks,' he said. 'Although we do have sourdough up here in the North, you know. It's all changed a bit since you were last home.'

'You could have told me,' I said. 'What do you think I went all the way to London for?'

Chapter Thirty Three

Chioma was right, even though she didn't know the full circumstances. I couldn't run away forever.

I phoned Lainey, considering asking her for help. I wasn't prepared for her shouting at me. Really angry shouting.

'Where have you been? I've left loads of messages on your voice mail. I've been worried sick.'

'I'm sorry, Lainey. I should have talked to you. There's no excuse.'

'I don't want an excuse, you idiot. I was worried.'

'Ok,' I said. 'Here's the truth. I didn't call because you, of all people, would have known something was wrong. I couldn't tell you and explain because it would have implicated you. And I still can't, for the same reason.'

'Jennifer Blake this is not helping. I am even more worried now.'

'Please, please don't worry. I am sorting it out, I promise. You will be the first to know. Only I need your help, please.'

She still sounded sniffy.

'You know I'll help,' she said. 'Don't whine.'

'Okay, if for some reason I end up locked up, can you please look after Wolfie for me?'

'You skipped bail, didn't you? And you promised if you ever went on the run, I could come with you. Like Thelma and Louise.'

Lainey was always good at putting two and two together and getting four. Lucky for me she didn't know this particular sum involved a catastrophically large unknown.

'I had a good reason. I promise, I will tell you all about it when I can.'

'Of course I'll look after Wolfie. And you can tell me all about it when I visit you in Holloway.'

'Holloway's been closed for ages, but I appreciate the sentiment. And I am sorry I let you worry.'

'To be fair, I'm more worried now.'

I pottered around the house, then went with Lucas and Wolfie for a long play in the park.

Wolfie was much better at walking to heel, especially now he was allowed off the lead for a good run. He wasn't too bad at coming back when called, either. In any case, he liked to stay close to Lucas.

All I was doing was putting off phoning Nick, or as I justified it to myself, waiting until a more reasonable time to ring him.

Back home, when Lucas was settled on the living room floor watching kids' TV, I was back at my laptop.

I went back to Simon Ward's page and instead of skimming, I started reading the various articles linked.

Two months ago, there was an interview in his local newspaper on the second anniversary of his son's disappearance.

Two whole years.

How awful for them all, and how terrible for Lucas.

It was a measure of the kid's intelligence and resilience that he had retained happy memories of his father and grandmother from the age of six, especially after being forced to tell such terrible lies about them.

In this article, as well as the one with Lucas and his nan and the panda, there were also photographs of his mother – Kim Ward, now Verity Gray. There were none of her boyfriend, who was supposed to be the source of the accusations.

But Kim had been training as a homeopath and an aromatherapist. She was ideologically set against Big Pharma, and "Western Medicine." She was into clean eating and veganism and against even occasional indulgence.

It all fitted with what Louisa had told me. It seemed what had started as an almost religious thing, a purity obsession, had led her into some much darker and more dangerous places.

Nick's articles about conspiracy theories and who was likely to fall for them had suggested New Age types were just as likely as the far right to embrace them.

Yet we are all prone to conspiracy thinking. We can all fall into the same traps because the world is complex and we humans don't much like thinking, properly thinking, for ourselves...

And to be fair plenty of people prefer a vegan diet and clean food without devoting their whole lives to Conspiracies'R'Us.

It seemed to me that what may have started out as a devious strategy to gain custody might have developed into a real set of beliefs because the groundwork was already there.

It wasn't necessary to blame Jed Shepherd, if that was his real name. Birds of a feather. And they had likely found more kindred spirits in Brighton, through the Karma Kafe.

In the interview, Simon told of the time Lucas was brought back to him hungry, after a weekend with Kim and her bloke.

He had misbehaved, so they had made him fast and meditate on his sins.

That was when he realised her beliefs had become extreme – she had starved her own child.

He had remonstrated with Kim and told her the boy was too young to fast. He thought she was under the influence of her new boyfriend. He took it all back to Family Court, applying for sole custody.

Social services stressed contact with his mother was important, but the Judge ruled the mother's visits should be supervised and Simon, as father, was awarded full custody. His mother, Lilian, moved in to make it easier.

Then Kim reported Simon and his mother as part of a Satanic paedophile ring, so social services were involved once again. There was talk of Lucas being taken into care while it was all investigated. There was a social worker who seemed convinced there was some devilry going on.

Kim and her boyfriend start harassing people online – not just Simon and Lilian, but friends and neighbours. They started up web pages and there were YouTube videos about how evil had contaminated the whole community. It all became very complicated. Eventually they accused the police, social services and the judge in the custody case as well.

Kim never accepted the judgement, although she put on a good show, until the day she collected Lucas from school. She convinced the teacher on duty that she had permission. Later still it turned out the new teaching assistant was also involved in the cult. It wasn't just a crime of opportunity – it was planned and orchestrated.

Once Lucas was gone, there were people theorising it wasn't the mother who kidnapped him at all. They claimed that Lucas had been sacrificed by his own father, as the main rite of the satanic cult. They even spread rumours that Simon killed Kim and her boyfriend Jed Shepherd too.

Simon was arrested at one point, before being bailed for lack of evidence. I certainly empathised with that.

I read it all and compared it with what I had observed for myself. I knew some of it was absolutely true, from things which Lucas had said.

I remembered him worrying I might starve Wolfie for being naughty in his training sessions, and my heart broke for the boy all over again.

Once Lucas was in bed, I phoned Nick. I'd already decided on all the things I wouldn't tell him. I wouldn't tell him I had kidnapped the child. I wouldn't tell him I knew he was a journalist.

But I would tell him anything else – just to persuade him to travel up to me.

'I need your help, Nick,' I said. 'I think I'm on to something, and I don't think there's anyone else I can ask.'

'I think Alex's real name is Lucas Ward. There's a news story, and it all seems to fit. I'm texting a link to the story.'

'That does look like the boy,' Nick said, 'but you've not seen him, have you?'

'I recognised the mother,' I said. 'Kim Ward looks exactly like Verity Gray, or is it the other way round? And the essential oils, massage therapy matches too.'

'It sounds like a nasty custody battle gone wrong,' he said. 'Perhaps we should tell DC Elliott.'

'There's no chance there's anything in the ritual child abuse stuff, is there? I mean, not the satanic stuff. But people do abuse children, and they do make up all sorts of scary stories to silence them.'

'I'm sure it's not. This interview tells us the whole mess was investigated, and Simon Ward and his mother were cleared. We should take it to the police. And DC Elliott has seen the boy, right? That should get through to him.'

This wasn't going quite how I wanted it to go.

I tried again, remembering he was a journalist. He was surely going to want a scoop.

'I think I have a lead.'

Then I lied. I hated lying. I wasn't keen even on lying by omission, but this was worse.

'I followed them,' I said. 'I found them again and I followed them all the way to this little town in Lancashire. Can you come up, take a look, and see what you think? Then we can go to the local police together.'

There was a long silence while he thought it through, then he agreed. He'd drive up on Sunday. I gave him the address of the local gastro pub, a stone's throw from Martha's house and told him I'd book him a room.

'Let me know when you arrive,' I said. 'I know where we can sit and talk it through in perfect privacy.'

At least I had another couple of days with Lucas, and I was going to make the most of it.

Chapter Thirty Four

Even though I'd made my mind up, I was jumpy on Sunday. How long would Nick's journey take – I checked Google Maps, but I had no idea what time he would start out.

We had our long play in the park early in the day. I didn't want to be out when he phoned. I wanted time to explain to Lucas. Not that I knew how to explain.

After lunch, I did try to talk to him.

'I've got a visitor coming today,' I said. 'I promised I'd help you get home, back to your dad and your Nana Lilian. I found someone who might be able to help, but I want to talk to him first before I tell him about you.'

'Okay,' he said.

'When he rings, I want you to go upstairs and stay in your bedroom for a bit. You can take Wolfie, if you like.'

'Okay,' he said.

When the phone finally rang it was only mid-afternoon. I admitted I was staying at my aunt's house, a few hundred yards up the road. I sent boy and dog upstairs, opened the front door and stood on the front step.

In moments, Nick was on the street outside the pub. I waved until I was sure he'd seen me.

I rushed him through the hall and into the kitchen and put the kettle on.

'Thank you for coming,' I said. 'I do appreciate it. Tea, or coffee?'

'Tea would be fine,' he said, sitting at the table.

I noticed I'd left lots of Lucas' drawings and art materials on the table, so I quickly swept them into a pile and put them on a working surface. Hopefully he'd assume it was family stuff.

'Do you want anything to eat?' I asked. 'I could make you an omelette, or...' I was prattling on, trying to avoid the difficult conversation ahead.

'I ate on the way,' he said. 'It's fine. I know this is weird, but sit, and let's talk.'

'It is weird,' I said. 'I know I'm obsessive about this stuff, but I have my reasons.'

'I have my own,' he said.

'I know, Mr Gamble. Were you ever going to tell me the truth about who you are?'

He was immediately apologetic.

'Nick Kennedy IS my name,' he said. 'Gamble was my mother's name. I've always used it for writing as sometimes, in investigative journalism, it's better to keep at a certain distance from the story.'

'And the part about you being a therapist?'

'Well, that's not entirely untruthful,' he said.

'I've read your article. The one that talks about Ben Goldacre's dead cat, Hettie.'

'I'm a better therapist than Hettie is a Nutritional Consultant,' he said.

'Perhaps because you're not dead yet?'

He laughed. A proper, whole-hearted laugh. It reminded me I did, in spite of everything, find him easy to trust. I liked him. It was that simple.

'Seriously', he said. 'I've been investigating this stuff so long I decided to take some real, certified courses in therapy. It interests me, and it can actually help me in my work as a journalist.'

'You mean, it helps you lie to people who don't trust journalists?'

He grimaced.

'There is that. Although I didn't know at the time you had reason to hate my profession. I didn't recognise you, except in retrospect I realised your name was familiar. But yes, it does make it easier to talk to people.'

'And Rory?' I asked. 'Is he real?'

'No,' he said. 'Sorry. I thought it made it more acceptable, you know. A grown man looking for a young boy. And with all the conspiracy theories around...'

'I thought you were uncomfortable about talking about him.'

I could understand that. I couldn't understand Lucas though. I thought knowing Rory had helped him to trust me.

He never said, 'Rory who?' Or, 'I don't know any Rory.'

It was like he accepted anything people said. Most of the time he seemed fine. But there was a sense in which he seemed out of touch with reality. Or maybe he was too scared to disagree with whatever people said. He was so confused.

'But you did see him? You did meet the family?'

'No,' Nick said. 'I talked to them online, when they were asking for advice about how to deal with an autistic child. I was on their trail, but I was a month too late, and you'd already moved into the house.'

'I saw a piece you wrote about conspiracy theories, and the likelihood something like pizzagate could happen here. Is that why you were looking for the Grays?'

'Yes,' Nick said. 'I do think it's like a cult, with branches all over the world. The Grays were as close as I got, and now they've disappeared again. And I am genuinely worried about Lucas.'

He took a breath and seemed to be wondering whether to say more.

'I know Simon and Lilian. They're lovely people. They are holding on to hope, but it's horrific. They've been waiting, hoping, for more than two years now. Missing their boy, and terrified about what might be happening to him.'

And I've made their misery last longer. I did my best, I know, and for all the right reasons, but I had added to their pain.

I wouldn't do anything differently, though.

'But people think the Grays are lovely too. DC Elliott. The people in the Karma Kafe.'

Wolfie bounds downstairs and into the kitchen, followed by Lucas, shouting.

'Bad dog, Wolfie. We are supposed to hide upstairs.'

Oh shit.

'Take him back upstairs, please,' I say, quietly. I can see from his face this was his rebellion, that he wanted to see what was going on.

And part of me was glad he had, because it meant he was braver than he was a few short weeks ago. And he knew we were talking about him, so why wouldn't be interested?

'I was about to tell you,' I said to Nick.

He was not, however, in any state to listen.

I sat very still and quiet as he ranted.

'What the actual fuck, Jen? You're mad at me because I lied about being a journalist and you have the kid stashed away here. You kidnapped him!'

I didn't think he'd finished yet.

He hadn't.

'How? Why? What? We have to get him home, Jen!'

'That's why I called you. I didn't know, remember. I didn't know any of Lucas' story. I knew this child was being abused, and I couldn't make anyone listen. But I didn't know who he was. Not until a short time ago.'

'The police will sort it all out. And social services.'

I lost my temper a bit then.

'That's not my experience,' I said. 'When my stepfather locked me in the vestry cupboard when I was sixteen, the police said I probably deserved it. They believed him when he said I'd stolen jewellery from one of the congregation.'

'Look. I get it, but that was a long time ago.'

I said, 'Have you seen the stories Simon Ward has shared? He was arrested! And I followed some horrible links down a YouTube rabbit hole, a whole warren of them, and I saw actual policemen on video, asking the child questions, planting horrible answers in his mind. Stuff the kid luckily didn't understand. So which police do we believe?'

We sat in silence for a few moments.

'I want your help,' I said. 'To get him home safely. But he needs help. He's too good. So compliant. How awful must his life have been that he easily ran off with a woman he didn't know. Just because she promised not to lock him up?'

'He is quiet right now,' Nick said.

Oh my God. What did he hear?

I ran upstairs and there was no sign of either boy or dog.

Thank God he had the dog with him.

'We have to find him,' Nick said. 'Where might he go?'

Of course, it was pouring with rain. Nick and I both had coats, but I was horribly certain Lucas had not. He would be getting cold and wet, and it was all my fault.

We tried all the favourite places. The park. The pottery studio – Sean wasn't in.

We walked down to the main road and I steeled myself and knocked on my mother's door. I stood there, dripping wet, waiting for her to respond.

'I've not seen your dog or your kid,' my mother said. 'Is that your fancy man, already? With your husband recently dead. Richard was right about you, you whore.'

Nick looked like he was preparing to stand up for me, so I glared at him.

'I know you too,' I said to her. 'I think I'll make sure you don't have my boy locked in any cupboards, if I may.'

I didn't wait for an answer, I pushed past.

I had long ago sworn nothing would ever get me in that house again. I hadn't known then how much I could care about someone, so those memories were as nothing.

He wasn't there, of course. If he had been there'd have been a dog barking either inside or outside.

It was a little bit satisfying to upset my mother more than she had me, for once.

We went back towards the park calling Lucas's name, and Wolfie's.

The rain slowed down and halted, but not before we were soaked through.

A woman in wellies and a rain hat with a small dog on a lead called us and half ran towards us.

'Are you looking for a boy and a dog?' she asked.

'Small boy, big dog,' said Nick and the woman smiled.

'He didn't know where he was staying so I took them to the police station,' she said.

'Thank you so much,' I said. 'We've been worried out of our minds. It's only been half an hour but -'

I was even more worried now. The police! They'd be able to sense my guilt as soon as I walked in there. Maybe they'd think I'd been abusing him, to make him run away.

Nick murmured reassurance.

'Could you point us in the right direction,' he asked the woman. 'We're only here on a short break and don't know the area well.'

'Of course, I'll walk you there. It's not far.'

I said, 'I thought I knew it well, but it's changed such a lot. I'm here to sort my Aunt Martha's cottage.'

'Martha Blake? I knew her well. You must be Jennifer.'

She started reminiscing, about how proud Martha had been. If there was any hint I should have visited more, or come back sooner, she gave no sign of it.

Mrs Greenhalgh went into the police station with us and spoke to the young constable on duty, who was sitting on the floor by a warm radiator playing with Lucas and Wolfie. The smell of wet dog was pungent.

'I found the matching pair,' Mrs Greenhalgh said proudly.

'Lucas, I was really worried about you,' I said. 'Come here for a hug.'

He got up and trailed over to hug me without any enthusiasm.

'Still upset with me?' I asked.

The police constable stood up.

'Are you responsible for this boy and dog?'

'I am,' I said. 'I know Lucas is far too young to be in sole charge of the dog. He was upset and ran away, and he was only gone for a very short time.'

'My boss would like a word, if you don't mind waiting. He'll be free in a few minutes, I'm sure.'

'Of course, that's fine,' I said. I was terrified. Nick put a hand on my shoulder and said, 'Don't worry, it will just be routine.'

The young constable went to the reception desk and made a quick call. I couldn't hear a word, though I was straining. Then she sat down again on the floor and carried on entertaining Lucas and Wolfie. What on earth might Lucas have said, to set off alarm bells?

Mrs Greenhalgh was chattering away with the young policewoman and telling her how she knew my Aunt Martha and how lucky it was she'd found us.

After almost half an hour, I was called in to Detective Sergeant Bailey's office. He asked if I wanted Nick to be present too, but I said, 'Oh no. This is all my responsibility. He's just visiting us, a friend.'

'So you are responsible for the pair of them,' he said. 'Look, I am not unreasonable. I know these things happen. But a young boy shouldn't be in sole charge of a large, scary dog. He's not strong enough to control him.'

I managed not to laugh at the idea of Wolfie being scary, because DS Bailey had a point. A dog like Wolfie doesn't have to be scary to be dangerous.

'You are right. I should have been much clearer with Lucas about these safety issues. He's never been out alone with the dog before, and he won't be again until he's got a mortgage and a dog of his own. It's all my fault – I didn't realise he was upset and had decided to run away.'

I held back on the story about Lucas' mum being in hospital – I'd only use that if there was no other way.

'The dog should have a tag with your address,' he said. 'The address on there is in Brighton, and the phone is switched off. Not even voicemail.'

'I am sorry. We are just staying here for a few days, I had no idea. But Wolfie is chipped. I am a responsible dog owner, I promise you. I can put you in touch with the Rescue Centre I've had my last three dogs from,' I said.

I was so nervous I was talking too much.

He looked at me sternly, and then relented.

'I find myself believing you, in spite of everything,' he said. 'And Mrs Greenhalgh has vouched for you, I gather. Just don't let this happen again.'

I babbled my thanks, relieved.

I heard Pastor Richard's voice in my head again, quoting the gospels. *Go, and sin no more.*

Chapter Thirty Five

We were all very quiet on the way home, except Wolfie who was a bit too pleased to have a new person to slobber on. Nick took it rather well, considering.

Once we were indoors, I suggested to Lucas he could go and have a wash and get changed, or into his pyjamas. It looked like he'd been rolling around in the bushes in the park. I turned the heating up and offered Nick a towel, as I roughly dried my own hair with the other.

'We can order a takeaway, if you like. Your choice, Chinese or Indian.'

Lucas managed a smile. 'Chinese,' he said, as I'd expected.

In the kitchen Nick had already put the kettle on.

'We've got to talk to him, find out why he ran away,' he said.

'I don't think that's a good idea. It's too much like what happened to him before, being interrogated. And he doesn't know you, yet. I think we eat and then talk quietly about what we plan to do. And ask him if that's okay with him.'

Nick looked worried.

'It's my fault,' I said. 'I should have prepared him and you, and we could have let him stay and listen. But maybe it was always impossible.'

'It might have stopped me from yelling at you.' Nick was almost apologetic.

At least it felt like we were on the same side now.

'I guess to Lucas it looked like it was happening all over again. Adults making decisions without ever talking to him.'

Wolfie bounded in – the early warning for Lucas' arrival.

He looked scrubbed clean, at least on the surface.

I wondered if he was growing potatoes behind his ears, and almost burst into tears as I realised that was a rare memory of my dad, from when I was only four or five.

His hair was all damp and scruffy and I wanted to hug him, but I held back.

'Where's your dirty clothes?' I asked.

He turned round to go and fetch them, and I said, 'Don't worry, we can get them later. Shall we order some food?'

I poured him a glass of milk and soon we were all sitting round the table and arguing about the food order.

'We must order two portions of ribs because they're Lucas' favourite, and I don't want to have to fight him for them,' I said.

Nick insisted on duck with pineapple and ginger, and I thought we should have rice and noodles.

'That list is way too long,' I said. 'But never mind. Wolfie will eat the leftovers, so long as he doesn't get at the bones.'

It wasn't long before the food was delivered, and we were all tucking in and laughing.

Lucas didn't look worried anymore. I hoped talking to him wasn't going to upset him – but it had to be done. At least now he was fed he would be too full and sleepy to even think about running away. All the same, I planned to take extra care to lock the doors later.

Once we'd finished eating – and there were no ribs left but plenty of rice and noodles for Wolfie – I cleared the table. I put the bones and the empty cartons straight into a bin bag, then outside in the dustbin.

I came back as Nick was pouring fruit juice for Lucas. He asked if I wanted some too. Soon we were all sipping on diluted pineapple and orange.

Lucas burped, and we all laughed, even Wolfie.

It was time to get started.

'I know you were upset earlier,' I said to Lucas, but I promise you we will not do anything without talking to you first, okay?'

He looked at me but didn't say anything.

'Have I broken my other promise to you?'

'No,' he said.

'Well, this is the same.'

'I don't want to go back,' he said. 'I want to stay with you.'

I could have wept.

'You want to see your dad again. And your Nana Lilian?'

'Yes,' he said.

'That's what we want for you, right, Nick?'

'It is.'

'You won't take me back to the place where you found me. To be locked up?'

'I won't. I promise.'

Lucas said, 'I was frightened when I was in the park. I thought someone was watching me. I was scared it was Mum and Paul, come to find me.'

I smiled at him. 'I don't think they can know where we are,' I said. 'But sometimes it's easy to get scared and imagine people are watching us.'

I told him the story about Robert Louis Stevenson, and how he had imagined the horses pulling the hansom carriages around Edinburgh were watching him.

He thought that was funny.

I suddenly remembered the title of one of Stevenson's most famous books and felt guilty as hell.

Nick said, 'I have an idea. I don't know why I didn't think of it earlier.'

I looked at him and nodded for him to go on.

'Lucas,' he said. 'Do you remember, a long time ago, when you had to talk to a nice lady called Kathleen?'

Lucas seemed puzzled.

'She had toys and things and she asked you to use the toys to tell her stories.'

'Oh,' said Lucas. 'I think so.'

'She asked you if you wanted to live with your dad and Nana Lilian, right?'

'Yes,' he said. 'She promised I could. And I went to live with Daddy again but then Mummy collected me from school and she told me Kathleen had changed her mind and said my Daddy was a bad man.'

Nick shook his head. Aghast.

I was more used to what had been happening.

'Lucas,' I said. 'I know we've talked about lies and truth. You know sometimes people tell lies, right?'

'Yes.'

'Telling lies is bad. But sometimes we have reasons to lie. And your mum, well, she missed you very much and so she told a lie. I don't know Kathleen, but I know she didn't change her mind. And your dad has been looking for you all this time. He misses you too.'

There were tears running down Lucas' face. It broke my heart, but at the same time, I thought it was a good thing. Crying is sometimes all there is that helps.

Nick started again.

'Lucas, I know Kathleen. She's my friend. She's helped me a lot with my work.' That bit was for me, I guess.

'How about if we take you to Kathleen tomorrow. I am sure she will talk to you and help you to understand. She will be able to talk to your dad and your Nana Lilian, and help sort everything out so you can go home.'

Lucas was nodding.

I said, 'You'd like to see Kathleen again?'

'She was nice to me,' he said.

I looked at Nick. 'Perhaps you'd best find out if it's okay with Kathleen.'

He went into the living room to phone her.

'I am sorry we frightened you Lucas,' I said.

He got up and came over to me and gave me a quick hug, before getting down on the floor and playing with Wolfie.

I guessed I was forgiven then.

Nick came back, looking pleased. 'I didn't give her any details – I didn't want to put her in a difficult position. I asked if she was available tomorrow, as I knew someone who needed her help. And she's promised she'll be in and has nothing else planned, so there'll be plenty of time for us.'

'Is that okay, Lucas?' I asked. 'If Nick drives us to see Kathleen tomorrow?'

He looked up from the floor and nodded before going back to scratching behind Wolfie's ears.

'Oh,' I said, 'I should have asked. Where does Kathleen live?'

'Brighton,' he said. 'Well, technically, Hove I suppose.'

'I guess I'd better pack some stuff then,' I said. 'I might well not be coming back here for quite some time. Oh, and I hope there's enough room for Wolfie in your car? I could always follow in Aunt Martha's car, I suppose.'

'I think we'd best all stay together for now. Wolfie will be fine,' Nick said. 'And I'll be off back to the pub and get some sleep. I'll be back here first thing after breakfast to pick you both up.'

I waved him off then started faffing around packing. I put Lucas' dirty clothes in the washing machine on an automatic wash and dry cycle.

I packed my own clothes in my suitcase and put the laptop in its bag. I put a few changes of clothes, and his spare PJs, in a holdall for Lucas. Even if he went straight back home from Kathleen's they'd likely only have six-year-old stuff for him. I added in his teddy plus all his art gear. Finally I very carefully wrapped up his vase for Nana Lilian, in three layers of bubble wrap, and in a cardboard box. His bag was heavier than mine.

The following morning, we were up ridiculously early. I peeked into Lucas' room, where boy and dog were still asleep. Wolfie was, as usual, taking up more of the bed.

Downstairs I set cereal out on the table, with bread and butter ready to make toast.

I made myself a first cup of tea.

The freezer was full of food so I left it switched on – if I was unavailable for any length of time, Mr Havilland could arrange for the cleaners to sort the house out.

I tried not to think that unavailable would probably mean I was in prison. It was as easy as thinking about a stick without a monkey clinging to it.

Nick arrived while we were washing up after cereal and toast.

'I thought we'd better make an early start,' he said.

I dried my hands before going to answer the door and took perhaps a little too long – he was looking worried.

'You thought we might both have done a runner, admit it?' I asked.

'I did wonder. Last night I contemplated asking if I could sleep on your sofa to keep an eye on you both,' he admitted. 'Then I realised you had called on me for help, so I was being silly.'

'Not entirely,' I said. 'I mean, I am worried about facing the music. But I know I have to face it sometime. And now I know, I have to do the right thing.'

'When did you work it out?'

'Maybe a week ago,' I said. 'I was looking for clues earlier, but it wasn't easy. And I didn't know who was right or wrong, and I told you – I have experience of how badly wrong the authorities can be.'

'You'll be fine,' he said. 'It will be obvious to anyone with any sense you had the best of motives. And I know Simon, remember. He's a very sensible guy.'

I smiled.

He looked at the bags. 'Do you need that much?'

'I could leave lots of my stuff, I guess. Just take the laptop bag. But we need Lucas' bag – the boy has lost too much already. And Wolfie's bits. Which reminds me – we should see if the dog guard fits your car.'

I grabbed myself a change of clothes from my suitcase and stuffed it in with the laptop, and then hefted the suitcase to the living room. Meanwhile Nick fitted the dog guard in place, put the bags in the well behind the driver's seat, which still left room for Wolfie in the boot with his rope toy.

'Best go to the loo before we set out,' I said to Lucas. I might not have been much of a substitute mother, but some of it came naturally.

I took Wolfie out first and locked him in the back of the car. Lucas happily got in by himself and let Nick belt him in. I quickly locked up the house, and settled into the front seat, handbag on the floor between my feet.

Nick was a good driver so I soon relaxed and dozed off. I woke up when my phone pinged.

Another text. I looked at it bleary eyed.

You pushed me to the limit. I pushed him. Cause and effect. It's your fault as much as mine.

Would this nonsense never end?

'Come on, dozy.' Nick said. 'Time for a toilet break and a snack?'

I hadn't even noticed we were parked at a service station.

Lucas had a smoothie with vanilla, taking it with him, and I bought a bottle of water, Nick had takeaway coffee.

'I need something to keep me awake, if you two are going to snore all the way to Brighton,' he said.

'Okay, okay,' I laughed. 'Let's have the windows open and talk.'

Nick taught Lucas to play a game of yellow car, which involved shouting out 'yellow car' when one was spotted.

I quickly became convinced the game had been devised before yellow became such a popular car colour.

The journey passed very quickly, but most likely it was because I didn't want it to end.

We stopped at Pease Pottage services and had a meal in the cafe. Me and Lucas had egg, chips and ham. Nick had a burger.

'I've never had a burger,' Lucas said, looking at Nick's with eyes wide open.

Nick sighed, and sliced a piece off, and let Lucas try it.

I stopped myself from saying Lucas had told me he didn't like burgers.

Lucas said,' Yummy.'

Nick smiled, swapped plates, and ate ham egg and chips while Lucas devoured his first burger.

After finishing our meal, I took Lucas into the ladies and waited for him, then cleaned the evidence of a very messy burger from his face.

Nick was waiting for us by the car.

Once in the car, I compulsively checked social media again. It was a habit it was impossible to break.

To my astonishment, it was all over the news that a man had been arrested for Matt's murder. I couldn't quite believe it.

Then I set it aside. It really didn't matter. Not compared to Lucas.

I quietly asked Nick if we could call in at my house before going to Kathleen's 'It will only take a minute or two. Promise.'

I didn't want to say out loud, because Lucas would be so disappointed if I couldn't find Panda.

Nick pulled up and parked in the layby outside the house. Lucas was still asleep, so I quietly slipped out of the car, thankful Sarah was nowhere to be seen.

I unlocked the door and stepped over all the post – and walked straight through to the kitchen. There was Panda, on the kitchen counter, as expected.

As I locked the front door behind me, I had the feeling of being watched, the hairs on the back of my neck shivered.

Robert Louis Stevenson's horses, I thought. Or more likely Sarah and Izzy.

With that thought I ran down the steps and jumped quickly into the car.

It wasn't far to Kathleen's house.

Lucas was sleepy, as I persuaded him out of the car, but he woke up and was delighted when I gave Panda back to him.

'Thanks, Aunty Jen,' he said. 'I knew you'd find her.'

Chapter Thirty Six

Kathleen Hart was very welcoming. Her house was smaller on the inside. I looked more closely and realised it was because the whole space was crammed with beautiful objects. The hall was hung with woven tapestry and embroidered banners. The kitchen was lined with rows and rows of mismatched blue and white china. It was cosy, rather than overwhelming.

She very much belonged in this house. She was short and round and soft with grey hair in an untidy bun, like a picture book grandma. She was obviously a warm person. Something in me finally relaxed.

Kathleen obviously recognised Lucas, who was still clinging tightly on to Panda. She said a quiet hello to him but made huge fuss of Wolfie. She recruited Lucas to help her open tinned fish – pilchards in tomato sauce – to put in a bowl for the dog, followed by a bowl of water.

I was dreading what the fishy smells would do in conjunction with Wolfie's digestion.

We were allowed out in the garden to run, but Nick and I pretended to stretch and relax, while boy and dog chased around, free after being cooped up in the car all day.

Nick introduced me to Kathleen and gave her a vague idea of what had been going on. She took it very much in her stride, with barely a raised eyebrow.

After we'd all let off steam. she took us into her therapy room. Again, I was entranced by the space. The walls were lined with shelves, floor to ceiling. There were many books, but also a wide range of toys and objects. I recognised a set of dolls from around the world. Small pottery animals of all kinds – pets, farm animals, and wild. There were dolls houses and miniature furniture. Toy cars and lorries, buses and fire engines. Toy boats – dinghies, and yachts to tugs and ferries. There were puppets on strings, marionettes, and glove puppets. Even Sooty and Sweep were present.

Kathleen started by settling Lucas on the floor with a selection of toys, still including Panda, and asked me to tell her everything.

I skipped what only mattered to me, except for explaining I'd run away from press attention after being accused of murdering my husband. I felt the need to add I hadn't killed him, and she smiled, nodding as if it didn't need saying.

For the first time I realised if I hadn't been accused of murder, if I hadn't been hounded by the press and more, I would never have seen those locks and bolts, I would never have found Lucas.

It felt a little bit like fate. But I realised too that I wouldn't have it any other way.

That explained why I was in the house, the one Lucas had lived in. I described my shock and upset with the locks on the outside of the middle bedroom door, and how it had reminded me of childhood. I confessed I had begun to obsess on it, so had tracked down Lucas's family – his mother and stepfather.

When I described breaking into the house and finding Lucas locked in his room, then going back to kidnap him – well, I think I finally shocked this calm woman who had seemed unshockable.

'That was remarkably brave of you my dear,' she said.

When she'd heard everything, she sat in meditative silence, her fingers pinching the top of her nose, her eyes closed. Pondering.

'Clearly Lucas must be returned to his family, to his dad and his grandmother, Lilian, as soon as possible. The way to do that is through the police. You do understand, Jenny?'

'I do,' I said. 'What is best for Lucas is most important.'

Then I laughed. 'In any case, I skipped bail, so am likely to be arrested as soon as DI Carstairs finds out I'm back. Although I daresay kidnapping is more serious.'

Kathleen looks stern. 'You perhaps shouldn't talk of it as kidnapping, my dear.'

'What worries me,' I looked at Lucas who was playing quietly, but also on high alert, listening to every word, 'is the police who were in on the conspiracy. I watched videos,' I said.

Kathleen nodded. 'Me too,' she said. 'As part of my duties to the court. They were seriously upsetting.'

Again, the pause for thought.

'I still have contacts in the police, of course. We may be able to make this go much more smoothly by contacting the ones who are still working on the kidnapping. There's a DI Coleman who I know, and she is very sensible and reliable. It's probably best if we don't involve the local police. But first, I'm going to break the rules. I don't see why you two should have all the fun.'

Kathleen's plan was to see if Lucas would respond to a gentle hypnosis session.

'I will be very careful,' she said. 'I promise I know what I'm doing.'

Nick nodded.

'I will help him to relax,' she continued, 'and then when he's in a light trance, do a little gentle exploration of what's been happening in the poor child's mind. Not a deep exploration – just enough to find out what kinds of things his mum and stepfather said to him. And then some post hypnotic suggestions to help him feel safe with the police and social services, and to prepare him to be reunited with his dad and grandma.'

Nick raised his eyebrows at her.

'I'm too old and tired to care about being struck off,' she said. "But you don't have to mention it to anyone if you don't want to.'

I was a bit concerned about hypnosis, knowing a little about false memory syndrome, but Kathleen was very reassuring. And if it could help Lucas, I was all for it.

'Do stay here in the room, as quietly as you can.'

At first Kathleen and Lucas were gently playing with the toys, entering into a bit of a fantasy game with fairy tale themes – princesses and knights and witches.

Lucas seemed a bit worried about witches.

Kathleen offered to tell a story, and opened a book and read to him, talking so quietly he seemed to drop off to sleep.

'You're not asleep, Lucas. You are very happy and relaxed. Remember, like last time? And you can answer my questions. How do you feel?'

'Sleepy,' he said.

'Now I want you to tell me a story,' she said. 'A true story. And it might be a bit scary but you know it's going to have a happy ending. You are safe. Wolfie is here looking after you.'

Gradually Kathleen drew out of him what had happened after his mum collected him from school. How she and Paul had taken him to live in the house on the main road, which was now Auntie Jen's house. How his mum and stepfather had become more and more scary. They kept telling him horrible things about his Nana Lilian and his dad and he didn't believe them but he was scared of them he knew he had to agree. If he didn't, his stepfather would smack him. Or he wouldn't get anything to eat. He said how bad he felt, and how guilty, that he's agreed to say terrible things about his dad.

'There's no need to worry,' Kathleen said 'It's the job of grown-ups to worry about the truth. And it's their job to keep you safe.'

Lucas said, 'Like Auntie Jen, who rescued me.'

At that, my tears started to flow.

Kathleen said. 'You're safe with us now. You will soon be having an adventure with the police and other grown-ups whose job is to look after you. Panda will go with you. And I will try to make sure you get to see your dad and nana Lilian very soon. You will remember all that happened to you, but held at a distance, like a memory that doesn't hurt any more. And you will remember how much Jen loves you, and Wolfie too.'

Kathleen allowed Lucas to fall into a natural sleep.

'He does seem to be quite resilient, and I've done what I can to help. But there's no doubt the child has been through more than enough already, and there's more to come.'

'One thing which troubled me, was how easily he came with me. I asked him over and over, and he didn't want to go back to his mum.'

'It's a good sign,' she said. 'He wanted to escape. He trusted you. And here you are, proving yourself trustworthy.'

We tiptoed out of the therapy room and back to the kitchen, leaving Lucas sleeping on the big beanbag, holding tightly on to Panda.

Once we were settled around the kitchen table, Kathleen said, 'Before I make those calls, I just wanted to ask you a few questions, Jen, if that's okay?'

I was a little worried, and it showed.

'I'm not trying to convict you, dear,' she said. 'Quite the reverse. If you would like to tell me what it is that made you do this brave and unusual thing. There must be a reason.'

I blushed.

'It wasn't brave, really,' I said. 'I was just terribly afraid and angry for him. I suppose it goes back to childhood. I was a lot older than Lucas, but when I was a teenager, my stepfather locked me in the vestry cupboard. He was the pastor of this little evangelical church, and he thought I was a sinner. Worse than a sinner, really.'

Kathleen nodded. 'You couldn't bear to think of it happening to anyone else?'

'I couldn't,' I said. 'I've never talked about this to anyone else before. I still feel...oddly ashamed and humiliated. I know better now, in my head. But my emotions...'

'Thank you for trusting us,' she said, reminding me that Nick was present. He'd been quiet, and I'd been caught up in her warm attention, I'd almost forgotten.

'It's a good first step,' she said, 'Talking to us. But you might want to talk to someone else, at some point. You deserve the chance to heal. And you are not in any way evil. Many people who've been subjected to such treatment lose their empathy for others. It's too painful for them to acknowledge, so they side with the abuser. You are stronger than that. Lucas was lucky that you found your way into his life.'

Nick just patted me on the hand. I was jittery and embarrassed, but that was somehow just the right thing.

Kathleen stood up. 'I'm going off to make those calls now. And I think it would be a good idea if you made any calls you need to make. I think it will be a few hours, but best you are prepared.'

I started by calling Lainey.

'You know I said I was going to need your help,' I said. 'I'm back in Brighton and am likely to be arrested in a couple of hours. Could you come and collect Wolfie, please?'

'Of course,' she said. 'Where are you?'

I asked Nick for the address and passed it on.

'Can you tell me what it's about yet?' she asked.

'I've still to call my lawyer,' I said. 'But you'll find out soon enough, I promise. It's worse than you can imagine, and maybe better too.'

She laughed.

'You absolute bloody tease. But I'll let you get away with it, sure in the knowledge your lawyer is gonna give you a hard time.'

'She really, really is,' I sighed. 'Thanks Lainey. You're the best.'

'I am,' she said. 'See you in an hour or so.'

Next up, Chioma. Now this was going to be difficult.

I didn't even get my opening sentence in.

'I've been waiting to hear from you. When are you coming in?'

'I'm in Brighton,' I said. 'I'll give you the address, and then I'll explain why I disappeared.'

There was an ominous silence as I read Kathleen's address out and Chioma made a note.

'I hope,' she said eventually, 'You have a good reason for me to convey to DI Carstairs why he shouldn't arrest you for skipping bail?'

'Well, the first reason is he must know by now I didn't murder anyone. I've seen the news. They've taken someone in for questioning in connection to Matt's murder.'

Chioma was disappointed. 'I was looking forward to telling you. Yes, it seems Amy's husband was arrested for murder yesterday morning. He hasn't been charged yet, though it appears they are opposing bail. But you still broke the law. Skipping bail is still an offence, even if you're not guilty.'

'Secondly,' I said, once she paused. 'I am expecting to be arrested for kidnapping in the next couple of hours or so. Which is why I need you here.'

It was the first time since I first met Chioma back at Uni twenty something years before that I'd ever known her lost for words.

Even so, it didn't last long.

I did my best to give her a summary of what had happened, in between the stream of loud expletives which seemed to erupt continuously from my phone.

'Chioma,' I said. 'You never swear. What is going on with you?'

'You are complaining about me swearing and you a fucking child kidnapper?' she shouted.

'He's a lovely kid,' I say. 'You'll like him.'

'That's not helping,' she said. Quieter now. 'But dammit, Jen. I had no idea when I agreed to have you as a client that you would make my job so interesting.'

'But you're coming, right?' A note of pleading entered my voice. I needed her. I hate needing people.

'Too damn right. I wouldn't miss this for the world.'

Chapter Thirty Seven

Kathleen came back into the kitchen.

'The London team who investigated Lucas's disappearance are on their way here,' she said. 'They understand about your other issues, Jen, but they will need priority access to you. Finding the Grays will be their main focus and you're their best lead.'

'In that case, heaven help them. But DI Carstairs is going to be after me too. I'm in demand.'

'I should tell you,' she added, 'A couple of social workers will be coming too. They'll be looking after Lucas, finding him foster parents.'

'Can't he go straight back to his dad?' I was distraught. 'I promised him.'

'I'm sure it will happen very soon,' she said.' Only after all he's been through, it's best to reintroduce slowly. Especially considering the lies he was told.'

It was sensible, perhaps, given all that had happened to him. Yet I still felt it justified my distrust of the system.

'Don't worry about him too much, Jen,' Kathleen said. 'I will be involved at all times as I already have an established connection with Lucas. It was a good decision from you and Nick to bring him here. I promise you did the right thing.'

Somehow, I trusted her.

After nearly an hour spent waiting, waiting for nothing to happen, I decided to go for a walk with Wolfie. I needed to walk off some stress. And I wasn't looking forward to saying goodbye to Lucas.

I looked in on him, in Kathleen's therapy room. He was still curled up asleep on the beanbag. I whispered to Wolfie and he lazily unwound himself from the boy, careful to leave him sleeping.

'I won't be long,' I said to Nick and Kathleen, who were drinking coffee at the kitchen table. 'I want to stretch my legs and give Wolfie a last walk.'

Nick laughed. 'Don't be daft,' he said. 'You're not going to prison.'

'Probably not,' I agreed. 'But you don't know DI Carstairs like I do.'

'We'll speak up for you, won't we, Kathleen,' he said.

'Speak for yourself,' she said. 'I know a hardened criminal when I see one.'

I was laughing as I let myself out of the front door.

I walked down towards the sea, Wolfie staying close to my heel. It wasn't far and maybe we could tramp across the pebbles and paddle in the sea before going back to confront, well, whatever lay ahead.

'You are going to be so spoiled at Lainey's' I said to Wolfie. 'Though I know you'll miss us, me and Lucas. We made a good team. A family.'

Wolfie woofed, in agreement I thought. Then he started barking more aggressively.

I wondered what was wrong and as I turned round, I caught a glimpse of sudden movement as a boot connected with Wolfie's leg. There was an awful cracking noise, and then scratchy white plastic sacking was scraped over my head.

I couldn't see a thing. I was hyperventilating and then I sneezed, and someone pushed me awkwardly and I fell, my head banging on what must have been the floor of a van.

I surfaced slowly from the blankness. Somehow I was sitting upright, tied to a chair.

'The bitch is awake.'

That was me, I supposed.

I recognised their voices. Embarrassing, in the circumstances.

My mouth was crammed full of musty cotton, and I was gagging.

I decided to keep my eyes closed and pretend it wasn't happening.

At least the hard kitchen chair was more comfortable than the floor of the van, which was the last thing I remembered, before I came round. I was itching to check if there was a lump on my head, but I was tied up too securely. I had bruises on my bruises.

My guts were grumbling so loudly the noise could be heard across town. I don't know how long I'd been out of it, but I was ravenous.

A sharp slap across my face and instinctively, I opened my eyes.

I was rubbish at pretending, so my kidnappers could see I'd recognised them. How on earth did they find me?

'Tintin, we meet at last,' I said. Or is it Jed?'

He slapped me again.

'I knew you were awake.'

He pulled at the gag, yanking a lock of my hair out with the knot. I refused to show how much it hurt.

'Where's my dog?' I asked, my voice controlled. As if I wasn't asking, at least partly, to provoke. Wolfie ran off, limping. I was pretty sure he was safe. Like me, he was a survivor.

'You're worried about a dog, you fucking monster.' The woman yelled at me. 'You took my kid.'

'I'm glad I did,' I said. 'He's going back home now, to his Dad.'

She started to wail.

I talked over her noise. 'What do you think you'll gain, by kidnapping me? You're not going to get Lucas back. The police are on the way and social services. I can't influence them. So what are you going to do with me?'

'You're one of them,' she spat. 'You don't deserve to live. We know what you people do, and we are fighting back now.'

Her phone rang then, thank God, and she walked into the hallway, talking in low whispers.

He followed her out. They hissed furiously to each other. Moments later I heard the front door slam shut behind them.

I was on my own, in this miserable, cold and abandoned house. I was pretty sure that was an improvement on whatever they'd been planning next.

I knew where I was then. I'd been there before. The house must have been empty for weeks. Perhaps since the last time I was there, based on the whiff of damp and the layer of dust on all the surfaces. I started rocking the chair, trying to manoeuvre over to the kitchen cabinets. Maybe there was a sharp knife in the cutlery drawer.

I wobbled the chair too enthusiastically, and it tipped over on to the floor, taking me with it. I landed square on the bump on my head.

Fuck. That really hurt. I felt dazed, woozy-headed. Maybe concussed.

Banging and clattering noises erupted at the front of the house and added to my confusion. This was amplified by heavy footsteps and loud voices in the hallway.

DC Dave Elliott was the first into the kitchen. I smiled at him from my uncomfortable position on the floor – we were old friends after all – but he refused to look me in the eye. He pulled open a drawer, grabbed a pair of kitchen shears and cut me free. He yanked me up by my arm, still not saying a word.

I was slow, but not that slow.

'You're going to arrest me, aren't you?' I said, holding out my arms, as he swapped the clothesline for handcuffs.

One of the other policemen remonstrated.

'Come on, Dave, that's a bit much. She's been tied up here for hours. She's not going to make a run for it, is she?'

Reluctantly he removed the cuffs. He still hadn't said a word to me.

I kept cheerfully talking to him, because I could see how much it was winding him up. Underneath, I was starting to think, to make connections. And I discovered that after all, I could pretend.

Before I had time to completely work out what was happening, I was carted off to Hove Police Station.

The desk sergeant took my stuff, which was basically phone, keys and wallet, and put me in a cell.

A police constable came into the cell. 'Since you're going to be here for a while, would you like a cuppa and a sandwich.'

'I'd rather talk to DC Elliott, if that's possible. '

'You don't get to decide who interviews you,' he said. 'Anyway, he's busy telling everyone he can you can't be trusted, and you've been leading him a merry dance the last six weeks or so.'

'Oh,' I said. 'I rather liked him.'

'He said you were charming. It wasn't a compliment.' The constable walked out and locked me in again, apparently worried I might sweet-talk him.

He came back with a barely edible tuna and sweetcorn sandwich and a cup of strong tea.

'May I please call my lawyer now.'

'I can call for you,' he said. 'What's the number?'

'It's on my phone, with the desk sergeant.'

'It will have to wait then,' he said. 'He's on his break.'

'I hope his tea is more drinkable than this.'

Maybe I imagined it, but the cell door slammed a little bit louder.

I dozed off on the very uncomfortable bunk.

When I woke up, I was very stiff and very thirsty.

Not long afterwards, the door opened again, and two new police constables came in, bearing tea and toast. They stood and watched me eat and drink.

'Come with us, please,' the young female constable said. I recognised her then. She had accompanied DC Elliott after the break in at the house. Lucy something, I thought?

'Oh, hi,' I said. 'I'm sorry, I've forgotten your name. You came with Dave Elliott when my house was broken into,' I said.

'PC Lucy Shelton,' she said, not even managing a smile.

'Am I going to be interviewed now?' I asked. 'I'm still waiting to call my lawyer.'

'We've been asked to take you over to Wimbledon Police Station,' she said. 'There's a DI Carstairs waiting to talk to you.'

She collected my stuff from the duty sergeant and then had a conversation with the other constable about whether they needed to cuff me.

'She did skip bail,' the other police constable said. 'And DC Elliott said she can't be trusted.'

'He's not exactly in a position to claim he has good judgement of people,' I said.

'What does that mean? Do you know what she's on about?' PC Shelton asked her companion. Anything rather than talk to me, it seemed.

'You'll know soon enough,' I said.

They decided not to cuff me and instead PC Shelton sat in the back seat of the police car with me, as the bloke drove us to Wimbledon.

I was totally exhausted by being driven around again after such poor sleep. I was almost relieved when I was shown into an interview room with DI Carstairs, who was actually waiting for me.

'Not a cell, then?' I asked.

253

He shrugged, passing me my stuff, which PC Shelton had been looking after.

'Is it okay if I call my lawyer?' I asked. 'Only in Hove they wouldn't let me.'

'Oh, they knew it was pointless as you'd be coming here,' he said.

'She was in Hove, as it happens,' I said. 'Probably still is.' Had no one told him about Lucas, and what I'd done?

'Would you like something to eat and drink?' he asked. 'I gather you've had a rough day and a worse night.'

'If I could have something reasonably palatable,' I said. Perhaps a bit better than stale black tea and a limp tuna and sweetcorn sandwich?'

He sent the young Police Constable off to find something edible. 'For all of us,' he said, looking at his watch.

In fifteen minutes, she came back with a selection of wraps and fancy sandwiches, layered salads and smoothies from Marks and Spencer's.

'I asked for edible food, not for you to cater a party,' Carstairs said, grumpily.

'I'm happy to pay for my share if I can have the duck wrap and the fruit salad,' I said, greedily.

Carstairs laughed, pushing them towards me.

'I guess I should have held back until I needed to make you talk,' he said.

After I'd eaten half the wrap and had a drink, I started talking.

'Do you think bail jumping trumps kidnapping,' I asked him.

He looked gobsmacked. I realised then he didn't know – they'd sent me over here, what, on automatic? This was odd.

'Your lawyer phoned a couple of times and told me you had an excellent reason for missing signing in,' he said. 'I saw the video. There's no question of skipping bail being an issue. Who kidnapped you?'

'Oh, that wasn't why I couldn't make it,' I said. Then I remembered Kathleen had warned me not to talk about it as kidnapping. 'There's no need to make it easy for them,' she'd said. 'Intention matters.'

'I want to interview you about Henry Thompson,' he said. 'Somehow I have a feeling you know more than you've been telling us.'

Chioma was shown into the interview room.

'Well, this has been quite the game of hide and seek,' she said. Then she looked at DI Carstairs. 'I sincerely hope you haven't started without me.'

Then she looked at the food on the table and added 'Any of that going spare? I'm starving.'

Chapter Thirty Eight

'May I have some time alone with my client, DI Carstairs?' Chioma asked, once she had eaten all the pastries and snagged the last smoothie.

Carstairs sighed and looked at his watch.

'I think we all want to get this over quickly,' he said. 'Therefore I'm going to do this a little differently.'

Chioma looked interested and alert. I wanted to go home and sleep, so I grabbed at the idea.

'Sounds good to me,' I said.

'Wait a minute,' Chioma said. 'Let's find out what's on offer, first.'

'Lawyers,' Carstairs said. 'Always so cynical.'

She snorted. 'Pot, kettle.'

'Jennifer Blake,' Carstairs said. 'I am officially releasing you from police bail without charge and with no conditions. Sign here, please.'

'Oh, brilliant. Does that mean I can go home?'

'I would appreciate it if you would agree to be interviewed first. I'd like to know what you can tell us about Henry Thompson.'

At that point he was called out of the office. Something about the kidnap team wanting to talk to him.

After a few minutes he came back in muttering darkly. 'I don't see how it's supposed to be my fault when Hove shipped you over here in the first place. What did I know about the kidnapping?'

He looked at me, questioning.

'OK,' I said, 'Can you explain to me why I'm no longer a suspect?'

'When you finally let us know you'd driven down to the seaside cottage on the relevant Monday, it was easy to trace your movements via CCTV. Your car numberplate,' he said.

'We were already looking but you narrowed it down by giving us the time and your route, and so it became a priority. We soon established the time you drove back home, and Matt's car was seen driving back towards the cottage afterwards.'

'Oh,' I said. 'I hadn't realised.'

'You'd have been cleared much sooner if you had told us everything. The pathologist also fixed Matt's time of death. It's never all that accurate, but it was clearly hours after you'd gone back home.'

'I'm sorry,' I said. 'I thought it made me look guilty, that I'd driven straight down there from the clinic. And I always knew it wasn't me.'

'Once we established the timeline, you were obviously in the clear. All that left was a concern that you might have been conspiring with Henry Thompson.'

'I don't know much about him,' I said. 'I only met him once. Oh, and he was at Matt's funeral, but he didn't talk to me.'

'Tell me about that first meeting,' Carstairs said.

'It was four, maybe five months before Matt died,' I said. 'It was a bit scary actually, because he'd obviously been watching me. He approached me in the park, where I was walking my dog. Not Wolfie,' I said, tearing up a little, 'My previous girl, not long before I had to say goodbye to her.'

Carstairs actually looked sympathetic. He had way more emotional range than I suspected.

'He asked me if I was Matt Taylor's wife. Maybe I shouldn't have answered, but I said yes. He told me he was Amy Thompson's husband.'

Well, this was what Carstairs was looking for, clearly, from the avid look on his face.

'And this was months before you and Matt separated, months before he died?'

'Yes,' I said. 'Look. I don't like talking about this. It's still painful. I'd just gone through another unsuccessful IVF attempt. And we were about to have one last try. At least, Matt wanted it to be one last try. I didn't even know who Amy Thompson was.'

'How is this relevant?' Carstairs asked.

Chioma reached out, and held my hand, switching unconsciously into friend mode. If I'd mentioned it, she'd have said, 'Even lawyers have friends, you know.'

Yes, I was deflecting with dark humour again. I've tried therapy and then there was counselling for the IVF, for me and Matt. I lost count of the number of times I was pulled up on it. But fuck that. I needed a coping mechanism and this one came naturally.

'He stood there, waiting. He clearly expected me to know what he was talking about. After an awkward silence, he added. 'You know? Amy Thompson. The woman your husband is having an affair with.'

Carstairs said, 'You did know about the affair, then?'

'Some stranger comes up to me out of the blue and tells me my husband is having an affair with his wife, and you think it means I knew? No wonder you thought I'd killed him. Obviously I checked it out. I found out he was seeing her, this young woman who had been a temp at the office – maternity cover, ironically. And of course I didn't tell you I knew in advance. You suspected me anyway.'

It was Carstairs' turn to look irritated. 'I knew you were keeping stuff from me. That's why I suspected you. Why on earth did you choose not to tell me everything. It was a murder investigation!'

'I'd concluded Matt had killed himself,' I said. 'I knew I hadn't killed him. You showed me that email he was in the middle of composing. Addressed to me. Saying he was sorry for everything. He wrote that he'd believed we might still have a future together, but I'd made it all too clear we hadn't. It broke his heart that I would never forgive him.'

'It was just general though, and you as well as his mother and everyone who knew him were sure Matt was not the suicidal type.'

'That must happen a lot, though? People often hide their feelings. Matt was never great at opening up when he was having problems of any kind.'

'But you did tell me he'd told you about Amy that afternoon, when you argued, and he left for the cottage. As if that was the first you'd heard of it.'

'It was the first I'd heard of it from Matt,' I said. 'He told me all about Amy. About their plans. Everything he had done behind my back. He told me no more IVF, because it was all too painful for both of us. He couldn't bear watching me go through it all. And he told me he'd sold his shares in the company, and his mother's. If I kept my own, I'd have lost control. It was up to me, whether I kept my shares and accepted a junior role, or took a generous offer, and after a period of well-paid technical handover – went on to do whatever I wanted. But he took the choice away from me. Yes, I was angry. As angry as I'd ever been. I didn't want him dead though. I was angry because of what he'd done. How stupid it all was. I loved him, that's the point.'

'But you didn't confront him before this, when you knew he was having an affair?'

'I didn't. I knew the IVF stress was a huge factor. I knew he was unhappy generally – I didn't know how much he'd grown to hate the business. He never told me he wanted to sell up, to retire. I was waiting it out and hoping.'

'And you had no further contact with Henry Thompson?'

'No, I said. 'We never talked again. At least, I don't know whether he contacted me or not. There were texts, emails...'

Carstairs asked me to explain.

'For the last few weeks, months even, I've been getting texts, emails, phone calls. Many of them very nasty and personal. Accusations of having murdered Matt – some of them were direct. Others suggested I had at least caused his death. I hadn't thought it might be Henry Thompson, though I'd wondered about Amy. I didn't know, and still don't.'

'Why didn't you report this to us. We would have looked into it and it's our job to investigate.'

'You thought I'd killed Matt. I didn't think it would help to show you other people suspected me too.'

'You didn't think,' he said. 'That's the trouble.'

I lost my temper then.

'I'd miscarried. I was hormonal. My husband confessed to an affair, He left me. He sold the company out from under me, which I founded with him, without ever talking to me. Of course, I wasn't thinking.'

'I'm sorry,' he said. 'We did try to allow for all of it. Really. But we also did keep on explaining it was important to tell us everything.'

'I was paranoid,' I admitted. 'I thought you wanted me to confess. I was stupid, and I am sorry.'

'If there's anything else you haven't told us?' he asked.

I looked at Chioma, because I didn't want to look at Carstairs. I shouldn't have looked at Chioma.

'I don't think so,' I said. 'If I remember anything else.'

'Just let us have access to all those texts and emails. Your phone call log.'

'I will,' I said, although I still wanted to hold them back. 'But I already handed most of it over to DC Elliott in Hove.'

'Okay,' he said. 'Well I obviously can't give you the details but we have heard back from the CPS. It seems probable Henry Thompson is going to be charged with murdering your husband. I suspect when it gets to court you will be called as witness for the Crown. As will Amy.'

Chioma interrupted.

'While we're talking about Amy, I think you should both know. The DNA test we requested has come back negative. The baby isn't Matt's. It's Henry's.'

I was genuinely surprised, and my face showed it.

Carstairs was also surprised. 'I wonder if Thompson knew.'

He meant Henry, of course. But I wondered about Amy, and if she had known. She had certainly been pushing hard for her baby's share of Matt's money.

'I think we're done for now,' Carstairs said. 'We've arranged for the Met Kidnap Team to interview you here tomorrow, for your convenience and theirs. I would keep a close eye on Ms Blake overnight, if I were you, Ms Igwe. She has form for doing a runner.'

'I was kidnapped!' I said. 'On the way to turning myself in.'

'I meant when you skipped bail and went on the run with Lucas Ward.'

'Oh.'

As he left the room I could hear him muttering about the Met again. Something about wishing them more luck with me than he'd had.

I did feel some small sympathy.

'You can stay with me tonight,' Chioma said, brooking no argument.

Once we were in her car, she looked at me and asked, 'What was it you kept back, about the Thompsons?'

'I'm sorry,' I said. 'I don't want to talk about it yet.'

'You might have to,' she warned. 'Especially if he pleads not guilty, and you're called as a witness.'

'Can I cross that bridge later?'

'Not too much later. It can't look as if you are using it in self-defence. They could still decide to charge you as well, remember?'

'Let's get tomorrow over first,' I said. 'Then I'll tell you all of it. I promise.'

'I'll keep you to that.'

At her flat we drank coffee as we talked. Chioma brought me up to date with what had happened when I was otherwise occupied...

'First thing,' she said. 'I know you'll want to know about Lucas.'

I'd been keeping it the back of my mind, devastated I hadn't been able to say goodbye to him.

'The good news is, they decided continuity was of supreme importance, and as Kathleen volunteered to have him, that's where he's staying.'

I started crying, happy for them both. Kathleen would look after him.

'The bad news,' Chioma continued. 'Is that you aren't allowed to visit him. Not until it's sorted out legally. I know it's unfair, but it will be alright. And Kathleen's lovely.'

'She is,' I said. 'I'm pleased about that part. I wish I'd been able to say goodbye.'

'Kathleen did it for you. She explained you couldn't be there, and said she knew you'd visit him as soon as you could.'

It all depended on his dad and his grandma though. I knew that. If they didn't want me to see him, I would never see him again.

'Kathleen never wavered,' Chioma said. 'And neither did Nick. Even when the police and the social workers were sure you'd gone on the lam to avoid facing the music. They both stood up for you.'

'And you did too,' I said. 'Thank you.'

'That's awfully bold of you,' she said. 'Anyone with any sense would have gone on the run after what you'd done.' She sighed. 'That's why I knew you hadn't.'

'Nick will want to tell you himself,' she said. 'But he was the one who rescued you. He found Wolfie, howling outside your rental, and talked to your neighbour Sarah, and worked out where you must be. He says you owe him the story, by the way. Oh, and I'm sorry, but Wolfie's leg was sprained. Lainey took him to the vet and it's all going to be fine.'

'The fucking Grays,' I said. 'I heard something but had put it out of my mind. Poor Wolfie. Nick told me off when he found out I'd taken Lucas. Told me the journalist must never become the story, and that's what I'd done to him.'

'He must have adjusted to the idea,' Chioma said. 'Last I heard that long form article was turning into a whole book. He's already talking to a potential publisher.'

She looked at her watch and sighed.

'We need to be up in the morning, to get to Wimbledon nick by 10 am. Time for bed.'

Chapter Thirty Nine

The Kidnap Investigation Team, including lead investigator DI Eileen Coleman, was late. And after we got up ridiculously early to get to Wimbledon Police Station for them too.

We were kept waiting for over an hour, and more than once I whispered to Chioma, 'Come on, Eileen,' and she laughed and warned me not to let that slip in the DI's presence.

My phone pinged.

Another one of those texts.

What did you say, bitch?

I wanted to text back, *'How long have you got?'* but thought better of it.

While I had my phone out, I emailed Sean.

'Hi Sean,

Just to let you know, I had to leave in a hurry. Will tell all later, it's a ridiculously long story and, well, I haven't been entirely honest with you. If you don't want to know me when you find out, I'll understand. But please don't discard Lucas' poop animal, will you? I'll be back some time to sort out and I'll collect it then, if that's okay, Jen

When they eventually arrived, it was DI Coleman and a young detective constable who introduced himself as DC Rod Fields. The rest of the team were still in Hove, unsurprisingly, trying to find leads on where the Grays might have gone.

The interview was recorded so I was hyper-aware I must be very careful how I answered questions, remembering Kathleen had warned me not to talk about kidnapping Lucas.

'This is not a time for any of your dark humour,' she had said.

I wanted so much to ask how Lucas was, and if he'd been able to see his dad and Nana Lilian yet – but I knew that was unwise too.

'Can you please explain to me how all this started,' DI Coleman asked.

'I moved into the Victoria Park house at the beginning of July,' I said. 'It was increasingly uncomfortable living at home. The neighbours – who've known me for years – seemed to think I'd murdered my husband. Of course, they all liked him – he was full of energy and friendly where I was quiet. I mean, I liked him too. I loved him...' I broke down a bit.

'This is incredibly difficult,' I said. 'I've only just been released from police bail and been told someone else has been arrested. I've spent months being the main suspect in my husband's death. And now this...'

'And now this is not nothing,' DI Coleman said. 'You know that.'

'I do, of course. Only I am exhausted – not just because I've had hardly any sleep for the past few days, but the stress and worry of months has an impact too. Please make allowances if I get a bit emotional.'

'We will,' she tried to smile but her face hadn't had the practice.

'It was on my second day there, when I was waiting for the office removal people, I had a close look at the middle bedroom. I knew it had been a child's room – there was dinosaur wallpaper. But it made the best room for my office. It wasn't overlooked and there was a great view towards the park.'

She wasn't quite tapping her fingers on the desk, but it was costing her some effort.

'After they'd set up my desk and computer and left, that was when I noticed the lock and the bolts on the outside of the room. And it triggered a kind of trauma response,' I said.

'I know it sounds all fake and trendy, but it is real, you know. As a child... Well, you don't need to know all the details. But I was locked up, in a cupboard, by my stepfather. Seeing those locks brought it all back. It preyed on my mind.'

She nodded, but I didn't feel I had reached her.

'Sarah, the neighbour, didn't think the previous tenants had a child. Lots of post arrived for them and I tried to find a forwarding address, but it was impossible.'

'And?' she prompted me.

'There was an official looking letter. I opened it, and it was from the Education Department, trying to arrange an inspection. The Grays were home schooling. That set off all kinds of alarm bells. Home schooling is perfectly legitimate,' I said, 'but sometimes it can be a cover for abuse. And looking at the dates in the letter, it seemed that the prospect of an inspection had triggered their move. Afterwards I couldn't get them out of my mind.'

DI Coleman was most interested in my interactions with DC Elliott.

'As I understand it,' she said, 'DC Elliott came out to the house when you had a break in, right?'

'Yes.'

'And nothing ever came of it?'

'Well, it wasn't kids, as was first suggested. I received an abusive text with an attached video, showing someone rummaging through all my stuff. It was clearly some kind of threat.'

'And why didn't you report this?'

'I did!' I was indignant. 'I handed it over, all the emails and text, as well as this particular one. DC Elliott promised to pass it all on to the Digital Harms Team.'

She looked at me very carefully.

'Then when you somehow traced the previous tenants, you claim DC Elliott visited them and returned with reassurance, saying the child seemed happy. The parents agreed they sometimes locked him in his room, but only for his own safety, and they used a baby monitor to keep an eye on him.'

'Yes,' I said. 'DC Elliott did what he could to reassure. He made it absolutely clear I was breaking the law, that I shouldn't open their post, that I should put this all behind me. And if I didn't, he would see I was charged with any number of things – from interfering with the mail, stalking, wasting police time.'

'But you didn't do as he asked, did you?'

'I tried. But I couldn't stop worrying about the child.'

'Please describe for the recording what you did.'

'I knew where the Grays were living, so I walked my dog past a couple of times. I saw them bringing packing boxes and then going out in their car again. I knew they'd left the child locked up on his own. An eight-year-old.'

'You didn't know he was eight at the time, did you?'

'I did not.'

'And you didn't know he was on his own. There could have been a babysitter.'

'I surmised. I was right.'

'What did you do?'

'I walked the dog round to the back of their house, found a spare key under a plant pot – it looked like it had been there for years, but it worked. There was no one else in the house. We went upstairs and I unlocked the bedroom door.'

'We?'

'Me and the dog.'

'Okay. I wondered if Nick Kennedy had accompanied you.'

'No. I've said before, and I'll say it again. He was not involved in what I did. I asked him for help when I worked out what had been going on and who Lucas was.'

'You are claiming you planned and executed this kidnapping all on your own.'

'I don't see it as a kidnapping,' I said. 'It was a rescue. And I didn't really plan. It was impulsive. I asked Lucas if he wanted to come with me, and he said yes. He came with me so easily I knew there was something deeply wrong.'

'But you might have been wrong yourself, about why it was easy.'

'I had no idea why,' I said. 'I really didn't. All the time we were on the run I became more and more worried about why he hadn't been reported missing. Why no one was looking for him.'

'And you didn't know who he was?'

'You can check my internet history,' I said. 'You can find out when I found the news stories, when I friended Simon Ward on Facebook. How I read all the stories and watched some of those dreadful videos, and even read the Family Court Judgement.'

'Once you knew who he was, you could have taken him to the police straight away. He could have been home so much sooner.'

'I wanted to make sure he went home to the right people.'

'That wasn't your decision to make, was it?'

'It isn't now,' I pointed out. 'I did my best. I take full responsibility for my actions.'

'And what if the case hadn't been so clear cut,' DI Coleman asked. 'If he'd been an ordinary naughty child, or an autistic boy, and the parents were doing *their* best?'

'They'd have reported him missing,' I said.

'And what would you have done then?'

'I don't know. I didn't plan ahead. I acted on impulse.'

'Yet you lifted keys and went back to the house a second time before you kidnapped the child.'

'Before I asked him to come with me, yes.'

'That sounds like planning.'

'Come on,' I said.

Chioma glared at me and DI Coleman's stern expression hardened.

It wasn't deliberate. I was under pressure.

'I was grieving. I was driven mad by all the stress. The miscarriage. My husband's death. All the suspicion. And the child was being locked up. Left in on his own. What if there had been a house fire?'

'There's one thing I don't understand. You say it took you over a month to work out who Lucas was. Yet he told you his name. He was eight. Why didn't you ask him questions? Why didn't you push him? It was because you wanted to keep him for your own, wasn't it? Because you had a fantasy of creating your own little family.'

I looked at her in silence for a few moments. It was important I get this right. Honest in every way.

'I did have that fantasy. He's a lovely child, and there isn't anything I'd like better. Except I always knew he wasn't mine, and I always wanted what was best for him. I didn't push him, because it was clear he was traumatised. He had night terrors. Some of the small things he let slip, well, it was obvious to me he'd been through some horrific stuff. I recognised it from my own childhood – an emotional rather than a factual similarity.'

Chioma said, 'You don't have to answer all this now. There's going to be plenty of time.' She could see the tears rolling down my cheeks. She knew how little I talked about my childhood.

'It's okay,' I said. 'DI Coleman is asking fair questions. And she has hit on the difficulty in all this.'

I paused, wiped my tears with a tissue from the pack Chioma pushed towards me.

'I don't have much experience with kids,' I said. 'But I know dogs. I've rescued traumatised dogs and I know you can't force it. You have to wait for them to heal. Over time, if you don't push, the stress response relaxes. Really, it didn't take long for Lucas. He's a remarkably smart and resilient little boy.'

I wiped my tears again and managed to smile.

'My rescue child. After all, I did bring him back. I needed Nick's help, but I made the move. I could still be playing happy families up north, if I hadn't genuinely cared about what was best for him.'

DI Coleman said, 'It wasn't your place to be judge and jury.'

'I know that. I've thought about little else these past weeks. And his mum – I know she's gone crazy, with all this satanic abuse conspiracy stuff. But she wanted what was best for her son too, I'm sure. I do know in that, at least, we are mirror images. We both thought we were right.'

DI Coleman wrapped up the interview.

'We're going to need to talk to you again,' she said. 'Please don't go anywhere without our permission.'

'I can go back to Brighton, right?' I asked.

'You may.'

'Even if I wanted to make a run for it, I haven't got my passport back from last time,' I quipped.

Chioma glared at me.

DI Coleman sighed. 'We'll make arrangements to interview you again, once we a little further into the investigation. In the meantime, if you'd like to stay here for now. I believe DI Carstairs would like to talk to you again.'

She stalked out, followed at a respectful distance by her DC.

'Well,' said Chioma. 'It's a good sign they decided not to put you on police bail again. I guess you are getting some leeway here because you brought the kid back.'

'You mean I did their job for them.'

'Please do not say that to them. I nearly died when you said *Come on*, to Eileen Coleman.'

'It's serious, what I did. I know that. At least it's only going to be one trial, not two.'

'Don't forget, you'll be a witness in Henry Thompson's trial.'

'Oh yes. We must talk about that soon.'

At that point DI Carstairs came in, with PC Dalton who was carrying a tray of coffees and chocolate wafers.

'Hello you two,' he said, all informal and cheerful, passing out drinks and sugar.

'I wanted to check again,' he said. 'You said you'd handed over all the texts and emails to DC Elliott?'

'Yes,' I said. 'I'm sure.'

'And you didn't ask him to keep it informal or anything?'

'I kept it informal by keeping it to myself, until he asked to see them. He stood over me and made me send them to him. But anyway, the video was a step too far. I was scared. I wanted it on the record, and I wanted it investigated.'

'That's odd,' Carstairs said, 'Because he doesn't seem to have logged them or started any investigative processes. The Digital Harms Team know nothing about it, and DC Elliott isn't on duty today. I'll follow it up. In the meantime, can you make sure I have copies?'

'I'll forward them on to you,' I said. 'I have screenshots of the texts.'

'I'm afraid I'll need your phone if I'm going to investigate the texts,' he said.

Reluctantly, I handed it over. Then I fished around in my bag and gave him my second phone.

'Oh,' said Carstairs. 'You really have decided to trust me. Thank you. I promise you'll have them back in a couple of days.'

I was glad I'd made sure not to send any incriminating texts on either phone.

'Oh, and one last thing,' he said. Almost an afterthought.

'Henry Thompson has been charged with your husband's murder. He was denied bail and is on remand.'

I burst into tears. Grief, or relief, or a complicated mixture of both.

'I am sorry for your loss' he said. 'I know this has been a very difficult time for you. But perhaps this will eventually bring some closure.'

Chapter Forty

I moved back into the Victoria Park house, wondering why I seemed to keep on needing new starts. Probably there was something wrong with my way of thinking about everything. I was after all still the girl who had been locked in the vestry cupboard, still the young woman who had thrived at university and the one who had established a successful business. There was no reason I couldn't also be the woman who had lost her husband and rescued a child.

I went to the DIY store, and asked an older gentleman dressed in the trademark black and orange for advice, bought the tools he recommended, along with Polyfilla and paint and paintbrushes.

For some reason I wanted to do this job myself.

I removed the bolts from the outside of the middle bedroom door, then filled the holes with Polyfilla. After it had dried, I painted the door and the frame with white gloss to match the rest of the paintwork.

I decided to keep the dinosaur wallpaper. Knowing Lucas chose it, and knowing he was now safe, I felt comforted by it. It was a kind of connection.

As I took the heavy old bolts downstairs, the doorbell rang. I put them on the hall table. As I opened the door, I was bowled over by a madly overexcited wolfhound, with a brace on his back left leg. It didn't seem to be slowing him down at all.

'I presume that's you, Elaine Margaret Westwood, hiding behind this big old dog?'

I heard Lainey laugh as I backed into the house, picking up the bolts on the way.

'Shut the door behind you and come into the kitchen. Tea?'

'Yes please,' she said. 'I brought doughnuts.'

I put the bolts down on the kitchen table, and turned my back on her, attempting to wipe the tears off my face.

I'd cried more in the last few days than in the rest of my life put together.

She noticed though.

'Oh, you big old dafty,' she said. 'Come here.' She gave me a big hug, which Wolfie soon broke up.

I put his water dish down and gave him a bowl of kibble, neither of which did anything to distract him from the plate of doughnuts on the table.

Lainey picked up the bolts.

'Are they...'

'Yes,' I said. 'I decided it was time.'

'God, Jen. You are brave. I'd never have dared.'

'Just a bit of DIY,' I said.

She glared at me.

'I know what you meant. I was more than a little crazy, I think. And I was also terrified.'

'But think of what might have been. Of all the awful stories we read where no one noticed, or people looked the other way. I'm so proud of you, Jen.'

I was still crying. The tears pouring down my cheeks.

'It's okay,' I said. 'It's catching up with me. I'm fine.'

'Have another doughnut,' she pushed the plate towards me.

The doorbell rang again.

I let Nick in, relieved I'd not eaten the last doughnut.

'Meet Lainey,' I said, 'My best friend and dog rescue fanatic. Lainey, this is Nick, my partner in crime.'

Lainey laughed. 'We already met,' she said, getting up and hugging him.

'You're home then,' he said, accusingly. 'Why didn't you text me, at least.'

'I was going to,' I said, defensively. 'I only came back last night, and I've been doing DIY. Oh, and DI Carstairs has my phones. He's planning to actually investigate the nasty texts and emails. Apparently *Call Me Dave* hadn't even logged them.'

'Oh,' Nick said, butting in. 'I have some very interesting info about DC Elliott.' He paused, dramatically.

'You going to tell us?' Lainey asked. 'Or do I have to set the dog on you.'

It wasn't much of a threat given that Wolfie was sitting eating scraps of doughnut out of Nick's hands.

'He's gone missing,' Nick said. 'He called in sick and then never showed up, stopped answering his phone. Eventually they sent a couple of PCs around to check, and he'd upped sticks.'

Lainey said, 'Am I seeing an actual pattern here, or am I imagining a conspiracy?'

'My contact says it was strange he was assigned to the break-in in the first place – it would never have been one of his usual tasks. Apparently he'd asked some guy who works in the response team to let him know if there were any calls to your address, Jen, and a handful of others, including the Grays' new address. It turns out they were all people involved in this group.'

'It was a conspiracy, then. You know, there was a policeman in one of those terrible videos, interviewing six-year-old Lucas, pressing him to say his Dad had done the most awful things. Cold comfort, but Lucas seemed to have no idea what they wanted to hear from him. He thought it was mostly about junk food, bless him.'

'The food purity thing,' Nick nodded. 'But this group, it was an inner circle in the online forum, you know? Where the Grays' photo was. They see themselves as moral crusaders, paedophile hunters. They don't trust the police to deal with it, because the police are involved in the cover ups. It all goes back to Savile and Cyril Smith, and the children's homes scandals – that's their justification. And it's all merging with QAnon stuff now, imported from America. O brave new world.

We were all a bit stunned, I thought. I'd been feeling uncertain of DC Elliott for a while, and when he arrested me there was something which felt off. I just hadn't imagined it might be quite this bad. I'd been confiding in DC Dave Elliott, and all the time he was on the other side.

'Elliott could have been looking for us, me and Lucas, all that time. Unofficially. I thought we were safe when there were no news reports of the missing kid, and he could have been after us.'

Nick said, 'He did try to put feelers out, it seems, but it was too big of a risk to follow through. He was very opportunistic. He was unlucky that Carstairs and Coleman were both on the ball, or he'd have gotten away with it.'

Lainey spoke. 'Just as well you're a nutter about not trusting anyone, Jen,' she said. 'I'll never complain about that again.'

'Pull the other one,' I said. 'And anyway, I did trust Nick, right?'

'Have you thanked him for rescuing you yet?'

'I haven't!' I was very apologetic. 'Sorry Nick. Chioma told me all about it. How both of you and Kathleen stood up for me, too.'

Nick said, 'That's better. It's about time you were properly grateful. And I found this mutt, as well.' He gave Wolfie the last bite of doughnut.

I laughed.

'And while you're feeling contrite, it might be a good time to push you for permission to write your story? I've been commissioned to write a long form story about Lucas's return home, and I'd like to include your part in it? Simon has agreed already.'

'That's fine,' I said. 'Although it probably has to wait until all the legal shenanigans are done with. You'll check that out first?'

'Of course,' Nick said.

'OK. But right now, I'd like to hear what happened from the horse's mouth. How did you work out where I was being held?'

'I don't think any of us realised you weren't back from your walk until the police team showed up,' Nick said.

'That's me. Instantly forgettable.'

He rolled his eyes, dramatically. 'The police were all immediately convinced you'd gone on the run, no matter what me and Kathleen said. Then Chioma showed up, and Lainey to collect Wolfie, and they started to worry until the boss policewoman...'

'The DI,' said Lainey, 'Eileen Coleman. And you a journalist too.'

'The DI,' he continues, 'suggested the best cover for going on the run was to make it look as if you planned to come back. And Lainey said that you weren't that bright...'

'Thanks, traitor,' Lainey said.

'I don't think they appreciated us,' Nick said. 'Or understood how stressed and tired and worried we were. Of course, we were joking but we were also terrified.'

'Anyway, I went to look for you. When I found Wolfie, limping and howling on the front steps of your house – thank fuck he made for home – and then Sarah came out and told me the Grays had been around a lot lately, while you'd been away, I put two and two together.'

'Well, thank you,' I said. 'I couldn't work out exactly what their plans were. In fact, I don't think they knew what they were going to do with me, but it was good to be rescued. I don't think they'd thought it through, beyond punishing me.'

I shivered.

Lainey said, 'They're never going to get access to Lucas now, surely. No matter what.'

'I shouldn't think so. If they're ever caught. I wish I knew who tipped them off though. Just a few minutes before the police raid.'

I paused, while my brain connected the dots. I was slow. 'It must have been DC Elliott,' I said. 'I thought he couldn't face me because of having to arrest me, but it was a different kind of guilt altogether.'

'Slowcoach,' said Nick.

'Oy,' I said. 'I've not had the time you have to put it all together.'

They laughed.

'I wish I could see Lucas. And Kathleen. Do you know how all that's going? DI Coleman warned me to stay away.'

'Kathleen's still looking after him,' Nick said. 'He's doing well, apparently. His dad and Nana Lilian are visiting every day and Kathleen thinks social services will agree to him returning home as soon as next week.'

'That's brilliant.'

I was still missing my boy though, and I thought Wolfie probably was too.

After they both left, I had dinner alone – well, not alone, exactly, with Wolfie watching every mouthful. I felt a bit deflated, somehow.

I didn't want to keep on working for the company any longer. And Stefan didn't need me anyway. He'd established a great team. I could have let go ages before.

I knew there was a long haul ahead, until Henry Thompson's trial. And I didn't know when, if ever, I would be allowed to see Lucas again, which hurt my heart.

Could I get started on my dog rescue, without knowing what was going to happen? Would I be charged with kidnapping?

I put the TV on, but nothing kept my attention.

I logged into my laptop for the first time in days. There was an email from Sean. Of course, I would usually have heard it ping on my phone. I hoped there was nothing in there to embarrass me in front of DI Carstairs.

Hi Jen,

What on earth do you mean I might not want to be friends anymore? I've known you since we were both ten. And of course, I won't discard Lucas' spirit animal. It's a snake, you monster. Not a poop animal. (I know, I know, it's a poop animal. And I added green glaze as he asked and it's even queasier now.)

Yours, Sean x

I sat there for an hour, like a pathetic teenager, interpreting that single kiss. Probably just an automatic thing, I thought. Some people always end emails with a kiss.

Chapter Forty One

A few days later, Chioma called me.

'DI Coleman is ready to see us again. She has a few more questions, apparently.'

'I thought we'd been through everything. She's not going to arrest me, charge me with kidnapping, is she?'

'I don't know,' Chioma said. 'It's possible, but I didn't get those kind of vibes.'

'DI Coleman didn't have any vibes, man,' I said. 'She's a cold fish.'

'You can be a bit harsh, you know. She's doing her job.'

'I'd find it easier to be less judgy if she didn't see her job as locking me up and throwing away the key.'

When we arrived at the police station – which was beginning to be a lot too familiar – D I Carstairs also wanted to see us.

'This will only take a minute,' he said. 'I wanted to give you your phones back. And to say I gave all the evidence on there to DI Coleman, so you wouldn't lose your phones again.'

Chioma said, sternly, 'That was a bit presumptuous of you.'

I said, 'No, he was quite right. I've got nothing to hide, and I get my phones back sooner. Thank you.'

DI Carstairs gave me a hard look. 'Remember if you think of anything else that will help us make our case against Henry Thompson, you must let us know.'

I distracted him. 'Any more news about DC Elliott?' I asked. 'Has he turned up yet.'

Carstairs shrugged. 'It didn't take that long to get out. Ah yes, that would be your journalist mate, I presume.'

'No comment.'

'I am sorry you were so badly let down,' he said. 'You were right not to trust him, it seems. That should help you with DI Coleman, anyway.'

While we were waiting for DI Coleman I sent some texts – to Nick, Lainey, and Sean, to let them know I had my phones back. I was looking forward to streamlining back down to just one phone again. No more confusion.

We weren't waiting long for our next interview. DI Coleman was less stern than before. I wouldn't go so far as to describe her as warm and friendly, however.

'I have some good news for you,' she said. 'We've had some long conversations with Kathleen Hart and with Simon Ward. Kathleen was full of praise for your strategy with Lucas. She said you have excellent instincts, and he was very fortunate you didn't push him. I was wrong.'

Suddenly I liked her a lot. Not many people admitted when they were wrong. Maybe she would be fair, after all.

'And Simon Ward says as far as he's concerned, you are the reason why Lucas is home.'

"Oh, is he back with them both? Brilliant.' I was full of smiles.

'Yes, he is. And as I say Simon Ward is grateful to you for all you did for him. In fact, he says if there were to be a prosecution he and Lilian will be witnesses for the defence. As will Kathleen Hart.'

Oh. That was unexpected.

'The CPS are very unlikely to go ahead in these circumstances. However, it doesn't seem quite right there should be no legal consequences. We are therefore proposing that you accept a caution for taking Lucas without the permission of his legal guardian.'

'What does that mean?'

'You'll have to admit your guilt, and you will have a criminal record,' Chioma said.

'And that's it?'

I was ready to accept, but Chioma asked for time to talk to me.

'Look,' she said. 'If you do the therapy course you've been on about, you won't be allowed to see patients if you have a record. You won't pass a basic background check. Stay strong. Trust me.'

I agreed, although I had no plan to see patients, I didn't think my options should be constrained.

When DI Coleman returned, Chioma said, 'Ms Blake has decided she will take her chances in court. With a jury.'

'I'll be a few minutes,' she said.

When she returned, she said, 'This goes against the grain with me, but I've spoken to the CPS, and they have agreed a trial will not be in the public interest. That will be all.'

'You mean, that's it?' I said.

'It is. You are free to go. Oh, and my name's Lena, by the way. Not Eileen. Not ever.'

Ah.

When DI Coleman had left the room, Chioma grinned at me and said, 'See, I was right. I always am.'

For once, I didn't even want to argue.

The following day, when I was walking Wolfie on the Downs, my phone rang.

It was Sean.

'If you're not too busy,' he said. 'I'm in Brighton today. Maybe we could meet for a coffee?'

'When?'

'Right now?'

'OK,' I said. 'Well, give me half an hour, and I'll finish walking Wolfie. You can come to the house. I'll put the kettle on the moment I get home.'

'Great,' he said, 'Only I don't know the address.'

'I'll text you. Where exactly are you?' I asked.

'Near the station.'

'Brilliant. If you pop down Trafalgar Street, about a hundred yards, there's a fabulous French deli. Fetch us some treats to go with our coffee, would you?'

He laughed and hung up.

I sat down on a huge stone and said to Wolfie, 'I think he likes me. Or you.'

Then I texted the address before we raced home so I could brush my hair and at least change into a clean tee shirt.

I was looking out of the window waiting like an idiot teenager when he arrived in a taxi. He was carrying a huge suitcase, and a white card cake box.

Odd...

'Don't worry about the case,' he joked. 'I'm not moving in. It's empty. I brought down a load of pots for an exhibition in the gallery on Gardner Street.'

He followed me into the kitchen, bringing the cake box, which he set carefully on the kitchen table.

'Oh, and before I forget.' He went into the hall, and I watched as he rummaged in the case and grabbed a parcel wrapped in bubble wrap.

'Poop snake,' he said, unwrapping it and setting it on the table.

I laughed, lifting it up for a closer look.

'God you were so right. That shade of green makes it even worse than I imagined.'

'He'll love it though. And he is very talented. Will you be seeing him soon?'

'Ah now. That's part of the long story I promised you.'

'That's what I'm here for,' he said. 'That and coffee.'

'Oh sorry,' I said, belatedly putting the kettle on. 'Instant okay?'

'Heathen,' he said. 'It will do, but it will be outclassed by my contribution.'

I put the coffee on the table as he opened the box. Two chocolate mousse cakes, topped with decorative gold foil. And two apricot tarts.

'Start talking,' he said.

'Okay,' I said. 'Buckle up. I told you I was hiding out in Aunt Martha's house because I was suspected of murdering my husband. I didn't do it. But I was on police bail, my neighbours were all looking at me funny, and there were journalists and photographers on the doorstep every single day.'

'You did,' he said. 'And I confess I looked it up online afterwards. If anything, you understated how awful it must have been.'

I smiled.

'I actually hid out here first. Only various things happened...'

I told him about the break in, the policeman, the bolts and locks. And I told him I'd kidnapped – rescued – Lucas.

'I knew there was something odd,' he said. 'You didn't have any siblings and the papers said Matt didn't either. I sort of assumed you were an honorary aunt.'

I told him the rest, finishing on the recent good news that I wasn't going to be charged, and Lucas was at last home with his dad and Nana Lilian. I hadn't been able to see him yet, although I lived in hope.

'And you worried I might not want to know you again? You idiot woman,' he said. 'Come here.'

And he hugged me while Wolfie pushed in between us, and then tried to slurp away at the pastries.

'I think we'd better eat these while we can,' I said, backing off from anything emotional.

We gorged on cakes as we talked some more, but about stuff that didn't matter. It was almost like having a normal life again, only a normal life that included butterflies in my stomach, the kind of butterflies that hadn't visited for years.

After an hour he said, 'I'd best call a taxi, or I'll miss the last train. I have the boys this weekend, otherwise I'd stay longer.'

'I can give you a lift to the station,' I offered, but he insisted on a taxi.

On the doorstep, with the big empty case, he turned and gave me a quick hug, and a peck on the cheek, which suddenly turned into the lightest and shortest and sweetest kiss on the lips. Then he was gone.

Chapter Forty Two

Filled with hope and optimism, there was one more obstacle to my freedom.

Technically speaking I still owed Chris Bailey and NRS Tech many more months of my time. On top of that he'd been seriously short-changed by my many absences – on the lam, being interviewed by the police, and coming up, possibly time in the witness box in court.

He'd handled it all like a true gentleman – never once complaining, even when it put NRS Tech in the limelight. I'd kept apologising, thinking all the while of how badly Matt would have reacted to a member of staff being so much of a bloody nuisance.

'Do not apologise,' he said. 'It's all good publicity, especially now you're known as the woman who did what was right no matter what it might cost her.'

'That's one way of looking at it, but there'll always be the *'no smoke without fire'* people.'

He grimaced.

'What a world,' he said.

'I wanted to ask, 'I said, 'If you would consider releasing me from my contract early? I'm perfectly willing to provide consultancy as needed, on a day-to-day basis. But really, Stefan and his team are brilliant. They make me realise I should have loosened the reins so much earlier.'

Chris nodded. 'It's what always happens with startups,' he said. 'It's hard to let go when it's your baby. Matt had realised that, I think, and you would have done so eventually. And of course, we will release you. I know you have your heart set on this dog rescue plan. I take it you've found somewhere?'

'Somewhere, and someone,' I said. Blushing. 'Maybe.'

'I am delighted for you,' he said, and enveloping me in a big hug. 'But you'll always be part of the NRS Tech family, and don't you forget it.'

'Americans,' I said to him, mock grouchy. He laughed. 'You're practically one of us now,' he said. 'And you are welcome here any time.'

I wandered round to Stefan's office saying hello to a few familiar faces on the way He stood up, greeting me with affection.

I asked about Elena, and he scrolled through some photos on his phone.

'She is gorgeous. Takes after her mother,' I teased. He didn't even realise I was teasing. He just agreed.

'I wanted to be the one to tell you I'm no longer part of your team,' I said. Even though I had secretly always thought of him as part of mine. 'I don't think you need me anymore, anyhow. I've agreed with Chris that if I am needed, I will always be available on a consultancy basis. And this may not be very professional of me, but seriously, if you do have any problems any time at all, call me. You don't need to go through Chris and make it official if you need a chinwag for half an hour.'

'A chinwag?' he asked.

'A natter, a chat,' I said. 'Just to talk things over, if you're stuck and need someone to talk to. Whether technical, business or personal.'

'That's very kind of you,' he said.

'I mean it. Seriously, you have been a joy to work with. And nothing flustered you, even...'

'It's been an adventure,' he laughed.

'There's one thing.' For the first time he mentions the kidnap.

'I read Nick Gamble's long form piece in the Observer, on Sunday.'

'Oh,' I said. 'I knew it had been published, but I hadn't dared look.'

"I know you probably don't want to talk about it," he said. 'But first off, I think what you did was very brave.'

'...and illegal,' I said,

'We all know sometimes what is legal and what is the right thing to do don't always go hand in hand.'

I smiled.

'I wondered if you ever found out who it was that was stalking you?'

'No, not really. It was more than one person, according to the police. I thought it might be my mother but well, I'd need to talk to her to find out. I'm not sure I care that much. At least, I'm trying not to...'

'This is a bit awkward,' Stefan said. 'But had you thought it might be your mother-in-law?'

I didn't know what to say. So I said nothing.

'I have a confession. She was here quite a lot in the first few weeks after the takeover. We all thought it was understandable. She'd lost her son and she'd been a shareholder, and she knew lots of the staff who were staying on... When she asked me if I could give her your new number, I didn't think twice. I'm sorry. I realise now I should have asked you first.'

I smiled at him. I knew how much courage it took to confess.

'You weren't to know. I'd likely have said yes anyway. And it probably wasn't her.'

He wasn't having any.

'But you'd have known Eve had your contact info then. And there's more.'

'I heard her talking to the receptionist a couple of weeks ago. She was crying, and she said she was sure you'd murdered Matthew. That she was devastated the police had ruled it out. She didn't believe it.'

I reeled. I couldn't believe she'd actually been telling people.

'Thanks for letting me know. I had wondered why the police wouldn't tell me why they took so long to close the investigation. They were so sure at first it was an accident, and then, suddenly, everything changed.'

Now I had the excuse I needed to confront her. I was longing to know how she felt about Amy, now we all knew baby Jamie wasn't Matt's son.

Chapter Forty Three

I hadn't heard from Amy since the revelation that Henry was Jamie's father. She knew Chioma would have shared the results with me, but still, I was amused. All those emails she had sent, when I was having so many problems, taunting me and pressing for money. And they just stopped.

Chioma was smug that she'd talked me out paying Amy a larger sum of money, but still thought it much more than she deserved. She'd warned me I wouldn't get it back, if, as was proved true, Matt did not turn out to be the baby's father.

Meanwhile, I wanted to have my money's worth.

I emailed her.

'Hi Amy

I was sorry to hear the results of the DNA test. You must be so disappointed, and I'm sure Eve is too.

Nonetheless, I would like to arrange a meeting with you to discuss what we do about the rather large payment I made, on the assumption that you were telling the truth about your baby's father.

Neutral ground would be best, I think.

I assume you're no longer staying with Eve, so if you could suggest a cafe which is convenient to you, I'm happy to do the travelling.

Hope to see you soon,

Jen, etc

I was planning to let her keep the money, but I thought a little threat might come in useful.

Her answer pinged back almost immediately.

Jen,

I'm a bit busy at the moment as you know. Looking after a small baby is rather tiring, although of course you wouldn't understand that, not having had the experience.

However, I do think it's best to end our relationship on a friendly and co-operative note. I'm sure we each have something the other wants. Even if it's only silence. I am back in my old home, supporting Henry as best I can.

There's a little Italian cafe at the end of the High Street in New Malden. Be there at eleven tomorrow,

Amy

Oh, I'd be there.

If I wanted her silence – and I hadn't decided on that part yet – then I was damn sure I could afford it. She didn't seem to realise she'd lost her bargaining power.

Even though I was five minutes early, she was there before me. Sitting in state with the baby in a sling, café staff huddled around, admiring Jamie, fetching and carrying. I noticed an upmarket pram parked by the front door, wondering if I'd paid for it.

I walked in, smiling. She didn't realise yet who she was dealing with, and her poker game wasn't as strong as she thought it was.

'Hello,' I said, cheerfully, as I sat opposite her. 'What a gorgeous baby. Jamie, isn't it? How lovely that your names rhyme.'

She scowled at me.

'Please could I have a pot of tea,' I said to one of the crowd. 'With a pot of water and milk and sugar. And some food? Would you like anything, Amy?'

The waitress disappeared and produced a menu.

'My treat,' I said to Amy. 'But then, I'm paying for it either way, right?'

I was struck again, as we waited for drinks and toasted sandwiches, how much she still looked like a younger and prettier version of me.

Funny how Matt thought that was a defence. 'It's why it made sense,' he said, not seeing how much it hurt me.

I wondered again if she'd known about the similarity. How much she had consciously planned, and how much was impulsive. It looked like a trap that was neatly designed for Matt, and he leapt right into it.

Once our food and drinks had arrived and the crowd of baby-worshippers had disappeared, I started the real conversation.

'He is a cute baby,' I said. 'Do you think he takes after his father, the murderer, or his mother, the manipulative, scheming bitch?'

She flinched a little. That was good. It looked like she hadn't realised I had teeth.

I carried on.

'Eve threw you out then, so you had to crawl back to Henry.'

'He always wanted me back,' she said. 'And once Matt was out of the picture...'

The words I didn't add resounded in my mind – because your husband pushed him off a cliff.

'And Matt's money was out of the picture, more to the point.'

'I'm not convinced it is,' she said. 'I still have leverage.'

'Henry's on remand,' I said. 'When I was arrested, they let me out on bail. You see the difference.'

'They don't have the evidence that will clear him,' she said. 'But I know the truth.'

'They have the evidence now to convict,' I said. 'DI Carstairs interviewed me. He also has copies of all my emails and texts. And that includes yours. Like me, he can recognise a shakedown when he sees one. When he asked, I answered.'

'Did you tell him you gave Henry the address of your holiday cottage.'

'No, because I didn't. You made that up because it was the sort of thing you'd do. Amy, he followed you. He already knew where the cottage was. I didn't have to tell him anything.'

She looked sulky, like a teenager. I was almost regretful Matt hadn't ever lived with her – he'd have hated that pout so much.

'Look,' I said. 'This is where it ends. I get it – you feel entitled to more. I will not be blackmailed. If you push anymore, I will take you to court for fraud, to get back the money I've already paid you. I know it will cost more than I will get back, but if you don't stay right out of my life from now on, I'm willing to do it. Understand?'

'Understood.'

I stood up, throwing enough cash on the table to cover the bill twice over.

'That's the last time I pay for you ever,' I said. 'See you in court.'

'I thought you said you wouldn't sue me?' she wailed, loudly enough that the waitress looked up, interested in the public drama.

'At Henry's trial,' I said. 'I'll be a key witness.'

And I walked out.

Chapter Forty Four

Nick phoned, asking if I was available for a few hours. I said yes, so he turned up with a picnic basket.

'Is this an apology for that Observer article?' I asked.

'If it needs one,' he said, warily. 'I thought I'd been fair.'

'More than fair,' I said. 'It's just a bit embarrassing. I doubt my mother would have enjoyed it.'

'Is she a reader?' he asked.

I laughed. 'Not usually, but no doubt people would be queuing up to share it with her. Anyway, I've decided I'm not going to worry about what she thinks anymore. I managed for twenty years – I guess I can learn how again.'

'Don't be hard on yourself,' he said. 'We can do that for you, now.'

I laughed again. It felt odd to have friends who I'd let close enough to really know me.

'The grille is still installed in the car,' he said. 'So Wolfie can come with us too.'

He drove us to North London, refusing to say where we were going. He promised Wolfie would have a good run, and I'd enjoy it too.

He parked outside a house I recognised from poring over old news stories.

'Are you sure this is okay?' I said. I was so nervous, I was trembling.

He gave me the poop snake. I don't know how I missed seeing him purloin it from the kitchen counter.

'Someone has to give this to Lucas, and I thought it should be you.' he said.

'I'm terrified,' I said.

'It will be fine. You were invited. I've not dragged you here out of the blue!'

I got out of the car while Nick opened the boot and grabbed Wolfie's lead. I was still fretting when the front door flew open and my favourite small boy ran down the garden path and threw his arms around Wolfie, before walking slowly towards me.

'Hello, Auntie Jen.'

I tried to control my emotions, but I seemed to have lost the skill.

I took the poop animal and offered it to him. 'Sean didn't forget,' I said. 'Does he look like you expected?'

'Better!' he said. 'He's a fabulous snake.'

I held my laughter back. He was so proud of himself.

'I'll carry him in for you, so you can walk Wolfie,' I said.

Lucas took Wolfie inside, making him walk to heel, while I followed with Nick, carrying the poop snake.

Kathleen was there. She hugged me, looked at the snake, and laughed heartily.

'Lucas?' she asked. 'Is it deliberate, do you think?'

'You're the therapist.'

'Did he not warn you?' she asked, meaning Nick. 'You seem a bit shocked.'

'He didn't,' I said.

'Men!' she said. Then added, 'Oopsy. I'm supposed to be better than that.'

'Not all men. But yes, Nick.'

Kathleen led us out into the garden where there was a barbecue going and a picnic table weighed down with food and drink. I put the poop snake on the table.

Simon Ward, looked up from the barbecue, and I could see he was nervous too.

'I know you!' he said, astonished. 'The lady who needed the Manchester train. I hope you enjoyed the bread.'

'It was delicious,' I said. 'And I'm sorry I lied to you.'

'No,' he said. 'I think you were brilliant and brave and there aren't enough words. Without you –'

He introduced me to his mother, Lilian, Lucas' nan, so I got another big hug.

Lucas was training Wolfie to sit, then lie down.

'Auntie Jen,' he shouted. 'Wolfie still likes cheese.'

We had a wonderful afternoon in the garden, eating, drinking and laughing.

At the end, Simon made it clear I would always be welcome.

'No matter what happens next,' he said, 'You're part of our family now. You'll always be Lucas' Auntie Jen. And we will always, always be grateful for what you've done for us.'

'I've never had much of a family,' I said. 'But it was worth the wait to find you all.'

Nick was mostly quiet, driving me home.

Finally he spoke. 'Was I really wrong, not to warn you? I thought you'd fret and might even decide not to come.'

'You were probably right. You bastard.'

'Oh, I'm forgiven then,' he said. 'You've been so polite this afternoon, I thought we weren't friends anymore.'

Chapter Forty Five

I felt a bit lost. As if I didn't know what to do with myself now I wasn't on the run, or stressing about being on trial for murder.

Ok, there was still plenty to stress about. I wasn't looking forward to being a witness in Henry's trial.

I knew I still wanted to start up my own dog rescue, and with an emphasis on therapy dogs. I'd done introductory counselling courses, after taking advice from Kathleen, but had no plans to work with clients directly. But at a step's remove, training potential dogs and assessing their suitability, I could still do my part to support children with trauma.

I travelled back home again, to Aunt Martha's house. It had technically been my own house for more than four years but would never feel like it. I had yet to decide what, if anything, to do – whether to put it on the market, or not.

Sean was on the doorstep within ten minutes of me texting him that I'd arrived. I couldn't remember when anyone was last this keen to see me, and I was trying hard to take it slowly, to keep my heart safe, but I already knew it was no good trying. It was already lost.

He had risked first, right? I couldn't hold back forever.

We ordered a Chinese feast and ate the tiniest possible amount before we looked at each other, smiling.

Who made the first move? It was probably simultaneous.

It was also the first time Aunt Martha's sofa had seen that much fun, ever.

We were back at the kitchen table eating cold fried rice and sticky ribs when the doorbell rang.

'You have two minutes to get back into your clothes,' I said to Sean, pulling on my kaftan and going to the front door.

It was my mother.

'The village telegraph's working well then,' I said. 'Come in.'

I took her to the kitchen where Sean was busy buttoning his shirt. She was outraged. I wish I could say it was like being a teenager again, but I never had much fun back then. There was plenty of catching up to do.

'Would you like tea? Some Chinese? There's plenty,' I said.

'No thank you. I don't like any of that foreign muck,' she said.

'More for us then,' Sean said. 'Hello Mrs Blake. I don't know if you remember me? I'm Sean Hunter. I was in Jen's class at school.'

I should have introduced him, but I lose all sense when my mother's around. I become as awkward and tongue tied as I was when I was young.

My mother looked at him, ignored his outstretched hand as if it was filthy – well, she'd worked out where it had been, I suppose.

'I was going to ask you round,' I said in the silence. 'I've not decided what I'm doing with the house yet, but I thought you might like to choose some of Martha's things, to remember her by.'

'The house should have been mine,' she said.

'That was up to Martha, don't you think?' I asked.

'You manipulated her,' she said. 'You had a devilish way of getting round people. Look how you got away with kidnapping that boy. It never worked on me.'

'You read Nick's article, then,' I said. I couldn't resist fishing, provoking her.

'I didn't give permission for all those lies to be told about me, about your stepfather, about your childhood.'

'Didn't Nick contact you and give you a right to reply?'

'I wouldn't dream of talking to him. I put my trust in God, not the representatives of mammon.'

I made a mental note to tell Nick who he was representing these days.

'How sharper than a serpent's tooth it is, to have a thankless child,' I said.

She glared at me. 'Where's that from? The Bible?'

'Shakespeare. King Lear,' I said, knowing it would enrage her more, as she wouldn't be able to remind me that the Devil could quote scripture.

I followed her around the house while she assessed everything, picking out the antiques which might have some market value. Not because she liked them, or anything of that kind. Nothing sentimental about my mother.

I didn't mind. If it made her happy, I thought, knowing nothing ever could.

'Is there anything off limits?' she asked.

'Just the kids' books. I'm taking those for Lucas.'

'The child you kidnapped?' My mother is horrified.

'The child I rescued,' I said.

My mother looked at the books.

'Winnie The Pooh is a first edition. You'll let me have that?'

'No,' I stood firm. 'It's for Lucas.'

'You always were a selfish, spiteful child,' my mother said.

'Says the woman who stood by while her husband locked her daughter in a cupboard in the chapel and left her there for hours. The one who called the church elders in to hold an exorcism.'

'We were at our wits end. We didn't know what to do with you. You were constantly disobedient.'

'I wasn't partying and taking drugs, Mum. I wanted to carry on at school in the sixth form.'

At that moment, I realised I had hoped my mother might have relented a little. That my generosity might make a difference, perhaps buy an ounce of her compassion. I hadn't dared hope for affection.

'I wondered,' I asked, "If it was you that was following me, who broke into the house.'

'Why would I?'

'I thought you might be angry I hadn't answered your letters. I thought you might want me back in your life, perhaps.'

'All I want from you is a donation to save the chapel roof.'

I started to laugh. Helplessly. A real belly laugh, although it did feel as if it might tip into tears at any moment.

I'd always somehow kept alive a spark of hope, that she might one day want to be my mother. It was never going to happen. I accepted that now. Oddly, that acceptance felt better than the hope.

'Can you promise me no child will ever be locked in that new chapel, in the dark? That no child will ever be told they are possessed by demons?'

My mother was silent.

'Not that it makes any difference. I wouldn't believe your promise anyway.'

She glared at me.

'You can have any of the stuff you want, except the books. If you sell it and donate the proceeds to the chapel roof, that's your business. I'm going to be here for a while, maybe two or three weeks. You can collect it whenever. I'll instruct the solicitors to give you access, supervised access, when I leave,'

'Can't I have a key?'

'I dunno. Did you let me have a key when I was sixteen? You didn't trust me, you said.'

'That was different!'

'I think not. My house, my rules.'

Childish, but it made me feel better.

I saw her out, and watched her walking into the distance, knowing it might be the last time I saw her.

I was sad for what I'd never had; not for anything real I'd lost.

Again, I felt a surge of gratitude to Aunt Martha who had given an unhappy and uncommunicative teenager a home, and encouraged her to study and go to University and build a new life. She'd never once complained when I'd not shown more gratitude, when I hadn't ever visited.

Back in the kitchen Sean was waiting for me, chewing on a sticky pork rib.

'Don't worry, I kept half for you. I counted,' he said.

He did know me, then.

After we'd eaten, and we were sitting on the sofa, stuffed to the gunwales, and cuddling, he said, very seriously. 'Your mum's not improved much, has she?'

'I did wonder if it was all Richard, but it's pretty clear now it wasn't,' I agreed.

I thought about what Kathleen had said, about talking to people about what had happened to me in my childhood. I wondered if it might have helped, if I'd been able to talk to Matt. I never had. There was always this shameful thing I kept from him.

'I don't really talk about my childhood,' I said. 'I know you have a bit of an idea, but it was so much worse than anyone really knew.'

I told him about being locked in the vestry cupboard. He was horrified when he realised I'd had a panic attack, triggered by being in his studio. I reassured him as best I could.

'It was good for me, really. Ironically, it was a kind of exorcism. And I love that you've transformed it, with all your art on display.'

'What was so dreadful,' I said, 'was that the Superintendent of the chapel knew I'd been locked in there.

He'd heard me banging on the door, trying to get out. He found the key and unlocked it but pretended that the door had just stuck. I knew he was lying.'

'That's why you couldn't look the other way,' he said, putting his arm around me and pulling me close.

I wriggled, and he laughed. 'Okay,' he said, 'I'll let you go.'

'It's not that,' I said. 'I just wanted to tell you about it all. I've bottled it all up for too long.'

'I'm listening,' he said.

I told him the whole story. Starting with Pastor Richard organising the prayer ceremony, at the chapel. How I'd been made to kneel at the altar, with every member of the congregation looking on, as he led them in prayer, asking for me to be released of the demon.

'He named the demons Defiance and Disobedience,' I said. 'I had been led astray from the true path of the Lord.'

'I don't recall you being much of a hellraiser,' Sean said.

'I wasn't. This was all because I wanted to stay on at school, and study Maths at University.'

'Jesus,' he said.

I laughed, although I was close to tears.

'One of the chapel ladies went to tell Aunt Martha,' I said. 'That was when she rescued me and took me to live with her. Mum wouldn't stand up for me. She wouldn't even say she knew I wasn't possessed. I went with Martha, because my mother didn't want me.'

'Oh, Jen,' he said, putting his arm around me again. 'I am sorry you went through all that. I wish you'd told me then.'

'I couldn't,' I said. 'I was too ashamed. Too humiliated. It's still hard even now.'

'You, my love, have nothing to be ashamed of.'

After we had polished off the rest of the cold Chinese – high emotion made me hungry, it seemed – Sean said, 'This is probably the wrong time, but...'

'The wrong time,' I said. 'Don't be daft. And anyway, you have to say it now.'

'I thought,' he said. 'I mean, I understand you're planning to sell up here, and I can see why you might want to leave it all behind. But had you thought of staying?'

'You asking?'

'Well, yes, if you like,' he said. 'I'll even go down on one knee.'

'Just going down will be fine,' I said, and now it was his turn to laugh.

'What I was thinking of though, is your dog rescue. The old farm up the road here is for sale. They couldn't make a go of it, and it would be perfect. It needs work, but there's plenty of room. There's a farmhouse and outbuildings, and plenty of space to build runs and kennels. And...'

'You've thought about this, haven't you?' I asked.

'I've thought about nothing else,' he said.

I looked at him, and I said, 'Well, there's a few things I need to sort out. But we can go have a look at this farm tomorrow, if you like. But in principle it sounds like a good idea.'

Chapter Forty Six

Two weeks later, I reluctantly returned to Brighton. I'd had a wonderful time with Sean, and I was waiting on surveyors' reports on the Old Brook Farmstead before we decided on our future.

I'd been doing some deep thinking on another question, and I called Nick, asking if he could possibly arrange another visit to see the Wards.

'I think Wolfie's pining for Lucas,' I said. 'It doesn't have to be a long visit, perhaps we can call in on the way somewhere else?'

Nick laughed. 'So now you want me to make up an excuse for you?' I'll see what I can do.'

A couple of days later he drove me to London again. I told Nick I was thinking of moving back north.

'To live in your Aunt Martha's house?' he asked.

'Well, no. Or maybe. It's not decided yet.'

'You're blushing. Come on. Spill.'

'Okay. I met someone. I really like him. There's a farm for sale, nearby, and it would be great for my dog rescue place. I'm a bit reluctant, because well, it's awfully close to where my mother is. Distance makes it easier to cope with how she feels about me. And how I feel about her, too.'

'You're the only person I know who could fall in love when on the run with a kidnapped child.'

'I didn't. Well, not then, it took time. And I've known him since I was ten, eleven.'

'That's okay then,' Nick said. 'Seriously, I'm thrilled for you.'

It was too cold to spend all our visit in the garden, though Wolfie would have welcomed rolling in the mud.

Lucas was delighted to see us again, and this time I got a hug as well as Wolfie. I'd been worried that at some level, he was holding on to some pain that I'd abandoned him.

In the kitchen, alone with Simon, I raised an idea.

'When I was reading all those interviews,' I said, 'and trying to work out what to do, I saw you'd always had dogs in your childhood and wanted to have one again.'

'Yes...' he said, warily.

'It's just an idea, and I will understand if you say no. He's a whole lot of dog. A handful. But he loves Lucas and Lucas loves him...' My voice trailed off.

'Do I have this right?' he said. 'You're offering to let us have Wolfie? But he's your dog.'

'He was our dog, mine and Lucas', for longer than he was ever mine,' I said. 'And I'd insist on visiting rights, of course.'

'I think that would be wonderful,' Simon said. 'I know Lucas would be ecstatic. Mum, well, she'd get used to it.'

'I thought it might give him a bit of continuity,' I said. 'Anyway, I'm opening my rescue soon, I hope. I'll have to get used to parting with them, once someone else needs them more.'

'It's extraordinarily kind of you,' he said. 'If you're sure.'

'I am,' I said.

'How's everything else going?' Simon asked. 'I know this trial must be hanging over you.'

'I'm so scared. I keep on thinking, what if they decide it **was** me? The whole thing is a mess. And I had as much motive as Henry.'

Simon looked at me, thoughtfully.

'You are the bravest person I've ever known,' he said. 'When you rescued Lucas, you did what you thought was right no matter what the consequences would be for you. You were ready to give your life up for him.'

'I still would,' I said, looking towards Lucas.

'More than that, you were brave enough to bring him home. That took courage too.'

I smiled at him through my tears.

'You can do this, Jen. I have faith in you. It shines through you're a good person. Tell the truth, and the jury will see that. I promise you.'

'I hope you're right,' I said.

'You'd better tell Lucas about Wolfie then,' Simon said.

I went out into the garden, and watched boy and dog playing for a minute, sure I'd made the right decision.

Lucas saw me.

'See, Aunty Jen, he sits when I say now.'

He did too.

'You're going to have to keep up the training,' I said. 'Maybe even take him to obedience classes.'

'Why will I?'

'He's your dog now, Lucas. He was missing you so much.'

Lucas was speechless for a moment, his mouth open. 'Are you sure, Aunty Jen? Won't he miss you too?'

'Maybe an itty-bitty bit. But yes, I am sure.'

I had the best hug ever.

The house was oddly quiet without Wolfie.

Lainey kept trying to persuade me to adopt another dog, and of course it would eventually happen. Possibly even before setting up my own dog rescue.

In the meantime, on Kathleen's advice, I took some more courses at the local college. I needed to know more about theories of trauma and trauma counselling, she said, before taking the plunge to include the training and placement of therapy dogs in my rescue plans.

'It's not all going to be as simple and natural as working with Lucas and Wolfie,' she said.

'Simple and natural,' I repeated and laughed.

'Okay,' she said. 'That's not the best way of putting it, I concede. But you do need some theoretical framework.'

Chioma phoned.

'DI Carstairs wants to see you,' she said. 'If you can come into the office this morning. He won't say what it's about, but obviously it has something to do with the trial.'

I was nervous walking into Chioma's office. Carstairs was already there, and they were chatting over coffee like old friends.

I sat down, braced for the worst.

'Hello Ms Blake,' Carstairs said. 'No need to look as if you're worried you might be breakfast. I've already eaten.'

Chioma snorted, having apparently forgotten she was supposed to be on my side.

'I am worried sick,' I said. 'In a few days I'll be on the witness stand and I am terrified.'

'I don't think you need to be,' he said.

'I wanted to talk to you about those texts and emails. I know you didn't want to hand them over, and I think now I see why.'

'Oh?' I said, in a small voice.

'You thought they were damning of you, right? I mean, I understand. When they started up, you'd been arrested for Matt's murder. You were on police bail. It must have been scary.'

'Just a little,' I said. 'That, plus you were apparently convinced I did it.'

'I knew you were holding something back,' he said. 'In an intelligent person, that's usually not a good sign.'

'Flatterer.'

'Anyway, we sorted them all out. The emails from Amy, fairly obvious. The unhinged ones, well, I can't prove it yet, but I'd guess your mother-in-law, right? Especially as they carried on while Henry no longer had access to his phone.'

'I thought so. Even though the language was not like her in real life.'

'It leaves these, from Henry. We found his spare phone, his burner, when we searched the house. Fingerprinting proved it wasn't Amy's. Also, the silent phone calls were from the same number. But when you read them all in order, it's more of a confession.'

'Oh.'

'I can understand why you missed it. You were all caught up with Lucas by that point. But listen. These texts tell a story. And they can only be from Henry.'

We're both on the same side in this. Why can't you see that?

I wanted to talk to you. There was no need to run away.

Why did you tell me? I know I started it, but you must have known how I'd feel.

I suppose you think I should face the music. No chance. You are as much to blame.

I tried to phone you, but I couldn't speak. I want to talk. Talk to me. Please.

Without you, without your refusal to help me, none of this would have happened.

You're as much to blame for this as Matt. You should have kept him in line.

You pushed me to the limit. I pushed him. Cause and effect. It's your fault as much as mine.

I listened, astounded.

'He couldn't handle it,' Carstairs said. 'It's not unusual. And he blurted it all out in texts to you.'

'They sounded mad enough one at a time,' I said. 'I'd never looked at them as a sequence before.'

'You should have trusted me, Ms Blake.'

'I never trust anyone,' I said.

'I can confirm,' said Chioma.

'I'll put all these into evidence tomorrow,' he said. It's a bit late as a submission, but it can't be helped.'

I was also holding more evidence back. I would have to ponder that some more – awful and humiliating as it was. With these texts, it wasn't quite so damning of me, perhaps. And anyway, it was equally relevant to Henry's motivation.

I was home when DI Coleman came calling at lunchtime. I was sitting at the kitchen table with my books, studying.

Initially I was glad of the interruption when I answered the door and recognised her.

She wasn't smiling though.

'Lucas has been taken again,' she said, straight off, while she was still on the doorstep.

Stunned, I led the way to the kitchen and put the kettle on.

'How? How is that possible? I know he'd recently gone back to school, but surely everyone was on high alert.'

'We haven't worked it out yet. It was the last day of term so they finished early – around lunchtime I gather. He wasn't there when Simon arrived to collect him, and we've checked all the CCTV in the area. There's no sign of him going off with anyone else, or on his own.'

'And the Grays? I know Nick has a contact who swears they've gone to ground in Spain. There are little - and not so little – outcrops of these cults everywhere.'

'There's no sign of them so far. I wondered if there was anything you found, anything at all, when you were trying to work out how to best return Lucas?'

'I'm sure I told you everything at the time,' I said. 'I watched so many of those awful videos and trawled through so many of those toxic websites, I was frankly glad to forget about it all.'

'I know,' she said. 'It's a real sewer. I'm sure these nutters have always existed but being online amplifies it – they find each other and wind each other up.'

'I'll talk to Nick,' I said. 'Maybe two brains and all that. He's steeped in it all, researching his book. I don't know how he can bear it.'

'Thanks, Jen,' she said. 'And to think I demanded you do no more freelance police work.'

'Poor Lucas,' I said, tears filling my eyes. 'I promise, if I think of anything I'll let you know straight away.'

When she left, I called Nick.

He'd already spoken to Simon and was also racking his brains.

'I'm sure there's something,' I said. 'At the back of my mind. But maybe I'm imagining.'

Nick suggested asking Kathleen's help – perhaps she could hypnotise, help me to recover lost memories.

The following morning, he came to collect me.

Together, we explained to Kathleen what we needed.

'The poor boy,' she said. 'We always say kids are resilient, because of course they have a survival instinct. Most of the time, except in the most extreme circumstances, they cope with what life throws at them. And he is a very bright and a very strong boy. All the same, this is terrible.'

'I don't know what his mother is thinking,' I said, 'Putting him through all this.'

'Of course you don't, Jen,' she said, smiling at me.

'I'm not breaking any duty of confidentiality to tell you that in general, the family courts recognise children should have access to both parents. Sometimes, it's better that the access should be supervised. Some people cannot bear to be denied anything they want – or even recognise that what they want should always be negotiated with other people. This is all covered in the courses you're doing, Jen.'

I nodded.

'Right, so we will see what we can do to recover any memories you've lost that might help. I promise you it's not at all invasive or dangerous. I won't lead you or prompt you. It will be a matter of relaxing and listening to me as I suggest you allow memories to float to the surface.'

I sat relaxed in the chair, half dozing, listening and remembering. It was bitter-sweet, thinking back to all that time with Lucas and Wolfie, running in the park. Sean too, and all the pottery. The morning he gave me a bacon butty.

I sat up, and almost yelped.

'That's it,' I said. 'How could I have forgotten.'

I scrolled back through the photos on my phone, until I found the one of Louisa with Verity, Lucas, Arthur and her then baby. Just weeks, at most before I took him – so well after he'd been snatched from the school gates.

I showed Kathleen and Nick and forwarded the photo to DI Coleman, and she phoned me immediately.

'I am sorry,' I said. 'If I'd told you all when you were questioning me, all this could have been avoided. Louisa Scott is the mother of Lucas' best friend Arthur. She was still in touch with Verity long after Lucas was snatched. She must have taken him.'

'Ye Gods,' she said. 'I'll let you know what we find out.'

When I got home to what I was expecting would be an empty house, Sean was sitting on a small holdall, on the top step.

'What are you doing here?' I asked.

'I heard about Lucas,' he said. 'And a little bird told me you were fretting about the trial. I came to support you.'

'Was that little bird called Nick, perchance?'

A person less like a little bird I had ever to meet.

Sean laughed.

'Blame me, blame me Nick, blame anyone and everyone. I don't care. I'm here, okay.'

'Okay,' I said, in a quiet voice.

So many people believing in me, and I wasn't capable of believing in myself.

He cooked for me, and we sat and talked over his special Spanish omelette, with a glass of red.

'I know you're still worried about committing to the dog rescue, up at the farm. But I think I can set your mind at rest, at least on one problem.'

'Oh?'

'Your mum,' Sean said. 'She's sold up and moved. I asked around, and no one knows where she's gone.'

'Oh,' I said again. I felt sharp pang, hurt that she hadn't told me, even though I knew it was stupid.

'I asked around. Someone at her church thought perhaps she'd moved to Spain. Easier on her arthritis, or something.'

I suppose that made sense. Although I never imagined it possible that she'd leave that church. It had been her whole life for so long.

I took a deep breath.

'Okay, I'll put an offer in on the farm then, if it's not too late.'

'I was hoping you'd say that,' Sean said. 'I would have moved for you, although...'

'No, you need to be near your boys,' I said. 'I know that. I don't want to take you away from your family.'

I poured us each another glass of red, and then I told him how DI Carstairs had put the texts together.

'He seems sure it doesn't implicate me. But he doesn't know all of it. I was too ashamed, embarrassed, humiliated. I couldn't tell him.'

He looked at me, seriously. 'Is there anything you've not told me? Because this is amazing. You're a real hero. Why would that be a problem?'

I looked down.

'There's something I've not told anyone,' I said. 'Not even my lawyer.

I told him everything. All about the document I'd found, and how it gave me a motive to kill Matt and how embarrassing and humiliating it all was.

When I'd finished, he said, 'Oh Jen. You are still carrying around these feelings from your childhood. You had nothing to feel ashamed and humiliated about. You didn't then, and you don't now.'

I hadn't seen the connection, but it was there, somewhere. All part of the pattern of keeping everything to myself, not trusting anyone, and internalising the blame for everything.

I smiled at him, through tears.

'It's not anything like as bad as you think. Your part in this – none of it is your fault. I know that you feel hurt and humiliated, but you have to tell your lawyer. Promise me?'

I did.

'Thank you for trusting me,' he said. 'You don't know how much it means to me.'

He talked me into phoning Chioma, and she agreed with him. I had to scan and email the documents. She said she'd talk to Carstairs, and that they would be passed on to prosecution and defence. That was it would all go into disclosure ahead of the trial.

'If we're lucky, Carstairs won't have submitted the texts into evidence yet,' she said. 'But it's not unusual in itself for the evidence bundles to be all in a muddle. You tell the whole truth about when you found it and why you didn't pass it on earlier. You're human. The jury will get it.'

Meanwhile, Lucas was still missing, and I was fretting. Obviously. What did the rest of it matter in comparison to that?

Chapter Forty Seven

I'd spent so much time worrying about being a witness in Henry Thompson's trial for the murder of my husband, that it was strange to feel I couldn't give a damn.

All I could think about was Lucas. I'd put on my precious necklace he'd made from polymer clay for me to wear to court.

The trial still mattered. I'd hoped for a time that it had been a stupid accident, or even that Matt had killed himself, unlikely as that had seemed. I'd only gradually come to realise that Henry must have killed him. Matt deserved justice.

My fear of public humiliation was as nothing. I didn't care anymore that everyone was going to know what Matt did to me, and why. All that mattered was that Lucas came safely home.

Simon Ward phoned to wish me the best for the trial. 'It seems a strange thing to say,' he said, 'But good luck. I hope it goes well.'

'I'd ask how you're all feeling,' I said, 'but that's a stupid question.'

'Wolfie is pining,' he said. 'We all are. It seems harder to bear, after having him home at last, and for such a short time.'

My head was still a mess, though. Would the jury understand why I'd been reluctant to talk about everything, why I'd held back information from the police investigation? The prosecution had a strategy to communicate it all, but then Henry's defence would have their turn and do everything they could to undermine me.

I knew I hadn't murdered Matt, of course. Any residual belief I had in the integrity of the police had been shattered by recent experiences – though not by DI Carstairs who had initially had me down as a killer. He turned out to be the good cop in the end. Maybe I should have told the truth, the whole truth from the beginning.

I was already on bail for murder when I found actual, documentary evidence, that was part of the problem. I was on the defensive by then, outraged at being a suspect.

Who would have believed me, simply based on hearsay? What Matt had told me was deranged, as well as illegal. Maybe Carstairs would have found the evidence eventually. I don't know.

Sadie Bell, the prosecution barrister, warned me in advance there were going to be difficult questions – from her, not from Henry's defence. 'It's best to spoil their arguments in advance,' she said.

It made sense, but I didn't have to enjoy it.

The moment I was on the stand, my nerves all came back. I was terrified I would make a hash of it, with my mind being on other things being so obvious, that the jury would read the wrong implication into it.

I touched the necklace at my throat, as if it were a talisman.

When I made the affirmation, swearing to tell the truth, I heard a snort. Eve was in the court, watching. She wasn't to be called as a witness. Her certainty that I, and I alone, was to blame for Matt's death didn't endear her to either prosecution or defence.

Sadie Bell stood, and my ordeal began.

I was on the stand for what seemed like an aeon. Most of my answers were uncontroversial, so unlikely to be challenged by the defence.

Yes, I knew about Matt's affair with Amy. Henry Thompson had told me. He was very distressed, yes. He had approached me in the park and told me there, three months before I threw Matt out.

I hadn't been surprised, exactly. Not because Matt was a bad husband, or a serial adulterer, but because he'd been unhappy and disengaged from everything. The IVF treatment and the sequence of losses had been hard on both of us.

I hadn't challenged Matt. I was waiting it out and hoping I'd get pregnant and the affair would pass.

So far, so good.

I mean, not good exactly, but it was all widely known. No one could contradict it or prove it wrong.

The first area where I was on shaky ground was the letter from Matt giving me permission to use the last remaining embryos. Exhibit C1 was the letter I'd taken to the clinic, and which our counsellor had handed in to the police.

It was, granted, a confusing story. Matt had told the clinic he no longer wanted the final embryos used. I hadn't known. I'd gone down to visit him in our cottage and asked him to sign my letter, giving me permission to use them. I'd had no idea that he wouldn't be alive to back me up. That was a key point.

If I'd known, I'd have assumed he would repent of his earlier decision. That was just Matt. He had loved me, in his own way.

I had searched through all the documents I could find, showing several different variants of Matt's signature. In the end, the handwriting experts had agreed it was his, to the intense disappointment – at that point in time – of DI Carstairs.

I thought Sadie Bell had done a good job of making all of this clear, but the defence would still be sure to try to use it to trip me up.

Then the humiliation began.

Sadie knew, and I knew what was coming. The defence barrister perked up – this was going to be his lever, he hoped. Patrick Neel, QC. I knew he was only doing his job, but I hated him anyway.

'Ms Blake, when you were searching for documents with Matt's signature, you found something else, didn't you?'

'I did.'

'A document with Matt's signature, and Amy's. A legal document of sorts.'

'If *of sorts* includes illegal documents, yes,' I said.

The courtroom was silent. The jury avid.

'Could you please describe the contents of this document to the court. Exhibit C2, everyone.'

'It was a kind of surrogacy agreement drawn up between Matt and Amy. An illegal arrangement, made after she became pregnant, that in exchange for a series of payments she would give up legal custody of her child to the father. Matt Taylor.'

At that point Eve lost control. 'Liar,' she shouted at me, across the court room.

The judge intervened. 'Mrs Taylor, I know this is emotionally draining for you. I am very sorry for your loss. But please do control yourself, or I will have no choice but to exclude you from the court.'

'Sorry, your Honour,' she mumbled.

Pity she didn't get thrown out. I didn't want her to see my humiliation.

'And both of them signed it.' Sadie continued.

'Yes.'

'Was this the first you had heard of this somewhat unorthodox and highly illegal arrangement?'

'It was not.'

'I know this is difficult, but please can you tell the court how you found out about this, and when. In your own words.'

'It was the day we split up. We had a huge argument, on the way back from the IVF clinic. It continued when we arrived home. Matt sprang such a lot on me all at once, it was overwhelming. First he told me he'd sold NRS Tech, behind my back. I did have a choice, even though he and Eve had sold their shares to the new owner. I could have stayed on in my own company as minority shareholder – still been part of NRS Tech, the company I founded and named, but I'd have had no say in its direction.'

'That was a shock, right?'

'I knew he was unhappy, dissatisfied. But I didn't realise how much. I was very angry, yes, but we could have worked something out.'

'But there was more,' Sadie prompted.

'He confessed to the affair with Amy.' I stopped. I didn't want to go on. This was already the most humiliating part of my life and it was about to get worse.

'I know this is difficult. Please, Ms Blake, Jen, please go on.'

The human touch, that simple Jen, near broke me. It was intended of course. It would make me more sympathetic to the jury.

'I laughed at him. Said I already knew about Amy. Asked if he thought I was stupid. I was stupid. I didn't know.'

I paused. Wiped my tears.

'He told me Amy was pregnant with his child. It was like being punched in the stomach, so soon after my last miscarriage. I told him to leave. To go, live with the woman. He could go off and have a perfect family and ditch me. The barren one. Leave me on my own.

But Jen, he said. *I love you. I don't want to leave you. Amy doesn't matter to me, not like you do.*

I swore at him. Told him to leave. Told him he couldn't have his cake and eat it.

Amy knows it's just a fling, he said. *I was clear from the start. She doesn't want the kid, either. Jen, the child could be ours. She's agreed to give up custody to me, as the child's father. You could adopt.*

I started weeping, quietly. Tears flowing.

The judge adjourned for fifteen minutes, to give me time to collect myself.

When the hearing started again, I looked at Eve. She was white a sheet. Looked as if she might pass out from shock.

Sadie gently asked. 'Please could you recount the rest of your conversation.

'I asked him if he was insane. If he realised the agreement wasn't legal. He said, yes, he knew. But it was what Amy wanted – money, not the child. *Of course she'd have liked to have me as well*, he said. *She's one for the main chance. But she'll take the money. I'm sure of that.*

He'd made a down payment, too, he said. There's evidence in his bank statement.'

Sadie said, 'Please see Exhibit 3 c.'

A few people gasped. They might well.

'Please carry on,' Sadie said.

'I said do you know how humiliating this is? I'm not stupid. People gossip. I've heard all about Amy. I know she's a younger version of me. And now she's pregnant with your child? How could you do this to me?

But that's the point, he said. *She does look like you did, when you were younger. The child would be ours, Jen. Or as near as makes no difference.*

I started throwing things. I kept on, breaking things and throwing them and screaming. Until he left.'

'And you'd had a previous conversation about surrogacy, right?'

'We had.'

'And what was the outcome?'

'He'd wanted to go abroad. There are countries where you can pay a poor woman to carry a baby for you. It was what he wanted to do with the last set of embryos.'

'And you didn't want that?'

'I did not.'

'It would have given you a better chance of having your own baby, and you still didn't want it?'

'I don't like the idea of surrogacy. Not for money. It's repugnant to me, to ask a woman who is poor and needs the money to put her health on the line. Remember, I know what the treatment is like, the toll it takes on your body.'

'And Matt didn't understand?'

'I thought he did, but apparently he managed to come up with a worse idea. With help from his girlfriend, Amy Thompson'

It took a lot of self-control to manage not to say, *that bitch Amy*.

Sadie asked the key question next.

'Did Henry Thompson know about this agreement?'

'I assumed he did,' I said. 'Matt had paid Amy a lot of money. I thought he must know. At first, I thought they were in on it together. But when I told him, he flew into a rage. He didn't believe me. I made a copy of the agreement and gave it to him.'

'And you didn't tell the police. Why, may I ask?'

'At first, I thought Matt had killed himself. I was just saving myself humiliation. But then when it became clear that he had been murdered, I thought it was my fault. That I'd given Henry the motive.'

Sadie referred to the texts. 'And this is what Henry Thompson means by this string of abusive texts he sent you?'

'I think so.'

Sadie asked a few more questions, and I answered on automatic, totally wrung out.

Yes, it was Henry's baby. This was eventually proved by DNA testing. But Matt had believed it was his. Amy too, or she'd pretended to. I'd believed Matt and Amy.

The judge declared a recess, so at least I had a break before the defence started on me.

Round and round it went. Why had I held back this oh so convenient explanation of Henry's motive. Why had I not produced this story in my defence, rather than allow the police to continue investigating me for murder.

Let those who are without sin cast the first stone.

I told the truth.

'I felt sorry for Henry. I understood what had driven him to murder, although I thought it had been in the heat of the moment rather than premeditated.

'I was grieving. I still missed Matt. I had loved him. I didn't think I'd ever have forgiven him. I had thought at first he'd killed himself because of that. The unfinished email to me, the apology, on his laptop. Even the police thought it was a suicide note at first.

'Once it became clear Henry must have killed him, it was hard. I was still humiliated. I didn't want anyone to know.

'Amy was constantly emailing and pressuring me for money for the baby.

'And I was getting nasty, vicious texts that could only be from Henry. Saying that even if I didn't kill Matt, I had set it all in motion. It had all been my fault.

'I couldn't believe he was justifying himself that way. He and Amy deserved each other perhaps. But he would have let me be prosecuted, maybe go to prison, for a murder he committed.

'DI Carstairs had pressed me. He knew there was something I'd been holding back – it was why he had suspected me.

Eventually I came to my senses. You'll understand, I was under a lot of pressure for unrelated reasons. I was finally able to confide in my solicitor. And so here we are.'

If anything, I think the defence made things worse for their client, not better.

Once my turn on the stand was over, I was exhausted, but I still planned to stay and watch how the rest of the trial unfolded. I felt I owed it to Matt.

Chioma talked to me, as we took a break in the waiting area, outside the court room.

'You did the right thing,' she said. 'I know it was hard, but the jury warmed to you. Your pain was visible. That's not humiliating, Jen. That's human. And the documentation, showing how damn crazy Matt was – well it helped explain the state you were in.'

'I was worried it would make them think I had killed him,' I said. 'It was certainly crazy-making enough.'

'But it made Henry crazy too. And those texts you produced proved it. They showed him unravelling.'

I was about to go back into the courtroom, when my phone rang. I had a call from DI Coleman.

'Get a wriggle on, woman. I need your help. They're in Brighton.'

Chapter Forty Eight

I raced home. DI Coleman was waiting in her car outside the Victoria Park house. She had the door open, waiting for me impatiently.

I didn't stop to ask any questions. I parked up and got into the passenger seat next to her. She had the door open waiting for me, impatiently. A taxi went past at speed and damn near took the door with it.

'Thank God you were only on the stand for a day,' she said. 'My team's busy scouring the area, but we were hoping you might help us track them down.'

'I'm catching up here,' I said, confused. 'Brighton?'

'Mobile phone signal,' she said. 'Once we knew who the likely culprit was it was relatively easy to get a warrant and the mobile provider has been very co-operative.'

'Oh,' I said. 'I thought Nick said he'd heard the Grays were in Spain somewhere?'

'Louisa could be on her way to meet the Grays, we think. Or vice versa. All bets are off at the moment.'

'What about her husband? Is he not being any help? He's not with them, is he?'

'We're not sure what's going on there,' she said. 'He's on some kind of business trip in the US and we've not been able to track him down yet. It looks like she waited until he was gone to set the plan in motion.'

I was still in shock, really. It was only a couple of hours after I'd been on the witness stand giving evidence in a murder trial and now I was off on a mad hide and seek mission in Brighton.

'CCTV gave us some clues as the route. It seems like some kind of magical mystery tour, to try to mislead us. So far they've been to Stonehenge and the New Forest. It's not how I'd travel to Brighton from North London.'

'It sounds like something's gone wrong, doesn't it? Surely if she's taking Lucas to his mother, going directly there would be for the best.'

'You'd think so. Travelling with a toddler and two nine-year olds is no picnic,' DI Coleman said. 'I'll bet she's knackered and locking down for a couple of days. The longer she's not been caught, the more secure she's going to assume she is.'

'That's not the way it works,' I said, with great feeling.

DI Coleman looked at me and laughed. 'I rather think you're in a different category than most,' she said. 'I don't think we'd ever have found you, if you didn't want to be found.'

'I'm glad you asked me along, but I'm not quite sure why,' I said.

'We reckon you're our best bet for recognising Louisa Scott. And reassuring Lucas, when we find them. You did great work in snapping that photo, but there's no substitute for having actually met someone in the flesh.'

'It's been a while. I mean, I'd even forgotten meeting her.'

'It's not like the telly,' DI Coleman added. 'We can't pinpoint a phone that closely, especially in a highly populated area.'

'Okay,' I said. 'If Louisa's anything like Verity, they'll be looking for vegan food. Karma Kafe first? It's not very likely, but it's all I can think of.'

'It's a good start,' she said. 'From what we found out the Karma Kafe was also a hub of cult activity. Might be somewhere they'd choose to hand Lucas over?'

DI Coleman parked outside the cafe. As we walked in, everything went suspiciously quiet. Lena had a print of a photo of Louisa Scott and the waitresses barely glanced at it, before saying they'd not seen her. The girl who I'd been friendly with before just blanked me. Well, I hadn't liked their flapjacks anyway. No loss.

After we left, DI Coleman said, 'I've been made more welcome in an actual den of thieves.'

'It's a bit counter cultural anyway,' I said. 'But I detected a bit of extra animus, I thought. Maybe Louisa has been here before us, or the Grays.'

By ten we decided it was pointless searching any more. The mobile signal had dropped out for a while, leading DI Coleman to worry Louisa had decided to get a burner phone.

I remembered how much damn trouble it was and how I kept getting everything confused.

After an hour or so, the signal pinged again. Perhaps she had been recharging.

DI Coleman's team had rooms in a B&B in Saltdean, and I invited her to stay the night with me and Sean at the Victoria Park house.

I introduced Sean and the DI and apologised to her. 'I never got around to sorting out the spare bedroom here, so I'm afraid I can only offer you the couch. But it is pretty comfortable.'

First, we shared an Indian takeaway at the kitchen table.

'You can't call me DI Coleman while we're fighting over the last poppadom,' she said. 'It's got to be Lena.'

'Sorry. I keep forgetting,' I said.

I set my phone alarm for eight am, thinking that was quite early enough when we were on the tail of a woman travelling with two nine-year-old boys and one toddler.

We were barely awake and sleep-drinking coffee, which Sean had made, bleary eyed, when Lena's mobile rang. She put it on speakerphone. It was one of her officers.

'She's on the move ma'am,' I overheard. 'The mobile signal's showing they're in Newhaven now.'

'Oh shit,' I said. 'We'd best get moving. The ferry leaves for Dieppe at nine.'

'We have posted alerts for all the ports and airports,' Lena said. 'But all the same, I'd rather we were there if at all possible.' She called the Newhaven Port Authority and officially requested their help.

There was a lot of grumbling but they agreed to check Louisa hadn't boarded, or the Grays.

By the time we got there, the ferry was on its way out to sea. No one had seen a woman with three children, or a couple with one child, and none of the names had shown up in bookings.

'Have you checked the other possibilities?' I asked. 'Have you checked Portsmouth, Plymouth, Dover. Gatwick? Shoreham Airport?'

'We are the police. We do know how this works,' she said. Then she relented. 'Louisa's not booked anywhere. It's my view she's meeting the Grays somewhere, though God only knows what name they're traveling under.'

We collected sandwiches, salads and take-away coffee from the supermarket before meeting with the rest of DI Coleman's team, which had been extended by a couple of volunteers from the Brighton force who remembered Lucas.

The mobile signal was gone now. She'd turned her phone off or run out of charge. Or was it more deliberate?

Between us we decided Dover was the most likely option. DI Coleman drove along the coast road, while the rest of the team split up – two to Gatwick, while the other two took the motorway, driving west.

'Google Maps says it's about two hours away,' I said. 'Same by motorway too.'

The mobile operator called when we were about fifteen minutes from Dover. We'd picked right – they were already in Dover. I was so worried. There were ferries from Dover at all hours – not just twice a day like Newhaven. My stupid lapse of memory had caused all this.

'You think it's your fault, don't you?' DI Coleman said. 'But consider this. If you'd told us, and Louisa had been questioned, they might have found someone else to take him. And we'd have no chance at all. This way there's hope.'

Then her phone rang again.

'Whoop,' DI Coleman was pleased. 'Louisa's just booked a ticket. For nine 'o'clock tonight. We can relax now.'

'What if she's deliberately booked it and they are off somewhere else now?' I asked. 'She's been leading us a merry dance.'

'Maybe she has, or maybe not. I am not sure she seems quite that bright to me.'

'We have to pass the time until nine,' I said. 'And given Louisa has dragged them round Stonehenge and the New Forest, maybe we should take a wander around Dover Castle.'

'Go on, then,' she said. 'It's a long shot, but we need to stretch our legs.'

'Which carpark?' she asked.

'Lower?' I suggested.

After Lena parked up, we bought two tickets and allowed ourselves to be talked into a guidebook before we wandered up to the actual castle.

It was huge. Even if they were there, we surely had no chance of finding them.

Just then we had another call. Louisa's mobile signal had disappeared again.

'What did I tell you?' I said. 'She's messing with us.'

I flicked through the guidebook, reading up on the gatehouses and towers and the huge stone keep.

'The curtain wall is nearly a mile long! We'll never find them.'

We sat on one of the many benches, watching all the tourists go by.

Lena said, 'Maybe we should check all the car parks? If they're here, she must have parked, right?'

We were arguing about what to do when the mobile operator called back.

'False alarm,' she said. 'Definitely in Dover still.'

Lena said, 'We might as well relax. We'll intercept them at boarding. It's the only way.'

I was still flicking through the castle guidebook.

'I know where they are,' I said. I jumped up and started running.

Lena followed me, grumbling.

'There's tunnels,' I said, gasping for breath. 'That's why the phone signal disappeared. The tour lasts fifty minutes. It all fits.'

I paused, looking around.

'I can hear him,' I said. 'I can hear Lucas' voice.'

I started running again.

'Just wishful thinking,' Lena said.

'No, that's him,' I said. 'But I still can't see him.'

'Auntie Jen!' a voice shouted.

There was a boy, running towards me, wearing a red hoodie. Behind him a woman with a toddler and another boy. She didn't know what to do, but her first instinct was to get up and run in the opposite direction, dragging her own two with her.

DI Coleman had a surprising turn of speed. She intercepted Louisa and had her in cuffs in no time.

'Auntie Jen,' Lucas collided with me, and wrapped his arms around me, hugging me tightly to him.

'I knew you'd come and find me,' he said, letting go.

'I had to,' I said. 'Wolfie is missing you.'

Then, he reached out his hand. 'You're wearing the necklace I made,' he said, touching it.

'I wear it a lot,' I said. 'It's my favourite necklace.'

I got on the phone to Simon at once. I didn't even give him a chance to speak, I said, 'I have someone here who wants to talk to you.

'Dad,' Lucas said. 'I'm sorry, I was so stupid. I didn't think.'

I could hear Simon sounding very calm and saying,' It's not your fault. It's never been your fault. Lucas, you are only nine.'

'I'll bring him home,' I said to Simon.

'No,' he said firmly. 'I'll drive down to you. You must be exhausted after the trial and everything.'

I was, so I didn't argue. Anyway Simon was crying. He'd held it together for his boy, and suddenly all that fear and foreboding had nowhere else to go. I quietly said goodbye and hung up.

'What happened, Lucas?' I asked. 'Everyone thought you were safely at school.'

'It was Arthur,' he said. 'We were in the playground, and he said, let's skip maths. We can slip out under the fence and go and get an ice cream from the shop. His mum was in the shop, waiting. She was cross with us and said she'd take us home. She took us to their house, and I wanted to call Dad but she wouldn't let me.'

'Then when I thought she was taking me home, she didn't. She kept driving and driving and she shouted at me for pestering her. Then she told me my mum was missing me, and only a cruel boy would not want to see his mum, and she was taking me to see her for a quick visit, and then I could go home to Dad and Nana. But I think that was a lie.'

'It probably was,' I said.

'I'll never be naughty again,' he vowed.

At that I started to laugh and couldn't stop.

Later that evening, when we were all together at my house – Lena, Sean, Nick, Simon and Kathleen sitting with me at the kitchen table, and Lucas curled up on the couch with Wolfie, I was contented. I belonged with these people, in some strange way. I liked them, and they liked me.

I almost didn't care what the verdict was in Henry's trial. I'd done my best. Told the truth and shamed the Devil.

'You know,' I said. 'I have a lot to thank Henry for, really.'

Sean snorted. 'Don't say that in public,' he said. 'You're talking about the man who killed your husband.'

'Oh, I don't mean that,' I said, blushing. 'No, I meant this. He told me about the affair. Then after Matt's death – he wouldn't stop pestering me. He turned up on the doorstep, for fuck's sake. He even made a pass at me. As revenge. Ugh.'

'I didn't realise that,' Nick said, 'until you mentioned it in court, on the stand.'

'I didn't tell anyone,' I said. 'But that was why I moved. Not just the journalists. So that's how I ended up in this house. It's how I found the locks on the middle bedroom door. If I hadn't, I would never have found Lucas, and all this' I gestured around – 'would never have happened.'

'It doesn't bear thinking about,' said Simon.

'It really doesn't,' said Sean.

Chapter Forty Nine

DI Coleman had been right. Louisa had no fight in her. Lena reckoned she was worn out by looking after the boys. More than once, Lucas had tried to tell strangers he'd been kidnapped, and wanted to go home. She'd managed to convince them all it was a joke, that he was angry because his dad hadn't come with them – anything that made him look like a badly behaved kid.

People didn't want to get involved. Why didn't any of them think to check?

The plan had been to take Lucas three days earlier, but her husband's business trip had been delayed.

That answered one question. Her husband wasn't involved. Probably.

She'd managed to stop the Grays from leaving too early, but then hadn't been able to get in touch with them. They were still out there, somewhere. On the run, again.

Meanwhile, at the Old Bailey, the jury found Henry guilty of murder. All that was left was the sentencing. None of it would bring Matt back, but it was, I guess, what they call closure.

Or almost.

I drove over to my mother-in-law's house. I sat in the car for a few moments, wondering whether I should confront her, or let it go.

My instinct was to walk away, and yet that instinct hadn't always served me well. She had, after all, tried to destroy my life and for what? Where did her conviction I'd killed Matt come from?

Amy, perhaps.

Eve answered the door.

'Hello,' I said. 'I think it's time we had a talk, don't you?'

'You never would call me mother,' Eve said, all injured innocence. 'I suppose it's too late now.'

It most certainly is, I thought.

Eve led the way into her lounge. She gestured for me to sit on the most uncomfortable chair but didn't offer a drink. Hospitable as ever.

'No Amy?' I asked. 'Of course not. She's back in the family home now, her and the baby. Henry will undoubtedly be going to prison for a long stretch though. I expect that will be fine with Amy.'

'I wasn't expecting you to care,' she said. 'But that was my last chance at a grandchild.'

'She was only welcome as long as she had Matt's baby. I suppose I should be relieved it wasn't only me who didn't make the grade.'

'Don't be ridiculous,' Eve said.

'I paid Amy a rather large sum of money, on the understanding she was carrying Matt's child. I know what it's like to feel cheated. By her, and by Matt.'

'She said you didn't pay her anything,' Eve said.

'You're relying on the word of the woman who lied to you about the paternity of her baby. She took advantage of Matt, and then she took advantage of you.'

'I don't know why you're here. If it's only to rub my nose in it, you can leave now.'

'I just want to know, Eve. Was it you reminded Matt that he only needed a majority vote to sell his shares.'

'We all knew. It was pointed out when I invested money in NRS Tech for my ten percent of the shares. What's wrong with you? Isn't ninety percent enough?'

'As it happens, I'd rather have been consulted. That's all.'

'You would never have agreed.'

'I didn't have to,' I said. 'You had the majority, between you. It was all just to avoid the discomfort of a discussion, was it?'

Eve smiled. 'Oh, it was so much more than that. Matt wanted to avoid conflict. He was always like that. But me, I got what I wanted.'

That was some comfort, I suppose. She'd manipulated him into it. Sure, he was a grown man and should have stood up to her. Just like he should have been capable of resisting Amy and her ridiculous scheme.

Weakness can cause far more pain than malice.

I continued. 'I've been into the office, Eve. I was talking to the staff and to my surprise, I discovered you'd been telling everyone I killed Matt for his money.'

'That's nonsense,' she said.

'I know it is, but I know you said it. DI Carstairs told me too.'

'Is it any wonder that's what I believed? You were so angry. You weren't even mourning him. All you cared about were those embryos. You even forged a letter...'

'I didn't,' I said. 'You were in court. You know Matt signed it. For all his stupidity, he wasn't a cruel man. I guess he inherited the kindness from his father.'

'What do you want of me?'

'Admit you were the person sending those cruel texts.'

She looked at me, mute.

'Oh, I know it wasn't you who broke into my house. You hired someone. That means it can be tracked. Who you paid. If I wanted to, I could ruin your reputation. What would people think of you if they knew you hired someone to break into my house, to take videos of all my stuff and email it to me, to terrify me.'

'I thought you'd run away. I thought you'd killed him. So yes, I did it.'

I hadn't expected it to be so easy.

'Will you leave now. I've lost everything. Isn't that enough?'

'I don't know if it is quite enough,' I said. 'I'll have to think about it. Aren't you even a little bit sorry for how you hurt me? Or is only your pain that matters?'

Eve started sobbing.

'By the way, I worked out which texts and emails came from you by the language you used. You're really not very creative. Perhaps you should sign up for poison pen lessons. It's funny it's all stuff you wouldn't dream of saying in real life. Just like a basement dwelling keyboard warrior. You're such a tight arse. If you let yourself loosen up a bit, perhaps you might enjoy life a little bit more.'

I stood up, and walked to the front door, to show myself out.

'I didn't kill Matt,' I said, turning back. 'I didn't need to. He really did bring it all on himself.'

I shut the door quietly behind me.

Chapter Fifty

Six Months Later

It was a gorgeous day. Sean was right after all. My stressing about our big celebration party being spoiled by rain was a complete waste of time and energy. It would also have been pointless worrying even if it had been pouring down, as he also pointed out.

There was so much to celebrate, the weather couldn't possibly have ruined it. We were finally settled in our new home, and the Dog Therapy Centre was ready to be launched on the unsuspecting world.

There was plenty of room in Aunt Martha's house for family and friends to stay over. My nosy neighbour from the Victoria Park house, Sarah and her daughter Izzie were staying there, and her wife would be arriving later. Simon, Lilian, Lucas and Wolfie had already arrived, along with DI Coleman, who we were all gradually learning to call Lena. I could hardly wait for them to drive out to the farm and see it all for the first time.

Kathleen was the first to arrive, calming me down with her presence. She had been supportive and encouraged me during therapy training and had even written me a reference. She'd personally phoned the course co-ordinator when he'd expressed doubts about my suitability. My notoriety was always going to follow me, I knew. On the positive side, I was beginning to get used to having people in my corner.

Lainey had quit the Wimbledon Dog Rescue to join me as a partner. She was already collecting an odd selection of candidates for the therapy dog training, all of whom she could justify, somehow. She was staying in Martha's house too, but an old farm worker's cottage was mid-renovation, and would soon be ready for her to move in.

Nick arrived on time, although he'd texted to say he might be late. He was full of excitement, after a meeting with his agent. His book about cults, *Conspiracy : From Lizards to Demon Children* was due to be published in a month's time, and he was planning a huge launch party – another excuse for us all to get together.

Sean's ex and their two boys turned up. I'd had to promise Jessica I wouldn't encourage them to adopt a dog.

'There's no need, Jessie,' I'd pointed out. 'They can always be volunteer dog walkers here, you know. Free labour counts as a win for both me and you.'

She was still one of the nicest people I'd ever known.

Lucas and Wolfie arrived, with their entourage. For me, nothing else mattered. All my family were here.

Sean put his arm round me and kissed me in front of them all. Lucas, now ten, said *Ewww*, in a loud voice and everyone else laughed to see me blush.

'Wedding next year?' Sean whispered. 'Maybe,' I replied.

My phone pinged.

I shouldn't have looked at it. Some habits are hard to shake.

It was an email from Dave Elliott. No longer a detective constable – now a full time conspiracist. As Nick had said, for some it was a profitable endeavour.

'You think you got away with it, bitch, but don't count on it. I will not forget. I know your sort. Rich. Connected. I couldn't believe you were actually arrested for murder, but now I see it clearly. It was all part of the cover up, wasn't it?

I don't know who else is involved. It might be everyone at your cosy little party. It may be some are dupes.

But you. You've been in this for a long time, haven't you? You were recruited as a child. Your stepfather knew. The local police knew. Yet still you thrived, became rich.

You monsters have been getting away with this for too long. It's a rot that runs deep in our society.

I promise your days are numbered. There are more of us now than there have ever been, more of us who take our part in the fight back.

We are not helpless anymore. You are not safe. None of you are safe.'

I showed Nick and he checked Google on his phone. Old habits die hard.

It had begun. The Truther Guy had a new series of YouTube videos placing me, Jen Blake, at the evil heart of the Satanic Temple in the UK.

I pressed play.

He promised a bombshell episode. The teaser started with a familiar voice, telling of a young girl who had been possessed by the Devil himself.

My mother.

'You were recruited to our cause very recently,' the Truther Guy said to her, 'but we recognise that you have been in this fight for longer than any of us. We salute your courage.'

Dave Elliott came up next.

Nick turned it off. We'd all seen enough.

My mother was probably in Spain, with Elliott and the Grays.

'I feel responsible,' I said. 'After all, Kim Ward only did what I did. She kidnapped a child, rescuing him from what she genuinely believed was a very great danger. As his mother. It's hard to blame her.'

Kathleen touched my arm, reassuring. 'The difference lies in what you did afterwards,' she said. 'You nurtured him and helped him to heal. You returned him to the family who love him. Most of all, you were right. He needed rescuing.'

'Will this never end?' I said, feeling like bursting into tears on what should have been a happy day.

Nick said, 'I don't think it does. My research shows it constantly changes to incorporate new mad ideas, but there's a core at its centre which is remarkably persistent. People want easy answers, they want to find some sense of meaning, and they can't engage with the actual everyday chaos of the world. Most of them are harmless cranks, but some are dangerous. As we have seen.'

Sean put an arm around me. 'Whatever happens next, you aren't alone in it. I think – 'he looked around at everyone, 'we can all promise you that. And we will do our own little bit to make the world a happier and safer place. One step at a time.'

There was a short silence, interrupted by Lucas and Wolfie racing between us.

'Let the party begin!' Sean said, shaking off the mood. Nick joined him at the barbecue, and Kathleen picked up a tray piled with canapés and started passing them round.

As I nibbled a cheese straw, I looked around and counted my blessings.

All we can ever do, as Sean said, was take life one step at a time. I was happier, truly, than I'd ever been. Looking back, I'd seen having children as the only way to find happiness and meaning in my life. Yet somehow I'd found what I needed by letting go of all of that.

Lainey had the last word. 'Perhaps we should start a Guard Dog section.' she said. 'Only, we're gonna need more German Shepherds.'

Any excuse for more dogs.

Wolfie settled beside me, his huge head resting on my feet, and Lucas settled next to him. Mysteriously, the last two cheese straws on my paper plate disappeared when I wasn't looking, and boy and dog had suspicious crumb moustaches.

I pretended not to notice. For now, all was well in my world.

Author's Note

Thank you for reading **Rescue Child**

If you enjoyed this novel, I would appreciate if you could leave a brief review on Amazon, or even just a star rating.

Do follow me on Facebook at *Ann Rawson Writes,* or you might subscribe to my *Ann Rawson Writes* substack.

Early Reviews

Captivating read from start to finish – 5 stars

What starts as a suspicious murder whodunit quickly evolves into something more. A good, enjoyable read that gets you thinking about how other people interpret the emotions they think they see.

Sarah Arrow

Original and warm – 5 stars

This books is in turns sweet and shocking, structured and surprising. It's the work of a master of the likeable authorial voice. A writer it's good to spend time with, spinning a take that you just HAVE to follow through its twists and turns. Run away with the Rescue Child!

G.P.

A Savage Art, my first psychological thriller, is now available on Amazon. This is the same novel as published by Fahrenheit Press in 2016, with a new cover.

Can revenge ever be justified?

Kate Savage is an artist who creates dark fairy tales from textiles.

Devastated by the death of her assistant and unable to accept the official explanations, she begins to dig deeper and finds herself being seduced into an erotically charged and potentially dangerous world.

Kate becomes convinced that Dr John Reed, a charismatic alternative doctor, is implicated in the apparent suicide of her assistant and is determined to gather the proof that will confirm her suspicions – even if it means putting herself into harm's way.

Selected reviews -

"Like the best dark chocolate, this is a bittersweet novel with more than a hint of spice. Beautifully crafted, it kept me in suspense until the very end – and I usually guess who did it well before that.

Marion Barnet, Textile Artist

A Savage Art is an absolutely brilliant read. Really, this is a novel worth reading with it's fluid style, the great story - one you won't want to put down and will leave you looking forward to whatever Kate does next, and certainly whatever A E writes next.

Babs Saul

...an utterly gripping plot with more twists and turns than Spaghetti Junction.

Olga Wotjas, Novelist

An excellent read. I knew it would be from the first couple of sentences. Good plot and subplots. This kept me engrossed, and made time fly on a long plane ride. Plane ride or not, I heartily recommend this novel!

Elle Dee USA

As intricately woven as the detail on one of the delicious corsets portrayed, this novel by A E Rawson is pacy and crammed full of information on both sadomasochism and fabric art, a combination that fits together surprisingly well. Sprinkled with enough dead bodies to satisfy the crime thriller fan and a hint of glitter to add a touch of magic, I genuinely did find it difficult to put down. I really couldn't decide who had murdered who on the way or which character was going to become a body next. Rawson kept me guessing all the way through. An intelligent and well written story which I thoroughly enjoyed. I look forward to reading the next one.

Judith Parsons

The perfect thriller set in Bohemian Brighton, UK. A textile artist becomes entangled in a dark world of torture and porn when she tries to make sense of her friend's death. The plot is full of clever twists and the characters are compelling. If you wished 50 Shades was better written this might be the book for you.

Carmilla Voiez

The Witch House, my second psychological thriller, is currently available on Amazon. Previously published by Red Dog Press, I decided to self-publish a Second Edition when they closed down.

Who can you trust, if you can't trust yourself?

Alice Hunter, grieving and troubled after a breakdown, stumbles on the body of her friend and trustee, Harry Rook. The police determine he has been ritually murdered and suspicion falls on the vulnerable Alice, who inherited the place known locally as The Witch House from her grandmother, late High Priestess of the local coven.

When the investigations turn up more evidence, and it all seems to point to Alice, even she begins to doubt herself. Can she find the courage to confront the secrets and lies at the heart of her family and community to uncover the truth, prove her sanity, and clear herself of murder?

Selected Reviews -

"I loved this book and recommend it as a January read for our book club.

Ann is a master storyteller. I couldn't put it down for all the twists and turns. I couldn't wait to find out what was at the next turn. The identity of the murderer was handled perfectly living the reader to speculate until the end."

Ida Horner

"Just finished this beauty by Ann Rawson, who writes quite unlike any author I've ever read before. An engrossing and gripping tale that will keep you guessing right to the very last page. The characters are so real that I hated some and was rooting for others. Brilliant."

Marney

Acknowledgements

As always, I owe thanks to a lot of people.

First, there's Marion Barnett, who worked hard to keep me sane, especially by reminding me that I do really need to pace myself.

Lots of people read this novel – some read early drafts and some the later ones.

After Ryan, Myfanwy Fox endured the most, and I am very grateful for her final line edit.

Graham Pugh read at different stages and tried his best to talk me out of a prologue. All mistakes are my own of course – but the prologue is not a mistake.

Lesley Lathrop and Salomé Jones provided useful feedback and generous encouragement.

Mark Bailey and Tone Hitchcock read earlier drafts, and their response helped me realise I did have a good story.

Everyone who read it found stray lapses into the present tense, resulting from an early unwise stylistic choice. If there are any left after endless revisions, then that really is all my own fault. Just to confuse the issue there are a few places where I deliberately slipped into the present tense for immediacy. Of course, that's not just an excuse!

Christine Miller and Cathy Dobson helped with some late corrections. And the brilliant Jacqueline Le Sueur uncovered some inconsistencies I'd totally missed.

Tone Hitchcock also created the glorious cover art, which I absolutely adore.

I am more grateful to all of you than I can ever express in words. You'll just have to settle for the interpretative dance.

Thank you all,

Ann Rawson, December 2023

Printed in Great Britain
by Amazon